all times
have been
modern

Also by Elisabeth Harvor

FICTION

Excessive Joy Injures the Heart

SHORT FICTION

Let Me Be the One
If Only We Could Drive Like This Forever
Our Lady of All the Distances

POETRY

The Long Cold Green Evenings of Spring
Fortress of Chairs

ANTHOLOGIES

A Room at the Heart of Things

all times have been modern

Elisabeth Harvor

VIKING
CANADA

VIKING CANADA

Published by the Penguin Group

Penguin Group (Canada), 10 Alcorn Avenue, Toronto, Ontario, Canada M4V 3B2
(a division of Pearson Penguin Canada Inc.)

Penguin Group (USA) Inc., 375 Hudson Street, New York, New York 10014, U.S.A.
Penguin Books Ltd, 80 Strand, London WC2R 0RL, England
Penguin Ireland, 25 St Stephen's Green, Dublin 2, Ireland (a division of Penguin Books Ltd)
Penguin Group (Australia), 250 Camberwell Road, Camberwell, Victoria 3124, Australia
(a division of Pearson Australia Group Pty Ltd)
Penguin Books India Pvt Ltd, 11 Community Centre, Panchsheel Park, New Delhi – 110 017, India
Penguin Group (NZ), Cnr Airborne and Rosedale Roads, Albany, Auckland, New Zealand
(a division of Pearson New Zealand Ltd)
Penguin Books (South Africa) (Pty) Ltd, 24 Sturdee Avenue, Rosebank, Johannesburg 2196,
South Africa

Penguin Books Ltd, Registered Offices: 80 Strand, London WC2R 0RL, England

First published 2004

(FR)   10 9 8 7 6 5 4 3 2 1

The lines quoted on page 322 are from *The Martyrology*, by bpNichol. Reprinted with permission.

Author representation: Westwood Creative Artists
94 Harbord Street, Toronto, Ontario M5S 1G6

Manufactured in Canada.

LIBRARY AND ARCHIVES CANADA CATALOGUING IN PUBLICATION

Harvor, Elisabeth
All times have been modern / Elisabeth Harvor.

ISBN 0-670-04440-7

I. Title.

PS8565.A69A64   2004   C813'.54   C2004-903541-X

Visit the Penguin Group (Canada) website at **www.penguin.ca**

For T, S, K, A, N, D, and for Faith,
Hélène LeBlanc, and Hélène LeBeau

In art, there are no generations, only individuals; all times have been modern

—Nadia Boulanger

A SOLDIER COMES to stand next to me as we make a wide swing away from the dock. He doesn't speak, he only squints out at the river as if he's spent years under orders to squint out at rivers. It isn't until we've sailed past the first island that he asks me to light his cigarette for him. But it's too windy out on the water, a big wind keeps blowing my hair across my eyes as I'm pretending to watch the mainland rising and falling and when I turn to glance back at him I try to make my eyes look intolerably sad. Tragic, even. Tragic with the knowledge that I have already lived an important and sorrowful life.

No, I tell him.

Why not?

Because I don't want to.

Why don't you want to?

Because I just don't. Why can't you light it yourself?

When he sets his hands on my hips so he can squeeze past me to stand on my opposite side, I get an attack of the shivers from the quick dents his cold fingers make on the bare skin between my sun halter and bathing-suit bottoms. But I try to look unimpressed: it's the night I've turned thirteen, after all, it's even almost the exact mid-point of the twentieth century, and I have a book with me, a birthday gift called *The Thirty-nine Steps* that's so exciting I feel sick to my stomach

1

from my need to reach the end of it before it gets dark. My parents are also parked in the first car, just behind where I'm looking back at Kennebecasis Island. But even though I'm feeling too chilled (in a hot-faced way) I don't want to go back to the car for my sweater because I don't want the soldier to think I'm upset.

"At least tell me your name."

"It's Kay."

"Oh Kay," he moans. "So why won't you light my cigarette for me, oh Kay? *Okay*, Kay?"

I can't do it for him. Besides, how can I do it for him when I've already told him so many times that I wouldn't? Because by now I really want to, I want to because I want my mother to see me do it.

But she might not even be looking and when the lights on the far side of the bay come into view he decides to light his cigarette for himself, then smiles down at me as I close my book. "Leaving me, are you?"

"Yes."

My parents are talking in low voices at the front as I slide onto the back seat and pick up the flashlight, then click it on and begin to read fast, leaping from one moon of words to the next and not looking up till I hear the boat threshing water, then the words get jumped by the jolt of landing as their meanings race past me—I hate this, I hate it almost as much as I hate falling asleep and getting bumped awake as we drive off the boat—but now the words are tipping again as we careen toward Saint John, the city where we'll be picking up a boy whose mother died three weeks ago, a boy named Derek who's going to stay with us for the rest of the summer and it's not fair that my brothers and my sister are away at summer camp and I'm the one who has to entertain him, I might even die myself if I don't reach the end of the book before we get to where he is, but just as we're turning onto his street I come to the final word, then we've bumped to a stop and we go up the steep steps to a tall house in the floodlit fog of Saint John, the house of Derek's older sister, Georgia Switzer, a teacher and poet who's a friend of my mother's. I always worry that I'll be expected to say something intelligent to Georgia but will only end up saying something weird and peculiar. She's also going to be my English teacher when I start high school in the fall. And so it's going to be awful, going into English will be like walking into a class taught by my mother, and when she opens the door to us her eyes look strange, too bright or too emotional, and she's not dressed in black as I thought she would be, she's dressed in three shades of tan—tan turtleneck sweater, darker tan circle skirt, tan ballet slippers—and when she tells Derek to run upstairs for his suitcase I'm surprised that it isn't gloomy in here, all the lamps are turned on and all the floors shine.

On the drive home, Derek sits next to me in the back while my mother sits sideways on the front seat so she can talk to us and I'm afraid of what she's going to say next, her dark-lipsticked smile is so ghastly and friendly. "Tell me, Derek!" she calls back to him. "Do you like to read?"

"Sometimes."

"Kay loves to read!"

I turn to look out my window, humiliated. It's as if she has just said, "We have recently discovered that Kay has a most remarkable talent, she knows how to read." One day last winter she even told a man who came out to visit our workshop in Scanlon Falls that he should go upstairs and entertain me. I was home from school, sick with a cold, and this man, who was very hairy and breathy, came up the stairs to my room. "I've been ordered by your mother to entertain you and so I've decided to read my poems to you," he told me, then he sat on the chair next to my bed and for the whole afternoon he read his poetry to me while I kept lying at attention under my quilt hoping I wouldn't need to tell him that I had to go to the bathroom. I wondered if his poems were bad poems and my mother didn't know what to say about them and so she sent him upstairs to spend the afternoon with me. But how could I tell if they were good or bad? All I knew was that he kept reading them as if they were hymns and he was singing them without the music. But at the end of each poem he would stop, wait for me to say something, and when I couldn't think of anything to say he would move on to the next poem.

My mother is asking Derek if he likes to sing.

Now he doesn't answer her. By now he's probably decided that she's incurably insane. He might even think I'm the same kind of person she is. But I've decided not to even care what he thinks, he's just a boy. At least the soldier was a grown-up. Or a sort of grown-up.

"Darling," my mother is saying to Derek, "you must call me Idona."

"Yes," he says.

"What about in the car?"

"Sorry?"

"Do you like to sing in the car?"

"I don't know, I've never tried it."

"We have a song in our family that we like to sing whenever we're on our way to Gondola Point. I sing: Here we go to Gondola Point! Then you and Daddy and Kay sing Gone-doe-la-point! Gone-doe-la-point!" She makes her mouth into a tiny "o" as if she's teaching idiots to sing and after she has sung the opening line she makes an up and down wavy motion with her hand to let us know that we are to follow her, and so we do, we sing in misery and gratitude all the way to Gondola Point.

MY MOTHER HAS GONE to Saint John to see her dentist this afternoon and so I want to find myself a book that's got love in it. I go down to the bookcase in the sunroom and pull two grey books down from the top shelf, *Remembrance of Things Past,* Volumes One and Two, then decide on Volume Two because I like the titles of the smaller books it contains: *Cities of the Plain, The Captive, The Sweet Cheat Gone, The Past Recaptured,* and now that I've decided on it, all I want to do is spend the afternoon reading it while no one can bother me. But on my way up to my room a door above me creaks to click shut. I know it's the door of the bedroom belonging to Derek for the summer and I know this because on this particular afternoon we're the only ones at home. I walk past his door and go into my room, close my own door, then sit at my desk like a student about to begin a history assignment. I used to look at books that were filled with pictures of gardens before I went to bed at night, or read mystery stories, but ever since school got out I've been reading books about nurses or horses and in one of these books a nurse even owned a horse and I'm hoping there'll be a horse in this book too. Or a man on a horse, a handsome dark man riding on horseback and seeing, across a vast plain, a golden city. Instead, I find myself making my way through a thicket of difficult words and French names (*campanile,* Marquis de Frécourt) and there's a boy who seems to be close to my own age although he has a much larger vocabulary—but then he's French—and this boy is spying on two men (a baron and a tailor) by peeking between the slats of a pair of shutters, and now here's a description of the tailor, a man who has "placed his hand with a grotesque impertinence on his hip, stuck out his behind, posed himself with the coquetry that the orchid might have adopted on the providential arrival of the bee...." I feel a throb of excitement on reading this, I so much love to spy on people, and the sticking out of his behind fascinates me too, it reminds me of certain childhood games that I used to think were really bad, and after the two men have gone into the tailor's shop and closed the door I race on ahead, rushing through the boy's plan to eavesdrop by passing through a kitchen to descend a service stair so he can hurry under the breadth of the courtyard to the place where there's a stairway up into a room next door to the tailor's shop. But then he changes his with all my fingers, then go back to the bookcase where I consider reading *A Town like Alice* again because I love it so. But I've already read it six times and have actually read the best part of it at least twenty times, the part just after World War II where Jean, the brave former prisoner of the Japanese in Malaya, meets the Australian soldier who survived being nailed to a tree for the crime of stealing chickens for her while she was on a forced march around Malaya with a convoy of British women, the part after the war where he's too shy and polite to her until they make a trip to an island off the coast of Australia and go swimming in the sea and Jean can see how wrecked the skin on his back looks because he was tortured for her sake. This is when she gets the inspiration to go back to her cabin and braid her hair into a single braid, then wrap her Malayan sarong around herself and walk barefoot out to where he's waiting for her. This is the best part because this is when she places her hands on his shoulders to say, "Is this bettah, Joe?" This is when he kisses and kisses her, then carries her in his arms into her tourist hut where her sarong keeps unwrapping itself even though she keeps trying to hold it pulled up over her breasts as she says, "Dear Joe, if you can't wait until we get married, it's really all right."

I would like to try this, I would like to lie down on my bed and wrap my nightgown sideways around myself like a bulky sarong and roll over behind my pillow and place my hands on its shoulders to whisper, "Is this bettah, Joe?"

But then I get an inspiration too, I'll ask Derek to play Scrabble with me, I should be kind to him, his mother just died a few weeks ago, and so I get out the box of letter tiles and go up the stairs holding the Scrabble board pressed to me like a school book.

Music is coming from his room when I knock on his door. The squeak of bedsprings comes next, then the sound of hopping on one foot, then the hops of two feet, and when he opens the door he smiles down at the Scrabble board and tells me he knows how to play a much better game.

"What's that, then?"

"Come on in and I'll show you...."

I can smell socks as I step into his room: socks and something else. Cheese, I think, my brothers' rooms also mostly smell of cheese, then he's saying that the first rule of this game is that he's going to think of a number and I have to guess what it is.

I glance over at his bed, his blue pillow slips. "Nine," I say.

His shorts seem to be breathing all on their own. "That was close," he tells me. "And so I'm going to have to give you one more chance."

Of course the whole point is to guess wrong. Even I know that. You win by losing. I think of older girls at school saying to boys in grade twelve, "See you tomorrow," and the boys in grade twelve tilting back in their chairs to say, "Is that a threat or a promise?"

"Fourteen hundred and ninety-two."

"Closer. But that's not it either."

"If nine is close, how can fourteen hundred and ninety-two be even closer? It doesn't even make any sense."

"It's true," he says, smiling down at me. "It's a great mystery." He's still watching me, though, in a thinking sort of way and so I'm not all that surprised when he shoves me (but only as if it's a joke) against the wall by his door, then taps me on a shoulder. "Rule number two: You have to hit my hand away."

When I lightly push at it, he touches my left elbow.

And so I touch one of his shoulders.

At this he sets his hands on my hips. But this time, instead of batting him away, I pout up at him, feeling plump in every part of my body. His hand drops lower down then and begins to rub at me in a way that makes me feel a sensation of such secret happiness that even though he's the one who's giving it to me he also seems to be the one who's standing in the way of it, it feels too private to have anyone else see it as taunts from my childhood keep singing themselves inside my head. So make me then. So I bet you wouldn't dare to. So I dare you. And by the time his hand has done whatever he's doing to me for however long we've imagined it will take for my mother's appointment at the dentist's to be over, I feel drunk, I'm ten thousand times more drunk than any flower after a visit from any baron or bee, then he's starting to walk me backwards toward his bed—and I want him to, I want to go wherever his guiding hand pushes me but at the same time I'm worried that once we're lying down I won't know what to do with my own hands—when we hear the warning gouge of tires in gravel followed by the slam of a car door and the tinier gouge of high heels walking fast across the wet yard of pebbles, then the dangerously innocent but also dangerously probing voice calling up the stairs: "Hullo, hullo!" And so I'm sure that my mother must know, I'm sure she knows everything. And besides, Derek is talking to me, he's saying in a low voice, "Go to your room now, *hurry* ..." and so I do go, but my heart is by now violently beating down where the ticking was and I'm feeling furious because we were interrupted and so I thrash around on my bed trying to make one of my hands be Derek's hand, but it's too small (and it's also too much mine) and when he doesn't come down to join the family for dinner and my sunburned father asks me if I know where he is, I can feel a cooler glance fall on me from the far end of the table as I say no. A glance on the lookout for some new slant in my gaze, in the way I'm holding my spoon. But when my immediate ancestor asks me how I spent my afternoon, I'm able to quite calmly tell her that I spent it reading a book by Marcel Prowst.

My oldest brother, back from the summer camp where he was the swimming instructor, shouts, *"Proost!"* While Idona—her lower lip still puffed up from the Novocaine—turns to appeal to our pink father. "Don't you think that a girl of thirteen is too young to be reading Proust?"

On the blackboard, Georgia Switzer draws wobbly lines of shields and troops, then sketches Joan on her horse as she tells us how stunning this year's play will be. "We'll have banners rippling in the winds blowing from fans mounted high up on the shelves behind the curtains in the auditorium," she tells us, "and we'll be getting superb posters too, big ones that will say SAINT JOAN IN SAINT JOHN, COME TO THE BATTLE, COME TO THE MIRACLE. I glance up, then quickly glance down again at my copy of Joan's speech, praying that Georgia won't ask me to read first.

But because I'm the only student whose name she knows she asks me to read first.

"Never again to hear the young lambs crying in the healthy frost...." I read in a high and clear little voice while she squints at me as if she's deciding that no army on any stage on earth will ever take orders to ride behind me. And then at the end of the class she tells us there's been a change in plans: we're not going to be doing *Saint Joan* after all, we'll be doing *I Remember Mama* instead.

Girls our own age now kneel next to our ankles to measure the hems of our long dresses and pinafores, boys our own age build the sets. And the night of our first dress rehearsal, girls our own age serve us spaghetti and beans in the cafeteria, smiling tenderly at us because we are the stars.

Nights of euphoria, these nights of the play, the tiled hallways of our school gone dim while we run up and down them calling out urgent news: Do this! Do that! Curtain call in ten minutes! But then it's not a matter of minutes, it's a matter of years, years pass and I'm working for my parents at their studios in Scanlon Falls, showing armies of tourists around the silversmith workshop, selling them rings, taking them into Idona's workroom with its wide view of the river. They gaze down at Idona's loom, at the fabric growing like patterned moss on its strings, then look down to study their hands, my father's broad silver rings on their fingers.

On the last day we're open for the summer—by now it's the summer I've turned twenty—a final car comes down the lane and I can't bear it, I can't bear to talk to one more tourist and pretend to be a charming person, the whole afternoon that I've been smiling and saying yes, this would be a perfect gift, the perfect thing, I've been longing to run down to the river for a swim.

This last visitor introduces himself as Alexander Oleski and his smile tells me he knows he is handsome. He's looking for a wedding gift and once he's found a silver bowl that will do, he admires the view of the river and so we walk down to the beach and sit on a round rock and he pulls the rings off my fingers, then shoves them onto my toes, the swampy air reeking of baked mud and grasses that smell dying and dried out, they're so reedy and fishy.

"These rings on your feet all look like wedding rings."

"They do."

"So maybe we should get married...."

I wonder if he's acting this way because he's really only shy. Unless he's a psychopath, I don't know enough about men to be able to tell. And so I invent a small smile, then look at my watch. "So how long have we known each other? Forty minutes?"

"It's much easier to love a woman if you've only known her for forty minutes. But if you won't marry me, will you at least have dinner with me? We could take the cable ferry over to Gondola Point and drive into Saint John...."

But by the time we get to Rothesay we're too ravenous to drive all the way to Saint John and so we turn in to the driveway for Shadow Lawn where we order roast lamb and cucumber soup and Alex talks about politics in a way that makes me understand a world I've never had any interest in up till now and this changes him into a more serious person—an incredibly handsome serious person—but at the same time the way he uses his hands bothers me, it's too rehearsed, he chops the air with his right hand, then a finger dials a phone number in the air, or at least part of a number, then he claps a hand to his heart as if I'm an audience he wants to convert. I tell him about a weekly music show I have on CBC Radio in Saint John, leaving out the information that I got it because the owner of the station is a friend of my parents. I'm very good, really, at leaving things out, I'm aware of this again when I refer to Shadow Lawn as a "family mansion for hire," then describe the dances I was invited to in this house when I was sixteen, leaving out the news that I was an utter social failure and was only asked to dance by the sons of friends of Idona's. But when we come out into the night, I forget all that, there's such a warm wind in the summer trees and a full moon in the sky and under its hollow light we take the ferry to the other side of the river, then drive over the hills leading us back to Scanlon Falls, where the studios and the main house look black and industrial, a giant black chimney at one end, a night factory surrounded by a wilderness of trees. We go into the main house to get two bottles of beer and as I click on the lights Alex admires it, its oddities, its stairs without railings, its ladders and inner balconies, a towering painting of a fat grey naked man washing his hair in a grey shower looming behind the oak table, paintings of fierce red and orange flowers with black throats, scribbles of green paint on their black stems, paintings of wild stormy skies, old maps on the walls, a hanging white face with blue paper streamers for hair. "I've heard about this house for years"—his voice is filled with wonder as he looks all around—"it's all so crazy and terrific and so legendary, really, and your parents are legends too."

"But they are actually very conventional people. As parents, I mean."

"All parents are that." But then he says, "Play something for me," and he rests an elbow on the top of the piano as I sit down on the piano bench to play and I so much hate being watched that I stumble my way through the beginning of Rachmaninoff's Piano Concerto No. 2 in C Major, then stop to say, "I'm sorry, but I can't play with you watching me like this."

"Oh. Sorry." And he goes over to the fireplace and sits down next to it and I worry that he'll feel banished as he sits all alone over there, breathing in the aroma of cold ashes and the rubbery dank smell of the meadow lilies. But I do play better after this, somewhat better, and after I've finished the Rachmaninoff, I play "I Only Have Eyes for You," then we walk out of the house leaving all the lights blazing and on our way down to the river we make a detour across the moonlit garden—its night scents deeper than sweet—then walk into the orchard. And when I lean back against a tree he kisses me. It's a deep kiss, a French kiss, but the innocent life I've been leading ever since my afternoon with Derek Switzer hasn't really prepared me for this kind of kiss, it's happened too quickly, I only know what an orgasm is like, not a kiss, and it's depressing to discover that I don't really like this kind of kiss, it's too much like having my teeth licked, it makes me want to hurry back into the house and brush them. But on our way down to the beach we hold hands and all at once I like him so much again, I feel so close to him, I like his voice, and I like the way we sit like two children on the same rock we sat on when the sun was still high in the sky, I like the way he's telling me that he plans to go to Europe next year. How lucky he is, to be leaving this boring country behind to fly far away, that would be the true happiness, I can see this now, it could even be the answer to everything, above all the solution to my not having made any plans for what I want to do with my life. I think of bombed cities, reconstruction, and how I could never pass up the chance to begin again, among foreigners. But he's not in the same mood he was in this afternoon, now he's speaking in a serious way about a future to which I have not been invited.

"But why are you all alone way out here in the country?" he asks me as we're walking up through the orchard again, his arm around my shoulders this time, his breath warm in my hair. "Where are all the other people in your family?"

"They've gone to a wedding in Boston."

We stop and kiss again, then I have to lean back against the nearest tree because he's slipped one of his hands inside my sweater to cup a breast and the way he's flicking one of my nipples is making me feel breathless. "They'll be back tomorrow night."

"But is that fair? To leave you behind to look after everything?"

"We drew lots. My sister wrote GO on six squares of paper, and on the seventh one she wrote STAY and I was the one who drew STAY."

Which is why—although I don't say this—I have to be the one to get away. "But I wanted to have a few days to myself anyway, it's so noisy here when everyone's home, American tourists take the boat over to see us, we're the big event of their day, even the big event of their whole trip if we can show them we love them enough." *Los Americanos.* My sister Vivi and I divide them into loudmouths, sweethearts, future friends. For there's no one better than the best Americans. And no one worse than the worst. Idona paints the eyes of the masks white every night and when she does a demonstration for the first group of Americans the following morning she paints little fishes where the blank eyelids were, misquoting Shakespeare—"Full fathom five thy father lies, these are fishes that were his eyes"—and she gets a laugh every time. But what I don't tell him is that I've been afraid on these long quiet evenings when I've been alone, the nearest two farms are a six-minute walk in either direction, in the summers it's not even possible to see them, they're too hidden by leaves, and so our house has seemed unsafe, the doors only hooked by small hooks and cheap slide-across bars except for the back door which has a real lock, a real key, anyone could yank the other doors open and walk barefoot into the house, any weirdo could make his way up from the river or down from the bluff and walk through the fields of grasses straight to here, where I am. And when I look out the back windows, it's not that the cedar bluff moves closer as it might do in a horror movie, if anything it seems to have stepped back and to have become even more tiny and gilded and medieval and sinister, as if a small perfect deer might go leaping in a perfect arc in front of it like a deer leaping in front of a wood in a tapestry in that golden light that's so perfect, so ominous.

Alex Oleski raises his arms up on both sides of my face, braces his hands against a part of the tree trunk that's above my head, then pushes my thighs apart with a knee. And so this is how it begins: I fall in love with his knee.

I'VE BECOME ADDICTED to the kind of kissing we did the night we first met, now I can't live without it, I want to get married sooner than soon, I'm thinking of the happiness (and the deep sex) of marriage as we look down at rings rising like gold handles out of slits in blue velvet boxes. "Sapphires," the girl behind the counter tells us as we peer even deeper, at a band of blue stones on sparkling display deep inside a glass case. *Can* they be? When the tag tied to the ring says it's been marked all the way down to thirty dollars? Alexander buys it for me and when we step out into the bright Saint John sunlight and I hold up my hand so we can gloat at it and inspect it, it's clear that it's only a ring of blue glass chips. My hand keeps on getting grabbed after this, by women my own age who stare down at it with diagnostic fierceness: "What are the stones?" And I respond in a low voice, trying to sound convinced and convincing, "Sapphires."

Meanwhile, the wedding draws near. We'll be having Beethoven's "Ode to Joy" instead of the wedding march. And no bridesmaids, no ushers. No best man, even. One of my brothers will stand, in a blue suit, next to Alex. And Vivi, in an elegant grey suit, will stand next to me. Everything done on the cheap, including the wedding dress, a tall and regal satin dress pooling into even more satin and bought on sale for fifteen dollars because it was worn in a fashion show and the model who was wearing it accidentally dropped a cigarette on its lace-and-satin train, leaving behind a tiny black hole that Georgia Switzer hides by stitching a white silk organza butterfly over it.

OUR WHOLE COURTSHIP was by mail. I used to write to Alex every night and really miss him, but the night before our wedding when he spends the whole evening flirting with women friends who've dropped by with gifts, I cry and tell him I don't think I can go through with it after all, and I mean it, then I'm afraid to mean it, and it's already here: a flurry of bells as we step out of the church into the dull November afternoon, the quick drive back to the house where one of the wedding guests tells us he hit a beautiful white dog on his way to the church. So that when Alex and I duck under the showers of confetti and snow—the first snow of this year—I can't shake the picture of the wedding guest leaping across the ditch while bearing the white dog to an open grave in a field, it so powerfully calls forth the image of a groom striding across a threshold with his new young bride lifted high in his arms.

We drive against a blizzard all the way to Moncton and when we run from the car to our hotel, snow stings our eyes, blows into our throats. But when we step into the bright shock of the lobby and Alex gushes over a vase filled with pink roses that's been placed on the front desk, all I can think is: Why does he have to gush like a woman? Of course I'm not at all proud of myself for thinking this. But although I'm not at all proud of thinking it, it makes me know something new about marriage: instead of having only one person to be ashamed of, now I'll have two.

Georgia Switzer's wedding gift to us—it's practically an heirloom, it's from 1922—explodes inside my new grey suitcase on the flight to Quebec City and my satin slips and panties end up getting drenched in historic champagne. But we don't stay in our hotel room to inhale the antique and alcoholic air, we're too eager to hurry out to the Plains of Abraham. Then we walk along the Boardwalk in a great wind and look down at the incredibly wide St. Lawrence River. Night, sex, sleep, a hurried breakfast in the windy lower town, then we have to run for the train to Montreal so we can get settled in the apartment Alex has found for us on Durocher Street, a street in the student quarter near McGill.

ON DUROCHER STREET we walk into a room that looks like a stage set: nothing in it but a bare table and a refrigerator. Although Alex has pasted red cardboard hearts all over the refrigerator door.

"But where is the bathroom?"

"It's just down the hall, we'll be sharing it with the tenants in 33C."

"And the kitchen?"

He opens a narrow door to reveal a hot-plate placed next to a tiny sink in a broom closet, then holds out a hand to me. "But come see the bedroom, it's fantastic, it even has a marble fireplace."

So our first home is really nothing more than two rooms and a bed. But why should we mind? We're going to Europe in the spring and so when I write to thank the wedding guests for their gifts, I describe it as a "real gem, we even have a hideous green marble fireplace in our bedroom and so it's all very grand." I also sign up with an agency that sends typists out for temporary work, but I don't tell Alex about all the times I am "let go." Sometimes it takes my new bosses two or three days to discover how inept I am, but I never get to stay for the weeks I understood they'd be needing me. I don't blame them for letting me go, I'm not a good typist, I'm too frantic, inaccurate. Only cooking redeems me the nights Alex brings unmarried male friends home for dinner and I concoct elaborate dinners in the broom closet.

IDONA AND VIVI are to sleep in our bed while Alex and I will go up the street to the house he lived in when he was a student to sleep in one of the empty beds there. I have the feeling this excites them, the idea of sleeping on this wide creaky bed where so much sex has (presumably) been happening, but they look very demure in their black berets—their Christmas gifts to each other—as we discuss the pictures from the wedding that have been arranged in an embossed white wedding album the photographer gave to Alex and me. (When we're alone we call it the condom album because we slot the condom packets into it, being unable to keep them in the medicine cabinet we share with the tenants in 33C. But luckily I remember this just in time and as Idona and Vivi and I are about to sit down on the bed to look at the photos together and Alex is distracting them by suggesting drinks of Martini Rossi, I quickly slip the packets into a pocket.)

After dinner we decide to go out to look for a store where we can buy pumpernickel bread for breakfast. But Idona wants me to stay behind for "a little talk," she hugs me around the waist as we bid Alex and Vivi goodbye, Vivi looking vivacious and unmarried in her black beret as she turns up the collar of her coat, then sweeps out into the starlit night with my husband.

"Here, sweetie," Idona says to me in her mesmerizing voice, "sit down beside me here, darling," and as we formally sit down side by side on the big bed again, she takes one of my hands in hers and strokes it over and over in a way that makes me feel drugged as she mentions little things she's noticed, her eyes shining, tender, but also, because they are too aware of their tender expression, somehow cold, strategic. "We all love you, we are all cheering you on, we are all hoping you can begin to make something of your life by becoming a success at being a happily married young woman. But darling, take your little kitchen for instance, you could have such fun cheering it up, you could really make it so charming and cosy, you could put up a few shelves and buy two or three bright blue pottery mugs and put a Picasso poster over the sink, or a Bonnard, one of those lovely breakfast scenes with a view into a garden, you could give yourself a beautiful view of a garden in France as you're standing at your grim little sink, doing the dishes. And you really do need to buy a new dishcloth, my darling, the one you have is so horrid and grey, Vivi and I were both a bit horrified when we saw it, it made us reluctant to eat very much of that terrifically delicious dinner you cooked, I'm sure you noticed that neither of us asked for second helpings."

No, as a matter of fact I didn't. But it's true that the dishcloth is grey, or a purple sort of grey, partly from mopping up grape juice on rushed winter mornings, but partly, yes, from the grey of never having been bleached or replaced and I see myself rinse the dishes in a great flash of hot water, then wipe down the tiny counter with a single sweep of the dish cloth so that I can sit down at the desk to write my collection of untrue words: real gem, green marble fireplace, all very grand.

"I'm telling you these things for your own sake, just to be helpful to you so that your new husband will be proud of you. It's not that I want to be critical of you because I don't, you know that, and you also know how very much we love you and that we're really just here to have fun...."

And so it goes until Alex and Vivi let themselves in, laughing and talking and making me feel frantic that they might overhear what Idona is saying to me while at the same time I'm even more frantic to overhear what they are saying to each other. I hear them tap the snow off their boots, then take bottles of milk or beer out of the refrigerator—beer, I think—then Vivi must be showing Alex something she's been reading in the paper because there's a silence of almost a minute in which I picture him reading it (reading it or kissing her) then I hear him laugh and say, "Yeah, that's true, the elections were rigged," and I begin to relax.

On the way up the hill to our bed for the night, he talks to me about Idona. "I'm surprised she doesn't want to stay in a hotel."

"The people in my family never stay in hotels. We prefer to sponge on people, we find sponging on people so much more amusing."

ONE COOL SPRING NIGHT we go out to dinner at Le Caveau and after we get back to Durocher Street, I come up the stairs a few minutes behind Alex because I've stopped to pick up the mail. I'm climbing the stairs slowly, wanting to have time alone, I seem to need more and more of it, although I also feel a need to keep this aberration a secret. But as I'm walking past the bathroom that Alex and I share with the retired schoolteachers in 33C, I hear the two old women talking behind their door in their mournfully loud and judgmental voices.

"It's all *slimy*. But the water around it is all *red*, so maybe it's *blood*—"

In the beautiful spring evening, I stop breathing to listen.

"Blood or beets," says the other one in her practical voice that's as low as a man's. She's the one who once told me that she used to work as a dancer. In Les Folies de something or other.

"You'd think she'd know better than *that*, it's just so disgusting. She's an adult, after all, or seems to think that she is—"

The other one laughs, then one of them turns the radio on.

When I let myself into the apartment, I can hear Alex in the bedroom talking to one of his friends on the phone. I go into the broom closet to splash my eyes with cool water, then under cover of the ten o'clock news, I creak out to the bathroom and close its door with an anguished stealth. It's a tablecloth the old teachers were speaking of, an embroidered white cloth with beet stains on it that I slipped under the bathtub to soak in a basin of warm soapy water, then forgot. How long ago was this? That we had pickled beets for supper? Weeks, but I can't remember how many weeks. It could even have been in the winter, I seem to remember snow falling on a mild winter evening. I fill the bathtub with hot soapy water and flounce the tablecloth around in it, but it really is slimy and also so greyly spotted with mildew that it can't be saved and so I bundle it up in a towel and hurry it into the apartment, and while Alex is out in the bathroom, taking his bath, I stuff the slippery embroidered damp wad of it into a garbage bag and carry it down to the back of the building where the garbage cans stand under the stars in a foul-smelling row.

THIS AFTERNOON I meet one of my accusers coming up the stairs as I'm on my way down to try out for yet another temporary job. A powdered old flapper who must once have been sly and jutty-hipped, she's the one who was the dancer. She's also the one who has the destroyed face, the voice of a man.

"Hello," I say. But the old dancer snubs me.

But now everything moves fast, in two weeks we'll be off, we'll be ready to fly. To Scotland on Good Friday, on Easter Sunday to Dublin.

IN DUBLIN we see a white van with a black swastika and the words SWASTIKA LAUNDRY painted on it. ("This is how much the Irish hate the English," Alex tells me. "If the Germans were fighting the English they couldn't be *that* bad....") Then we hop over to London, go to the

London Zoo, a haze of green on the trees, leopard spots on the silk print top worn by an American starlet walking down one of the zoo avenues with a lover or bodyguard whose square face is the ill red of a brick.

Then it's down to Italy for a month where five little boys in a small town in Tuscany skip along beside our German motorbike, pelting pebbles at our bare ankles. "Tedesco! Hitler! Mussolini!" Dancing up and down on their little stick legs to jeer at us. But our first evening in Paris we run into friends: the two cyclists we met in Venice, Gunilla and William, then go with them to a club in Montmartre to hear a singer whose voice is too ruined to be imploring. In her black sweater and black skirt she looks exactly as I dreamed a real chanteuse would look and the Parisians in the audience listen to her with their eyes painfully closed. Only a heavy handsome Greek (or at least he looks like a Greek) leaning against the wall to my right keeps looking around, his cool gaze passing over the small crowd, then passing over Alex and me. I sit on a small bench shoved back against the wall, then pull off my sandals so I can feel the music in my feet, and when I look up again and see that he's coming over to sit down next to me, I feel a dropped flutter in my belly.

"Mademoiselle," he whispers in his exciting foreign voice, "d'ou venez-vous?"

"Canada," I whisper back.

"D'accord."

"D'accord?" I smile up at him. "What do you mean by that?"

"Mademoiselle, pleeeze, put on your shoes, we do not permit people to be wearing their bare feet in this club."

WE COME BACK to London to stay for a week on Birkenhead Street with the two Polish aunts Alex knows from the times his parents brought him for visits to Warsaw. Anita and Karolinka: two dignified old women who are a little remote. In fact within twenty minutes of our arrival, I get the impression that they want us to go. After a strange dinner of anointed little Polish dishes they turn off most of the lights and go into their downstairs bedrooms, goodnight, goodnight.

Alex and I lie on our sleeping bags at the top of the house and whisper about them in the dark.

"They want us to go," I whisper.

"No, they don't. They're just very reserved."

"When I tried to help them out in the kitchen after dinner tonight they sighed."

"They sigh because they're old, they get tired."

"I really hate sponging on them." (Especially now, when they are being so unpleasant. Especially to me, I think but don't say.)

"But you've said yourself that you come from a family of spongers."

"I know, but I still hate it, I've always hated it. I'd rather stay in the worst dive of a hotel. And they don't just sigh, either. They also elbowed me out of the way when I tried to help out. And whenever I asked them a question they didn't even bother to answer me."

"I find that very hard to believe."

"Are you suggesting that I'm making it up?"

"I just said I find it very hard to believe."

But our worst sin of all is our German licence plate and in particular the white metal tongue with the D for Deutschland on it, I know this because tonight when I go to the window to take a bedtime look down into the rainy London garden, I see the two old women down on the wet driveway three stories below me, both with their raincoats caped over their shoulders and both giving what looks like some sort of bizarre attention to our motorbike. Anita, in a safari hat and her Wellingtons, is squatting and winding something (gauze?) around a part of the licence plate while Karolinka is posed with strict medical immobility beside her, an assisting nurse in a white cotton nightgown, in her free hand a flashlight that she keeps beamed on the D. Or on what was the D before it got hidden by its bulky mitt of gauze and adhesive. I call out to Alexander, "Alex! Come quick! Anita's bandaging up our motorbike!"

After this we take to referring to her as Adhesive Anita. It's a story to us, a useful anecdote. She was bandaging up our German licence plate in the rainy dark, I plan to write in my journal. So the neighbours wouldn't see it. She looked like a ravaged Christopher Robin in her short-legged pyjamas and a safari hat and her Wellies. But I won't write this until we've reached the outskirts of London—which I hope will be soon—I'm too afraid that the two old aunties from Warsaw, both compulsive dusters, will just happen to dust open my journal and read it.

WE CONSIDER LIVING IN STOCKHOLM over the winter, but we'd only know William and Gunilla and they don't even live in Stockholm, they live even farther north, in darkest Uppsala. Stockholm in winter would be banks of candles everywhere, or so I imagine it, the whole city a windy cathedral, Swedish girls with medieval but photogenic faces posing in depressed Stockholm doorways, it's too north, too dark, and so we end up spending the long rainy winter in Copenhagen instead. Everything is so wet: wet cobblestones, wet Radhus Pladsen, rainy grey Baltic Sea, grey parks with tracts of frosty grey grass and grey monuments until the rain rains all the frost away.

Then it's back to Canada again. To Ottawa, where we have two babies, then join the Committee, a group of activists and pacifists that's made up of Quakers, Unitarians, Marxists and Trots. The women go to buffet suppers at one another's houses on windy spring evenings, husbands in tow, although many of the husbands are by now conducting affairs with unmarried women—Alexander has already had at least one affair—while it falls to the wives to merely have little crushes. Afraid of losing our children, most of us only flirt, while all around us, younger women swallow a small blue pill along with their vitamins every morning, the notorious little blue freedom pill that makes it possible for them to walk up to the buffet of husbands to take their pick. But the flirtations are lovely too, I'm convinced of this the night I'm standing chatting to another woman on a lawn in Alta Vista, one of Alexander's jackets caped over my shoulders, its empty sleeves hanging down, when Vic (an adored husband, at least by me) comes up behind me to press the sleeves against my bare arms to warm me.

On a hot fourth of July the members of the Committee go to stand in two rows flanking the driveway up to the American ambassador's house, we stand in silence as his guests cruise slowly past us, a long parade of men in seersucker suits, their women beside them, wanton and sleepy in slippery dresses. Followed by a hush, then a roar, then two cops on motorbikes, then the future prime minister (we already know it's just a matter of time, he is *such* a star) coming at a good clip up the road, jaunty wave to all from his small open car.

But I love to read novels too much to ever be a good revolutionary. You can hide away from the world while you're reading and it saves you, it's like sex in this way. And so all I want to do is lie down on the tan India print tablecloth that I've spread out over the lawn and read book after book on the long hot afternoons, not pour coffee for the members of the Committee who come to policy meetings at our house or stay up late to make supper for Quaker women from Boston whose trains don't get in until two in the morning. I'm also forever hiding things: hiding fashion magazines, hiding anything the people we know will consider trivial and when a deserter from the American army comes to stay with us our second summer here I also try to hide my dislike for him. Light-eyed, in his late twenties, his gaze suggests harsh times, the frontier, a body hard as wood. He also has an air (especially at mealtimes) of being accustomed to so very much better. Three much more appealing Americans arrive the day after he leaves. Two men from the deep south and a woman from New York City. They've driven all the way here from San Francisco in an old hearse they've painted white, a white coffin roped to its roof and packed with leaflets. I feel proud to have the white hearse parked in our driveway, proud to have our neighbours see the brave company we keep. One of the men is a vegetarian, when he called to tell me this an hour ago, I spooned the main part of the casserole out into a smaller Pyrex dish for him, leaving behind the chopped-up wieners and the melted web of mozzarella, and now I watch him as he eats it to see if there's a moment when he tastes a criminal hint of the wiener, but it's fine, he eats without flinching, and after dinner they leave us for more militant and thrilling cities, to be followed by an American professor from Princeton, a courtly shy man who drinks cocoa with us in the kitchen, then asks us if he can use the phone out in our hallway to call his wife. "Hello, sweet darling!" we hear him call to her across the miles, but then Alex gets up from his chair and closes the door. I would have left it open, I would have eaves-dropped. And after we've all gone up to bed, I'm the one who lies wide awake the whole night the professor sleeps in the bedroom next to ours, it's so electrifying to have someone so magnificently thoughtful so near.

A Marxist from Toronto arrives next, a knapsack of notebooks strapped to his back. He lets it slide to the floor as he commandeers our den. Has an imperious voice and manner: His Gruffness. Has also tried to give angularity to his big bossy rump by stuffing packs of cigarettes into his back pockets. Expects me to bring him coffee and tea and above all expects me to keep the children at bay. Who, maddeningly, seem to think he's tremendous. The first two days I tiptoe around him, bent on accommodating him, but tonight when Alex gets home from work I whisper to him about the Marxist ("He's obnoxious") and as he's hammering tacks into the long horizontal print of Picasso's *Guernica* above the sofa, he whispers back, "Look, it's only for one more day, let's ask him to babysit, then we can check to see what's on at the Nelson...." And so we walk hand in hand into the range of furious typing. Which comes to a clattering stop two or three seconds before Alex knocks on the door. And when our resident tyrant calls out "Come in!" we open the door to see him yawning in a highly pleased way, then he zips up his jacket. Lord, this radical boy is clairvoyant, he's so clearly on his way out for the evening. "Think I'll take a wee break, think I'll go take in a movie. *A Hard Day's Night* is playing down at the Nelson...."

WILLIAM IS HERE. And agrees (because of the fog) to stay overnight. At midnight we're still out in our cool kitchen drinking wine and cracking walnuts—a baronial sound in the foggy fall evening—then while Alex is locking up for the night, William follows me up the stairs when I go up to fetch sheets and a pillow for him and after we've reached the bedroom level, we stand in the doorways of my babies and listen to their breathing while I whisper their names and ages to him and he whispers the ages of his three daughters to me. Then it's on up to the third floor where he sits on the windowsill drinking his wine as he watches me dip my way around the low canvas army cot to pull the blankets up over the sheets. But he must notice that I don't like to be watched because he reaches over to a low bookshelf and pulls out my copy of *Women in Love*. "Oh no," he says, smirking down at the book. "D.H. Lawrence. And so do you actually like this guy?"

"Yes, I do. I love him."

"What's to love?"

"Oh, the way he catches the intensity of the feelings, the fights between his men and women...."

"But the guy was such a fascist, such a tiresome autocrat." He takes excited little sips of his wine. "A pedantic hedonist," he says.

"I like that," I tell him. "Pedantic hedonist. But wasn't he too passionate to be a hedonist?"

"Too passionate? Too much of a petty fascist dictator is more like it."

"Speaking of fascists, how's your Nazi novel coming along?"

"Gone into hibernation …"

I poke his pillow into a flowered pillow slip. "Runaway American soldiers and Unitarian women have slept on this cot. And sexy Marxist men."

He smiles one of his watchful small smiles. "Can't say I'm enticed."

I'M TOO LIGHTLY DRESSED at breakfast this morning (in a skimpy top and billowy silky trousers) and so have to dance from one bare foot to the other while I'm shaking the bacon across the hot silver face of our new stainless steel pan. Whenever we have guests stay overnight, I don't dress in the jeans and boots I ordinarily wear, I'm like a girl of fifteen bent on wearing something new because I can't be myself. And when I'm serving William his bacon and he says in a low voice, "Well, I don't have to ask you how *you* slept," I don't dare ask him what he means, I just have to pray that I didn't go up to the third floor in my nightgown (or without it) to pay him a visit in my sleep.

After Alex leaves for work, the boys totter down the back stairs to play in their sandbox, but William and I stay where we are, at the breakfast table, talking about *Sons and Lovers,* and in spite of the fact that he shouts his opinions, I feel grateful for them. "No one I know here ever talks about books, although a few of our Quaker friends have read *Portnoy's Complaint.* But not for literary reasons."

"No one," he tells me, "reads *Portnoy's Complaint* for literary reasons." But at this point the sound of the mail being forced through the mail slot startles us, magazines and bills pushed through to lie scattered on the floor. Only a postcard addressed to Alex in a flowing script makes my heart skip, but how private can it actually be, if she (whoever she is) has written her lover a note on a postcard for even the mailman to see? And rebelliously thinking, If the *mailman* can read this, *I* can read this, I flip it over and look down to read:

Comrade Oleski:

If I had of knowed you would be at that lie-in at La Macaza, I would have took a big truck and drove over you myself to rid this great country of ours of one more hunky Commie for sure.

M. Grey

I hand the postcard to William on my way out to the back porch, then run down to the garden to my babies, but they are still here, still safe, still playing a busy game of motor sputters and happy cries. I don't want to say to them, "There's someone out there in the wide world who means to do our little family harm," but I will if I have to. In the meantime the sun shines down on the trees as it has always done and when William comes down the porch steps to sit next to me, I look down at the postcard to say, "The handwriting makes it look as if a lovely and innocent young woman wrote this postcard, someone who teaches small children how to sing."

"Yeah. It's also someone who's faking the bad grammar. Someone who wants to come across as an East European fascist thug so illiterate that she's picking an obvious alias like M. Grey."

Flies swarm near the jam on William's toast as I try to picture her: a woman in a red suit whose mouth has been lipsticked into a black heart. The kind of woman who hums to herself in a satisfied, malevolent way. A smug crazy woman who might do any bizarre thing at all if she took it into her head to just do it.

"I do know that for weeks I won't want the children to play outdoors by themselves." And I look down at them in their sandbox, such small boys still, boys so small that they can walk while squatting.

"What do you think Alex will think of it?"

"He won't give a damn, he'll tell me she's a crackpot, he'll tell me to ignore it."

Once William has driven away, I sit with the postcard still in my lap, in love with Alexander again. He's worth it then, the misery of living with his moods is worth it, he is doing such brave work in the world. I go through the bills in the perfect sunshine, not really paying attention to them until I discover that one of the envelopes I mistook for a bill is an envelope with Alexander's office address printed on its upper left corner. But it's been addressed to me. I open it to pull out a letter typed by Becky, the office receptionist—the initials (B.T.) have been typed in the lower left corner—then look down to read a letter that Alex has apparently dictated to her so she could type it to me:

Dear Katarina Oleski,

I am writing to once again bring to your attention a hole in one of my good black silk dress socks. I would be most gratified if you would deal with this matter as expeditiously as possible.

Yours respectfully,
Alexander Oleski

If only he had been willing to type up the letter himself and not exposed me to the scorn of a woman my own age, I might have hurried up to the sewing room to darn the damn heel. But now I don't feel obliged to, I'd rather just sit here and hate him for his clumsy whimsy. Which is perhaps just as well since his sock would in all likelihood only have ended up all bumpy and puckered. And so I stay out in the sun with the boys, struck by the revelation that a postcard that could only be called hate mail should have filled me with love for my husband while on this very same morning a letter from this very same husband has arrived to sweep all this new love away.

Days pass, years pass, only one spot of colour bobs in the dim afternoon as I walk past the war memorial, then cross Elgin Street: a deep pink umbrella borne on a slender steel stick by a woman whose bare legs are also sticks, sticks of tan bone. Ancient apparition of fashion, she appears to be frightened of everything: the rain, the traffic, the armies of civil servants, their faces pale beneath the shelter of their dark umbrellas. I glance over at her, thinking the usual—I don't want to grow old! I don't want to die!—then look quickly away, and in looking away see Vic Elderkin crossing against the light on Wellington Street. I need to escape. I need to hide. I need to hurry, but I need to hurry slowly. Feeling apprehensive and ridiculous, I step into a green shop where everything smells of green suede and wool, squeeze past rows of green kilts, push my way past racks of green sweaters, end up at a row of suede jackets, pick up a green cuff, peer at it as if my life depends on my correctly reading a price tag.

But he must have seen me out on the street because he's followed me in here and my heart's still beating too fast as I hear him say my name.

I look up. I pretend to be startled to see him. "This is so amazing. So you're back in Canada again."

"I always did plan to come back, Kay."

32

We're left with a silence after this until he says, "And so are you planning to buy anything in here?"

"I like the green jackets," I tell him, hoping to give my escape the dignity of an actual errand.

"Go try one of them on, then. And one of the kilts too."

Once I'm behind the hazy beige curtain I draw on the cool slippery newness of the jacket. But the kilt is so bulky that it makes my legs look too skinny and white. I study my face in the mirror for a doubtful moment, then draw back the curtain to step out onto the bristle of the carpet in my bare feet.

He's sitting on a chair at the back of the shop like a husband, reading his paper.

"So," I say, trying to look amused and ironic as I hold my splayed fingers lightly pressed against the low pockets of the jacket, "What do you think?"

He looks up. "Great kilt. Is it expensive?"

I lift up the price tag that's hooked to its waistband. "Ninety-nine dollars."

"I won't buy it for you, then. But I will buy you a coffee."

It's still raining, but more lightly by now, as we walk down Elgin, then turn onto Queen, Vic talking about a Spanish course he took in a little town in Guatemala at the foot of a volcano.

"An active one?"

"Active enough," he says as we walk into a chilled place with green wallpaper and black posters of water lilies floating on glassy black lakes while Oriental music trickles nearby. Confetti dots are sprinkled along the red path of the carpet.

"They must have had a wedding in here," I say as we sit down in one of the tall booths.

He smiles. "And so how's Alexander?"

"He has the flu. But otherwise he's fine."

The waiter sets down glasses of water and menus. But we tell him we only want tea.

"And the boys are fine too. Last week I bought them guns."

"Guns?"

"Two little revolvers inlaid with fake mother-of-pearl."

'The ultimate pacifist buys guns for her babies."

"I did it because Tom had nothing to shoot at the other children with except for a twig or a finger and so he kept getting attacked. And so I bought both the boys pistols at Zellers and now Alex and I have a new manifesto: Let our children be children, let them play war, let them be happy."

But now our waiter is back and so we are quiet as we listen to the awkward pure sound of tea being poured, then I wait till he has gone off again. "But a real gun in the house would be a whole other story. I'd be too terrified that I'd walk in my sleep and shoot someone."

"Someone whose name begins with an A?"

"Or someone whose name begins with a K."

"The next thing you know you'll be buying a TV."

"We've already done that. We bought an old set from the colonel next door. And it's turned Tommy into a maniac...."

"He's been deprived for too long."

Could he really be talking about us? One afternoon three years ago he took Benno and me for a drive to the Rockeries, the cold sun shining down on the high hill of stepped gardens, Benno running ahead of us on shy excursions and singing songs that seemed to be celebrating some kind of well-behaved happiness. When we got back home he hopped down from the van, ran around the side of the house to play in the back garden. The colonel was all at once in the picture too, watering his lawn, assuming a moronically casual expression to gaze over at Vic's windshield, trying and perhaps also managing, in spite of the reflection of sun and windy leaves in the glass, to see in. And so we could only sit tightly holding hands until Vic lifted my hand onto his thigh, then pressed his hand down on my hand.

A MALE VOICE IS SINGING "If You Don't Know Me by Now," his voice plaintive one moment, a warning the next as I walk among thickets of garters, then disentangle what looks like a black net swimsuit with black velvet leaves pasted to it, the whole nubile contraption attached to black garters.

Alex is on his way down the stairs as I come into the house. "What kept you so long?"

I slip off my coat, taking care to leave the soft pink bag containing the sexy contraption lodged inside a sleeve. "I got off the bus on the way home and went for a walk."

"In the rain?"

"It's really only a faint mist by now. I also bought you a bag of bananas."

He walks ahead of me down the hallway to our bedroom, his tall black socks pulled up to a height that makes his pyjama legs balloon out, giving him a sour but comical look, and when we get to our room it smells stale and infected, dark leaves are crowding at the windows in the early evening wind.

He fishes a black book out of a box. "Look what I just found."

I open it to see a photograph of a stone frieze of Adam and Eve that I taped inside its front cover when we were still living in Europe. Fig leaves—stylized, primitive, their stems thick as black handles—hide the medieval stone genitals like two ping-pong paddles that have burst into leaf. My first entry is even from stony Bruges:

We are now in Bruges and after a late lunch went for a walk in the mild afternoon, breathing in the cool air of this grey city's inherited stillness, its Groeninge Museum and (even) its vile canals. Yesterday we also visited the Basilica of the Holy Blood and saw the Christ, so pale that he looked as if he'd been painted with skim milk except for where the kisses of the faithful had worn the thin paint down to the shiny bare wood of his knees. Then it was off to the cathedral where Charles the Bold and Mary of Burgundy lie buried and, to recover, lovely hot baths, then a quick dash out to a local hotel for an astounding supper of rabbit and prunes cooked in beer.

"Notice how you refer to Jesus Christ as 'the Christ.'"

"You think it's pretentious?"

"Don't you?"

"Yes, I do." But I feel deeply in love with it nevertheless.

He bites the top off his banana. "From the French. From the Russian. From the Portuguese."

I still have to smile, my younger self pleases me so.

"And here's an antique airmail letter from that madwoman, your mother."

I stay sitting on the side of the bed to read it:

Sweet little Kay and dear handsome Alexander,

Always so good to hear. Please write as often as you can. Although we do know how rushed life can be—how fantastically evasive time is, how quickly it evaporates, how soon the clock strikes twelve, etc., etc., etc., and yet a few words of news of your beloved selves is wonderful to receive—even though we do of course also know that we are as constantly in your thoughts as you are in ours. Hope all is as fine with you two dear ones as it is with us. Much much love and kiss kiss,

Idona

I remember this letter, it was waiting for us at American Express in Rome and I carried it (pressed between the pages of my passport like a square blue mountain flower) all the way to Paris. Where I finally slit it open to read it, then handed it across the coffee cups to Alex. When he read it he laughed. He already knew the sort of family he'd married into. "By the way, what's for supper?"

"I thought I might just throw together a stew. From the lamb."

"From the lamb. From the Czech. From the Swahili."

On my way down the stairs I hear the slam of a car door and peek through the round window to see the boys in their shining yellow rain ponchos racing across the lawn like invaders, so sturdy and rosy that they look like the baby children of giants.

W HEN WE MOVED to an ugly street in the east end last summer, the boys both in high school by now and Alex living on his own on the top floor of a house in LeBreton Flats, our street still smelled of the dried fragrance of its sooty gardens. But winter turned it bleak, a glare at the windows, even if the early March sun shines hotly through the plants on our windowsills, then moves in its quick arc across the sky as I change the beds and pour myself a glass of wine, then drink down two cups of coffee as an antidote to the alcohol before I pull on my coat and run down the stairs into the cold end of the day, slam myself into my car. But it's just too very damn cold, please let it not snow, this is my ardent winter prayer as I speed past the Shinto shrine lookout and the frozen river and park behind Union Station, then hurry to the Byward Market. I need to buy tulips. Tulips and Swiss coffee and a Black Forest cake with almonds and rum in it.

To the deli first, European aroma of disinfectant and ham, buy the coffee, buy the cake, then on to the moist claustrophobia of the flower shop, don't linger here either, don't let nervous resentment turn you into a spendthrift, then the dash out to Uplands to meet Idona's plane, the bare trees whitened by frost as my car swings between them down the grey highway.

Then the first view of Idona: grey fur Cossack hat and her fair hair brushing the collar of a long coat whose ivory leather has such a greyish cast it could once have belonged to a nomad.

"But where's your professor friend, Idona? Wasn't he planning to come with you?"

"He won't be flying in until midnight," she tells me as we're walking out into the cold evening. "But what about you, sweetie? Do you have a boyfriend right now?"

"No," I tell her. "Not at the moment."

"That's too bad, darling. It would be so nice if you had someone to take you out places."

When I think of being with a man, I think of being in bed with him, I don't think of being taken out places. "But I hate all that," I say darkly. "Going out. Dating." And I do. I despise the very word *dating*. Where men are concerned, I don't want to date, I want to be saved. But I tell her that I just want to be close to someone.

"Yes, of course," she says, sounding offended, even almost frightened. "I didn't mean to suggest that you shouldn't also want *that....*"

I shove her suitcases into the trunk, but as soon as we're off she begins to speak of her new friend. "A really brilliant man. But in spite of all that brilliance, really just so awfully, awfully dear and kind."

I frown as I turn out of the parking lot in the dim winter twilight.

"Henry Bix Goodison, his name is, and he's really just so considerate. Which is so amazing, really, especially when you consider that he's such an incredibly important man. And such fun to be with, and so I really do feel most awfully lucky—"

"What do you mean by important, Mother?"

Already knowing, of course. Meaning position. Position and impeccable manners and lots of money to keep position and impeccable manners afloat. But there's only the sound of the highway ringing beneath us in its sad Canadian drone until she pulls off her gloves, then neatly draws them on again to say, "Do you miss him?"

"Who?"

"Alexander."

"Why in the name of God should I miss Alexander?"

She turns to look out at the blank little white houses that are by now flying by, but I don't need to see her expression to know it, I can feel it, in the cold car. "I just meant that Alex is a very fine man as *well*," she tells me, speaking directly to the night on her right. "Idealistic. It surely must be possible to miss a person like that. Just because you're divorced from him doesn't mean you have to be spiteful about him...."

Whenever I look back on my marriage, I see myself reading. I'm reading while the boys take their naps, I'm reading a novel propped up next to one of my cookbooks as I cook, I'm reading in the bath last thing at night, I'm opening *Heart of Darkness* to see a small rain of sugar or salt fall into the water. When I had to pack the books for the move to the new place, *Neurosis and Human Growth* was all swollen and wavy from having set sail in the bath, its chapter on narcissism blurrily underlined, long or short paragraphs that must once have deciphered Idona for me, for beside these underlined segments her initials appeared everywhere in the margins—M for Mother, I for Idona—M and I, M and I, M and I—flurries, whole battalions of them, the maternal initials. But "M and I" could also stand for Me and I, this is a frightening thought, although I'm quick to point out to myself that a true narcissist couldn't have thought it. But I don't want to start any fights with Idona and so I only ask her if she remembers what people in Ottawa call Confederation Square.

"Something amusing, I seem to recall."

"Confusion Square."

The view of the bridge that's so spectacular on summer days, turning Hull into Helsinki above the bold blue of the water, now only looks dim and hazy, lights pricking into life here and there, and once we get to Sussex Drive, its Georgian houses look elegantly repressed and historic in the grey winter evening. "It's really a beautiful old town, isn't it? Never mind all its cow-town names." But I actually love these names— Tunney's Pasture, Mooney's Bay, Patterson Creek, Brown's Inlet—even though I also long to live somewhere else. Somewhere animated by feuds and opinions and fashion and gossip, somewhere electric. Montreal, New York, Toronto, Chicago. "I mean," I say to Idona, "what *is* this? Is this a farm that we're driving through, or is it a city?"

"But all these funny old farm names are rather sweet, really."

"Once the boys grow up, I might move to Montreal, it would be so much cheaper to live there. And so much more thrilling …"

"But I thought you loved your job here."

"Sometimes I love it, sometimes I hate it."

"I've been looking at you, sweetie, and I've been trying to decide what would help you. I really think you should do something different with your hair."

In the mornings I braid it into one big braid, then jab hairpins into it as I pin it up at the back.

"You'd be a much prettier girl if you'd only cut it shorter, let it breathe a little. Turn to your left so I can see it better."

"That might not be all that brilliant an idea, Mother. Not while I'm driving."

"We're coming up to a red light."

I brake, then turn my head to my left so that she can peer at my braid.

"Do you know what your problem is? It looks too fuzzy. A braid should be sleek."

It is, I think, going to be a terrible week.

But I need to slow down to park behind the cathedral. "I used to take the boys down here in the winters, on their sled." On the long walks of their childhood, the cathedral's statue of the Virgin Mary shining high up in the sun, a devout golden peanut gazing out at Hull and the hills from between her twin stone filigree spires. "Listen, I have to stop off at a pharmacy, but just for a minute."

"What for?"

"Just small things. Vitamin C. Toothpaste. A prescription …"

"For what?"

"A sort of sleeping pill."

"Oh, don't get into that, little Kay. Taking drugs. I've never ever taken sleeping pills. Not even when Daddy died and I had so much to cope with. And not when your stepdaddy died either."

I hurry down the windy street to the pharmacy. All I ask is not to be accused of anything. Although in my heart of hearts I of course ask for more, since—contrary to what Idona imagines—I often fall in love. Even with men I only see on the street, above all with men who carry their purpose swiftly in a way that seems too preoccupied to be sexual, but that somehow, because of something thoughtfully wise and considered in their eyes, seems the most sexual way of all for a man to be.

WE CLIMB THE STAIRS into the stale dimness and after I've hung Idona's swish coat in the hall closet I turn on lamps already positioned to shine down on arrangements of tulips. But all these aimed lights are a hazard because they also pick out flaws and shabbiness: the hole in the beige carpet that always makes me think of a hole in the heel of a woman's stocking, a pink plate with a banana skin gone tropically black on it. But when Idona gazes brightly all around the room to say that it's quite charming, really, much more charming than it looked from the outside and where are the boys, I tell her that they probably just had a few things to do after school and when I come back to the front room with the tea things, she squints up at me. "Aren't you terribly hot? In that big heavy sweater?"

"Not really."

"You have such an attractive little body, you should try to look more feminine."

"My body's too thick...."

"Of course it's going to look thick if you wear such chunky boots, such chunky trousers."

"These boots are combat boots, Idona. The height of fashion. Or they used to be."

"But why are you forever wearing black? Because black is not really your colour, sweetie."

"I wear it because it's practical," say I, her impractical daughter.

The real truth is that silk shirts in many colours are my downfall: mauve, rose, teal blue, moss green, ivory. But now there's the sound of boots clumping up the stairs and I pray that Idona will see how truly fine and good my boys are. Of course they aren't always good, they can be monsters, they can be mopey, they can be insufferable, they are adolescent boys after all, and so before they come into the front room I also pray for them to make a good impression. And as they come in they do: they shake hands with Idona and when she holds up her cheek to be kissed, each boy shyly kisses her.

EARLY ON THE SUNDAY MORNING that Henry Bix Goodison is coming to tea, there's a quiet but persistent knocking on my bedroom door and to stop the maddening rap-rap-rap of it, I cry out in terrible voice, "Who is it?" Then open my eyes to see Idona peek in. Pertly awake and dressed in a pair of ski slacks and a shaggy silver sweater that gives her an unfairly young look, she whispers, "Darling Kay, do you know where my toothbrush is?"

"What time is it?"

"I don't know exactly, darling, but it must be close to eight—"

I hitch myself up on an elbow. "The boys! They'll be late for school—"

"But it's a Sunday," she whispers.

I pluck up my watch so I can squint at it and see that it isn't close to eight or anywhere near it, it's only six-fifteen. I want to flounce around in my bed then, make her understand once and for all how truly monstrous she is. "This is the only morning of the whole week that I get a chance to sleep in!"

Under her miffed look, she seems trembly, as if she might cry, and so I don't dare set her off. "Look," I say. " I'll help you look for it when I get up, okay? Please leave me in peace until then. And don't wake the boys either, let them sleep!"

After I've heard her footsteps pad off, I get out of bed and push a chair tight against my door. Then I throw myself back into my bed and haul up the sheets, pound my pillow in a muffled rage. But my heart keeps beating in such pure hopped-up anger that I might just as well just give in and get up. But no, I won't, I'll just lie here and seethe and remember how she used to talk to Vivi and me about sex and the importance of "pleasing a man." And yet there was something about her lectures that was too uneasy, exploratory. Under the guise of giving us guidance she seemed to be trying to find out what we knew. Behind her back we would exchange mocking looks. We were adolescent girls, after all, and as adolescent girls it was a point of honour for us to believe that our parents' sex life was either non-existent or dreadful. As I sit up, then draw on my dressing gown, I think instead of getting dressed to go out, the nights with their bright stars and unwritten endings a stand-in for the future itself, the good luck we saw coming to us, but now I only feel drunken with crossness in it as I step out into the pure glare of the morning to see that Idona's door is shut. It even looks as irreproachable as a tombstone with the bright winter sun on it and it's this awful blamelessness that makes me understand that she must have gone back to bed and even gone back to sleep.

And it's true, she must have, because it takes her another two hours to come down to breakfast in a silk dress that looks very untried in the world, very new. "Sweetie, the front room is looking just too awfully boring. Let me revitalize it for you."

Revitalize: a word I remember from my childhood. Revitalize, beautify, finalize, spunky. I glance back at her over a shoulder. "Feel free." And so she goes off to collect baskets from other rooms, gathers up all the bunches of tulips and pokes them into a single black vase. I go down the hall to watch the transformation, see her hide a cushion with a grey-freckled patch of mildew on it behind a black cushion, then tumble lemons into Mexican baskets placed in the hot path of the sun. "You see how much more charming it looks...."

I agree, it does, but now the buzzer is buzzing and so she has to clatter down to the door to let Mr. Bix Goodison in, then leads a virile bald man up the stairs. A man in his late sixties, but powerfully, alertly in his late sixties, long black hairs grow down his wrists. "So you are the lovely daughter of this lovely lady," he says to me.

And when we sit down for tea Idona turns to me. "Don't the boys want to come down? And meet Henry?"

"Oh, I don't think they can. They have so much homework right now...."

Henry smiles as he stirs his tea. "They do their homework to music, I see."

As the afternoon passes slowly by, the talk keeps needing to be fanned back to life—the snow, the weather in general, the follies of the prime minister's wife—and not long after Henry leaves, Idona calls an old friend, then comes out to the kitchen to speak to me in an urgently subdued voice. "Frannie wants me to come and have lunch with her tomorrow, but I want to drive out to Kingsmere with Henry and so is it all right if I tell her the boys are sick and I have to stay home to help you look after them?"

I'm stirring a green soup that keeps swelling up and it seems to me that Idona's request is turning me into her mother. For here she elegantly stands, her shaggy silver sweater pulled down to the hem of her classy silky dress, a woman who has not washed even one single dish. Madam Dolittle. "No," I tell her. "It is not all right. If you want to tell lies to Frannie, don't tell her a lie that has me or the boys in it."

I TELL THE BOYS about this conversation tonight at dinner (Idona is still out on her Kingsmere date with Henry) and they pretend to cough, then get so carried away by the theatre of it that they clutch at their stomachs and pretend to throw up.

"And anyway, what would she have done for you if you actually *were* sick? Sit on your beds and force you to listen to stories about her love life?" I don't know whether I sound acid or wistful, asking this. No, I do know: I sound like someone who's trying to sound acid, but who's too wistful to manage it. After they've carried their custard into the front room, I stay sitting at the kitchen table reading *The Citizen*, the radio turned to the CBC. I should turn to a music station, because with the CBC there's always the danger that I'm going to be educated against my will or shamed into thinking worthy thoughts. I hear the ticks of rain on the windows, switch to a station that plays weepy pop. But Idona and Henry must be back in Ottawa by now, Idona must be walking into the Château Laurier and loving the scale of it, the majesty, the gigantic pear-shaped crystal chandeliers ending in hitched-up ropes of glass beads and crystal pendants, the eyes of the doormen so clearly letting her know how superbly she does indeed measure up, the satisfying hotel mix of the noble and cosy in the looming old landscapes that look as if they've all been painted on brooding afternoons in darkest Scotland. She's already told me that she's not planning to have sex with Henry until their wedding night, but I can still imagine her thinking how terrific it would be if she could just stay over there with him and have her breakfast rolled in on a hotel trolley every morning, a breakfast as dazzling as a perfect winter morning—snowy linen, serenity, black coffee, pale juice in crystal glasses—instead of shifting for herself as she's had to do in the sloth of my place, and so it's all too easy to imagine her saying to Henry, "You'll never believe what I found in Kay's kitchen when I opened a cabinet above the sink to look for a drinking glass. A hairbrush and a mitten. And three library books. All overdue. Plus a teacup with petrified cornflakes dried on the inside of it. Kay must *drink* her cornflakes when she's in a rush in the mornings. She doesn't even have a boyfriend, not one who's in evidence, in any case." But Henry might defend me. Even if she says, "All she wants to do is write bitter little stories about her family. And her own little life is so deadly *dull*. She has her two boys and her job at a little publishing house but as far as I can see nothing the least bit thrilling ever happens to her...."

But now she's back, I can hear her come in and as I go out to meet her she's brushing the rain off her silvery leather coat, then we all go over to the sofa to watch the evening news—sunlit scenes of brutality, sounds of gunfire, her perfume an insistent sweet reek in the room— and I keep feeling a childish urge to blow at the grey fur dandelion bloom of her Cossack hat, she's still wearing it, if I blow at it I just might make it disappear and she might disappear along with it and so it's a relief when she hangs it up on a peg in the hallway and we all troop up the stairs for bed. And once our little world is in darkness except for the lamp in my room, I squint against the light as I write in my notebook:

Rain at night is what I love most, I feel we are safe then. Wars & carnage are what make me think of sunshine. Of course I won't feel really safe (or happy, either) until we're alone once again. If only Idona would *go*. Darling diary, I count the days.

DIM SNOWY SUNDAY, muffled and slushy, the boys still asleep. Unless they are only pretending to be sleeping while secretly reading up in their beds, not wanting to come down and be polite to Idona. I want to escape from her too and when I hear the final flops and ticks of the dryer coming to the end of its cycle, I hurry down to the basement. I'll just stay down here and fold laundry. Fold the laundry and take my time folding it. Smooth out every sleeve, every pocket. But it's not to be: I've just scooped out a great soft armful of hot clothes when I hear the phone ring and as I run upstairs to it, I can already hear Idona's voice crying, "Whom should I tell her is calling, please?" *Whom*, I think, my heart indignant, oh, please, Mother dear, please do not put on grammatically incorrect airs with my friends, and as I'm on my way into the kitchen I'm greeted by her urgent, "It's a *man*. Someone named William Lindstrom."

"A voice from the past," I whisper as I carry the basket of warm laundry over to the counter next to the stove. Then I come back to accept the phone from Idona. "Hello," I say warily.

"A voice from the past," says William Lindstrom.

How can he possibly have heard me when I was taking such care to speak low? "William. Are you in Ottawa then?"

He is, but only for a day and a half, so could I meet him tomorrow for lunch.

"That sounds terrific."

"You sound a bit constrained."

"A good idea might be to talk that over tomorrow at lunch." I glance at Idona to see that she's over at the stove by this time, rubbing at its chrome knobs and dials with a pinkish damp cloth, doing a poor imitation of a woman deeply lost in her thoughts.

"Does this mean that the voice that answered the phone belongs to your mother?"

"I believe so."

"Is she right at your elbow then, listening in?"

"Actually," I tell him, "it's a favourite spot."

His voice has a smile in it that tells me I'm really quite good at this sort of thing. And I myself think I'm not at all bad at it.

"And what favourite spot is that?" Idona calls out to me after I've hung up the phone.

"The restaurant where I'm to meet William for lunch."

She comes over to sit down at the table across from me. "Tell me about him. Is he handsome?"

"Extremely handsome. With a reddish gold beard. A giant, but a friendly giant." But I also can't help thinking of the straight shining hair that's so at odds with his booming voice. If only he would cut his toddler bangs. If only he wouldn't *shout* so.

"What sort of work does he do?"

"He's a sociologist. But he's also writing a book."

"Oh," she says.

I can understand her disappointment, for I too am writing a book. And worse: have already written a book, *The Dangerous Meadow,* a slim little novel that I've hidden away in my sweater drawer for the duration of her visit. "A book he refers to as his Nazi novel."

"Are there Germans in it?"

"No," I say. "Academics."

But she doesn't smile.

Above us I hear footsteps, the sinking cry of the flush. I reach two mugs down from the cupboard that's cantilevered over the sink. "In fact, after Alex and I split up, William used to visit us sometimes and help me with things. He put up this shelf. He helped the boys fix their bikes...."

"He's keen on you then."

With invented conviction, I say, "Yes he is." But I haven't seen him for over two years. I don't even know if he and Gunilla are still together. They've split up at least once, then reconciled again. "The boys are awfully fond of him too, they call him Sir Will—"

"You must tell me more. Is he romantic?"

The tea could be steaming hot iodine, it looks like such a fatal tincture against the grey glaze of each mug's interior. I want to say to her, But of course you're a strategist and a stock-taker, like all romantics, and I think of how Alex used to call me not only darling but dearling, and not only dearling but dearlingest. "Romantic enough," I say. "Romantic enough for *me,* anyway. But what he is most of all is an excellent father. And an *almost* excellent husband—"

Everything in her face shifts at this, the happiness is kicked away and locked up. You led me on, her eyes say. And her voice says, "I hope you won't have anything to do with him then."

THE PLACE William and I have agreed on is close to Confusion Square, a tall and very old brick building, painted a matte black and with a lot of brass rails and greenery in it as well as little alcoves down at the back, where the maître d' seats me. No sign of William, though, and after an anxious few minutes I get up and push my way past the pink door at the back of the dining room so I can check on how I look in one of the full-length mirrors in the washroom. My glasses have a tint that's a glamorous plum. I take them off, put them on, peer at myself with and without them. Without them, I look like a shell-shocked lily. But Idona's visit wasn't really all that terrible as parental visits go, it's only left me feeling the usual: a little destroyed, a little superior. We even managed not to have one single big scene. The worst moment didn't come till the very end, out at Uplands, when the look I'd spent her entire visit trying to avoid was diagnostically aimed at me, a look that seemed to be powered by an irritated pity as she began to tug at my shirt collar and bat at my coat sleeves. I blot off my pink lipstick and wonder if I should ask William about Gunilla. How she is. I don't think so. But as I'm on my way back into the dining area I can see him coming down the steps to the lower part of the bistro. I wave to him, a tiny restaurant wave, and when he reaches me he holds me at arm's length so he can take a proper long look down into my eyes, then he tells me that I look fabulous. I have no idea if he really means this or if it's only the sort of thing he shouts at women every day of his life. But I'm not being fair to him, his eyes—he's watching me while pretending not to as he's drawing off his scarf—are thinking a lot they're not telling. And his hair is no longer combed down in shining bangs either, now it's wiry and combed back and looks damp, as if he's just had a swim or a shower. He pulls off his parka with a noisy healthy rustle of chilled nylon. "Usually I'm William the Prompt but today I got a call from a client just as I was on my way out of my hotel."

His calling himself William the Prompt makes me think of the children in *To the Lighthouse,* of how they were nicknamed after the kings of England: the Ruthless, the Fair, the Red, the Wicked. "But wouldn't punctuality be a sad thing to be revered for, down through the ages? Wouldn't you rather be remembered as William the Wicked?"

He smiles. "The forecast said snow, but you'd never know it, it's so cold and bright out."

"I know!" I shiver. "The glare." But in here the glare doesn't seem like a glare at all, the sun is pouring so warmly in through the tall windows that I can smell it on the silky backs of the linings of all the fur coats. But will we find anything at all to talk about? I smile back at him again and say, "So."

"So," he says. "I think we should have wine."

When our menus arrive he orders the veal Parmesan, I order the shrimp curry, he orders the house wine. Our waiter is already beginning to go bald, but the rest of what I can see of his body is amazingly hairy. Dense black hair, soft as fur, is even growing in the shells of his ears. An ape, but a gentle ape. He collects the menus with his great hairy hands, and after he's swung off through the greenery, William sits back to study me with solemn affection. "I've missed you," he tells me.

"It's really good to see you again too, William."

And by the time we're eating salads that have a musky odour of woodlot rising up from broken-off chunks of raw mushrooms, the conversation is jumping from one thing to another: his children, my children, the music scene in Thunder Bay, a recent trip he took to Chicago. But the main course has arrived by this time and as we begin to eat he makes me think of a bear from the reign of King Henry the Eighth, a great dancing medieval bear, an iron ring chained to one of its ankles, and once the wine has begun to warm my throat and breasts, his chest begins to seem very warm to me too, broad and healthy with a bear's healthy layer of fat on it, beaming out a great hibernating bear's pleasant warmth. And how really pleasant all of this is anyway: the shrimp curry, the wine, William talking; he's the sort of man who can sit and rub one side of his chest as he talks—he's rubbing it now, in concentric circles, over his heart—and it doesn't seem self-centred, it only seems warm, which makes me remember a conversation I had with him the spring after Alexander moved out. We were sitting on the floor of somebody's summer house out in the Gatineau Hills and I could feel the selective fever of the fire's burn down the length of one arm and the coldness of the flagstones too, in front of the fire. A coldness that seemed both medieval and suburban as it penetrated the thin cotton of my long skirt, then made me ache all along one of my thighs. But then one of William's partners, Stan Sadri, came over and stood, head bowed, listening in, until he hauled off his tie and started to draw the point of it in a weak-ankled dance up and down my shy arm.

As if he is psychic, William now begins to speak of Stan Sadri. "He went west. But the guy I got to replace him is a problem. Basically, the man's a masochist. A masochist and an alcoholic."

I spear a shell of lettuce with my fork, shove it over to a small lake of vinegar and oil, move it around and around in it, then after a small silence say, "I think I might be a masochist myself."

"Really?" He studies me with a thoughtful gaze that seems to be incubating a belch somewhere deep inside itself. He wouldn't have thought so, he tells me. He looks at me with careful attention. "You don't mean whips and blindfolds, do you?"

"No," I say. "Or at least I hope I don't. I actually think my cravings lie more along the lines of …"

"Along the lines of …?"

"It would only be an anticlimax if I told you."

"Try me."

I shake my head.

"*Tell* me."

How did we get into this mess? We were talking about Stan Sadri, we were talking about Stan Sadri's replacement being a masochist, and in anxiety I plane my hair back from my temples as if I plan to experiment with it in some way. Do it up in a twist or a topknot. But then all at once it seems flirty *not* to tell him, a kind of tease, and so very fast I come out with it: "Being spanked."

"I could spank you," he says in a voice that's wonderfully low, for him.

"I wouldn't let you," I tell him.

He picks up one of my gloves and pulls at each of its long leather fingers. "Strange words. Strange words, coming from a masochist. Why not? Why wouldn't you let me?"

It's a question that asks more than the question it seems to be asking and on this account I know it has to be carefully answered. So that even before I've finished saying "Because it wouldn't suit you," I know it's the wrong answer.

"Why wouldn't it suit me?"

"Because you are too nice, William."

"I am not too nice."

Now he is definitely offended, and quite rightly so, and all because the man who took over Stan Sadri's job is on his way to turning into a drunk.

"Word of honour," he tells me. "I am not nice."

"I believe you. Really."

"We could go back to my hotel room right now and I could spank you...."

All around us, civil servants are cracking open new conversations, their laughter forceful, coldly happy. I wonder what they would think if they could overhear this conversation between William and me, a conversation that just has to be, in its own careful way, wilder.

"I can't. I have an appointment with my dentist at a quarter to four."

"I could drive you there. In fact, we could go down to my hotel right now—"

Our waiter is back again, holding a tall pink plastic menu close to his chest. But we shake our heads to dessert and once we're alone again, I wonder if William considers my refusal of dessert to be acquiescence, and I begin to feel a kind of genital equivalent of the giggles, and when he asks in a voice as seductive as the devil's must be, "Are you tempted?" it does seem to me that the only humane response must be to say yes.

Out on the street I slide an arm through his, but then can feel from the tension in his arm that my arm is too wifely and so I withdraw it and pull up the hood of my coat. It's starting to snow lightly, an early spring snow, fine as dust but with pin-pricky stings in it. "I'm feeling a bit anxious about this."

"Don't be." Then he tells me that he's in good physical shape, that I need have no worries on that score, that I mustn't worry that he won't be able to "perform." I can't look at him after he says this because it never even occurred to me to wonder about how he'll perform, I just want this to be over and done with. And he's not really attracted to me either, he can't be. He can't be because I'm not attracted to him. And so I hope he won't feel hurt when this doesn't work out. But I can't very well say, "I'm only doing this to get the kind of experience I can use the next time I'm with a (more thrilling) man."

Snow sparkles in his hair and his beard as he tells me that he can't think of a single instance in his life when he's ever been moved to hit someone. This must be because he's so huge that people tend to steer clear of him. Even as a child, he tells me, he towered. Even in the sandbox, other children (their pails only half filled with sand) backed away from him. Spanking a woman—sexually or otherwise—has never been one of his fantasies, and yet he now finds that it has a certain appeal. But I hate all this, I don't want to get hit, I don't want to get slapped or hurt, I hate violence, it makes me sick, I'm thinking of something much more sexual and fondling than this, but now he's telling me that the last time he was down here he was sure we'd end up in bed together. "But you told me you were very into masturbation back then."

"I did?" I blush in the cold, pretending not to remember, although I can remember it all quite clearly enough. We were at a Sunday afternoon party out in Rothwell Heights and William (wearing an unbuttoned shirt over his black bathing trunks) was leaning toward me as I extolled the virtues of sexual self-reliance. A little drunk, we'd traded slogans. The one I remember liking best is one of his: NO BODY LIKE DIS BODY. But now we're coming into the Lord Elgin to find it crowded with the baggage and cries of a group of women who are all dressed alike, in ham-pink plaid skirts and green blazers. Members of some kind of marching band and incredibly happy to be away for a few days from husbands and children, their excited voices calling out to each other, nicknames or last names, while I can feel my back go slick as I splay my fingers inside the silk privacy of my long coat's deep pockets.

When we crowd into the elevator the band members gaze down in mass sorrow at the toes of their shoes. I don't feel their eyes on the backs of my legs until William and I get out on his floor. And once we've stepped into his airless beige room he's the one who does the housewifely things: turns on the lamps whose gold lampshades are the size of parade drums, turns down the dull brocade bedspread that looks as if it's been stolen from a royal bed in a museum. But as I unbutton my silk shirt he moans, making me hate myself for deciding that his moan sounds like a moan that has been moaned many times before, in many hotel rooms, but I can't lie to myself, I'm feeling extremely detached. He comes over to me then to pull off my boots. So much gallantry makes me feel awkward, a child, and when we stand and begin to kiss, I can feel the relief of not being exposed to his being able to read anything more in my eyes.

"*Bed,*" he groans, and he pulls me on top of him as we fall back onto the Javexy sheets, where we kiss skilfully, passionlessly, until he tells me that he has a condom. "Are you afraid of the plague?" he whispers, and when I respond with what I'm sure is an uneasy smile in my eyes, "I am afraid of *every*think," we laugh in deep unison, as if I've just made a brilliant ironical joke.

He raises himself up on straight arms then, looks down at me. Like a god gazing down at what? Scenery? His own creation? "Don't go away," he whispers, "and that's an order." And he hitches himself up into sitting position, then tells me that he'll be coming right back.

The sound of running water comes next. One discreet blast, then another, then he's beginning to brush his teeth. But the industrious hopeful sound of the brushing makes me feel so edgy that it's a relief when the bathroom door opens and he comes into the dim room toward me, his erection solemnly bobbing.

Tenting the sheet up for him—and again I feel like a wife—I can also feel how cold his tongue is in the wine-warmth of my mouth, and his breath is cold too, a cool peppermint breeze high up in slippery mountains, and the kissing means nothing, just as before, and we have sex as dutifully as any married couple on a Saturday night and afterwards he stays lying heavily on top of me, telling me stories. I feel bathed in his sweat, I feel clamped to the bed by his benign Nordic weight. But at the same time I keep stroking back his sweat-dampened hair and kissing him along his salt-beaded hairline and rubbing my nose in the scratchy and salty bush of his beard as if I want him never to leave me. And for five or ten minutes I really don't want him to ever leave me, it feels so good to be pinned down by such a warmly breathing-in, breathing-out heaviness—and in particular by such a breathing-out heaviness that now and then it makes his belly go tight as a drum as his mouth keeps grazing my eyelids and my mouth—little licks and kisses—although now and then he makes a quick detour to dip down to lick the little hollow at the base of my throat, a sensation that makes me feel happy and useful, as if I've been turned into a salt-lick at the edge of a forest, the kind that the deer come out to, in the foggy early mornings, for a quick taste of salt before they lift their lovely heads to the dawn. Now he's telling me that the first night he was in Chicago he slipped his contact lenses into a glass of water on his bedside table because he forgot to pack his lens solution, and that later that night, overcome with thirst but not quite awake, he drank them. This makes us laugh happily, then he holds his arms straight up in a yawn. "But to go back to this spanking business again: Alexander wouldn't oblige?"

"No. No, he wouldn't."

"Were you ever spanked as a child?"

"No. Or at least not that I can recall."

"Were you ever threatened with a spanking?"

"Now and then."

He lowers his arms to fall into a conductor's gesture. "So there you are then. You're still waiting."

I still don't want it to happen. Not here, not now. "Or maybe it's the sound of it," I say. "Or the idea of the sound of it. The applause that announces coming attractions. Unless it's the punishment before the crime...." Or maybe the craving comes from being adored in that part of my body when I was a baby, little spanks, although if someone had asked me two days ago if I thought about this sort of thing often, I would have said, "No, not often, it's just as if this part of my body has a mind of its own and the way it expresses it is with the low hum of occasional craving." And yet now that it's been at the heart of everything that's been both said and not said for over an hour, it seems to me that I've never thought of anything else. That I've never thought of anything, day in and day out, but wince after wince exploded in a way that needs to be fuelled not only by squeals and grunts but by the most tiny and happy cries, something quite separate from passion, almost its opposite, passion being so much more important and driven. Whereas *this*, this other, would make me feel completely pure, completely silly, and completely young. But the man would have to want to do it to me, and William doesn't. Or wouldn't. And besides, I wouldn't even want him to.

"But suppose *I* was the one who wanted to be spanked. Would you spank me?"

"No," I tell him.

"And why is that?"

"I don't think you could ever convince me that you'd even want me to."

"Suppose I could, though."

"The answer is still no."

"Don't be cruel."

"It just seems to be a more womanly thing, to want to be spanked."

"So for women it's womanly, for men it's pathology."

"I know, I know," I say in a soothing, guilty voice, "I know it's not fair...."

He looks at his watch. "We need to get you to your dentist."

Then we're driving south on Bronson into the afternoon glare and I'm glancing over at him to watch him squint into the low sun as I turn up the collar of my coat. He must be feeling a bit sad too, after such a wasted afternoon. Still, it's an afternoon that it could be entertaining to write about (his anecdotes, my apprehension) and so I say, "Will you write about this?"

"No," he tells me. "But *you* will," then he sings the praises of Gunilla and his three daughters until he has to slow down for a hefty blonde in a short dark plaid coat to stride to the other side in front of his car. He turns to look after her, then says that there must be more goddamn beautiful women in Ottawa than in any goddamn city in the whole goddamn Western world. Then he turns more dutifully to me: "Listen, this was lovely."

But he's wrong, I think as I hurry away from him along the strip of pavement leading to a tower equipped with drills and picks and other miniature and glinting instruments of torture, the very last thing in the world I would want to do is write about this.

THE PEOPLE I MOST FEAR meeting are other writers. Above all this afternoon, when I happen to be much too untidy to allow another writer to see me. Above all a writer who's as big a star as Della Kuhnert. And so I try to squeeze very fast past her, on my quick way somewhere else, but at this same moment she turns and I see that she, too, has no wish to be seen, so much so that I can easily imagine us asking ourselves the same two questions: Does *she* live around here? And, if so, are we likely to run into each other often? When I get to the cash registers I unload my onions and clementines in a rush, then look up to see that she's just arrived at the end of the line next to mine and is already suggesting that we go out for coffee at the tea room next door to Stationery House. Which is where she tells me that a movie is to be made of her latest novel. "That's wonderful," I say unhappily, trying to think of what work news I can offer in return, but I can't recall that I've accomplished anything in particular.

"My husband has to fly off to Bombay next week, and I've decided to go with him."

Her husband, her husband, what does he do? But now I remember, he's something up on the Hill, a deputy minister or parliamentary assistant to someone, but I can't bear it, all the movies made from all her books, all the trips to exotic places, her whole satisfactory orderly life. But Bombay or no Bombay, it seems to me that she has a rodent-like mouth as she neatly chews at her pastry, her sparkling eyes now shrewdly assessing me. There's something so crisp and dainty about her that it couldn't take anything very shocking to make her gasp, albeit prettily. "And how about you?" she asks me. "Are you still writing?"

"Still at it," I tell her. "Still an addiction, still an affliction."

"And you're well?"

"I'm fine. I just didn't get enough sleep last night."

She (forcefully): "How *awful* for you." But then she goes on to say that this is just not an area where she's ever had a problem. "I suppose this is because I work very hard and am consequently tired when I go to bed at night, and so I go straight to sleep."

An exchange that makes me warn myself never to become friends with her. I even begin to suspect her of wanting to lure me into complaining, so that later, behind my back, she can tell people what a complainer I am. "It was nothing," I say. "It was only the one night. So no harm done."

I don't run into her again until one warm afternoon the following spring. Mutual dread. Or perhaps only I am feeling the dread, she seems to be in high spirits. She praises the winning story in the *Saturday Night* competition in a tone of voice I find reverentially fascist and after she's given me a lift home, I invite her in, but as we're walking toward the scuffed door of number 208, I hear a dainty wail behind me: "But do you feel *safe* here?"

"Considering how wrecked it looks, how could anyone possibly think there'd be anything to steal?"

Once we're upstairs she goes to the sofa in my front room and settles herself, looking like an expectant black monarch butterfly posed on a lily pad, and when I bring the teapot out to the coffee table she surprises me by saying, "Are you divorced yet?"

"Yes," I tell her. "But my timing was bizarrely bad because we signed the decree nisi two months before husbands were forced by law to give half their pensions to their former wives."

"But I thought he was the one who left *you*."

"Not really. But someone has to do the actual physical leaving. And it usually falls to the man to do the gallant thing and just go."

"The gallant thing?"

"But it *is* the gallant thing, don't you think? To be the one to play the cad?"

"But Alex is such a great guy, I'm sure he doesn't need a law to tell him to do the right thing."

"Our sex life was good," I say, speaking in a dreamy judicious voice, like a madwoman. "And it began to seem wrong that it was so right when everything else was so wrong."

"I'm not sure I follow you."

It was the sex, really, I tell her, that held us together, it was so depraved and efficient.

"Depraved," she says in a soothing but uneasy voice. "Exactly how do you mean that?"

"I only mean that I didn't love him any more." But when I tell her that I've just bought her most recent book she beams up at me. "Oh, lovely. And so now you must tell me which parts you liked best."

I go to the tallest bookcase to pull it out, then stay standing to read little bits of it here and there, because I can understand why she wants this, can understand why she (or any writer) would want to hear another writer say, "I *really* like this, but I think this part on page twenty works even better, and *this* part, just here on page fifty-three, works incredibly well too, it really made me laugh."

She sits on my sofa looking so happily grateful and so generous, really, that when she tells me that no one in this country writes better, I'm bewildered. Is she talking about *me*? Is she saying that no one in this country writes better than *I* do? Because how could any writer dare to say such an openly adoring thing about herself? And I'm all at once filled with a startled affection for her, I even remember how she once told me she totally loved a story of mine, but no, she's been talking about herself because now she's saying, "And I think the reason I'm the best is that I'm just always a writer, being a writer is everything to me...."

"Your book does have a certain purity," I say darkly. But by purity I mean that there's a certain privileged innocence about her, about her and her book, the innocence of a person who, on principle, has no use for the truth. "But overall, I must confess that I find it suffers from an unbearable lightness of being."

She looks over at me, still apparently hoping for the best, her wavy orange hair bound back by a scarf of leafy chiffon. "But apart from that, you really liked it, didn't you?"

How can I answer this? When what I dislike about her book isn't just one thing, it's everything? But having said too much, I don't have the courage to say no. I even say yes. And after she has driven off, I carry the *Saturday Night* over to the sofa so I can read the allegedly wonderful story. And find it too arch. So of course it would win, it has the requisite deadness. Although afterwards, born of bitterness, there's the usual bonus: the vehement recklessness that leads to good work.

The room is a pale yellow with a nautical decor. One of the chairs has a back that's the steering wheel of a yacht, and two of the armchairs have marine slipcovers: white anchors and white boats on cobalt blue linen. And on the walls two paintings of two identical sailboats sailing on two not quite identical heaves on the swell of two identical seas.

I pick up a copy of *The New Republic,* read the beginnings of three different articles. After ten minutes have gone by, the door to the consulting room is at last pulled open by a blazered woman in her sixties, a harsh-faced doctor in a collegiate-looking grey skirt, narrow knife-pleats in it, a woman who makes me (in panic) think: But I don't want to tell this person anything!

It's no better once I'm seated across from her in her consulting room. I watch her watch me shrewdly as I describe my fatigue and my inability to make a decision, any decision. I don't make decisions, I tell her, decisions are instead made for me, on my behalf, by life.

"Married?" she asks me, looking down at her questionnaire. "Divorced? Higher education?"

"Divorced. But I never went on to get a higher education."

"Why is that?"

"I married young, had children."

"But your children are no longer babies, surely?"

"No, but they're still in school. And in any case it costs money to go to university."

"True, but there are also student loans, I believe." She glances over at the *New Republic* that I've brought into her consulting room with me and when she looks up, I avoid meeting her eyes and study her ugly green floral blouse instead. "And you do seem to have rather intellectual interests."

"I was in love with someone," I tell her, in spite of everything a little in awe of her beautiful Scottish accent. "But he was married. He was married and I was married...."

In fierce (or bored) silence she waits.

"But he went to Africa, then got a divorce and married someone else."

"But this was quite some time ago, I gather."

"Yes. When my children were babies."

"Are you sexually active at the moment?"

At the moment? Well no, actually, I want to say to the awful doctor. Not right at this moment. "Recently," I say. But can I count having been to bed with William for an hour on a single afternoon over a year ago in the Lord Elgin Hotel as being sexually active? "I was recently sexually active, but only briefly."

The large room, meanwhile, feels asleep, great carpeted acres of sun warm it. "But do you not work?" I hear the offensively marvelling voice ask me.

"Yes. At a small publishing house."

"And is your hubby still in the picture at all?"

Hubby and hobby: the two silliest words in the English language. "Only on Sundays."

"And what about hobbies?"

"Hobbies?"

"Do you have any?"

"No. Except that I write. But it's not a hobby."

She seems startled. "Books?"

"Recently I've only been writing stories."

"Have you published any of them?"

What a mean, unimpressed question this question is. I look out the window. "A few. Also a short novel. But that came out nearly eleven years ago."

"Eleven years ago," says the unpleasantly meditative voice. "That's a very long time ago, is it not? And you've not had anything published since?"

"A few stories here and there. A story in *The New Yorker*, actually."

When she stares at me, astounded, I say in a fake humble voice, "Which felt like a bit of a fluke, actually."

In her richly impatient voice she brings the session to a halt. "Look, I could suggest psychotherapy for you, but I don't believe it's what you need at this moment." She gazes up at me with a sensible Scots coldness. "Go to school," she tells me. "Better yourself."

Walking down her steps to the street all I can think is: what a wasted afternoon! And why would I want to go to school, in any case? Of

course a degree would mean I could teach. But the thought of standing up at the front of a lecture hall while I wait for the noise of the
latecomers to settle down so that I can pontificate to a sea of unimpressed or hostile faces fills me with panic. And they would know; a
class always knows when a teacher is terrified.

WHEN ALEX OPENS HIS DOOR, his smile suggests that we share an
old, old joke (our marriage) but when I hand him a stack of his
books and he asks me if I have a job lined up in Montreal, I tell him
no, I'm taking a year off to work on my novel.

"How many years is it since you first started to work on it? Twelve?
Thirteen? And why Montreal?"

"Because I can live so much more cheaply in Montreal."

"Even in Montreal you can't live for free."

"I have enough money saved up."

"After the next referendum, you could even be living in another
country."

"I doubt that will happen."

"Who knows what will happen?" And then it's the old litany: Go
to school, learn to teach, you can't go on living like this, working for
next to nothing while you dream of becoming a writer.

I take umbrage at the "becoming," but he holds up a hand. "You
know what I mean. You also know that so very few who do it are
able to make it. Of course I do know that you work very hard
at it...."

In a tiny voice, tiny and outraged—out of pride! because it makes
me feel stodgy and dull to be told that I work hard at it—I say in an
affronted voice, "No, I don't!"

"You do, you do, I know you do. But you've got to stop being such
a recluse. You've got to go out into the world and meet the sort of
people who might be inclined to do you a favour or two."

As I turn to walk away, he shouts after me, "I also meant to mention my cousin Magda to you! She's looking for a receptionist! For three days a week! You'd still have four days every week to write!"

He's never had any faith in me and now he even wants me to be a receptionist.

"I adore you!" he yells furiously after me, and I turn to look back at him. "Don't live in a dream world!" Then I understand: he wasn't shouting that he adored me, he was shouting that he implored me. But why did he marry me? Because I had a beautiful voice—he cannot abide a harsh or shrill voice in a woman—because I knew nothing about the subjects he was an expert on (politics, architecture) and because, therefore, he could instruct me. Because he barely knew me.

I'M AT THE KITCHEN SINK when I see Benno being blown down the lane in the rain. He looks briskly sad in his long black coat, his black derby, and when he unlocks the door to our part of the house, a lonely breeze blows in from the hall, then he comes to stand in the doorway to the kitchen. "You'll never believe this."

I'm shaking a pat of butter around in the cast iron pan. "I probably won't."

"He hit me."

"Who?" But I already knew.

"Dad."

"Why in the name of God would he do a thing like that?"

He says in a tired voice, almost an untethered voice that's climbing so high it might end in tears, "It was about my hat. He wanted me to take it off when I was at the table and when I said no he started to bat at it, pretending he was just kidding around, you know how he is, always has to pretend everything's a joke just so long as he gets his own way, and so then I said, 'Don't do that, okay? Leave my fucking hat

be,' and then he shouted at me not to shout at him and so then I
shouted at him and so he hit me."

I know what Alex thinks, he thinks a boy coming to the table with
a hat on his head is rude, he thinks Benno's behaviour is lower class, he
thinks it proves that I haven't brought the boys up correctly. I say in a
fierce voice, "I'm going to phone that father of yours right now—"

"Don't say anything at all to him, I beg of you."

AFTER BENNO HAS GONE OFF to his first year at Stanopolis, I pack
what's left of the boys' childhood books—*Titus Groan, The Wizard of
Earthsea, The Left Hand of Darkness, 1984*—so hard to believe that
soon it will *be* 1984—and when I begin the more difficult packing,
I miss their help. They've always been such speedy if unreliable
packers, leaving behind manila envelopes stuffed with tax receipts
and single boots, single mittens, or pelting bottles of spices into cartons
packed with notebooks and cutlery. I spread newspapers out on the
floor, walk past a photo of a bride at the altar of a cathedral, her tulle
veil running from the chancel all the way down the length of the nave.
But when I kneel on the floor to wrap up a pair of glass candlesticks,
I can see that she isn't a bride after all, she's an uphill shot of a
snowed-in highway running between black trees and grey mountains.

THE VASTNESS OF MONTREAL, after green little Ottawa, still feels tragic to me. The grey metro station that sits below the grey road leading up to the grey Villa Maria convent looks out over the sunstruck but grey world of Decarie Boulevard, while down on the platforms the people waiting for their trains seem to be meditating on their monotonous lives. And when they at last rise up on the escalators, then walk out into the windy sunlight of downtown, the great grey stone cathedrals rear up as the tiny downtown people hurry past them, bent on reaching their sad destinations.

But Benno is already here, living in genteel squalor in a rooming house run by a Sri Lankan, a person of general (if hysterical) good will, his roommates old Anglo drunks and ex-cons who carry stolen bloody steaks hidden deep inside the satin inner pockets of their overcoats. On my first Sunday night, he sets out for my place in the October twilight, takes the metro to Villa Maria, gets off the bus on Côte-St-Luc and walks down Randall Avenue and it must be the name of my street that leads me—when he's only ten minutes late—to be haunted by that dirge of a song, "Lord Randal, My Son," and above all by the words "O, where have you been, Lord Randal my son? O, where have you been, my darling young one?"

A WINDSTORM my first week here blows all the leaves down from the trees so that my boxy rooms are now flooded with an uncanny light that elates me as I run down to the basement with my basket of laundry. First wash in the new city! But the basement turns out to be a medieval warren. Walls battleship grey, all the doors painted the building's statutory dull orange. I keep opening the wrong ones. The last one I open leads into a short hallway that smells of old damp, detergent, swept decay.

When I turn a corner, I see two black rats with their backs and tails to me, feeding on something, I gasp and stop. Why don't they run? But then I understand: they're dead. I can't bring myself to step past them, my legs feel too thrummed, instead I walk backwards out of the hallway, then turn and climb the stairs to the floor where the concierge lives.

Madame Goreau, a slender blonde, dried out as a husk and with a fawn cardigan hung over her shoulders, opens the door. Her eyes even carry an entertained smile, as if she's just been told a lovely joke. But what if I only imagined the scene with the rats? I've often enough been electrified by the sight of rats or mice on sidewalks or streets, dead rodents that have turned out to be dead leaves, dead gloves, dead mounds of rags. Once, with a horrible hop of the heart, I even saw a white rat hanging by its tail above the dashboard of a Volkswagen Beetle. But when I got closer to it I saw that it was only a dirty white fur ballet slipper, suspended by a silver ribbon and madly spinning. "This may sound very weird," I tell her, "but I just saw two dead rats down by the entrance to the laundry room."

The pleasure in Madame Goreau's face oddly increases.

"Did someone put out poison?"

"My husband did. But then we always get a rat or two in the building's back wing every fall. Don't worry about it. My husband will go down and dispose of them."

THREE MORNINGS A WEEK I work for Alexander's cousin Magda, a British architect who does house renovations. The other two partners are often away. Away in Europe or away giving lectures at McGill. And so her office is nothing like the big office on the main concourse whose summer students are a flock of fashionably faded tropical birds. Walking past the open door of the big drafting room, I sometimes hear the tropical screech of their laughter.

The noise in the back wing of my own building is another matter. It's no longer the antidote to loneliness it was at the beginning. Now it interferes with my sleep, now I tense up when I hear the woman above me moaning and dropping things (bags of rocks?) on the floor. Sometimes I spy on her from a window, watch her come into the courtyard. She's a redhead, an old beauty, and walks with the majestic, sanctimonious dignity of a madwoman. As for the moaning, it begins the minute she lets herself into the room directly over my head. Then a chirp like the chirp of a bird. The door of an oven? There's also music coming from every direction. A drum from directly below, hard rock and calypso from all around. On my second week here, when I turn on the television to blot out the music coming from too many directions, I happen to catch the last few minutes of an interview with Della Kuhnert. She lightly laughs, making me recall the afternoon she came to tea and how little (or how well) we understood one another, her voice sounding so airy and affected that it makes me picture myself hiding in dense foliage as I peer at her from within a grove of poplar trees, out to where she's prancing in the bold sunshine of anecdote.

Dark days of rain follow, but then December comes on in earnest, enduringly cold, snowless. But rain in the winter always makes me feel hopeful, especially if it starts at bedtime. I fall asleep thinking of how good the city will smell in the morning—of fog and soot and rain on the snow, and of how I'll be able to walk down the street with my coat open. But tonight furniture is being moved around in the room above my bedroom. The legs of the same little table, it sounds like, being scraped back and forth over my head, over and over. I do finally fall into a deep sleep, but then wake up startled, in total darkness, somewhere between three and four. The noise is much louder and by now I know it's no table. It's a rat chewing through the concrete wall near the head of my bed. I flash up, whimpering, no longer able to tell exactly where it's trying to burrow through. It seems to be close to my head, but when I pull the bed away from the baseboard, it seems to be coming down from a corner of the ceiling. And then from the closet next to my bureau. But there's nothing in here and no holes in the baseboards either and so I run to the hall cupboard and paw through a carton of shampoos and face creams till I find my hammer. Then I turn on all the lights and tap delicately with my hammer and by the time I've finished my tour of taps, there's silence.

At the office, the first happiness is always the pleasure of being alone to take in all the order and sunlight, the place having filled itself up with light ever since sunrise. On ordinary mornings I love everything about it—the desks smelling of oiled oak, an armchair that's upholstered in a fabric the corroded red of a sumach. The times I come into it alone like this, the first one, it's almost as if it loves me back. I sit down at my desk, slide open a drawer, slide it closed again. My little empire. But this morning I can only think of my own place and how there are just too many bad things: fights in the night and smashed glass in the hallways and the rats and the wrong kind of running down the stairs, but it's the rats most of all that make me decide that I'm telling myself lies about how much pleasure my job gives me.

At noon the architects from the mezzanine have pushed three of the cafeteria tables together to make one long banquet table and one of the architects is standing at one end of it getting ready to blow out the candles on a birthday cake. As I edge past him, he steps back and bumps into my elbow, knocking me off balance so that I stumble, then land on one knee as everything on my tray makes a graceful slide to the floor.

The next few moments are spent in our joined retrieval of a hill of coleslaw and the shining noodles from my chicken noodle soup, a glistening heap on the dampening carpet, the architect picking up the fragrant cinnamon mush of the baked apple with his napkin. And while I'm over at the garbage hatch, dumping my spoiled lunch down the chute, he drops to one knee as well, to gather up my scattered cutlery like a boy kneeling to play a game of pick-up sticks. In fact I've seen him before, we've passed each other on the sidewalk two times already, glancing at one another both times. He's dark, perhaps Slavic, his face is so broad, even a little pugnacious, but he's looking quite humble as he pushes a new tray along the cafeteria rail, picking out a new everything for me. I choose a table far from the party table while I watch him pay for the new food on the tray. Then he comes walking over to me with it, smiling contritely, and even smiles down at my baked apple as if it's the comment of a friend who's amused him: "Those baked apples look sort of lethal even at the best of times."

"Bad apples," I say, glancing down at it. "This also happens to be what the concierge of my building called the tenants who lived in my apartment before I took it over."

He sits down at my table. He glances over at the others, but he sits.

"For a while after I moved in, I was afraid that these bad apples would try to break into my place, but it never happened. Although last night I could hear a rat chewing in the walls. Chewing through concrete. It was like having a miniature road crew drilling right behind where I was sleeping—"

"That sounds pretty disturbing." And for a moment I'm afraid he's going to look down on me because I so clearly live in a slum. But he even matches my rat story with a rat story of his own. "I shared a house with eight other people my last year at McGill, a big old family mansion up on the mountain. The place was a hovel, but a hovel equipped with chandeliers, sweeping staircases, cockroaches, fireplaces, rats ..." He leans back in his chair. "But I've noticed you down here before. You work for Magda?" And when I say yes, he continues to study me, smiling slightly. "So," he says. "Speaking of rats," and here he gives me an even more fetching smile, "is Magda a rat?"

Because my answering smile feels too revealingly quick, I ask him how, exactly, he means that.

"I didn't mean it the way it sounded."

I have the feeling he did, though. But he says it's an architectural term. "Architects who like to talk theory tend to refer to the rationalist types as rats." He translates a few other terms I've heard Magda use: constructivist, deconstructivist, *post*-deconstructivist, modernism, po-mo. "Po-mo means postmodern," he tells me. "In the lingo. The thing is, the literary theorists stole all those labels from the architects, but it's not such a bad thing, really, to be a rat." And he tells me about a time he worked for a team of architects who were heavily into theory. "So heavily into theory that we didn't actually *draw*, we *talked*...."

But voices are calling to him from the birthday table.

"And so they went under. But here's a thing you might do while you're waiting for the concierge to deal with the situation down in the basement and this is go into all your lower-down cupboards and stuff up any holes and all around the pipes with steel wool. Rats have a hard time chewing through steel wool."

But now he really has to get back to the long table, the irritated others are calling him again. "Come back, Michael! Come back, Galbraith...."

I thank him for his advice about the steel wool. "If you hadn't tripped me, I would never have known that."

He's walking away from me backwards. "Any time you want advice about rats you just come to me!"

MONSIEUR GOREAU ARRIVES with a carton of steel wool wedged into an armpit, and in each hand a foil plate heaped with something that looks as deadly as poison millet. He slides one of the plates under the kitchen sink, sets the other in the bottom of the closet in my bedroom. After he leaves, I lift out all of my skirts and blouses and carry them to the packed closet out in the hallway because I don't want to wear anything that has the smell of rat poison in it. Then I run a warm bath and sit up in bed reading *The Golden Notebook* and am struck by how modern it is, how modern it's stayed, the women in their corduroy trousers talking about their problems with men. But once I've turned out my light, I lie awake thinking about the architect's face and the way he looked when I caught a glimpse of him through the big windows of the mezzanine office when I was on my way home just before supper. He was standing with one of the other architects at a long drafting table, looking down at a blueprint. Both men had rolled up their shirtsleeves, and their arms were A-framed as they stood squinting down at their plans, their neckties, narrow and black, dipping down into two matching pools of bright light.

I NEED TO GO to the dentist but don't want to dip into my savings and so I decide to sell two of my silver rings and a Tolmie drawing of a young wife in stretch slacks holding a fat baby in her arms that I once won at an Ottawa bazaar. I phone the ad in to the *Gazette* and when the woman who takes the call gets to the Tolmie drawing, she spells the name Tolmie out for me to make sure she got it right:

T as in terrorist
o as in opera
l as in lazy
m as in me
i as in I …

And everything gets sold. Once I've gone to the dentist, I even have enough money left over to buy a new raincoat and a handful of beads from the Bead Emporium, but in the end the whole exchange makes me feel like a country bumpkin who leads a cow on a string to market at dawn to proudly return at sundown with nothing but a bag of bad beans that are supposed to be magic. Warning myself in this fable-like way, I psych myself up to ask Magda for a raise—*m as in me, i as in I*—but I can't bring myself to do it. Instead, whenever she sends me out on errands, I sit for fifteen extra minutes in one of the glassed-in sidewalk cafés on de Maisonneuve, drinking Turkish coffee and feeling enigmatic and free.

WE'VE HAD A WEEK of bright days, the trees coming into hard new bud and sharp leaf. Out of sync with the season, Magda and I both catch colds. I also continue to feel hopeless about making my escape from her. The old refrain: she's pregnant, she praises me, she's also the only person in Montreal who ever touches me, usually when I've worked overtime or done her some minor favour. She'll give me a light hug, then a winced, sideways embrace. And hungry for contact with human warmth, human skin, for an hour or so after this I'll experience the world as more tactile and hopeful, even though her crisp hugs also always make me feel a longing to be in the arms of some man. But one Friday afternoon in May, she invites me over to her place, tells me if I insist on doing my laundry we can pick it up and bring it to her house. "Then while it's in the wash we can sit out in the sun and work on curing our colds."

Her house is a white house perched on a cliff in Outremont, a stone stairway leads us up to it, and after she's let us inside she tells me to do the tour. "I'll be with you in no time...."

And so I wander. Past a library, past a long room that's shady and cool, up three steps into a dining room that's all windows, down a hallway to a great sunny kitchen. An unguided tour of what money can buy: space and light, a sloping back garden. Money can buy you the country in the city, it's as simple as that.

I feel like a waif, a waif who no longer has her legendary craving to sleep in, since poverty (like a lover) is too much always on her mind. What if I end up having to share an apartment with some hostile, wispy woman? When what I'll above all require is the solitude that can teach me the severe pleasures of freedom? Just let it not be my fate.

I go to study the photos pinned to the corkboard next to the stove. An early shot of Magda and Russell sitting on a bed in a hotel, Magda on Russell's lap. Russell has an electrocuted look: pinpoint pupils in bleached, exposed-looking eyes, refugee shock of black hair (even though he was born in England), a navy blue suit. But the real surprise is the bride. Slim then, her hair drawn up into a high spray of fair curls, her primly amused way of sitting and her weary secretive smile give her a sexy look. But footsteps are coming my way, and now here's Magda saying in the briefly humble voice of the addict, "I shouldn't smoke, I know it," then she pads around in her stocking feet, opening and closing cabinet doors and once we've got the wash started we carry our drinks out into the sun. I sit down on an aluminum chair and Magda drops onto a wicker chaise, pinches back her skirt, undoes a front garter, then with a roll of a hip undoes a back garter so she can begin to peel down a high-sheen black stocking.

I try not to stare. At work I must have assumed that her glossy black stockings were the legs part of black pantyhose. A garterbelt fits in with the earlier Magda, though, she who so witchily sat on the lap of her electrified husband. "Is Russell coming home for supper?"

"No, he sends his regrets, he has to clear up a backlog of patients."

Washed by relief, I understand how much I've been fearing the assessing gaze of a doctor, above all the gaze of a doctor with such bleached and accurate eyes. What if he should merely glance at me and know all: my loneliness, my envy of their exquisitely faded rugs, my resentment of Magda, all of it. But I must be brave and ask her for a raise. Here. In her beautiful garden. I tilt my head at the angle of one who has made the decision to bask. But all I can bring myself to say is "It's so wonderfully peaceful back here."

Magda, flexing her toes in the hot sunshine, placidly agrees. "It's paradise."

"I'll be so happy when I can get out of my terrible apartment. It's pure bedlam there."

"What part of the city are you thinking of moving to?"

"Somewhere near the office, I hope."

Magda offers her white pregnant legs and her pregnant pleased face up to the sun.

"The rents must be quite a bit higher in that part of the city, though, that's a worry."

"Oh, I don't know," says Magda in a voice that has a whole series of yawns in it. "Look on the bright side, you'll be able to walk to work and so won't have to lay out cash for a metro pass."

I stare at her, astounded. *Rich people,* I think, they have an answer to everything, and it's a foolish answer, but no one dares tell them so. Because they are so innocent, you even end up feeling a horrible pity for them. Unless it's not pity. Unless it's just the lull before revenge. Because what you really want is to see them damn themselves utterly, that's why you won't give them even the tiniest chance to redeem themselves by talking back to them, that's why the more inane and brutal they are the more you are *glad,* the more it gives you the right to hold even more crimes against them. I think of my gloomy little apartment, of how there's always a damp cardigan buttoned onto a hanger and trying to dry out and how (wanting to steer clear of the basement) I do my washing by hand in the bathtub, kneeling to it like a woman at a riverbank. If I finish it before I leave for work in the mornings, I come home to find the dim rooms muggy and cold, eerily shrouded in damp flowered sheets. But why be angry, it's so lovely back here, and I close my eyes and imagine lying in the arms of a lover, the heat of the sun.

"I know what I'm going to prescribe for our colds: chilly vodka."

I open an eye. "Chilled vodka?"

"Hot vodka. Made with hot chili peppers. You drop chili peppers into a quart of vodka for a month. It's an old Russian recipe."

A ladylike creak and she's gone, but now her voice is already back again, just to the left of my shoulder. "Toss it back the way they do it in Russia. That way the vile stuff won't burn your throat."

I do as I'm told. But it makes me gasp.

"And here's a chaser."

I drink it down in one swift medicinal swallow.

"Hey, there, Oleski. Take it easy. You'll be flat out with the tulips if I don't slow you down here."

It's true. The garden's red tulips and green lawns are spinning greenly around me, then we're back in the kitchen—tilted now—and Magda is pulling a bowl of asparagus out of her fridge, then glancing at me oddly. Eat something, for God's sake. I don't want you to black out in my kitchen.

I eat a plum, pour another glass of the fizzed golden wine. A door slams, it's Russell, he has bags of deli food with him: caviar, a mayonnaise with flecks of old dill in it. Smiles at me. Decided to come home after all, hunger drove me to it. His dark hair is wet, combed back. Starved, he says. Went for a swim at Mel's place. He doesn't look at me too intently, I don't think. Corn on the cob, let's cook it up. Then Magda is saying we like to live simply, eat simple food, and the steam rises up from the big black pot with the ears of corn in it. Lots of butter, says Magda.

We need napkins, says Russell.

We need *bibs,* says Russell.

Funny, I say. The way people say ears of corn.

Russell and Magda both laugh, then Russell says: Ears of corn and the legs of the lame and Magda talks about a woman in Athens who made the most charming mistakes when she tried to speak English. Remember, Russ? The woman with the limp who ran that terrific restaurant on Kolokotroni Street? Then it's all the bargains they've picked up here and there and I keep trying to listen, but I'm in love with the food, now it's all hot garlic bread with hot garlicky butter and the sucked, baskety taste of corn on the cob. Did you buy baskets? I say. Where? says Magda. Anywhere, I say. I think I need to know this much. How much did you give this poor girl to drink? says Russell. We were curing our colds, says Magda. Let's make coffee, for God's sake. Russell says this, then somebody brews it as I look out the window and see that the garden has gone, then the talk turns back to Magda and Russell's travels and a place near Cadiz where they found a villa for sixty dollars a month and crossed over to Morocco to buy piles of caftans and rugs for next to nothing because Arab friends tipped them off to where all the best bargains were. And I want not to lose the knack for it—being middle class—no matter how critical I secretly feel of people like Russell and Magda for owning so much and denying how much guilt they feel for owning it by making so much of how little they paid for it. All the cut-rates and discounts. All the rugs and baskets that they've bought for a song. But there's also the thrill of being let in on so many of their tips and secrets, now we're in the car, we're veering in a plunge down the mountain, the city shuffling itself fast past us: a deep curve and a dip, a turn to the left, another dip, then we're here. "At my charming wee slum."

"Nonsense," says Russell, peering in at the alleyway to the back wing with too patrician an interest. "It looks perfectly nice."

"Great," I say, gathering up my sack of clean clothes and again I experience a plunged sensation, feel quelled, like a Victorian maiden aunt who is condescendingly adored, one of the family, her whole future accounted for. "And thanks, too, for a really terrific evening, it was really great. And for the drive too," and then I actually lose track of what I'm saying and begin to babble, itemizing all the things I'm grateful for—the food, the conversation—I even go so far as to say "It's also just so totally great to have clean clothes," but here, just in time, I stop myself from adding "for a change," and instead say, "really terrific, thanks a lot ..." I'm hugging the laundry bag to myself by this time while also worming my way backwards out onto the sidewalk. Already my face is aching from having said thanks and terrific too many times in quick succession.

"No problemo," says Magda, smiling up at me from the front seat with too hugely radiant a smile.

"Thanks again. Thanks for everything."

I can feel their eyes on the backs of my legs as I walk the paved gang-plank up to my building. A duet of smiles, married people's smiles. Benevolent? Falsely benevolent? No, it's worse than that, I'm compiling a terrible list of the bad things they might now be saying to each other:

Not the greatest place to live, is it?
Do you think she's involved with anyone?
God, I doubt it, she just seems too sad ...
If only she'd just relax and not try so hard.
I know! The way she kept thanking us—!
Yeah, that kind of gratitude, I guess she doesn't realize it,
the way it can make people feel just so put on the spot....

And all of the list to the beat of another list: *poor thing, poor thing, poor thing, poor thing.* To all of which I can imagine a psychoanalyst making the comment that whether Magda and Russell are really saying (or even only really thinking) such things about me is not really the point. The point is that I am thinking such things about myself. True, true, I admit it, going up my stairway, but it still makes my legs feel zingy from being stared at, as if self-consciousness has started something circulating along the pathways of blood, a humiliated sparkle halfway between an ashamed itch and a fever.

HANDS NEAR MY HANDS inspect a hill of avocados next to the lemons. "I didn't recognize you at first," the owner of the hands tells me. "The dark glasses, the hat. And so are you wandering around the world incognito today?"

"I think I'm only wandering around the world infectious." And as if to prove it, I pull a Kleenex out of one of my sweater sleeves and sneeze.

He goes to the cash register to buy an orange, then carries it back to me. "It seems to be my fate to keep buying you things to eat. Unless you're only sneezing because I've triggered an allergy in you. In which case, for your own protection, I should really be warning *you* to keep well away from *me*. By the way, what happened to your hair? Is it still there?"

I feel odd, feverish, flirted with, nearly delirious as I turn my back to him, then lift up the back of my hat to reveal my pinned-up plump braid. I can feel his eyes move up my body to my hair, I feel like a specimen, I feel as if I've exposed my own entrails or some more explicitly sexual part of myself. But then I need to sneeze again and when I turn back to him I can see that he looks entertained as he holds up his hands in surrender, then he's walking away backwards. But from his retreat at the front of the store he calls back to me, "The last time I saw you, I seem to remember walking away from you backwards too!"

"Yes!" I call from the aisle stocked with the soups. "I do seem to have that kind of effect on you!" I blow my nose again, feeling dreadful. Although *reverence* is the word that occurs to me. I am overjoyed that I inspire you to that kind of reverence. But he has already gone.

ONE OF THE WOMEN from the mezzanine office is standing at the tray rail when I run down to the cafeteria on Monday afternoon. A stylish woman with a hooked nose who has drawn her white-streaked silver hair back into a bun and whose patterned tobacco skirt dips to her ankles.

I tell her I love her skirt. "Is it Indonesian?"

"From Burma. *These* are Indonesian, though," and she holds out her wrists and jiggles her bracelets, then lifts a wedge of glassy lemon pie onto her tray. She's wearing a scarf tied so high up around her throat and in so many clever knots that she looks very French: both convalescent and chic.

"I've been wanting to ask you if there are any openings for a receptionist coming up in your office—"

"There *is* a job opening up in a week or two. So come on down and see one of the bosses."

"Should I ask to speak to Michael Galbraith?"

"We have too many Michaels so we just call him Galbraith. But you could see any of them, really."

So I should really go in there tomorrow then, since it's one of my days off.

But I don't. I work on my novel all day except for a few minutes in the morning when I dye a pair of curtains and a shirt with Ritt's Scarlet dye. And when I go out to Mi-hee's store to buy bananas in the late afternoon, I leave home without scrubbing the pink haze from the tub.

On my way back, I see William sitting on my front steps. When I get closer I can see that he has a blemished band of pink blur on his forehead. He walks down the steps to embrace me, an embrace that says: I expect nothing, I promise you....

Then up in my apartment he carries his flight bag into the bath-room. Why is the tub all pink, he'll wonder, then might conclude that the pink is from pink bath salts or some other esoteric female pink bath elixir or foam. There's a whistle, the roar of the flush, but the door that opens next is the front door, it's Benno. I hand him a peach. "Listen, Bennie, William's here. Remember him? You used to call him Sir Will...."

"I'll go, then."

"Just stay for a minute. Just to say hello."

When William comes back, I turn to him. "You two would remem-ber each other, I'd imagine."

William smiles at Benno. "Well, you've not grown any shorter, I'll say that for you," then Benno excuses himself, bolts to the bathroom. A few moments later we hear him call out, "What have you been *doing* in this bathtub? Sacrificing virgins?"

We laugh as he comes out to the kitchen to get another peach. We also want him to stay. But he has to go.

"Wait here," I tell William after Benno has gone, and I go into my bedroom to put on my transformed shirt so I can model it for him.

He's unwrapping a bottle of wine when I come back. I do a slow twirl. "Tell me what you think of my re-vamped Ritt's Scarlet blouse."

"Putting on the Ritz," he says as we carry our mugs of wine out onto the balcony to sit in the mild sunlight, sit and talk until the flowers in the nearby window boxes become whiter in the dimming light. He can't believe that I'm still sending stories to *The New Yorker,* but I tell him that their rejection letters are so tender and always seem to hold out at least a small bit of hope. I quote some of them to him. "I enjoyed reading these stories so much." "Keep in touch." "Please think of us again."

But when he smiles and says, "Sure they're polite, they hate to lose a subscriber," I confess that on some level I've already given up.

"They're already too much in the habit of turning me down. I'm down at the back of the class and also a Canadian. Although if anyone down there will publish Canadians they will." But I should stop: I'm rambling, contradicting myself.

"You'll bounce back."

"But some people don't want you to bounce back. They don't like to have been wrong about you in the first place, their pride in their own ability to make dire predictions about you has been wounded. And so the very last thing in the world they want to give you is a second chance."

"But why is it so important to you? It's only a magazine. And it's also so often a downright tame magazine. Besides, you've already had a story published there. Didn't you? A year or two ago?"

"It was over six years ago, William."

"So? Isn't that enough? Once in a lifetime?"

"I know that sometimes there'll be weeks when I'll rail against it. But then there'll be a week or two when there are such amazing things in it that I'll feel ashamed, feel there's nothing better. Sometimes I even think that North America is made up of four countries: Mexico, the U.S., Canada, and the New Yorker. Not to be confused with New York, the city. The New Yorker is a country all on its own, a protectorate you subscribe to. And what comes in the mail is its quaint or idiotic or astounding manifesto." I talk about pretending to read it all through my childhood, tell him about bringing it back from the mail box, inhaling the glossy self-confident American smell of it. "It was the first grown-up magazine I tried to read," I tell him, thinking back to the bizarrely wispy Victorian housemaids on the long-ago covers. I even begin to speak rhapsodically of that whole New England world, so crowded and verdant, all that lively intellectual history evoking the Fogg Art Museum, cobbled streets, the best America. "Besides, some of the very best stories I've ever read have been published there."

"Don't let it become Heartbreak House for you."

But when he tells me he wants to fall in love again, I tell him I'm finished with love. "I've totally renounced it." But how can I renounce what I don't even have? After he's gone, I read and make notes. The pump is primed by reading, even if what I write is only a snippet, only a word with an arrow shooting it across the page to another word. I write "blemished pink band of blur," then turn off my light. The bad nights are the nights I put off going to bed because I'm too lonely to go to bed. Or I'm not impressed enough by myself. I'm not impressed enough by what I've written.

A FADED BUT ELFIN REDHEAD gets out of a car in the parking lot as I'm crossing de Maisonneuve after lunch, the seat of her seersucker skirt gone saggy, then I see that the man who's getting out on the driver's side is Galbraith. Are they lovers? They can't be, she's too asexually serene. I walk fast in order to reach them before they've pushed their way into the building and when Galbraith glances back at me, he says, "Good."

"Good what?"

"Good you got your hair cut."

On my way back upstairs, my hair feels as soft as a shaving brush against the bare parts of my shoulders, but the afternoon passes by too slowly, nothing to relieve its passing but the scrub of Magda's eraser, the flick of her lighter, until at last I hear a yawn. Followed by Madam Yawn herself: "I'll have to leave a tad early, Russell wants to bring a visiting doc home to dinner."

When the door clicks behind her, I go into her drafting room, pick up her bottle of nail polish, pull out the tiny brush that's coated with lacquer, splay the fingers of my left hand, ready to stroke the red gleam onto each of my nails. But stop myself just in time. My painted nails will be ten pieces of evidence for her to see when she comes in tomorrow morning. Besides, I hate the smell of it. I also need to rush in case Mr. Pick-Up Sticks decides to leave early and so I root around in my bag for my Wild Musk. *Damn,* I keep crying to myself, *damn, damn, damn* (a kind of prayer), but I can't find it and so I only comb my hair, then as I run down the stairs I see through the tall slits of glass in the stairwell that it has started to rain.

"Galbraith? In the main drafting room, just beyond the next door."

When he hears footsteps, Galbraith glances up, then does a parody of a man steepling his fingers. "So. Are you planning to build a house?"

"I'm looking for a better job, actually. And I wondered if you are the person I should see...."

"You can see any of us. But come on down to the back, it's more private down there."

I follow him down to a row of dim rooms smelling of carpet and rain, see rolls of drawings stacked into pyramids on shelves. In the end room, he lifts a stack of sketches from a chair and bats the dust from it, but when I sit down on it, it feels like a chair in a chairlift over a wide valley, it's even upholstered in some sort of puffy grey cotton that's as soft as a ski jacket, making me experience such a tipped sensation that I seem to be rising in hitched-up increments, high over my own life. I tell him that Magda and I get along well enough. "But the pay is so low that I'm having a bit of trouble...."

"Keeping the wolf from the door?"

Yes, I say, liking his use of this particular idiom, his knowing that life is a fable.

"I don't quite approve of raiding the staff of a colleague," he tells me. "But no, that's not true. I just don't like the idea of raiding staff from a colleague I'll be running into every day down in the cafeteria."

But when I ask him if he's willing to do it, he places his right hand over his heart. "The fact of the matter is, you weren't happy with Magda. You came to *me,* after all."

On the way home I pass the glass café where I sometimes hide out from Magda. But I only want to think about the way Galbraith was so reproachfully personal, I only want to dwell on the way he looked at me when he glanced up and saw me walking toward him, a look of such kindled sexual surprise that it lifted me up, then dropped me back into myself, an infinitely more euphoric person. I repeat to myself the part of the conversation where he said, "*You* came to *me,* after all."

Magda could very well use the words *after all* as well. "After all I did for her." Or even: "So she's not the reliable person we thought she was, after all." To which I could respond: "I have to eat, after all." Or: "After all I went through with that apartment, I had to find myself a new place."

A *godsend.* Magda used to call me that, also *My right hand,* and as I'm crossing to the Vendôme Metro I remember walking up the sidewalk toward the back wing of my building, my sack of laundry hugged to me while Magda and Russell sat watching to see that I got safely inside and it's as if the whole centre of truth in a person can be located in the back, and in the backs of the legs. Being looked at, from behind, by watchers in somebody's car. Feeling the terrible gaze of more than one pair of eyes.

THE WIND IS EXTREME as we step out into the rainy night together, it blows my hair every which way (my hair that he likes), it even almost blows his words away as he offers me a lift home. But once we've slammed ourselves into his car, he glances over at me. "Giselle happened to mention that you're a writer."

"Yes. But I've only written one book."

"What's it called?"

"The Dangerous Meadow." And I'm struck, as I've never before been struck, by the comedy of this title since it sounds like a children's book about a meadow that's home to a family of ludicrous monsters. Who clearly represent—but it's the very first time I've noticed this— my mother and father and brothers and sister and me.

"I'd like to read it. In fact, I've been wondering if there's some way I could read something you've written...."

"I'd be happy to lend it to you," I tell him. But I really wouldn't be, I all at once have such a fear of his reading it and finding it too female, irrelevant.

"No, no," he tells me, an arm stretched along the rim of the seat behind me as he turns to look back over a shoulder so he can back his car out of the parking lot, "don't lend it to me. I would of course like to buy it. Although I must confess that I don't read all that much fiction these days."

"What do you read instead?"

"Books on politics and history. Books on architecture. Books about cities, the future of cities...."

I'm moved by his formality, his reserve, his grey suits, and am also moved by (or at least am too aware of) the flinch of the inner upper thigh of his left leg in his suit trousers, his unpanicky hands on the wheel or shifting gears, a white shirt cuff shooting out from his suit jacket when he reaches over to the dashboard for his book of street maps. But a man in a suit, why do I find this sort of man so secretly appealing? Particularly when so many of the men in suits are so clearly such idiots? My love for men in suits would also be a puzzle to anyone seeing the two of us together, especially tonight when I'm dressed as some kind of neo-hippie in a raincoat, my long skirt gone wet below my knees from the blowing rain and my feet wet and chilled because I'm wearing the same kind of sandals St. Francis of Assisi wore when he talked to the birds. I must love men in suits because when I was in my twenties men were much too scruffy to wear suits. I must believe men in suits to be pragmatic but passionate, even if they are the sort of men who would admire women in suits. And I am not now, nor have I ever been, a woman in a suit.

"I'm actually on my way to a little street off St. Denis to get a bite to eat, and it just occurs to me that you might like to get a bite to eat too...."

I say yes, that would be marvellous.

All afternoon I've known that I'm about to be fired, ever since walking past his office after lunch and overhearing him defend me to one of the senior Michaels ("But she hasn't done anything wrong...."), I've been feeling wary and accused. Although very grateful to *him*. But walking down the steps into the restaurant I'm again aware of how carefully he's watching me and again I wonder exactly when he'll give me the bad news. And when he does, how I'll respond. At least I'm being given time to prepare for such a moment, and in fact have had time to prepare ever since last week, really, when the rumour that the firm had just lost a major contract had run through the office. People, the rumour went, were going to be let go. A lot of people? At least two or three. And doesn't my knowing how things stand have to be better than sitting and flirting with him in pathetic innocence? Not that I even remember how to flirt. And yet I have such a clear memory of loving to flirt, I used to so love the whole repertory of glances bestowed and withheld, I so loved to get caught up in the musical beat of all those barely suppressed smiles, all that sweet (or cool-sweet) repartee. But was this really me? I no longer believe I ever knew how to be that cool or confident.

But over dinner he talks about cities and above all talks about a legendary and beautiful city in Africa where there are no cars and where the streets are lined with primitive communal dwellings five or six stories high that were built, incredibly, over four hundred years ago. "They keep the narrow streets cool, darkened by shade. A city of carts and horses and bicycles. A city on the east coast of Africa...."

"I would love to go there, it sounds like paradise."

"It is. And the air is really clear and smells of the sea. But since there can be trouble even in paradise it also smells of horse manure."

I smile as I slip off my jacket, hoping I'll look more appealing in my frail peasant blouse, then pick up my gleaming spoon and begin to sip at the fragrant clear soup—the bistro, like the night and the rain, being a bit gleaming itself. But when I tell him that I used to be married to an architect and that we toured Europe on a motorcycle trip that was a kind of honeymoon, I'm aware of wanting to hide the fact that I must be older than he is (by possibly six or seven years) although he seems not to have noticed, but then perhaps it doesn't matter to him, or wouldn't, possibly he doesn't consider me anything other than an employee it's now his sad duty to deliver bad news to. "And then when we were living in Copenhagen for a year, we shared an apartment with another architect."

"And you were practically still only a kid, right? A kid living with two architects, that must have been pretty horrible."

"Really it wasn't. I was the only one who didn't have a job, and so I spent a whole year just reading. There was a library of books left behind in the apartment. *Women in Love. Tropic of Capricorn* ..." I take a sip of wine, remembering the part of *Tropic of Capricorn* where Henry Miller writes of doing a favour for the madam of a brothel in Paris, and how the madam (wanting to do him a kindness in return) offered him a "free fuck in the Egyptian Room." Then there were all those long dark walks I used to take, late in the foggy winter afternoons, past all the sex clubs, past all the smart stores smelling so expensively of teak and leather, their glass scaffolding holding displays of the clear glass lamps and candlesticks that could so stylishly illuminate the deep Scandinavian night of four in the afternoon. "In a lot of ways, Europe was just such an incredible education for me."

"In what ways?"

"In charm. In depravity. In other lives. The great thing about the apartment, too, was that we got it on the black market and so we didn't have to be on a waiting list for years and years. But the owner, a sort of Dracula woman living in Paris, wanted to check us out and so she wrote to us to say that she wanted to meet 'the two men,' then she flew up to Copenhagen after arranging the whole thing like an assignation. The two men were to meet her at the main railway station at three in the afternoon."

"But how were they supposed to recognize her?"

"From a painting of her that she'd left hanging over our fireplace. She had black hair and her lipstick was a gash of violent red. We thought she was totally hideous, of course. She was also in the nude."

His eyes look entertained. "So then the two architects went off to meet her...."

"And were gone for so long that I began to be afraid that she'd kidnapped them, but at last I could hear them laughing as they were coming up the stairs. It turned out that she'd come to meet them in a sparkly evening dress and very high heels and the whole time they were trying to promote themselves as excellent tenants she kept calling them 'darling' and blowing smoke in their eyes." I lift a pack of my Dutch cigarillos out of my shoulder bag, offer him one. "And she didn't want to let them go either, she fancied them so."

He lights mine, then his, then leans back to exhale, studies me through the smoke.

Now. He will tell me now.

But he doesn't.

And when we're climbing the damp stone stairs to the street and I stub a toe on one of the steps he holds a hand down to me, although once I've regained my balance, we let each other's hands go. But as we're walking along the narrow street on our way back to his car, he surprises me by glancing over at me to say, "I needed you."

Words that make a splash, set off a depth charge in my heart.

"... last Saturday night ..."

Another depth charge ...

"... when I was at a party playing charades."

What a tricky little sentence this has turned out to be after all, the way it has meanly changed course and is by now merely running out of steam as it's running downhill.

"And I was supposed to be a writer, I was supposed to be Thomas Hardy. And people kept saying, 'Did you write *The Idiot*? Did you write *Middlemarch*?' And I kept having to say, 'Damned if *I* know, I'm only an architect. I don't know any of this stuff, I'm only a literary impersonator here.'"

So he has a very teasing flirting style, then. But then I already knew that.

We drive west until he turns off the road to one of the lookouts so he can show me the view out over the lights of the whole city (or at least the whole city on this side of the mountain) because there are vistas that he wants to point out to me. "The city in the area of the financial district—down on St. James Street—is built on such a monstrously heroic scale that you feel like a little mouse scurrying along some of those narrow old streets, even the foundation stones can be ten feet high."

I can so clearly picture him scurrying along the foundations of those mammoth stone buildings, a roll of drawings tucked under an arm, just as I could so easily see the narrow dirt streets in the city in Africa. But when he asks me how long I've been in Montreal and I say eight months, the tone of the conversation changes again when he says, "How was it at first? Were you lonely?"

"Yes, I was." A small silence follows my saying this until I sigh a little theatrically to say, "This is how lonely I was: if anyone had told me I seemed to be lonely, I would have taken offence."

He makes a sound that's halfway between a laugh and a groan of sympathy, then stretches an arm behind me again. "There's actually something I need to tell you."

So this is it, then.

"It's been really great having you at the firm," he tells me, his eyes brightly dark with the moment's disciplined emotion. "And also great that you've been able to write such literate letters in both official languages...."

"Giselle helped me a lot with the French ones. With the idioms."

"Good," he says. "But as I know you already know, we've just lost a big government contract and so we're going to have to let several people go."

In spite of the fact that I've been braced for this announcement the whole evening, I nevertheless feel a surprising contraction in my hopes, it's as if I've just drunk a painfully cold glass of ginger ale and am too intensely feeling its vaporous sting rising up through my nose to my eyes. I wipe them impatiently with my fingers. It's not even the thought of losing the job that's so unbearable to me, it's the thought of not ever seeing him again.

He reaches across me to open his glove compartment, pulls out a box of Kleenex. Pulls up a Kleenex to offer it to me.

"Thank you." I blow my nose. "Sorry."

I'm aware of the wince of his nearest thigh as he reaches out to stroke back my hair. "Christ, what can I say? I'm so sorry too."

I BRING HIM TWO LETTERS that he's asked me to type and when he sees who it is, he closes the door behind me, then holds his arms up like a flamenco dancer and does a quick little sideways dance step. But then he looks concerned for me. "Sit down," he tells me, and he pulls out a chair for me, then goes to sit on his own side of the desk.

When I sit, he asks me if I've been looking for another job.

"I haven't, actually. I thought that for a little while at least, since I've got a bit of money saved up, I might just work on my novel...."

"Don't be too quick to finish it. Since I haven't yet had time to buy your first book."

"I would rather you didn't read it, in any case. It would make me feel a bit awkward to know that you're reading it."

"Am I at least allowed to buy it?"

"Yes, buy it."

"Buy it, but don't read it?"

"Yes."

It's my last day at work, and all the architects have gone off to a meeting at City Hall. Only four of them come back, just before five, then they all leave again. Galbraith does not come back, but I stay at my desk, inventing small things to do. But when he still hasn't come back by ten to six, I pull on my raincoat and hurry out into the windy wet night, all at once afraid he'll come back and find my having waited such a mystifying thing for me to have done.

I go to the library, then home. But I don't want to cook, I just eat albacore tuna straight from the tin while I look at the paper, then end up dribbling spots of fishy oil down on my shirt. I'm rubbing the stains from the silk under hot water when I hear my phone ringing.

And so now here's his voice in my ear, he's so sorry he didn't get back in time to say goodbye. "But I've just bought a bottle of wine, and wondered if I could drop by in half an hour or so."

I say yes, that would be wonderful. "But could we make it an hour from now instead?"

"I'll see you at nine, then."

After we've said goodbye, I stand beside the phone for a few moments biting my hand. But then I move fast, toss my untidy life into drawers and cupboards and after my shower pull on the contraption I bought in Ottawa years ago, it's practically an antique by now, its lace so old it might even go up in a puff of black smoke, but it doesn't, its black velvet leaves and petals even still have such tensile strength that they are able to make my breasts look uplifted, youngly plump. But now it's time for the sad but necessary addition of my clothes, and so I pull on a black top and a long tan skirt that has a pattern of fingerprints in a daffodil yellow. Fingerprints or thistles. In the light from the yellow-shaded lamps I hope to look golden in it. Then I hurry into the front room, try to see it as Galbraith will see it. It's boxy, anonymous, but an old wicker sofa has been upholstered in an improbable fabric—a bold red corduroy, he might like this at least—and with luck he'll have a quick impression of bright cushions and posters. And books, lots of plants, drawings by the boys, and above the sofa the long print of *Guernica,* all that pain so cartooned and made festive, a pale Picasso-style profile being blown out from a window like an elongated bubble blown out of a child's bubble pipe and above it a banner blowing into a fist holding a lamp that illuminates all the scattered (but exuberant) body parts. I'd like to take it down, but it could be the sort of thing an architect would like—the odd dehumanized figures and all that grey and white—and so I won't take it down, I've got nothing to put in its place, for one thing, and I still have to light the candles. But just after I've coaxed three of them into flame, I hear a knock on the door and blow them all out in a panic so that he has to step into a room whose air is heavy with the fragrance of burning candle wax and sulphur.

He comes in, his eyes very alive as he presents me with a bottle of wine wrapped in green florist's paper. "It smells like a cathedral in here...."

"Or hell."

He laughs and I'm struck by how French he looks, how Montreal, in his black jeans and black turtleneck as he asks me if I'd care to share a glass of the Médoc with him.

But while I'm out in the kitchen, rinsing the wineglasses, I hear his footsteps, then his voice behind me: "So. How have things been?"

"Oh!" I say, turning to glance back at him. "Things ..." I try to think. "How have they been? They've been fine."

"Maybe we'll get another contract soon, then we can hire you to come back to us again."

"Really, I'm fine. This turn of events might even just be a blessing that's in the disguise of a bit of bad luck."

I can see him steal a glance or two at the disarray in my kitchen and I wonder if he sees me as an impulsive and untidy cook. Or worse: as some kind of slattern. There are battered cooking pots hanging on the walls, pots and glassware waiting to be washed in the sink, a zebra-striped red cotton pelt cut in the shape of Africa drooping from a string in front of the rickety glass door to the fire escape. He goes over to it, draws it back to look out. But he won't be able to see anything but the gas station, a toxic blue and white in the night. "That's not my best view, of course."

"No," he says, smiling back at me. "And we should thank God for that."

The glasses I'm setting out on a tray are so crudely made they look as if the glass-maker stuck his ladle down into a batter of bubbly bluish-grey glass, then stirred it so nonchalantly that it's as if a haze of brown has been baked into the rim of each glass, like a rim of pollution.

When we come back out to the front room again and he goes over to the tallest bookcase, he pulls out *The Brothers Karamazov*. "Here's one I've read. Two or three years ago."

"Did you like it?"

"Yeah, I did, I liked it a lot. I took it on a trip down to the east coast, then spent a week on the beach at Aspy Bay, deep in the Russia of the Karamazovs and the serfs while I turned the pages to the slow crash of the surf."

I consider what a short (but long) step it would be to lean my cheek against his warm back. But I only ask him what else he has read.

He runs a thumb along the spines of the books in the tall bookcase, looking. "Not this, not this, not this, not this. But here's one I know. From long, long ago. *Portnoy's Complaint*."

"Did you find it—how can I put this?—reassuring?"

"It did me the favour of convincing me that I wasn't sexually unique."

I laugh as I sit down on the sofa, then hike up my knees to hug them to me, pull my long skirt down over my toes.

But now he's peering at the *Guernica*. "You're a fan of Picasso?"

"Not really," I say, flattered that he cares enough for me to be subjecting me to a creepy interrogation about taste. "I just tacked it up to hide the gouges in the plaster. It was just something I already had. Left over from my marriage."

"The guy was quite the hack in his way," he says, smiling back at me over a shoulder. "Don't you agree?"

"I almost took it down before you came, but then I thought no, it's dehumanized and grim and so Galbraith might actually like it."

"Thanks," he says in a grim voice, his eyes looking pleased, flirted with. "Thanks a lot."

And I smile back at him thinking maybe I'm getting the hang of this, the tender verbal abuse that flirtation is, the conviction that the other person enjoys being tormented for the crime of being too much on your mind. "But my parents did have one Picasso print that I loved. A woman with only one eye. Or else she had stacked eyes. I used to lie back in the water and look at her while I was taking a bath."

He comes over to sit down beside me. "You liked to take baths?"

"I loved them. Every afternoon when I got home from school I couldn't wait to step into the bath."

"You wanted that much to be clean?"

"No, no, it wasn't that, I just wanted to sink back into the water and recover from school."

He looks over at me as if he's drawn to me. And yet he talks as if he's not. City politics, building methodologies, an implied optimism of scale, cities gone dead at night, cities that are urban wastelands because they haven't been given a vibrant downtown core. "And so we're going to have to keep on living with some really bad buildings that aren't going to go away."

"Yes, it's very sad," I say. But I'm much too aware of the itch and stretch of the little black net swimsuit to give cities much thought. So that when he pours another glass of wine for me, then one for himself, I drink mine down in one swallow, then jump up to ask him if he would like something to eat.

"That would be great. But could I use your phone? I just have to make a quick call."

I tell him that the phone's in my bedroom, then I go out to the kitchen where I don't bother to turn on the overhead light, there's enough illumination with the cold weak light that's coming from the fridge. But is he calling a woman, I wonder. Calling to tell her he'll see her tomorrow. Or calling to tell her he's on his way over just as soon as he can get away from here.

When he comes out to join me, I pull out a jar of olives, the big red wax apple of a gouda cheese. "Want an olive?"

"That could be nice."

As I'm slicing the cheese, he sticks his fingers and thumb into the jar and pulls out three or four olives. Then I do the same, and for a few minutes our fingers keep bumping into one another in the chilled sour water, then there's only the sound of chewing as we eat olives and slices of Gouda in the dark.

But once we've come back into the front room the conversation is awkward again. More city politics, and also so many more ideas about urban renewal and the need to humanize space that I try to come up with something more startling and personal, with anything, really, to shake us out of our boredom, but nothing comes to mind, and at ten to twelve I'm not really surprised when he looks at his watch, then stands, pulls on his windbreaker. "It's getting late, I really should go—"

But before he leaves he tears a page off a memo pad that he's pulled out of his windbreaker pocket and prints his home phone number for me. "Call me. If you start to feel depressed."

I smile down at the square of white paper. "You sound like a doctor writing a prescription." But my having said this sounds so tactless and heartless. So ungrateful, really. And so I quickly say, "But I'm sure to be calling you. I'm sure to get depressed! And thanks for everything. Thanks for coming by." Except that now I sound much too poised and social and so I say in a more emotional voice, "I really wanted you to."

And yet a testy melancholy seems to live on in the air as I walk with him to my door. Where we might do anything: joke, repress a yawn, kiss. But we only say goodbye correctly, then I tag along after him as he walks out to the elevator and touch his windbreaker sleeve lightly as a way of saying goodbye.

After I've heard the elevator sink to the first floor, I feel restless and sad. At the same time I feel a cagey relief, as if I've been spared some unimagined humiliation. Although not the humiliation of getting undressed. So that I put off going to bed because I can't bear to see the evidence of having dared to have hopes. Instead, I read for an hour or so, then go back to the round table to pick up the memo page with his phone number on it.

I consider calling him to say, "I'm already depressed. And so I need you to come back here immediately," but when I look at my watch it's too late, it's already ten to one.

A moment later my doorbell rings. It has to be him, who else could it be, but after I've buzzed him back in, I go to the top of the stairwell to make sure I haven't let a stranger into the building. It's him, I can see his scalp shining through his dark hair as he's turning to mount the fourth stairway and so I stay where I am, looking down on him as he's coming up. But do I really care for him at all, I wonder, and I decide that even though he's kind and intelligent, he's not really my type, a man with clever artistic tastes, a man who likes to talk about politics instead of movies or books. "Did you forget something?"

"My pen," he tells me, and I can feel his glance on my hips as I'm walking away from him to go into my bedroom to see if he left his pen in there when he was using the phone. But then I hear him call, "It's okay, Kay! I found it!"

I come back out to the big room, happy that it's been found and that he can be on his way again.

"It was just here, on the table. I was writing out my prescription for you, remember?"

Then we're at the door again and I'm smiling at him for being so kind about my little prescription joke and we're talking in whispers because it's after midnight and the whole building is asleep. "Did you get all the way home? And then have to drive all the way back across the city again?"

"No," he whispers, smiling in a way that tells me he knows that because I'm a woman I want the triumph of this. "I just drove over to Encore Une Fois for a coffee."

"What a bad hostess I am," I whisper back. "*I* should have offered you coffee."

"No, no, you were fine. But the whole time I was sitting over there drinking my coffee I kept hearing your voice saying 'I really wanted you to,'" and he reaches out to shove back my hair, then with two of his fingers he outlines my mouth as if to say "I really do have to do this." And when his fingers come to rest for an instant, I move my head back and forth so that my lips can still be caressed by them, then I move in close to him and we sink into the relief of a real kiss and everything gets jumbled, later I'll have the time to marvel at the sequence: how we so soon got to be kissing on my bed, moaning little moans that seem to be saying I want this, I've been wanting this, my tan skirt and his priestly black clothes and tan windbreaker in a little heap on the floor, his mouth sucking one of my nipples through the black net making me so concerned that he'll end up with a mouthful of black velvet petals that I have to whisper, "Wait, I can fix this," then I'm working my breasts out of their confinement while his other hand is down where I most want it to be and his voice (sexually hoarse, amused) is croaking, "How do I get this goddamn contraption undone?" And I'm croaking back, "It has little snaps...." a detail that under more ordinary circumstances might make us laugh or even make him moan "Oh, *baby*," but he doesn't, we're too far gone for jokes, too far gone into the urgent bliss of the moment, the necessary mechanics of the thing, everything has to happen now and it does, it isn't until nearly half an hour later that I whisper to him, "I'm so happy you came back," words that I want to say, even though I want (even more) to say I love you, but it's too soon to say it and it might only be sexual gratitude, tomorrow I might change my mind again, but how could I, feeling the way I feel tonight?

HE LEFT A BIT before sunrise and I (a woman without a job) slept in until eleven, then stayed lying in bed another half hour, going over the sequence of the events of last night, casting my memories back to the way his hands on my body made me feel so owned and abundant. And my hands too: planing them over his hips and around to his back to reach the crevice at the base of his spine and then the little hollow above it, the spot that I've read somewhere has a direct connection to the nerves in the cock, *cock* being a word I couldn't even use (except in bed) even as recently as last night—and I try to imagine how a man would feel, picture myself as a man looking down to see it swinging between my tanned woman's thighs, then see myself, or some woman who resembles me, adoring it, doing things to please it, see it comically and majestically rise, think with guilt of Alexander because I never adored that part of him except for its ability to make me happy, and yet I don't really feel guilt because he didn't deserve whatever he missed in not being loved by me, being too unloving to have earned real love, or so I conclude, adoring my darling new friend and wanting to make him and all of his body parts happy, wanting for the first time in my life to be both inside and outside another person's skin.

A PAINTER FRIEND of Idona's who lives on a leafy street off Côte-des-Neiges invites me for tea and I bring Galbraith along with me. On our way there, I tell him that our host comes from down east, from Lunenburg. "He's an alcoholic and I haven't seen him for years, I just remember him as someone who's really gifted and mean."

"Does he have a wife?"

"A woman named Jean. Who was once a beauty, I think."

And still is, when she comes to the door, a beautiful gnome in burgundy corduroy trousers, her long silver hair cut in long bangs, black socks in brown sandals.

In the den, Billy Burhoe O'Hara gets up from the deep suck of a black leather chair to shake hands with us. Smell of leather and an exhausted success. He seems shaky, his eyes fierce behind a film of blur. On the coffee table there's a big picture book with a photograph of a long hill in Ireland on the cover, a slope the uniform green of a desk blotter. Jean lifts it out of the way to make room for the drinks tray.

Billy sings old songs as he pours apricot brandy into tiny clear glasses. He sings "Why Can't a Woman Be More like a Man?" And then he sings in a shaky voice that makes us cast down our eyes, "Fly Me to the Moon."

But now the conversation has moved on to Montreal and what do I think of it, then Billy tells Jean to take Mr. Galbraith up to his studio. "But not you, Kay. You stay down here with Billy."

Once the footsteps have reached the landing above us, Billy leans forward to peer more closely into my eyes. "And so where did you find yourself such a beautiful boyfriend, my darling Kay?"

I hear his *where* as *how* and because I feel he's being condescending to both Galbraith and me, I say in a cool voice, "He's more than just beautiful, Billy."

"A bit short, is he not?"

"We're the same height, actually." But this is not true. When we're in our bare feet, Galbraith is two inches shorter than I am. But does this matter? In fact, I'm filled with admiration for the mismatched couples I see on any street on any given day: willowy women whose cocky little boyfriends don't even rise as tall as their smiles. "And I met him at work, he works with a team of architects at an office on de Maisonneuve."

"An architect," says Billy Burhoe O'Hara, and in saying this, he seems to have become gleeful, alive, shrewd, rejuvenated. "And so the man can think as well."

"Of course he can think, my darling Billy. He's very intelligent."

"Good," says Billy in a brisk disappointed voice. "By the way, Kay, how old were you when you and I last laid eyes on each other?"

"About ten, I think. Ten or eleven."

"You must have been older than ten, Kay. Since Jean and I were at your wedding."

I smile in apology. This is true.

"But look at you now," says Billy O'Hara. "You look even more like your mother than she does. That's what I thought when I saw you come walking up the street. I thought you were Idona. Idona's double. And since she's such a looker, it should mean that you're a great beauty too. But you're not, somehow, you're more like a parody of her."

A flinch in my heart makes me feel the need to tell myself that my lips are fuller than Idona's lips. And I have more emotional eyes.

Billy pours me another glass of port, then looks up at me with his own sad, ex-sexy eyes: "But hey, darling, don't let it get you down, you're sexier than she is."

I glance around the room in search of an object that will give me a topic so I can change the subject, spot the book with the long green hill on its cover. "Ireland," I say. "Alex and I went to Ireland. Long ago." And I think of Dublin, so serene and smelling of malt, its rows of Georgian houses an illuminated grey in the pale Regency light. Where did Yeats live? Where did James Joyce live? I was an uneducated girl in those days and so it never occurred to me to ask. On Easter Sunday we walked in a snowstorm to St. Stephen's Green, watched the snowflakes fall down through the leaves to come to rest on the cherry blossoms. "It snowed the whole Easter weekend we spent in Dublin."

"Did you go to Howth?"

"Howth?"

"Yeth."

When I smile, he says, "Howth *Head*."

"No, we went for a walk in the Wicklow Hills instead."

"My *dear*, you should have gone to Howth *Head*. Because Howth Head is where Molly Bloom stretched herself out on the wild heather for Leopold Bloom and said yes I will yes ..."

After Jean and Galbraith have come down from Billy's studio, Billy takes me up to see his paintings, stacked against walls and hooked onto giant vertical columns of chicken wire. They are all either of women or of fields and skies that have been plowed. Grey skies plowed into furrows of red and curdled gold, intensely green fields plowed into furrows of purple and black loam. And in the paintings of the nude models, the legs of the women are flopped out, the thatch between their legs bisected by the fiery red labia, the crimped pink of the clitoris making it look like a livid parasite, a kind of furious specimen worm. The thatches are all black except for the one that's grey, to match the model's blunt-cut silver hair, her face a bulbous flushed version of Jean's face. A younger breast than Jean can possibly possess juts from a loosely opened blue kimono that has huge white Matisse flowers drifting over it, the nipple of its greyish breast a thick and pert whorl of pink paint.

I go from field to field, nude to nude. "Very vivid," I say. "Very alive."

But Billy doesn't seem to hear me, he's instead pulling out more canvases from behind a tall curtain, wanting to show me more and more paintings.

On our way back down the hill at the end of the afternoon, I ask Galbraith what he thought of the paintings.

"Bloody violent. And what happened, by the way, while I was up in the studio looking at the paintings with Jean? Why did he want you to stay downstairs with him? Did he make a pass at you?"

I decide not to tell him the parody part. "He told me that I'm sexier than my mother."

"That's a pass," he says.

IN THE MORNINGS, when he's ready to leave for work after one of the nights I've stayed over, we stand at his door, and when we kiss our last kiss, we're grafted to one another, we're lovesick insects, we breathe the same breath. But once he has gone, I have to breathe on my own again. And sometimes it's even a relief to be alone so I can think of him unimpeded, without the interference of his actually being here. He has a gift for making everything significant, this is his great gift to me. I've already been here, off and on, for three nights so far, three nights and five days, but I still can't shake off the conviction that I'm a refugee from my other life, a life that now seems to me to have been lived in a truly sordid and dangerous place. Even if my old place is cosy and has lemon geraniums sitting on sunny windowsills and curtains that are a coarse factory cotton, dyed a harsh blue. But here I'm struck by the pure possibilities of a handsome abstinence and carefully staged tables and black leather chairs: the forethought, the chasteness, the skylights, the interior tracts of clear air and clean light. I walk through his rooms and breathe in the serenity, the cool order, admire the black leather sofa, the three grey canvas safari chairs with their tan leather straps in place of armrests, the four very large but low-hung paintings in slender gold frames, each canvas painted a dead adhesive-white, but with strips of the white torn away here and there to expose a background that looks like medicated netting, and on this medicated part of the canvas very dry brush strokes—drier-than-dry black scaffolding on one, dry smears of red and black thumb prints on the three others.

I do plan to go back to my own place most nights though, I sleep so much better when I can sleep unobserved, and it's from my own place that I phone Benno. When there's no answer, I call Tom at the Toronto restaurant where he's working for the summer.

I hear a crash, an avalanche of cutlery, as I wait for him to come to the phone.

"Things are sounding a bit violent there...."

"We're assassinating the boss with cutlery."

"Is he pretty awful?"

"He's a bit wacko, but he's not all that bad a guy either. Not great, but not terrible."

"I'm just calling to let you know that if you call me and I'm not at home, I can be reached at this new number I'm going to be giving you."

"How come?"

"I'm staying part of the time in the apartment of a friend I used to work with. A much more pleasant apartment than my own. And in a much more beautiful part of the city. A really French part...."

"Cool."

"There's even a computer here and I'm learning how to use it."

"And she doesn't mind?"

"She?"

"The friend you're staying with."

"The friend I'm staying with is a man, actually. One of the architects from the office where I used to work...."

"Oh Ma, no, not another architect. Not another hypercritical neatnik. It's going to be the story of you and Dad all over again."

"He's not at all like Dad."

"Look, I don't want to hurt your feelings, but it's got to be said: you're something of a sexual innocent."

"I was married for fifteen years, that must count for something."

"But you don't learn anything about sex by being married. Marriage is where you learn how to forget what you knew."

"You forget how to flirt, you mean."

"That too."

It's more or less the same story when I reach Benno. "So who is this guy? And are you going to marry him?"

And when I say who knows, who can say, he says, "Look, I don't want to meet this person, so don't invite me over for dinner and expect me to be all phony and polite and a lovey-dovey goody-goody little sonny boy to you, okay? Because I'm just not available for that kind of charade."

They make me smile. But then the whole world makes me smile. Even the butcher on Duluth and the boy I buy bagels from on St. Viateur make me smile when, out of guilt—for it's hard not to feel like a kept woman when Galbraith is paying for all the food—I shop as critically and inventively as a housewife from Paris or Avignon, then try one delicacy after another from the French and Italian cookbooks I find on the shelf above his stove. A recipe for trout in wine. Calf's liver with fried grapes, even though I've never yet met a man who cares for liver. To have it turn out to be amazing will be a kind of triumph then. And so this is how I've begun to spend my afternoons, in languorous cooking sessions, stopping a little before five to take a shower and rub body lotion into my arms and thighs, then going over to the bookcases to look at all the books about architecture: *The Architecture of Utopia, Ornament and Crime, The Image of the City, The Death and Life of Great American Cities, The Mathematics of the Ideal Villa and Other Essays, Delirious New York: A Manifesto for Manhattan.*

And after dinner when we go into his office for my lessons on the computer, even only his outstretched arm brushing my hair makes me feel swoony. There's even a feature where the word *No* appears six times in a long vertical column, but by one strike of a key I can turn every No to a Yes. A metaphor for these new and unbelievably heavenly days. Days in which I play my music on his tape deck all day long, music that makes me cry from sheer happiness, a happiness that makes me under-stand why the words *sheer* and *happiness* are so often paired like lovers, they are so undiluted, so absolute, so opposite to their opposite others (sheer fall and sheer folly) and so I dance in large loony pirouettes, dance to whatever the music is, whether it's Bach's Suite No. 3 in D Major or Mr. L. Cohen's mesmerizing monotone bringing the news that hey, that's no way to say goodbye. I don't work on my novel, happiness has taken away all my ambition, all my hopes for myself as a writer. If I type anything new on Galbraith's computer it's only the sort of thing an adolescent girl would type. Things about adoring him, about being bathed in his shine. And so I try to pull myself together, bring a notebook from my apartment over to his place, flip back and forth through it, find a note about a dead moose I saw in the woods years ago in Scanlon Falls, an iridescent brooch of flies feeding on one of its eyes, find notes about Alex: "He lifts a wrist to his glance, then taps at his watch face with an index finger, a woodpecker pecking at the hour for me, right down to the minute...." And many notes, too, about our boys when they were babies: Tomasz wrapped up tight as a talcumed papoose when I brought him home from the hospital and how there was nothing in the refrigerator but a pound of butter and half an old grapefruit, and how cluttered the kitchen was, with its stacks of dirty dishes in the sink, dirty floors, how I gathered up a pair of pink rubber gloves and a diminished grey mop to bring into the front room to Mrs. Noakes, the woman from Homemakers who was to help out for two days but was at the moment only sitting stiff as a man come courting on the sofa, how I tried out the vaguely aristocratic voice Idona tended to use when she spoke to the farm women who came to our house to clean on the weekends. "If you could start with the dishes, perhaps …" How at this offensive suggestion, Mrs. Noakes rose to say in a grand and affronted voice, "Oh no, madam, I do not do dishes or wash floors. I am not a char, I am here to look after Baby." How I turned away and left her, then sank onto the mattress on the floor of the master bedroom (euphemism for the only bedroom) wanting her to leave, but feeling afraid of her for some reason and ashamed that I was afraid. And so I couldn't tell her to go, I wanted Alex to do it. But I doubted he would: when he was pushing the baby and me out to the taxi in a wheelchair he kept calling flirty things out to the student nurses on their way onto the wards while I felt stick-legged and sexless as he pushed us toward the daylight, hearing him joke over the top of my head with the fast-walking, fast-talking younger women. How all the next day there was baby drill: bath, diaper practice, Q-tip dipped into alcohol, then carefully worked all around the little withered stump of what was left of the umbilical cord, Tommy's diapers stained with what looked like raffia, like seaweed. How after I'd changed his diaper and snapped him into one of his terry stretch-suits, I'd nuzzle his stomach and whisper any old endearment at all to him: Silly old kingpin, Mister Tummie. How his frail, hungry wail in the night way out of a cathedral—"tattooed forearms"—he holds his arms straight out toward the view of the city.

"You tell this story like a real Catholic boy."

"But I am a real Catholic boy. Or I am a real lapsed Catholic boy. Who was it who said that it's not possible to be both a Catholic and a grown-up? My father isn't even a Catholic, he's a Presbyterian who's descended from a long line of Scots mechanics with a bit of French thrown in—Galbraith probably means muddy hill or great in battle or some such noble thing—but my mother is as Catholic as they come and at home I spoke only French until I was ten."

"Were you born first or in the middle or at the end?"

"So far at the end that I was a mistake. But I was totally adored by my older sisters." He caresses my rump, then moves the flat of his hand up my spine, shoves a hand up through my hair, shimmies his fingers through it. "Which must be why I'm still so attracted to older women."

"So that's the attraction."

"It's one of the attractions."

I think of the older women I've seen with younger men lately. Their tired charisma. The wistful melancholy in their sexually thoughtful eyes. "I should practise my French with you, mon amour."

"You should. We could practise it in bed."

"We could. We could play tapes of some of those orgasmic French love songs. Je viens, tu viens, je viens, tu viens, je viens, tu viens, je t'adorrre mon amourrr ..."

"You're right, they're totally corny and bad. But what's your favourite thing to say in French?"

"Zut, alors!"

He smiles. "Is that from a children's book? Because I don't think anyone says 'Zut, alors!' any more, not even in France ..."

"Then I'll choose 'Quoi faire, quoi dire.' Or does that sound very affected?"

"Something a woman might say, more than a man."

And when we lean on the gate he whispers little things to me about my body and I admire his "anatomical equivalents," then make the confession that I find it hard to say some of those words. "Except when we're in bed."

"But in bed is where they happen to be most appreciated."

"Just as long as I'm a wild woman, right?"

"Right."

"And so," I ask him after we've been quiet for what seems to have been a very long time, "am I?"

"Are you what?"

"Am I wild enough?"

"Almost," he tells me.

When I was younger I would have brooded if a man had dared to say such a riskily forthright thing to me, but now I only feel curious. "What's missing?"

"There are just a few little refinements I still need to teach you."

Which makes me spoofily sing him a song in the voice of a woman who's flirtily pleading with a man to teach her certain sexually useful techniques. (And do it tonight.)

He thinks he can arrange that. "But I didn't know you could sing. Or at least I didn't know you could sing like that. So sing to me some more."

And when I sing, "I'll sing to him, each spring to him, and worship the trousers that cling to him," he says, "Now *there* is a song."

Over dinner he tells me he has to fly to Washington for two days. "Come with me, why don't you? It'll be more fun for me if you come along. And don't worry about having to pay for a ticket. This one's on me. Then instead of flying right back, we could take the train up to New York City and have dinner with my cousin Monique who's still trying to get over her divorce from a madman."

THE TRAIN is a civilized American train. A glass vase filled with daisies has even been set on the table in the first car, and tables and cane chairs face forward in the passenger cars. Across the aisle from us, two women who are both wearing steel-rimmed glasses have cleared their table of newspapers to lay out scissors, construction paper, sequins and feathers for the little girl who's now singing to herself as she glues a beard of magenta feathers to a grey moon. "American children are kept busy every single minute of every single day," I say in a low voice to Galbraith but he has already closed his eyes, then I close my eyes too and don't open them until we get to what must be Baltimore because the words JOHNS HOPKINS appear to the left of the flash of a bridge under a high cold sun, colossal letters that seem to require an anthem as backup music, but by now Galbraith is resting his head on his arms like a schoolboy who's fallen fast asleep while beyond him the swampy fields of pale grasses and cattails are slightly moving in the wind, *Father and Son Moving Company* painted on the upper half of a building that looks like a grain elevator and seems as far away as the horizon. We're already coming into the deep rusty poverty of Newark by this time, then coming fast into New York. So we're here, we sleepily stumble out into the wind and bright light, the streets blowing with papers and litter as we hail a taxi and go to our hotel, then change into fresh clothes for New York and rush off to meet Monique, the cousin who's an interpreter at the UN, an alert and shining-eyed person who takes us to dinner at a Cambodian restaurant on Thirty-first Street and over dessert tells us about the Russian men in her life, the Russian ex-husband, the Russian ex-lover, the present Russian lover, tells us about the two most deeply depressing industrial cities in the Ural Mountains—Perm, Chelyabinsk—tells us that when she makes a mistake in translating either French or Russian into English at the UN there's no time to linger, no time to brood and dwell, she has to let it all go, she needs to have already moved on to the next thing. Being an

Galbraith tosses me a cigarette, but I don't catch it, it drops in the muck near the toes of my sandals. God, how I wish he wouldn't do this to me, I hate the way he expects me to be on the ball every minute, but of course he only wants to show me off to his cousin and Josette, and so I call out, "Oh damn! Sorry! The only thing I've ever been good at catching is the flu!" But he wants to give me another chance and so he tosses me another one, a high close toss that even a toddler could catch. Even so, I just barely manage to intercept it, then drop my twig into the water and let the cigarette hang out of the corner of my mouth, but then take it out to sadly inspect it before I sing:

> *Loff's always been my game*
> *da dee da da do*
> *Vhot's a girl to do*
> *Can't help it …*

The liquid deep gulp of a paddle pulling back in the pond below comes at the end of my song, then we all watch a gondola moving with silent swiftness past our table, the gondolier having unloaded the night's final cargo of tourists somewhere off in the trees, while above him the crescent moon shines next to a single bright star, the only star to be seen in the whole New York City sky.

We say goodbye to Monique and Josette at the corner of Thirty-third Street, and after we've returned to our hotel room on Madison Avenue and made love in the hot sticky night, we lie and talk for half an hour before going to sleep, outline each other's eyes with a finger, outline a mouth, a nose, snap at a finger like a snapping turtle. Until I ask Galbraith what he thought of Josette and he says, "Mademoiselle Chatterbox?" And then, after a debating sort of silence, "Attractive. In fact, extremely attractive."

"But what if she never stops talking?" I ask this in what I hope is a neutral voice, even though I've been so sickeningly plunged into jealousy, its hot and cold lunge.

"That could be a problem." And in the momentary lull in the noise at the heart of New York I can hear the tiny glisten of sound his smile makes when he smiles in the dark.

OUR FIRST MONDAY BACK in Montreal we end up going to bed at five in the afternoon, the sun pouring in over us, my mouth moving over his body like a suctiony sea anemone, my mouth biting his fingers like a minnow, bites meant to express sexy ownership, and he's undersea life too, the little fishes that are my lips bumping against him, licking and nibbling. All day long, I dream of him and I don't even write anything that I'm happy with, I don't even have anything to write about except for my exhausting happiness—but it doesn't even quite feel like happiness, it's too agitated to be happiness or I'm too unaccustomed to euphoria or I just long for solitude, I don't even read any more, I've forgotten how to make even the most amazing book matter to me, I only read when I'm reading to him, it's not the fiercely devout reading I like to do on my own, it's a performance in a way, a small act of love. Besides, I don't really have the time to read, being in love requires too much thinking or at least too much recollection, I could spend all of every day going back over the ways he has looked at me or hearing his voice say the words he has said to me, memories that stay with me long after I've become aware of my aching legs, my sweaty back, and above all wanting—more and more, it seems—to be used to the point of ruin. But other times there's no need for all this wary euphoria, sex with him is so deep, so much itself, so like an ambush I believe in, the tenderness reserved for afterwards, not before, what we reward each other with for having come through the war.

THROUGH THE PETAL SLITS of the mailbox in the lobby on Randall Avenue, I can see a manila envelope waiting for me and before I've even completely retrieved it I can see that it's the return of one of my stories. And worse: the letter is only a form letter and someone with the scrawl of a child in grade two has written across the bottom of it, "Good luck with your writing!" If there's anything I despise, it's being rejected and then wished good luck. Although God knows I must *need* good luck. I unlock the door to my apartment, but when I step into the sour but sunlit warm air, I forget what I came for. But then I remember: my sandals. I find them on a low shelf at the back of my bedroom closet, but they all at once look much too flimsy and cheap, as if they've been cut out of shellacked paper.

I carry the story to my desk, slide it into a drawer. Now all I have to do is water the plants and go back to Esplanade. I want to cook something amazing, to make my other life matter. But a postcard I haven't even looked at yet turns out to be from Della Kuhnert who even signs it Love, Della.

We've just received a carton of books and old *New Yorker*s sent to us from Canada, reminding me that the last time we met and had coffee, at the Stationery House—sometime last year?—you

119

mentioned a story in *The New Yorker* that you thought I might like. But now I can't think what it was, our conversation was so hurried and scattered. Was it that strange story set at a Mexican resort? I liked it, parts anyway. As for Paris, we are having a fascinating time here and today was an absolutely wonderful day—we spent the entire afternoon sitting on chairs in the Luxembourg Gardens, reading. Not a single Frisbee, and everyone so splendidly behaved.

The phrase "everyone so splendidly behaved" so exactly describes both Della and everything Della writes that I have to smile. And since when has Della sent me postcards? Or signed them "Love"? And how did she get my address? From Alex, I suppose. I go down the steps to the street and try to let the sadness drain from my eyes, try to compose myself to be a citizen of the world again, try to convince myself that my sorrow is a ludicrous sorrow in the hierarchy of sorrows. But how can this be, when I'm struck dead in the heart by it? When no one else must ever know that I've been rejected? Not even Galbraith. In fact, Galbraith is the one who must not know most of all and when he gets home and we carry our glasses of beer up on the roof, I stay firm in my resolve not to tell him. I'm not even tempted to tell him after we've come back down to his apartment again and are still so hot from the sun that we have to lie down to recover on the black and grey Navajo bedspread on his low wide bed. At least I'm not tempted to tell him until he says, "You seem sad."

"It's really just nothing."

"I doubt that it's really just nothing."

"It's just that a total idiot wished me good luck today." And so now it all comes tumbling out: the story of my rejected story and how offended I felt when I was wished good luck. "Why isn't sanctimony a sin that's punishable by death?"

"Because if it was, there'd be nobody left on the planet." And he rolls over to me to untie the flowered belt of my dress. "What's this called?"

"It's a wrap dress."

"Can you unwrap it?"

I shimmy across the bed, feeling flushed, then stand up to unwrap the floral halves of my dress as he stubs out his cigarette and squints at me through his last exhalation of smoke. But when I start to pull off my panties he says, "Come here. Let me do that part."

I lie down next to him again and feel him shove them down. A great moment always, no matter what, then he stretches an arm across the pillows to say, "Rest your head here," which is when the phone rings, and so he has to roll away to reach for it on the table next to his side of the bed. "Yes, just a moment, she's here." And he rolls back to me again, eyebrows raised to warn me as he whispers, "It's a woman."

It's Idona, and after we've spoken for a few minutes I hold the receiver pressed to a shoulder, but then change my mind and press my pillow over it so that I can smother it completely. "It's my mother," I whisper. "She's at the Ritz-Carlton with her new husband, and they'd like us to come and have dessert and coffee with them tonight at eight o'clock and so do you want to go?"

"What about you?" he whispers. "Do you want to?"

"Only if you do."

"Maybe we should, then," he whispers back. "Just for an hour or so."

After I've said goodbye to Idona, her call having ruined the idea of sex, ruined everything, we sit up on our own sides of the bed and yawn, our backs to one another as we slip our feet into our sandals, then go our separate ways: Galbraith to take a shower, me out to the kitchen.

I bring his dinner out to where he's reading *Le Devoir* in the front room, then go back to eat mine in the kitchen. But after ten minutes have gone by, he calls out, "What's she's like?"

"She's a law unto herself!"

"Is she beautiful?"

"Yes!"

A bee drawn to the honey of the word *beautiful,* he buzzes out to the kitchen, sets down his plate, then belches. "Just my inarticulate way of saying this was delicious."

Idona used to roll down her stockings and kick off her silky panties, then peer back at her reflection to unhook the webbed panels of her garterbelt: lacy black flies and black clots of spiders caught in a contraption whose knock-kneed black garters hung foolishly down. "I was infatuated with her when I was a small girl, I thought she was so smart and beautiful. And since she was crazy about undressing in front of us, I have a feeling she even liked to turn her wee babies on. When she had her back to us and was pulling down her panties it was like she had these two huge white breasts...."

"Conveniently placed low down on her body so that her babies could reach them."

"You're right, do you know that?"

"I do know it."

"But the thing that's most important to know about her right now is that she keeps getting married. Getting married, you might say, is her most favourite thing to do. And in the process of getting married she also annexes property to herself...."

"She sounds like a medieval queen."

"Yes, she does. And she *is.* And her clothes have changed radically too, from husband to husband. When she was married to my father she used to wear handwoven skirts and run around barefoot. But after my father died she married an academic and bought herself nothing but stern little suits in Ultrasuede...."

"How many husbands has this woman had, for God's sake?"

"Henry, her present husband, is her third."

On our way down the stairs, I think back to Galbraith saying "Come here, let me do that part" and how each word was a single syllable and therefore so unlike the words I loved when I was growing up, words like *splendiferous* and *supercilious* and *supposition*. "On what do you base that supposition," I used to say when I was fifteen, hoping to pass myself off as the sort of girl who was amused by life and therefore truly cool. But how much better the shorter words are, short words in bed, short words in the rain as we drive down Parc, like *damn, damn, damn* when we can't find a parking spot close to the hotel and have to drive as far as rue Ste-Famille and so get drenched on our long run back to the Ritz-Carlton, hopping from puddle to puddle.

Then we're here, inside all the grandness and meeting the foreign dignitaries—my regal mother and her consort, Henry—and once we've done the introductions and sat down, I poke one of the linen napkins down the front of my dress, I so much need to separate the damp flowered fabric from my wet skin, but Idona says in a low voice, "Don't do that with your napkin, little Kay."

"But it's so freezing in here. And the air conditioner is shooting all this incredibly cold air straight down on us. Couldn't we at least move to another table?"

"I don't think the hotel staff would like that, sweetie, they seem to be so overworked as it is."

I slip my cold hand into Galbraith's warm hand. "Aren't you freezing too?" But his eyes are already dreamy from the wine and the talk he's having with Henry and he only gazes at me with a vague tenderness and so I can't allow myself to fuss any more, all I can do, beneath the protection of the tablecloth, is fold back my damp dress, then squeak closer to him so that I can press my cold arm against his dry sleeve and my cold thigh against his warm thigh as I drink up vast quantities of the burning, warming wine.

When the dessert arrives—eclairs floating on puddles of chocolate—Idona wants to talk about Princess Diana and Prince Charles, wants us to speculate on whether their marriage is happy. And when no one takes her up on it she begins to tell a story about how the Danish royal family, long ago, back at the turn of the century, coped with the fact that all eyes were on them up in the Royal Box by saying the same meaningless words to one another over and over: "red paper, blue paper, white paper, red paper, white paper, blue paper, red paper ..."

I adored this story when I was a child, I adored any story that involved people playing tricks on people, I so much loved playing tricks myself, above all on Idona, but now I hear it as a sad story since the king and queen weren't even witty enough to say scandalous things to one another as they sat above the tiny audience below.

And when Galbraith and I come out again into the humid warm night, our clothes dry at last, I slip an arm around his waist. "So?"

"So?"

"So what did you think of my mother?"

"She seemed quite aware of herself, I suppose, that was my main impression."

"That is *so* true." I hook a thumb over his belt and lean against him and kiss him, then run a hand through his hair even though I reproach myself (but not too much) for touching him so much, but I have to, it so much consoles me in some way, it so much consoles my own skin.

"So what were you two talking about while I was talking to Henry?"

"Red paper, white paper, blue paper, red paper, white paper ..."

GALBRAITH CAME HOME last night smelling of the sooty city and the rain. "Listen, I invited one of the students who's working with us for the summer over here tomorrow night—"

I could already picture this student, young and bashfully sweaty and flushed, extracting his arms from the sleeves of a schoolboy raincoat.

"But she can't be here in time for dinner, she'll just come for dessert and coffee."

Ah. A she. And I felt a small squirm of unease as I pictured her coming into the apartment, a brushed and shining young woman, a teardrop of rain poised to fall from the point of her collapsed umbrella, her eyes lovingly seeking out Galbraith's eyes above a breathless hello.

"Tess, her name is, and she has a real southern drawl."

Dessert was a chocolate cake with a deep seam of black in it, black as a seam of loam soaked in rum, but we held off eating it till Tess arrived at seven. Fair-haired, frank, open-faced, she seemed too candid and practical to be fallen in love with. And too pugnaciously smart in a way, too independent. Even if she came from North Carolina, a state she referred to, with a mocking smile, as "the progressive state." She addressed us as "y'all" as we talked about American foreign policy and cheap places to stay in the American south. And when it was time for her to leave she shook hands with me with serious warmth as she emotionally said, "Ah have never met a Canadian who wasn't intelligent, Ah have never met a Canadian Ah didn't like."

At which point Galbraith made us laugh by raising an eyebrow at her to say, "Well, honey, Ah guess y'all just has not *met* that many Canadians yet."

But today he's had a tense day with a client he's building a glass box for, up on top of the mountain, and when we come back down from the roof and he sees the footprints I left on the carpet after my bath, along with my hairbrush and earrings and two magazines and a damp towel flung down next to the two enlarged thumb prints of damp left by my wet rump on his Navajo bedspread, he yells at me, "What the hell's been going on here, Kay? This room is a shambles!"

Flushed from beer and sun, I glance over at him, astounded. "What are you talking about?"

"I'm talking about *this*. This incredible carnage ..."

"Isn't your choice of words a little melodramatic?" But I nevertheless transform myself into a cartoon dynamo, toss the scooped-up magazines and my hairbrush and the towel onto a chair, hook my earrings into my ears, strip off the damp bedspread with the speed of a testy nurse, then ominously fold it until it's in a plump cube that I can toss at the chair to land on top of the damp towel. "If you intend to be so prissy, I don't think we should even begin to consider having sex...."

He sits down on his bed. "So now I'm being prissy. When, as far as I can see, my only crime has been to suggest a reasonable degree of order."

"Where, in the name of God, has there been *dis*order?"

He laughs an amazed and unhappy little laugh. "You really think there hasn't been? Consider this room. And also consider when you're cooking, for instance, the way when you're making just one single little recipe, you need at least seven pots and five mixing bowls and then you beat the eggs with a whisk and consequently end up getting egg foam and basil flakes all over the stove."

"Basil flakes," I say, trying for the deadpan tone of a comic.

"I know it sounds petty, but after you went home on Tuesday night I had to spend over an hour in the kitchen, cleaning the stove and trying to wipe all the food marks off all the walls."

How humiliating this feels, but also how irritating. "But don't you have a cleaning woman come in to clean for you every Thursday morning? Isn't this the reason I never stay over on Wednesday nights?"

"But you can't push these people too far, or you'll lose them." He looks over at me and I see a flirty twitch in one of his eyelids. "You must at least be middle-class enough to know that."

"There was certainly a time when I was at least middle-class enough to know that."

"Last week Maria asked me if I'd had someone in to cook for me, the walls in the kitchen were so spattered ..."

"If I'm bringing so much chaos into your life, why do you even care for me, then?"

"I ask myself."

"I'm going to go for a walk. And please don't follow me. I need to be alone."

"I have no intention of following you."

"Could I have a cigarette, please?"

He tosses a cigarette to me, and when I manage to catch it (quite an elegant catch, actually) he says in a cool voice, "Bravo," then digs into his jacket pocket for a packet of matches, tosses it to me with a watchful smirk. "You might also find these somewhat useful."

I take the stairs to the roof, come up to meet the view out over the green city. But how clear and lonely the air up here feels! I walk swiftly to the chimney at the far end, make myself small enough to sit crouched behind it so that if he comes up to look for me he won't be able to find me. I wish that I'd had the foresight to bring my notebook up with me since the last thing in the world I'd want to do is go back down to get it. And so I only scoop a little mound of pebbles together to drop my ashes into, then sit brooding and wondering if he's really had all that bad a day at work or if I'm just making excuses for someone who's a domestic fascist. Or worse. A psychopath, a sociopath, a rapist, someone deeply evil, a killer. In spite of the fact that we've been so close, I barely know him after all, as his childish and mean little tantrum has all too obviously made clear. One morning last fall when I was on my rushed way to work, a woman who was in the habit of rudely shouldering her way past me in the Randall Avenue lobby came running along the hallway toward me, her eyes lit by fear, her hurrying trot frantic, a bobbing glint at her ears, then came the frenzied sound of a door being unlocked, the roar of the caged beast within, the woman's strident apologies escalating into a scurrying whimpering that had run, like musical notes, up the scales of terror. Whatever had this rude woman done? Spent the night with another man? Her whimpers chilled my eavesdropping heart as I ran down into the safety of the September city, the safety of not belonging to anyone, the beautiful safety of being alone. Because sometimes I feel so tired of everything. Even love. Because happiness in love is the most work of all. I think of Alex too and wonder how much my two neat-niks are really alike. They are really *hideously* alike, why didn't I see it? They make me think of a story I once tried to write about a young wife whose husband goes north in the summers and the photos he brings back home with him: shots of splayed-legged sea-planes with stitched wings and pontoons, tethered to flashes of blinding lakes, silver suns. Tethered to flashes and the sadness of a marriage that's not working out. A marriage tethered to flashes of blinding rage, blinding stupidity, silver suns.

I expect to find Galbraith in either a sulk or triumphant when I come back down to the apartment, but he's gone. And how clinical his place all at once feels, all the cold stainless steel in his kitchen, too cool a breeze blowing in through the windows. I unwrap cubes of beef from their bloodied pink paper, chop them into smaller cubes, yank open the bottom drawer of the fridge, grab out what I need, kick the drawer shut, run a blast of water over the cutting board, slam it onto the counter. I certainly don't plan to let on I hear him when he comes in, I'll just keep on chopping the weepy onions, the long green hair of the chives.

Ten minutes later I hear the front door open, hear it close again. "Kay?"

I scoot what's on the cutting board into a pot. One of the seven pots, take note. Then I do a fierce little chop, chop, chop.

"I'm sorry," I hear his voice say. "I'm a jerk, I'm a control freak, please turn around."

"I can't, I'm washing a carrot so I can behead it."

"In that case I apologize again and again."

"But I'm the one who ought to apologize. For not being middle-class enough to meet your requirements."

"Well, it's true. You're not middle-class, but you should be glad, you should be overjoyed that you're not a member of the smug and pathetic bourgeoisie...."

I cut and snip, again do my deranged little chop, chop, chop.

"The fact of the matter is, you're an aristocrat, an anarchist...."

More slicing and dicing, more scooting of mushrooms into the pan.

"This must be why you have no standards."

I drop minced chives and tomatoes into halved green peppers, spoon pesto over them. "It's just too damn bad that your last name isn't Godwin, then we could all call you God for short. I would also like to know how long you've been counting the bowls and the pots."

"I was speaking metaphorically, Kay. I also have a gift for you, so please turn around."

I litter the salad with crumbs of cheese, butchered shreds of red peppers. "I'd also like to know if there are any other ways in which I am being monitored." I've no sooner said this than I think of the haze of moisture I too often leave on the counters in the bathroom, but he is, thank God, much too clever to mention this now.

"No," he tells me. "You are not being monitored in any other way."

I go to the table to spread a yellow batik cloth that has a pattern of black flowers and black beetles on it.

He comes up behind me. "Did you bring this tablecloth from your place?"

"I was just trying to bring a little colour into our life over here.

Just trying to make this cool and collected and unflappable apartment of yours just a little bit less pure and less helplessly stern."

"Helplessly stern?" He laughs so hard he has to sit down, he's so weakened by laughter that he can't help himself.

"So what did you get for me?"

"A book I found at the secondhand bookstore over on Monkland."

"Ah yes. The store where the beautiful Icelandic girl works."

"She's a bit dull, our Miss Iceland. But I bought you *Mansfield Park* since you happened to mention a few nights ago that you've never read it." He has something else for me too. He stands, holds out a hand. "So come on."

But I only poke my hands into my pockets, then follow him into his bedroom, sit down on his bed.

He sits down beside me, tells me to close my eyes, then lifts up my left hand and slides a ring onto my wedding ring finger and I feel the deep uneasiness of being proposed to. And how can his timing be so stupidly bad? But when I open my eyes I see that the ring (a folklore chain of silver hearts on a dull band of black) is a ring he must have bought from a street vendor. "It's beautiful," I tell him, and although I've warned myself to stay angry with him, I kiss him to thank him.

I DON'T KNOW whether it says I'm a grown-up or a coward, but I would much rather take notes than fight. If I were in the army I would be in espionage, not the infantry. But I also see myself as a kept woman, a woman who's been swimming from class to class, having gone several rungs down the ladder of class with the move to Randall Avenue, then with the move to Esplanade having turned into a woman who has at last begun to climb up again, away from the hold (the hold that has rats in it, smashed glass in the hallways), a woman who's an expert at floating, treading water. Which can't be good in the

long run. And so I lift *Ornament and Crime* onto my knees to use as
a table when I sit down on Galbraith's bed to write:

I've decided to move back
to my own place, but I'll call you.

Then I gather together my jacket, my hairbrush, my lipsticks (A Rose
Is a Rouge, Ultimate Wine), lock the door, slide the key under it,
hurry out to Avenue du Parc to catch a bus down the hill to the metro.

Up in my alien and stilled apartment I sit on my sofa and picture
Galbraith finding my note, then driving to a bar and having sex with
a prostitute or a lovely young girl. Or with Tess, perhaps there was
something there and I just didn't see it. I see myself at his funeral,
conduct my own little experiments with loss. I want to be loved, I
want to adore, I want to do good work, but I also so much sometimes want not to be bothered. I pick up a memoir set in Africa that
I took out of the library last week, my plan being to write a review
of it and mail it off to the books editor at *The Gazette,* along with a
note asking him if I can write the occasional review for the paper. If
I can't be a writer, I can at least write reviews. I turn to the chapter
on Gabon, a country of curses and colonial exploitation, of innocence destroyed and beheaded corpses, a country that's tribal-Nazi,
conspiratorial, a country of voodoo acts and vengeful concoctions.
"A country custom-made for paranoids," I write in my notebook. "A
country in which paranoia is a deeply necessary response to everyday
life." I read another five pages, make notes on the way an African
hunter, after he has killed a monkey, forces the end of its tail down
its throat, then throws it over his shoulder so he can carry it (or wear
it) like a shoulder bag as he makes his way through the forest. "Like a
tourist in the forest," I write, but then worry that I might seem to be
mocking the monkey. "And if you can actually forget that the monkey

is dead, the image of it being worn like a handbag even has the comic practicality of a boy or girl wearing a monkey as a shoulder bag while walking through the African jungle in a children's book ..." But my heart won't stop thudding and I can't stop wondering where Galbraith might be, what he's doing, what he's thinking right at this moment, and so I pick up the phone and call him.

He doesn't say hello, he says, "I was just sitting here trying to devise a way to apologize to you even more abjectly."

AFTER I'VE PULLED MY DOOR to click locked, I need to endure my tiny moment of torment: did I to turn off the gas? I think I must look pious (pious or neurotic) as I bend my listening ear to a crack in the door to try to conjure up the coffee-pot in my long galley kitchen. I listen to see, at least until I'm able to picture the top of the stove with no pot or pan on it.

"It's locked, Kay. So off we go. To La Pâtisserie de la Gare!"

"The Pastry Shop of the War?"

"No. The Pastry Shop of the Station."

In the car he sings, "Or the Pastry Shop of the Nation!" And when we get to La Pâtisserie de la Gare we buy hot garlic bread for our trip out to Lennoxville to drop off a few sketches at the house of one of his clients. On the way there we stop near Acton Vale to visit Felix, one of his brothers, a goat farmer who lives with his wife and three children in a white house at the end of a long country road.

Felix asks us if we'd like to go for a walk up on the hill. And so we set off, the children fighting to hold hands with me while the two men walk up ahead, their hands in their pants pockets and much too far ahead for us to overhear them. They glance back at me once or twice, though, as if to locate my position in the distance behind them and when I reach the top of the hill with the children, Galbraith hugs me as if he hasn't seen me for weeks and the children take off, racing down the hill to giddily roll around in the leaf-lined hollow at the bottom of what Felix calls "our mountain."

The melancholy tinkle and gong of goat bells adds a long sadness to the country afternoon, a counter-melody to the awkward conversation and the way Felix keeps staring at me, and when Galbraith walks into the woods, leaving me alone with him, I inhale the clean wind, say that living in Montreal makes me miss the country so much. "The clear air."

"Yes, we do have that."

After a few more awkward moments I tell him that I too need to pay a visit to the trees, and when I do, I can see blue and white vertical stripes among the leaves of the poplars as I walk into the grove's windy privacy, but to reach Galbraith I have to take a path so narrow it's almost medieval and I walk it thinking there's something slumped and female about a man urinating out in the wild, no matter how male the man, and at this moment he glances back at me over a shoulder. "I'll be right with you," he calls to me, and when he comes down the path he says, "You came looking for me because you missed me, right?"

"That too. Felix and I also couldn't think of anything to say to each other and so I escaped."

"This is what tends to happen with Felix. Monsieur Taciturn, we used to call him."

"And so now you've seen our notorious little wood," Monsieur Taciturn tells us as we come out onto the meadow. And his voice sounds bitter, the voice of a country dweller talking ironically (and, he damn well must hope, ironically *enough*) to two dolts from the city. "Our main scenic event." So that we all look to the children to save us when they run back up to us again, breathless, each wanting to take a turn being swung between us so they can swing their short legs back and forth as we lift them up high on our way down the hill.

When we get to Lennoxville, I wait in the car while Galbraith takes his sketches into a pink stucco house. I pull my book out of my bag, open it to a chapter set in the rain forest, and when I look up from it I see how faded this street looks, how like the past, everything bleached and genteel and historic: pale leaves blown back in the wind, formal pale brick houses. Time seems to have stopped, at least in Lennoxville. But at last the front door of the pink house opens and Galbraith comes down the path to the car.

On our way home we drive over a high bridge, then he backs up. "Let's have a look at the beach." While we're on our way down the path from the highway, we can see that we aren't to be alone: a man and a woman are standing far below us in the water. But once we've got down to the beach and have settled ourselves on a slope of stones bordered by a narrow hem of sand at the river's edge the swimmers (as if at a signal) dive under the water, then quickly pop up and shake themselves, the woman in a streamlined tan bathing suit, a hefty vanilla stripe running from left armpit to thigh and the man very manly in spite of the fact that his long-legged brown cotton shorts are clinging wetly to his body in a womanish way. Then they storm the shallow water like gods, and when they've slushed their way in as far as their ankles the woman, who's been walking behind the man and kick-splashing the backs of his legs, gives him a sharp slap on the behind, and at this he joyfully wheels around to scoop and flail great sails of water at her.

Escaping, crying with laughter, she falls on the water, the man lunging after her to wrestle her till he's ducked her. When he brings her pantingly up, his fists tightly holding her hugged from behind, she violently pumps her knees up and down in the river to force him to let go of her. When he stills her by kissing her, she rewards him with a showy loud gasp of pleasure, and at this he dips under the black skin of the water, then pops up with a leafy yellow boa of seaweed, drapes it over her shoulders.

I sieve a stream of sand down onto Galbraith's hand. "Don't you hate loud people who are such show-offs about being in love? They make me think of the kind of lovers you see in the metro, the ones who cling and kiss as if there's a war or a revolution but when the train roars into the station it turns out they're only going off to shop at the Faubourg."

They are insufferable, he agrees.

"What I really want is a love that's illicit, a love that no one will know about, only us."

He squints over at me. "You're older than I am, that's pretty illicit."

I lean back, my arms braced behind me. "Your brother kept staring at me in this incredibly diagnostic way, did you notice?"

"Felix is always like that, don't give it another thought. He only asked me if I was serious about you. And I told him yes. After all, we fight, don't we? That must mean we're serious about each other."

He sounds so young. And not even all that certain. The loud woman in the river, meanwhile, is certain of everything and is by now sitting in the lap of her lover's crouched panting squat, tying the boa's leafy ends in a loose knot over her glistening breasts. They then rise from the water and come promenading toward the beach as casually as if they've been strolling down a city street on a holiday afternoon, then duck to pick up their towels, walk away.

Now that we're alone at last, we pull off our clothes at the water's edge and walk down into the river, sinking, then gasping as we feel the shocking bob of the cold water rise between our warm thighs. But then we only swim for three or four minutes, wanting the whole time to scramble out into the sunshine and collapse, beached, on the slope of hot stones. And once we've come out and rubbed our arms and legs dry with the sleeves of our shirts, we climb the path to the car, then roll down the windows to let in the hot breeze as we race past burnt-out woods, blots on stilts, groves of windblown leaves while I stretch an arm across the seat behind him, then sigh with pleasure, I'm feeling so rinsed by a healthy cool from the deep cold of our swim. "Tell me who your first sexual experience was with."

"With one of my cousins. She was nineteen and I was sixteen. And she helped me."

"Did you really need any help?"

"You're right, I really didn't. And who was yours?"

"A boy who came to stay with my family the summer I was thirteen. But we couldn't go all the way because we were interrupted. Which was lucky. Although at the time I was furious. And then he didn't come down to dinner that night and after that whenever he glanced over at me I would look away. Meanwhile, up in the privacy of my own room I thought about him all the time...."

"But of course."

But now night is coming on and we need to be on the lookout for twin spots of green lights transfixed on the borders of dark: deer coming out of the woods bearing antlers mounted on their heads like elaborate weapons, then stepping delicately down the embankments. As if they've come out of the woods looking for water, but the grey stream isn't a stream, it's a highway.

HIGH LITTLE VOICES imitating British pop singers are singing "And he loves her ..." as we walk down the hill at the western end of the park in the hot evening sun and when we look up to see where the song is coming from we see five little boys sitting in a row on the limb of one of the park's most ancient trees. Galbraith takes off his jacket and opens it out on the grass, then I pull off my cardigan and spread it beside one of his jacket sleeves so we can sit down. This makes the boys sing their song very much louder, then begin to throw pebbles at us. At first Galbraith catches them and lightly tosses them back, but finally he gives up and we walk over to the bridge to look down at the rushing dark stream while he talks about how much he loved one of his older sisters. "And I'm still in love with her, even if we have nothing in common. Except, of course, for our love for me."

We smile down at the black water, its busy gurgling.

"In high school," he tells me, "I had the lead in *An Enemy of the People*."

"Were you nervous?"

"I must have been, I shouted my lines."

"My first theatre experience was when I was cast as the Virgin Mary in grade three...."

"Inspired casting."

I feel pleased. I am teased, therefore I exist. "My brother Freddie had to carry a pineapple sprayed with gold paint on a silver tea tray and he had to sing in a high little voice, 'Myrrh is mine, its bitter perfume....' But what I remember best is walking to the store with him when we both were still too young to go to school and how we saw a new bride and groom—Jack and Arleen—lying on the swing seat on their veranda, and Jack was, as we would have put it, 'feeling' Arleen's legs. But as we were walking slowly by, inspecting the spectacle while pretending not to, Jack lifted up Arleen's dress and pulled down her underpants and started to spank her with a Bible. This made her squirm and try to reach down and get her underpants back up over her bare behind, but at the same time she seemed to really want to be prevented from pulling them back up, and so it was clear to us that she must also be loving it. After that we used to make five or six trips to the store every Sunday afternoon, but we never saw Jack spank his Arleen again."

Galbraith smiles. "The Bible's a witty touch. I'm also trying to remember who it was who said, 'Sex without sin is like eating a boiled egg without salt.'"

"That's so perfect."

"But what were Jack and Arleen like otherwise?"

"Jack came from a family of freethinkers who never went to church—they couldn't bear the boredom of the dull Sunday sermons—but they were the ones who mowed the cemetery lawn and tended the graves of the dead. But Arleen was a little bit religious, the times I went to Sunday school I would sometimes see her at church. When I was very small, Jack's grandparents were even still alive, I loved to go to their house because they were so fragile and ancient and sweet, like a confection. And when the children of Scanlon Falls would make their annual Christmas visits to each house to see what people got ..."

"That's what you'd do for fun out in the country? Go and look at each other's presents?"

"It sounds pathetic, I know, but it was only till we were ten or eleven. And every year when we got to Jack and Arleen's house, Arleen would show us the boxes of pyjamas covered with cellophane and serve us cake and tea and allow us to pretend we were grown-ups. I didn't even remember the Bible incident, not then. It wasn't until I was an adult that I began to think back and remember the sequence of things and ponder exactly what I knew when." But at this point we hear a rustle and glance back to see the five little boys crouched close behind us, five excited little boys who now race off, whooping and shrieking.

After dinner we go to McGill to see a movie about a young French conscientious objector who is imprisoned during the Algerian War. In the final scene the son crouches to talk to his parents through the prison's chain link fence while the prison guards stand at attention behind him with their guns, waiting to march him back inside the main compound and as he's being walked away from his little father and mother (their hands turned into spreading claws by the diamond-shaped wires of the fence) the mother calls out after him what seem to me to be the most beautiful words a parent can ever call out to a son or a daughter, "I am so proud of you!" But could I bear to see one of my sons in prison, even for a just cause? I know I could not. Having children has turned me into a coward. I want them to be good, but not dangerously good. When they were babies I wanted heroic futures for them, but now that they're growing up, I only want them to be happy. I talk to Galbraith about this as we're on our way back to his car, tell him I want them to be happy more than I want them to be good. "And how good can that be?"

"Don't worry so much," he tells me, and after we get home we carry bowls of green grapes up to the roof, then lie under the sky's wash of stars, milking the tart grapes from their stems until the night gets too dewy and cool and we have to go back down again, get ready for bed.

But once we've turned out the lights for the night, he looms over me to say, "So should I spank you with a Bible now?"

I smile in the dark. "I'm not sure I'm religious enough."

"Religious enough for what?"

"Religious enough to find that thrilling enough."

"What about a hairbrush?"

"No!"

"What about being tied up with dental floss?"

"That would totally terrify me. I'm not trusting enough."

"I'm running out of implements, Kay."

"So how about the human hand?"

"The human hand, then...."

"It's what I would want. A hand, not an implement."

"Whose hand would you like?"

"Whose hand do you think? But can we please just have plain sex, please?"

"Okay, but I have to warn you, I'm going to be thinking about this, I'm going to be considering it...."

Talking about it makes me want to do it. At the same time I feel shy, as if all my bashfulness has rushed to collect itself down at the site of so much possible male attention. But this is also the night that he tells me he loves me.

I tell him that I love him too, tell him that I've been wanting to tell him ever since the night he first came over to my place. "But I didn't want to say it until you said it first."

"Why? Because I am the *man*?"

"No, of course not," I tell him. Feeling offended. "For another reason."

"Tell me."

"It was the only way I'd be able to tell if you really meant it. And also, I must confess, because you're the younger one. I was afraid that if I said it first, then you might say it too, just to be polite."

"Hell, I'm not *that* polite." But after a small silence he says in a puzzled voice, "The difference between our ages can't be all that great though, can it?"

"I don't even want to know. After all, even when you were sixteen you probably could have passed yourself off as a father of three."

I can hear him smile one of his night smiles in the dark, that sexy tiny crack of sound that you need excellent hearing to even hear.

"And so for all I know you're only twenty."

"It's true that I cultivated the worn-out look."

"Did you have a long string of girlfriends?"

"More or less."

"My grandmother had such beautiful legs and such a young way of walking that even when she was in her eighties, men followed her in the street."

"But what happened as they passed her and sneaked a peek at her face?"

"They were shocked and appalled."

"Okay, so mock me. I know men are bastards."

"What did you write today?"

"I wrote about you," I tell him, hugging him from behind. "About how great thou art."

He's pulling strips of the white meat away from the roast chicken set out to cool on a pottery platter. "So go ahead and poke fun at me. Let it be open season on your devoted lover."

"Look at the parsley. It's been cooked so long it's turned black."

He digs into the stuffing, feeds me a bloated prune. "Everything's black in here. Black is beautiful, baby...."

I laugh softly against his back, but then worry that I'm being too clingy, too boringly adoring, and so I go and sit down on the sofa in the front room and watch the hot breeze blow the curtains in.

But he calls out to me, "Come back here!"

"What for?"

"I need to be hugged while I eat."

"No!"

"Why not?"

"It's not good for you."

"It is so good for me. I can't digest my food unless I'm hugged."

"No."

"Obey me."

"No."

"Why not?"

"It's not good for you to be obeyed."

"I'll just have to deal with you when I've finished this bird."

And I think yes, deal with me, I want you to, and the words *deal with me* all at once sound so sexual that they make me want to turn and laugh into a shrugged shoulder like a crazed ballerina.

He comes out of the kitchen and sits down beside me, then glances toward the bedroom.

"Right now? But it's so sunny," I whisper. "Shouldn't we wait till it gets dark?"

"The only way this is going to work is if you obey me, Kay."

Benno's white face flashes past me in a metro train going fast in the opposite direction to my own rushing train, making me feel how vast Montreal is, like revolutionary Russia. And when I call him after I get back to Galbraith's apartment he tells me that when I saw him he was on his way home from the dentist, that he's going to have all of his wisdom teeth pulled at two o'clock.

"Will you have to go on antibiotics?"

"Just as a precaution, the dentist said."

I call him an hour after his extraction is supposed to be over, but there's no answer. An hour later he's still not at home. Ten minutes later I dial part of his number but then hang up, not wanting him to think of me as a hysterical mother (because being a mother is like being a boy in high school, a boy who panics halfway through calling a girl to ask her for a date). But what if he's gone out to a bar and mixed 292s with alcohol, then collapsed in an alleyway? After one last attempt to reach him at five, I run to the metro. My name for his alley is Drug Alley and in my panic as I'm racing east on the train, I picture needles on the ground, a carpet of silver pine needles in a lethal forest.

A girl is leaning against a brick wall on his narrow lane, a young woman with dried-out brownish hair and kind eyes who's wearing the get-up of an innocent hooker: beneath a white raincoat, a pink bikini with an iridescent sheen to it.

"Pardonnez-moi, mademoiselle," I say to her in my stilted French, "mais avez-vous vu un jeune garçon avec un manteau noir qui habite dans cette rue ici?"

"Oui," she says. "Je le connais...."

"Il est mon garçon." Or is *garçon* a waiter? "Il est mon fils, I've been trying to reach him by phone but he isn't at home, I'm worried that he didn't take his antibiotics ..."

"L'antibiotique ..."

"Oui," I say. But what is the French word for teeth? Toothpaste in French is *dentifrice,* and so teeth should be *dents.* And wisdom? La sagacity? I point at my own teeth. "Les dents de sagacity."

"Ah," says the girl, mystified.

"Au revoir," I say, as if I'm leaving her forever, then I walk up the hill of wet paving stones to knock on Benno's door and peer through his window. I can see the futon and the floor surrounding it and crumpled bits of white paper that look like haphazard white tulips in the room's sub-aquatic dimness. And it isn't a terrible room, it's even recently been renovated. But it looks too forlorn in the rainy grey light, its decor a young man's decor: totally wrecked and abandoned.

In the metro I'm drawn by a more urgent music than any I've ever before heard down in these tiled caverns. Coming from the far end of the eastbound platform, it's music that's not quite a train and not quite horses' hooves and not quite music either, but somehow all three. People have congregated in a large semi-circle to watch a man who looks like a homeless person playing a tiny red guitar, almost a toy guitar, a man with a drunken boxer's face and fly-away hair. Shock is in the air—how can a person who looks like this play like this?—for the melody seems not to be a melody that anyone knows, it's scurried and drummed out of somewhere too private for that, it's played with too dedicated a malice. People seem to be humbled by their awe, all that awe at war with all that pity, and one by one they go forward to drop coins and bills into his guitar case. But the player only plays on, looks up at no one. I want to give him money too, but I don't drop my coins into his guitar case until I'm running to the train. Even after the doors have closed, we all stand staring out at him as we are being borne away, watch him as he's bowed over his tiny red guitar for as long as we can, we've been so stilled by his mad sorrow, and in fact he makes me worry so much about Benno that I get off the train at Atwater and hurry through the underground mall to look for a phone, then stop off at a deluxe cave whose spotlights are aimed at trays of feta and black olives in polluted dark water, find a wall of phones next to the plums and dial him again. But his phone only rings and rings.

Galbraith is lying on the sofa when I let myself in. He's pulled off his shoes and there's a rich male smell in the room, the odour of black leather shoes that have recently been stepped out of and I breathe it in as I set the plums down on the coffee table. "I was out foraging for food at exorbitant prices," I tell him, then sit down beside him, lift his feet onto my knees. "So what have you been up to while I was away?"

"Just the usual bachelor indulgences. A little pornography, a little self-abuse, a little espresso with cognac."

"You say *cognac* as if you want to break the word's back."

"I'm just trying to be sexy and French."

"But isn't our own private pornography enough for you, babe?"

"Yeah, it is." But then he says, "Yes and no." And then he says no. "Well, you know how it is. I'm a man, and so no known quantity of pornography is ever actually going be quite enough for me. But don't take it personally, it's just a corrupt male thing. It's not personal, it's biological."

Beyond our balcony the night is alive with voices trying to outdo each other, strident drunken voices switching back and forth between

French and English and when we step out outside, a swarm of fireflies floats down, then a shower of what looks like confetti on fire followed by the burning tip of a tossed cigarette. Galbraith stamps on it. *"Tabernac!"* he yells upward. "Watch what you're doing up there, idiots, we are not an ashtray!"

I slip into his room to try Benno again. Still no answer. I'll make myself wait for another ten minutes before I go to the phone again. And once we're eating and I excuse myself to go back to it, I sit sideways on his bed so I can keep my face turned away from him. But when I come back to sit down beside him he tells me I should write a story about an architect. "You could have him say some of the pretentious things *I* say: 'sense of the sublime, infinite vistas ...'" He laughs, scratches a foot through a sock. Then he looks over at me, asks me what the matter is. "This has been like having dinner with a zombie."

When I tell him he says, "But would your son want you to interfere?"

"No, he wouldn't," I say unhappily. "But I'll have to, if it's to save his life."

He reluctantly agrees to drive up and down the streets of bars that are close to the downtown universities, and after he lets me out, I walk up Benno's alleyway in the warm dark, his black window already convincing me that he's not inside and asleep, his place is too vacant, without information. I knock hard on his door, on his window, peering in through the glass until my eyes become accustomed to the dimness. But there's no one lying on the pale coverlet that's been spread over his mattress.

When we stop for a red light at Côte-des-Neiges, Galbraith glances over at me. "Once you get in touch with your son, don't ever tell him that we went out looking for him, he wouldn't like it."

I say I won't, then close my eyes. But when we get back to Esplanade I go straight to the phone. To my amazement, Benno answers it on the second ring. And when I tell him that I just want to warn him not to mix painkillers with alcohol he says in a sullen voice, "Don't you ever do anything but worry?"

"I do a few other things."

"But that's your chief pleasure in life, isn't it? Worrying?"

"I wouldn't go quite that far." But now I can hear Galbraith coming down the hall from the kitchen. "Listen, I can't talk any more right now."

"Why? Is your *friend* coming?"

"You'd like him if you knew him."

"I doubt it."

"I'll call you later in the week."

"If you must."

This is supposed to be a joke (or so I hope) and so I say, "I must."

Galbraith sits down beside me, watches me set the receiver back in its cradle, and when he asks me if that was my son I bow my head and hold a hand over my eyes before I say yes.

He hugs my shoulders. "So he's fine then, don't cry," and he flops back onto his bed, pulls me down next to him, then whispers, "Do things to me. Because I'm just a boy too and I'm in need of your attention."

WHO ARE THE SEXY GODMOTHERS to women? Passing on what they know? Women's magazines are the godmothers, women's magazines have dedicated themselves to teaching women all their sexual tricks, they teach women to write little messages on the arms of their lovers, then button their shirt cuffs while warning them that there's to be no peeking until three o'clock, no peeking at messages that say things like "When you come home from work tonight, I want to kneel before you ..." The husband of the woman who wrote this told her later that night that he'd read her message that morning just after arriving at work and that he hadn't been able to think of anything else the whole day, and when I'm not able to get her message out of my mind either, it occurs to me that sometimes writers know too much about words, writers know ten different ways to say the same thing, whereas someone who's heartfelt and not a writer can think of only one way (but it's the right way) and so while Galbraith is reading *Le Devoir* with his coffee, I sit down at his desk to write the magic words of the magazine wife on a sheet of paper, fold it and slip it into his jacket pocket, then pat the pocket. "Don't open this till three o'clock this afternoon."

I'm surprised when he phones me at three-thirty to tell me to meet him at a bar on Duluth. Because if he's already read the note wouldn't he want me to wait for him at home? He can't have read it. Unless he's read it and for some reason disapproves of it. But how could he disapprove of it? Unless some man he knows has told him about receiving an exact replica of this note, or perhaps he himself has already received an exact replica of this note from one of the women who's preceded me, it makes me sick to think that this might already have happened, I can feel my face get hot as I wash my hair in the shower, as I pull on my black dress, my black sandals with the wide tan suede straps, as I lift on my dark glasses on my way to the bar, then sit tensely watching the late afternoon crowds of Montreal women walking in the direction Galbraith will be coming from. But now here he comes, and now that I've caught sight of him I can see that he doesn't see any of these women, his expression is so completely private with thought, his face is so concentrated on something else, so filled with one thought or one problem. He's frowning too, he's frowning into the bright sun, and although he still hasn't seen me, I can't break my gaze, I don't even want to blink, and then he does see me, and the joy that rises up in his eyes (a radiant look that seems to me to be filled with a kind of honoured gratitude, the look of love, just as the songs say) won't allow me to stay sitting, I have to stand, because after all I am honoured and grateful too, and when he gets to my table, he only touches me on a wrist, then says, "How much do you owe here?" And when I say, "Four dollars," he takes a ten-dollar bill out of his wallet and slips it under a teacup, then doesn't even want to wait for the change, he instead cups my elbow to steer me under the awning and out into the sun again, then says in a low voice, "I didn't get a chance to open your note until half an hour ago. So let's go home...."

And so we walk to Esplanade on our way to our rendezvous with one another, but we are doing it by not speaking and not even holding hands as we walk side by side. It makes me think of being on the outside of certain sexually glamorous relationships in high

school, the ones that everyone in the school was in awe of, the ones
where the lovers wouldn't even be high school royalty, they would
merely be two students in grade eleven or twelve who were not even
the most gorgeous or most cool, instead they were the ones who
were most revered. They would walk side by side and never once be
seen to speak to one another, never once be seen to even hold hands,
their eyes would forever be aimed at some private memory or horizon
of passion or intimacy, and yet because of the intense privacy of
their sexual life they were a public phenomenon. People, even innocent people like me, seemed to understand that what they had (the
wordless connection they had) had nothing to do with flirting or
teasing or clever repartee, it was serious, it was the real thing, the
real dedicated humourless emotion, it was the most sexual possible
absolute devotion.

I understand all this, that Galbraith and I are not to give one
another knowing looks, that we are not to touch, that my right wrist
is not even to knock against his left wrist, not even by mistake, and as
we're walking like this, alone but together, I think of the magazine
article and the note the wife wrote, and how I must never reveal to him
that the note I wrote wasn't even my own idea, but something I got
from a magazine. Even though all the love words must, after all, be in
the public domain, and must have been in the public domain ever
since the first eavesdropper overheard a man and a woman wanting to
make each other happy on their pile of furs. And, really, aren't men
more pragmatic about sex than women are? And so would he even
care? As long as I did what I did, wouldn't that be the main thing? Love
has never been about originality after all, it's always been about
thrilling the other person so that the other person can thrill you. I'm
nervous though, as if I'm auditioning for a more difficult role in our
sexual drama, but it could only be the solemn approach to it that's
making me nervous, this and the fact that although we've done this

before, we've never done it when it's been ushered in by such formal anticipation. But by now people are staring at us as if we are refugees or as if we've been in an accident.

Then up in the apartment the late afternoon sunlight seems stale, the windows still closed against the heat. We don't open them, Galbraith only opens the door to the balcony, then takes off his jacket and loosens his tie. We each have to pee after this, then we each have to drink a long cold drink of water, then as I step backwards out of my sandals he comes up behind me and sets his hands on my hips as he kisses me on the back of my neck and I feel weak from the walk home in the hot sun, weak when he detours to pick up a cushion from the sofa, but once he's leaning against the wall of his room, the cushion dropped at his feet, I step onto it and we kiss, the cushion making me quite a lot taller than he is for a kiss that weakens me to the point where I do in fact need to sink to my knees as he takes my face between his hands to say, "From the time I opened your note I haven't been able to think of anything but this...." And even though this is almost word for word what the husband in the magazine said to his wife, the words feel completely new to me, they topple down on me with so much emotion.

THE SUN MOVES across the calendar, by now it's already August, the nights are already cooler, cool enough that we are inclined to stay in, one of us reading in one room, the other one reading in another room, and it's as if this kind of love at one remove makes me feel the most trusting tenderness for Galbraith, just from knowing he's near.

I've also been invited to go back to work again, to help out for two weeks, and so now in the mornings I stand next to him in front of his bathroom mirror as we prepare for the day. How happy I feel on these primeval mornings, even if I also feel like an imposter who's only pretending to live a normal life while the aromas of café au lait and sunlight on newsprint fill the rooms with an urban importance. Even out in the day the world seems too cinematic to be real as we step into the breezy sunlight, an illusion that persists even after Galbraith drops me off at the entrance to the park, our plan being that we'll arrive at work at different times so as not to attract unwanted attention. He'll be one of my bosses again, after all, and we don't want to be teased.

It's only late in the evenings of the nights I stay with him overnight that I worry that I might call out some inappropriate thing in my sleep. Or that I won't sleep neatly enough. And so we've settled into a routine where I sleep over on Monday, Thursday, Friday and Saturday nights, the other nights he drives me home. It's what he does when I have to go away for a day to give two readings at St. Michael's Hospital in Toronto. Although when he offers to pick me up early in the morning, to drive me to the bus terminal, I say no. "It's so fast to get there on the metro." And this is what I really want: to hurry alone down the stairs to the trains. But he insists, possibly because he's convinced that I won't get there on my own.

I can only sleep for a few hours, then there's no point in even trying and so just after sunrise I throw back my duvet, go to my typewriter, type up a new section of the novel while I'm still in my nightgown. Then the frantic search for Scotch tape and scissors, followed by rushed coffee, rushed bowl of soup left over from last Sunday night, but now he's already here, and it's only six-ten and he's upset because I'm not even dressed yet. "But I don't understand. Why can't you get everything set out the night before?"

I pull on my grey skirt, zip it up. "Will you please stop accusing me?"

"But why couldn't you have thought of making these changes last night? When you had time to prepare?"

"Because it's in the nature of this kind of last-minute inspiration that it comes to you at the last minute!" I call out to him as I'm on my way into the kitchen for my watch.

When I glance back at him, he's looking at his own watch like a husband.

"Just please go down to the car! Just please leave me alone up here so I can get ready!"

"But what do you still have to do? We're already late."

"Just *go*, please. I just need to be alone up here for three minutes."

"Not until you tell me why."

"Just to check things."

"What things?"

"The stove, other things."

"This is beginning to sound very obsessive compulsive, Kay."

"It only happens when I'm tired! And so will you please just *go?*"

"I'll give you three minutes, then. But not more."

Once I've heard his footsteps go down the stairs, I go back to the kitchen, stand in front of the stove, order myself to concentrate. Because if I don't concentrate, I'll start thinking of other things, then I'll have to begin all over again. And if I have to begin all over again there'll be no end to it, I'll have to keep doing it until I'm more and more unconvinced that the stove is off or the kitchen faucets are off and I'll miss my bus and Galbraith will never speak to me again, my relationship with him will be over.

I stand in front of the stove and warn myself: "You have my permission to touch each element, but only once." I then reach out and pat them—one, two, three, four—then hold a hand cupped under each faucet. "Off," I say to the Hot tap. "Off," I say to the Cold tap. Then I grab up my canvas bag and my raincoat, lock the door, run down the stairs as if I'm being pursued by my faucets.

When I push open the main door to the street I see Galbraith toss his cigarette out the driver window, then reach over to open my door for me as I come trotting toward the other side of the car. And once I've slammed myself in, we're immediately off, racing east above the speed limit at six-forty on this brilliant fall morning.

"Sorry!"

"Only one sorry?"

"Meaning?"

"Meaning you always say sorry at least four times. Sometimes even five times."

"Sorry, sorry, sorry, sorry, sorry."

"What's the name of the hospital where you're giving the reading?"

"St. Michael's." I look out at the perfect morning. "And so you can see that they've not only sanctified you, they even worship you so much that they've actually named a hospital after you."

He doesn't smile, he's not going to indulge me. As for me, I have no plans to appease him, it's too much like being married again. And on my birthday too, which I most certainly don't plan to mention. "What are you going to do after work today?"

"Felix is coming into town and I'm going to meet him for a beer."

I try to imagine it. "Still older than you are, is she?" I arrange for Mr. Taciturn to say. Then I arrange for Galbraith to respond, "Yes, she is. I don't predict any change there, actually. At least not in the foreseeable future." I gaze out at the streets, still so quiet and asleep and tall-doored and correct. At this time of day even the city is dewy. "It's an amazing morning, in any case."

He won't look at me, he's concentrating on the traffic.

I picture myself free of him and alone on the bus, how I will breathe laxly, truly alone and unobserved for the first time in weeks. Just to be. Just to breathe in the calm (although also awful) bus air.

At the terminal he switches off the ignition, then turns to me. "Don't take anything I said too personally."

"What can I say? I always take what you say personally."

"Come here."

I move into his arms and he strokes back my hair. "I'm a maniac when it comes to catching planes and trains. To say nothing of buses. But you know what I want you to do? I want you to go into that hospital that's named after me and wow all those guys on their dialysis machines."

"At least they won't be able to get up and leave if they don't like what I'm reading, they'll be a captive audience."

"I thought I was your captive audience."

I drag my canvas bag out from the back seat and hope that my smile is an older woman's smile, a little cynical, a little amused, even though I'm afraid it's only a smile that adores him, comme d'habitude and typical moi.

He squints up at me as I'm walking past his side of the car, and when I reach out a hand to him, he grabs my wrist, draws me back to him. "Call me when you get in tonight."

"But I might be very late."

"No matter how late."

No matter how late, no matter how late, the words sing inside my body like love words as I climb onto the bus. And the bus isn't any help either, trundling out of the station in its bumpy, aphrodisiac way, then heading south, miles of yellow leaves blasted apart by its speed and the early fall breezes, then we're driving across a wide valley that's a rural wasteland of hulking industrial barns and hydro pylons strung over the low hills. But I'm only thinking of sex and tenderness, certain glances.

At eleven we turn onto a driveway over crunched gravel, come to a stop in front of a dark wood chalet set in rolling green farm country, then walk across a sunny concrete plaza that's walled by weeds to a lodge that's bright with late morning light. I follow the other women passengers into the washroom where there's already a crowd in front of the sinks and mirrors, young women outlining their eyes, repairing the damage from so many hours of sitting still. Two little girls who come out of two of the flushing cubicles, pulling at the backs of their jeans and looking cranky and damp, are followed by three older women who begin to soap their hands—viciously, distastefully—at the round dirty sinks. I splash my eyes with cold water, then cup the cold water in a hand, drink it. There's no taste of chlorine in it, it's water from a deep well in deep country. But the sinks make me remember taking trips with Tom and Benno when they were small enough to come into the women's washroom with me to wash their hands in the water blasting from the bruised chrome taps, good little boys, wobbly from the exhaustion of watching one scene replacing another scene, the world whirling around them, too much to look at, I couldn't have believed then that they'd turn into two big guys who would flinch if Alex or I bumped into them or touched an elbow in a moment of affection. Galbraith was like this with me one morning last week too and looked at me so moodily that I wondered if he'd had a bad dream and out of a whole cast of shady characters I was the one who did him wrong. But now we're being herded back into the bus again and more miles of grass follow, more hills and towns, then at last we're here: squeal of streetcars, clear jolts of excitement.

At St. Michael's I take the elevator up to Urology where a tall nurse tells me that none of the patients can understand English. Only a potter from Antigua, a round-eyed man who has only one kidney and who's walked over here from another ward, is able to understand me. For him I read:

Over here snow falls
on mistakes of the heart

as mounds of footprints
harden into ice

As I move on to another poem, a man in a bed near the sinks begins to snore loudly, and when I look up I see two nurses in a nearby drug pantry smirking in my direction, then it's over and I'm being led away by Louise Archer, the social worker who set up the two readings, an elegant woman with straight silver hair who's wearing a slim grey ferny dress under her lab coat and who gives off a fragrance that's more peppery than floral. She leads me down polished hallways to a room where fifteen or sixteen people are waiting for us on chairs hitched into a circle. A churchy arrangement, but at least the patients here seem to have been primed to be glad to see me, and not long after I've begun to read they begin to interrupt me, but the interruptions (relevant or irrelevant oddball experiences from their own lives) are somehow relieving. And at least they are awake. It's only when I'm reading a section that makes a reference to sex that they become extremely quiet (frightened, even) and so I skip ahead to read them a poem about childhood. At some point during this poem, Louise must have left the room and it's not long after this that one of the male patients begins to ask me about being a child at school. In a Donald Duck voice he asks me if I was grateful to my teachers. I say yes, to some of them. Then a greyer man sitting next to him asks me if I was grateful to my teachers for teaching me about William Shakespeare. Yes to this too. The Donald Duck man then asks me, "Did you know that Shakespeare drives a Corvette?" But at this same moment a door is pushed open, and an obese ebony woman steps into the room bearing a white birthday cake with a single fat pink candle stuck into it, then Louise and all the patients sing "Happy Birthday" to me. The two men who talked to me during my reading continue to give me more details about Shakespeare's life (as he's living it now) while they are eating their cake. And after it's all over, Louise puts an arm around my waist as we're walking down the hall to the elevator. "I knew it was your birthday today because when I called you last November to invite you to read for us and we talked about dates, you told me that the date I'd picked out for you was your birthday. And so I just made a note of it, then two days ago I put in an order for a birthday cake with the hospital kitchen. But I also want you to know that the two guys who talked to you about Shakespeare are both paranoid schizophrenics, they're two very ill guys, and today was the first time that either of them has spoken a word to *anyone* for over a year. We were all just so impressed by that."

Perhaps they recognized one of their own kind in me, but nevertheless her words elate me as I push open the hospital's EXIT door and walk out into the late afternoon of the hot thrilling city. I'm in a state of euphoria as I recall the way the day has moved from the ridiculous to the sublime in three little hours. But then all's well that ends well, as the owner of the Corvette once so wisely said.

In the free time I've got left before the next bus leaves Toronto, I visit a bookstore, then walk up the steps to a cathedral, lured up to it by the drift of pale leaves and the formal weak light on its stone steps, go into its hushed interior to sit in one of the pews so that I can breathe in the ecclesiastical smell of dry wood and old velvet. But I'm only marking time, I only want to get back to Galbraith.

I half sleep as the bus races back to Montreal under a sky of bright stars. And below the stars the dim fields, the black trees. We might be driving at night somewhere in Africa, but by the time we reach Kingston just after ten, the stars are lost behind fog. The driver gears down to stop at a restaurant that's both banal and hallucinatory and I find a pay phone to do as I've been longing to do the whole day and call Galbraith.

"Where are you right now?"

"In Kingston. Or somewhere outside Kingston, the fog's so dense out here it's hard to tell."

"Come and stay with me tonight. It's closer too, just take a cab from the station."

It's foggy in Montreal too, high and low blurred lights in the mist, then the swift silent drive in the cab to Esplanade, polished granite in the lobby, a towering madman getting on the elevator when it cruises to a stop on 3 at two in the morning, a man with a decayed look who's dressed in a gold satin dressing-gown and whose glance takes me in with such a weary distaste that I say hello out of the conviction that it will be best to make eye contact, to indicate that I'm an upper-class sort myself and people will definitely come looking for me if I go missing or get murdered.

He doesn't reply and when the elevator stops at 5, he follows me out, then with a small bow turns right as I'm turning left. When I reach Galbraith's apartment, I close the door behind me in a rush, lean against it as I lock both the locks, go straight into his bedroom, sit down beside him to kiss him, but he's so deeply asleep that he turns away from me with a groan.

Out in the kitchen I drink a bottle of beer, then go back to the bedroom to undress in the dark. Galbraith sleeps on as I slip in beside him thinking the words I would say if he were awake: Here I am, sweetheart, and here is my body, as requested, my time away swims in my head, I'm so insane from exhaustion, but when I come back to bed after getting up to pee in the night he turns to me to whisper "You're back," then falls asleep again and the next time I open my eyes it's morning and he's gone.

I tie on his kimono, go to the door to the balcony to see that it's raining, rain falling in the mild and listless but lovely misty city morning. But by the time he comes back from work, it's sunny and he's carrying a large photograph of sailboats bobbing near the industrial fretwork of a bridge in bright sunlight. No, the sailboats aren't sailboats after all, they are the billowing walls of the Sydney Opera House, he tells me this as he gets his hammer out of a drawer in the kitchen, then carries the photo into his bedroom. I can hear him hammering up a hook for it while I'm rinsing lettuce for a salad, then he's coming back to the kitchen. "Come look."

I follow him to the doorway of his bedroom. "It still looks like sailboats all herded together in the sunlight. It's so astounding that it's an actual building...."

"Architecture as deception," he tells me. "By the way, thanks for coming here instead of to your own place last night, even though I wasn't in any state to indicate my appreciation."

"I sat on your bed, hoping to wake you. I even gave you a kiss, but you apparently thought I was a mosquito," and as we're carrying plates of bread and the salad out to the coffee table, I tell him about the strange man I met in the elevator in the middle of the night. "A huge and seedy psychotic guy in a gold satin dressing-gown."

"This whole building is filled with these entitled old boys. Rich ancient old boys who've never had to grow up. But did he frighten you? I shouldn't have asked you to come here so late at night. If anything had happened to you it would have been my fault. Do you ever think that? That some request you made of someone could put them at risk?"

"I think this way all the time. With my children. I'm always afraid that my need to reassure myself that they're safe will actually put them in danger, that they'll unlock their doors in a hurry because they hear the phone ringing, then will completely forget to take their keys out of the door—"

"And all because you called...."

It spooks me to even talk about it and so while we're both out in the kitchen serving ourselves our carbonnade, I tell him about the patient who snored all the way through my reading in the kidney unit, then dramatize the scene in which the schizophrenics asked me questions about Shakespeare's Corvette. I've just begun to describe the surprise of the birthday cake with its single candle when he interrupts me to say, "But why didn't you tell me it was your birthday when we were on our way to the bus station? Jesus, I wouldn't have acted like such a schmuck...."

As we carry our bowls of beery stew into the big room, I tell him I didn't even think of it. "My birthdays don't even hold all that much interest for me any more." But as I'm blowing on my soup, he sings to me:

Mon trésor Kay,
C'est à ton tour,
De te laisser
Parler d'amour....

"That's such a great song," I tell him as we climb up to the roof. "And it has such a beautiful melody. Not at all like the militaristic and tedious birthday song that people sing in English." Then we lie down under the stars, a faint swarm of them over this green part of the city, and when he says, "I have a confession to make," I turn to him and kiss his shoulder. I feel happy. Happy and unafraid.

"You remember the night we first kissed? Which was also, coincidentally, the night we first had sex?"

"Vaguely."

"Vaguely!" He lunges for me, tickles me until I gasp and twist. "I happen to know for a fact that you consider it a night to remember."

"I do, I do...."

"So here's my confession: I tricked you that night. I came back because I wanted to plant my pen somewhere in your apartment, but I told you I'd forgotten it. And then while you were in your bedroom looking for it I was taking it out of my windbreaker pocket to set it on the table that's on the way to your kitchen. And that's when I called out to tell you that I'd found it."

"So it was a trick in a good cause then, since it made everything happen."

"It would have happened anyway, one way or another."

"But do you think we went to bed together too soon?"

"Only women worry about that, men never do. And besides, by then we'd already known each other for five months. I already knew that you were totally crazy about me."

"Yes, I was."

"Was and are."

"Was and are, was and am, was and will be, world without end, Amen."

"So." (Rolling over to lean on an elbow.) "Do you believe in God?"

"Do I believe in God."

"Don't repeat the question, Kay. Answer it."

"I believe in prayer."

"And therefore also in God."

"And therefore also in some idea of God. Or in some idea of a just and kindred spirit."

"Do you believe in the afterlife?"

"I believe in the soul."

"Do you believe in the soul's survival?"

"I know that I want to." I squint over at him. "And what about you? Or is this Catechism Night on Esplanade and I'm the one who's supposed to answer all the questions?"

"But you wouldn't describe yourself as being in any way conventionally religious...."

"No. My relationship with God is personal, I hate organized religion."

He rolls away from me, lies flat on his back again.

"I started believing in God when my children were small and were late coming home after school or playing with friends, I felt so at the mercy of chance. And when they came safely back to me I would express my gratitude to God."

"How would you do that?"

"I'd say, 'Thank you, God. Thank you, dear God, my darling....'"

"So your relationship with God was fairly erotic."

"It was just a relief to have someone to thank. And it turned out that God was the someone."

"What church were you christened in?"

"In the Anglican church."

"Which is practically Catholic, right?"

"It's the closest you can get to being a Catholic if you are a Protestant."

"And your children were also christened in the Anglican church?"

"They weren't christened at all."

"Not at all?"

"Not even a little bit. But why so many questions? From a man who's a lapsed Catholic?"

"The Catholic boy never dies." And he tickles my face with one of the weeds that he's pulled out of the roof garden, walks the tickle up my legs, up my arms. "So," he says. "So when you were at the hospital that's named after me, there was just one single pink candle on your birthday cake, right?"

"Right."

"And so how many candles would there have been on it if your actual age was accounted for?"

"This is beginning to sound like a problem in algebra."

"So do it, then."

"No."

"Why not?"

"Because it doesn't matter."

"But what if it matters to me?"

"Does it?"

"It does in the sense that I'm aware of the fact that it's something we just never discuss, and I suppose what brings all of this on is that I did have that beer with Felix yesterday and he asked me two questions. One, is she a Catholic? And two, how old is she? And then today when I was having lunch with my friend Gus and I told him that I was seriously involved with an older woman, he asked me how old. And so both times I had to fake it, pretend that I knew."

"So what did you tell them?"

"I told them you were thirty-six, even though you seem younger. At least to me." He looks over at me. "So what is your true and actual age, baby?"

My heart skips and races, wants to race far away. "Why is it necessary for you to know this?"

"Aren't you even curious to know how old *I* am?"

"Not if you're even younger than I think you are."

"But if we should happen to break up over this, wouldn't it be sort of horrible but also sort of fascinating that it was a birthday cake that began our love affair and it was another birthday cake that brought it to an end?"

"Why would it be sort of fascinating?"

"Because of the irony of it all. And because you are such a student of human nature, mon amour."

"Right, then. So let x equal the age of Galbraith, and let y equal the age Galbraith thinks Kay has attained. If Kay's actual age is $x + 8 = y$, then how much is y?"

"x equals twenty-eight," he tells me.

I'm astounded. "I would have said you were older. Maybe even thirty-five, thirty-six."

"And so now what does y equal?"

"It's just too depressing to give you y."

"Come on, you promised. I told you my age, you have to tell me yours."

"If I do, it will change everything."

"No, it won't."

I've hitched myself up on an elbow by this time and can feel how my eyes are only fixed in careful doubt as I look down at his face.

"I mean, how bad can it be? Even if you're as much as ten years older than I am, we could still live with it, couldn't we? It's only numbers."

"And if it's more than ten?"

I can see his eyes begin to look frightened too. "So you're ninety-two."

"I'm forty-five."

He too is astounded, this much is clear, and so I try to feel flattered.

"And here I was feeling guilty for telling Gus you were thirty-six."

I can't bring myself to say thanks, I'm too afraid. "But my boys are both at university."

"I did know that." His left knee is unhappily jiggling. "I suppose I really didn't want to know, and that's why I just never did the math. But I still cannot get over how young you look."

An hour later, when we're getting ready for bed, he sighs as he pulls off his shirt, then turns his bare back to me to show me a mole on his left shoulder. "Does it look black to you?"

I pull the hat of the gooseneck lamp in a downward swoop so I can shine its light on the mole, click on the lamp so I can peer at it. "No, it's brown."

"You don't think it's a malignant melanoma, then?"

"No, I don't. Because you're right. That would be black." And when I ask him if he'd like me to give him a back rub, he at once turns to lie belly down on the bed. But by the time I've poured a dollop of lotion into my left palm, he's already asleep. I rub my hand on my thigh to make it unslippery enough to snap out the light, then sweep my hands up his back over and over, it feels like such a deep thing to do, the repeating slow lunges like rowing without oars in the dark.

W HEN I HEAR HIM come down the hall to the kitchen, I'm hulling strawberries at the sink, it's a sunny afternoon between five and six, my back is turned to him and I'm wearing one of his upside-down work shirts as an apron, its sleeves tied around my waist like bulky apron strings and I can feel his gaze take in my hips and I get a feeling that he's wondering if I'll ever get fat. Or he might be thinking: But her legs are still slim, her arms are still slim. *Still!* I could tell him that *still* is a cruel word if you are a woman and that I'd prefer for him to think that no one in his right mind would ever dream I'm only five years away from fifty. But when I look back at him all I see is how startled he looks and so my face must all at once must have a preoccupied slackness that he's never noticed before. And so I make a huge effort to sound young when I say, "Hey! I didn't hear you come in."

He tells me to close my eyes.

As I close them I can feel a belt of cold beads being slipped down one of my shoulders, then I raise a hand to my throat and run my fingers over hexagonal Braille as I hear a click. "Hey, they feel beautiful. Thank you, mon amour," and I go to the bathroom mirror to see that I'm wearing a choker of beads made out of black jet. Very handsome, if a little funereal. He's still brooding about the age difference, then. I wonder if he'd be surprised to know that I've been brooding about it myself. About the fact that he's only twenty-eight and therefore only seven years older than Tom. If only he could be thirty, and therefore only a decade over from me. But how could that help? He'll be seventeen years younger than I am till the end of time. "This is really stunning," I tell him as I come back into the kitchen again. "And so sexy, too, in a depraved Victorian sort of way, I really love it."

When we hug I hope he's discovering new virtues in me in spite of everything: that I don't have the volatile dampness that so many older women do and that my voice hasn't turned shrill, or at least not yet, and since his hug is a listening hug—listening, testing—I hope he can feel how strong I still am.

At bedtime we sit propped up against our pillows and read. I glance down at his book and see the words "mesmerized pathology," words that so uncannily describe my feelings for him that I should tell him, but I only go back to the movie reviews. "Listen to this," I say. "'Into every life must fall a little comeuppance.' No, listen to this: '*She* teaches him manners, *he* teaches her larceny …'"

"Listen to *this*," he says. "'The city and the book are opposed forms … there is no single point of view from which we can grasp the city as a whole … writing a book, one pretends to an omniscience and a command of logic which the experience of living in the city continuously contradicts....'" He closes the book and sighs. Enjoying himself, I think. "Continuously contradicts. Sounds like a marriage." He yawns. "So tell me why you and your husband split up."

"The nights we used to discuss divorce were our happiest times. These were our most deeply married times, the times we'd lie in bed late at night and whisper about divorce. But here's a story that will tell you the whole story of our life together: when we were out in public he would swing hands with me and lift one of my hands to his lips. But only if someone happened to glance our way."

"Did he sleep around?"

"Only twice, actually, and not even with any of the women he was crazy about. Whereas I was forever falling in love and dancing too close to the men I liked, then writing them long letters, not knowing how much men hate and fear getting letters. I'd also agree to meet them places, then make excuses not to show up. So you could say that I was actually the more unfaithful one."

"He had affairs, though, and you didn't do that."

"But his affairs were so brief and boring, they were nothing. I fell in love much more often than he did and so I was much more unfaithful than he ever was, in my heart. Still, I must have been angry with him, because I did dream of poisoning him...."

"What with?"

"Years of sweet pies and cakes."

"That doesn't sound too evil."

"We were also just never alone, we always had people living with us. Students from Ethiopia, deserters from the American army during the Vietnam War."

"You were an adult during the Vietnam War? When I was only a little guy of eight or nine?"

I roll over on my belly, hoping to lure him into admiring the swoop of my back. "When you were a little guy of eight or nine, I was already a married woman with two little babies."

"God. Hearing you say this makes me feel like I'm in bed with a monument."

I slide off my watch, smooth cool lotion down my arms. "Thank you, Galbraith."

"Sorry," he whispers. "But it must have been pretty fascinating to only be in your twenties at such an important time in the world's history. Did you feel that? Did you feel it was an incredibly exciting time to be young? When so much history was happening? To be at the heart of it?"

"Alex was the star, I was only the star's groupie. But I still did feel deeply good. And when we did our slow march through Ottawa on our way to Parliament Hill and people came out on their verandas to watch us as we walked silently by, I felt doomed and noble, like an early Christian."

He laughs and pounds his heels on the mattress. "God, I can see it. I can see you as an early Christian, you must have been hilarious."

"I suppose I was, really."

"I don't think I've ever even talked to someone who was already an adult that long ago. Apart from my parents. Someone who was actually *there*, I mean. Way back when."

"Way back when? You make me sound like a relic."

"A relic I want to fuck," he tells me, rolling toward me. "But why are you wearing these? Are you getting your period?"

"I think I might be, I've been feeling so heavy down there." But how happy I am, relic though I am, to still be young enough to be asked this particular question, and I kiss him deeply, wanting to bring us back to who we were before I turned myself into a young married woman of twenty pertly smiling down at him as I poured him a glass of milk when he was only a child of three.

Fog MOVED IN over the city during the night and it was a misty fall morning when I hurried to the front window so I could watch Galbraith get into his cab. But his smaller self, five stories below me, seemed preoccupied, patting the pockets of his raincoat, and although I stayed at the window ready to wave, he didn't look up.

Two mornings later he called me from a phone in the hotel lobby in Victoria and told me about an early morning walk he took yesterday along the seawall. He might also get a chance to design a community college close to the ocean. But then I could hear laughter, other voices, and when he said, "Quoi faire? Quoi dire? They're already here," I wanted to tell him I love him, but I was afraid that the others might be too close by, and not wanting him to feel he had to say I love you back I said, "I'll probably be in bed by the time your plane gets in."

"Taking the requirements of both parties into consideration, I'd have to say that there simply could not possibly be a better location."

How adorable this was.

But this morning he calls to tell me that there's been a change in plans, they've got the contract for one thing, which is a challenge and a miracle, and so he's going to have to postpone his flight until Sunday and not get into Dorval until well after midnight. "And so

I'll probably be bushed and just want to go to my own place and go right to bed. But I'll be going in to work on Monday morning and so I'll call you from there at noon, then we can work out where or when we'll have dinner on Monday night."

Where or when. And when he doesn't call me at noon on Monday, I park the phone next to my typewriter and type up several pages of old notes. I try not to keep looking at my watch, but I look at it every other minute. Two o'clock comes, then after a long time it's three. At five past three I call his office.

"Just a moment please!" sings the voice—I think it's Giselle's—then I can hear the phone ring in one of the cubicles.

His hello sounds rehearsed, irritable, No, it's worse than that, it's a voice only pretending to be irritable—a voice only faking an impatience with the world—while its irritability is really intended for me alone. And meant, in a cowardly way, to warn me. But when I don't speak, it becomes human again. "Hold everything, I just have to close the door here." Footsteps walk away, walk back. "Kay, this is you, right? Can you say something please?"

"I thought you said you were going to call me at noon."

He lowers his own voice to a matching whisper. "Darling, I *know*. But it's been a total madhouse here today. We've had conference calls ever since I came in this morning at ten. And we even need to have a meeting at dinner after our final meeting here at seven and so I won't be able to have dinner with you at all tonight, I won't even be able to drop by until sometime after ten."

I TRY TO PICTURE THE FUTURE without him, the sensible sunlit years when all my pleasures will be trivial, asexual, and when I wash my face and then look up at it in the bathroom mirror, it's a worried blur above the embroidered gleam of my slip. I pull on a mole-coloured silk shirt I know he likes and a straight black skirt to go with it, spray lemon cologne on my arms, on my ankles, and when the bell rings at twenty past ten, I unlock my door, then sit on an arm of the sofa while I listen to his footsteps come up the stairs. Then he's in and he looks awful as he sets down his briefcase. "Aren't you glad to see me?"

I stand, although I don't walk toward him. "I'm always glad to see you, you know that, but I'm also puzzled. Please tell me what happened."

"What do you mean, what happened?"

"You came back east a different person."

He pulls off his raincoat and hangs it over the back of one of the chairs, then sits down at the table. "I went for a walk on the beach every morning and I thought about us, that's what happened. And then Max, one of the West Coast architects, invited me home for dinner and so I met his wife and his two little boys and these two little guys were so absolutely great, you would have loved them too, you would have been crazy about them. And Max's wife was this really lovely woman. Actually it was incredible, how much she reminded me of *you*, Kay." At this he smiles at nothing in particular. "As I pictured you at twenty-six or twenty-seven...."

How I dislike this, being put into competition with my younger self. I walk over to the window and pretend to look out as I say in a cool voice, "When I was twenty-six or twenty-seven, I was spending all of my days dreaming of other men." And when I turn to look back at him I see that he looks pious but also—and I am terribly relieved to see this—at least a little bit jealous.

"But you were still only a really young married woman back then, with two little children."

"It's the easiest thing in the world to daydream about other men when you're still only a really young married woman with two little children." And so I tell him that while I was helping my babies build their sand-castles at the edge of the ocean, I used to picture a man's hands shoving down the straps of my bikini top and while I was lacing up the skates of my toddlers at the rink another man would stand behind me, pressing himself against me while he was unzipping my skirt.

But he ignores all this to say, "And so we really do have to face facts here. I want to have children. And in fifteen years you'll be sixty." He stares at me in a haunted young way so that I can see the full horror of this, for him. "While I'll only be forty-three. And I don't think you would be happy, either, having a young husband trailing behind you when you're getting on in years, a nursemaid of a young husband walking two or three paces behind you, carrying your raincoat and your medications and stealing little peeks at other women...."

"Yes, it could be very sad," I say. "I can see that now. But it's also true that we can never know what the future will bring. By the time you turn forty-three you could be suffering from some terrible degenerative neurological disease and if we're still together I could, at the age of sixty and still in excellent health, be pushing you around the malls in your wheelchair, your bib and your catheter and the pharmacy bag with your medications in it all stuffed into the basket hooked to the handlebars."

He laughs. A light, unhappy little laugh. "Or we could both be in wheelchairs, we could both be gaga." And he stands to pull on his raincoat, but then he sits down on the sofa again and leans painfully forward to say, "If it's any consolation to you, I don't want whatever it is we've had here to be over, either."

I press my fingertips hard to my eyebrows on hearing this, but when I get tearful and walk toward him to tell him that I wish we could have just one more night together, he stands up again and I can see that he's almost afraid of me, he almost wants to back away from me, a boy wanting to get away from a mother who's turned suddenly wild.

"But we can't," he says helplessly.

I follow him to the door where we hug one another with a dry hard embrace and he says "Kay" in a quiet little moaning voice, then he lifts my hands away from his chest, forces them down until they are only empty hands hanging down at my sides so he can make his escape down the stairs.

I go straight into my bedroom and drop down on my bed, in tight pain until I can allow myself to cry, to feel the long pain of loss, the long night ahead of me. But I stop to listen when I hear the door open again, hear footsteps come my way, hear his voice say my name, then feel the bed tilt as he sits down on it and runs a hand over my raised hip, then strokes back my wet hair until I say, "I suppose I should check to make sure it's really you."

"It's really me. And I'd like to stay here tonight...."

I wonder if he can feel that even the ends of my hair are wet. "Only if we don't have sex."

"That's okay. We don't need to."

I raise myself up on an elbow, but keep my back to him. "Because I couldn't bear it. Not if we're never going to have it again," and I hiccup a little, then blow my nose. But he wants to have sex, I can feel him wanting it, I can feel him decide we need to do it, we need to go so deep into it that there's only love in it. Love, but no sex. If we are going to get through this, then we need to turn it into a sacrament, unless it's only the Catholic boy in him who must be thinking this, then he's kissing me again while crazy things whirl around in my head, a kind of riff on I'm vexed again, perplexed again, thank God I can be oversexed again, and he's whispering, "We have to, it's the only way" as he's aiming a sideways hand up what feels (in all this dampness) like the nylon glisten of my pantyhose and we're both small factories of heat as I raise my hips to help him pull them off, then he helps me pull off my panties that by now must be smelling too swampy from a day when too much has happened, then I tell him I'm getting my period.

"Then having sex will keep you from getting cramps. Because it always does."

I roll over and unbutton his shirt and unzip his fly, only now and then still hiccuping a little while I tell myself not to think, not to think ahead, not to anticipate pain, who knows what will happen, only be here, as they say—as *who* says? as everyone says, as the universe says— only be here now.

Sometime in the night I turn to him in the dark. "But why can't we just be together until you meet someone else?"

"But how could that possibly be fair to you," he whispers. "Picture us sitting down to dinner one night and me saying, Okay, I've met her, and so it's all over for you, sweetheart. And besides, as long as I'm with you I'm not going to be meeting anyone, and the reason I'm not going to be meeting anyone is I won't even be looking, because how can I even be looking when I'm still with you?"

This makes my eyes fill again, it's so sweet (unless it's really just so very damn shrewd) and after he falls asleep I lie awake thinking of having a baby with him and the three of us living in a kind of mad borrowed bliss together, but I also know that I no longer have the stamina to cope with having small children underfoot and doubt I could tolerate the creaky cry of a baby for even a single afternoon to say nothing of its whole childhood and the endlessly hard and endlessly endless adolescent years. And when it at last begins to get light I get up and set off a series of tinkles as I slip a dress off its hanger, then on my way out of my room close the door behind me with a tiny click.

At ten past seven he comes to stand in the kitchen doorway while I'm at the sink, pouring myself a cup of tea. "Promise me you won't do anything rash."

I glance back at him over a shoulder, then reach up to a shelf for the basil flakes, the notorious basil flakes. But I'm not sure he remembers the basil incident. "Like kill myself, you mean?"

"The thought did cross my mind."

After he's had his shower he ties on my African robe, the one that has an iodine-brown backbone that looks like a tribal X-ray on a background of black cotton and because of its wide cut at the shoulders (and because he is short) it fits him spookily well. Then he sits down as if nothing very significant has happened, although as he's spreading jam on his toast he says, "Now that you won't have me as a distraction, you'll be able to give more time to your work."

"Yes, that will be wonderful." And I consider telling him that for me life has always been either all love or all work and since this was all love it kills me to lose it. But he's already looking at his watch. Damn, he'd better dress.

I'm braiding my hair into a stumpy braid when he comes to stand beside me so he can comb his hair and I understand that this is another part of our life together that I'm going to miss, being part of the domestic rush with a man in the mornings, watching him watch his own eyes in the mirror in the non-vain or half-vain way I believe most men watch their morning reflections. To watch his eyes watch his own eyes as he knots his tie, his thoughts already on the morning ahead, there's something dreamy but pragmatic about this: the morning briskness of a man checking himself out in a mirror with the look that says I am a man, and therefore I understand the world. At least up to a point.

But it's already time for him to go, then everything happens too fast, I follow him to the front door where we hug for the last time, then he turns away from me quickly and runs down the stairs.

WHEN HE COMES OVER again and we have sex, it's the new kind of sex, sex that's in mourning for the sex we used to have. It ends with my stroking his hair back from his damp forehead. "So this is how lovers get to be friends."

A week after this, Benno and I are spooning up our cold cucumber soup in a dim refugee light when the doorbell rings. I jump up from the table and run to the bathroom mirror, drag a brush through my hair, hear Benno call out, "Is that him?"

"I think so!"

"I'm not staying, then."

"Yes, Bennie, thank you, I do need you to go."

"I want to go whether you need me to go or not." Then he's gone and I can hear the sound of his boots running down as lighter footsteps are on their way up, then Galbraith comes in. "A young guy coming down gave me this incredibly dark look as I was on my way up."

When I tell him it was Benno, he pulls off his raincoat, then drops down on the sofa. "Well, let's just say he made it perfectly clear that he wanted to beat me up for breaking your heart."

We sit at the dark table and talk for over an hour, then stand holding hands as we agree that we should make a real effort not to see each other any more, it's too hard this way. But after he leaves, I fall onto my bed and cry with my whole body, the way young women cry.

THE WINTER WAS HARD. I got sick, I caught one cold after another, I was writing only about sad things: the winter after Tom left home for university, for instance, and how without him around the house to organize us and be our bossy connoisseur, Benno and I ran out of cutlery, or at least out of spoons, until there was only one spoon left in the cutlery drawer. "What do you *do* with them?" he asked me one morning as he was pulling on his parka. "Throw them out with the lettuce leaves?" But all on their own they just kept ending up in the kitchen midden under heaps of coffee grounds and eggshells. And then it was weeks before I could manage to remember, even when I was downtown after work, to go into a hardware store and buy new ones. In the meantime we couldn't even eat our porridge at the same time in the mornings but had to take turns with the spoon. Benno used to make jokes about it, he called it the House Spoon. One morning when I was late for work and we both had to eat at the same time because Benno was also late for school, I let him have the House Spoon and I got out the aluminum measuring spoons and ate my egg with the almost flat little half-teaspoon, my porridge with the wide shallow tablespoon. But the memory is painful to me, and wanting to redeem myself in the eyes of my youngest son I take an oval serving platter down from a cupboard and use a spoon (for I am now the owner of a dozen spoons once again) to spoon corn relish into one section, baby pickled onions into the next section, smoked salmon into the third, dill mayonnaise into the fourth. Then I mix up the batter for oatmeal cookies and once they are in the oven I phone Benno to invite him over for supper.

EVEN MY JAZZ TAPES sound so teasy and busy they make me think of headaches, of the wiry buzz of tiny machines, I only want love songs, that maudlin lonesomeness. At last April arrives, a grey dawn in the most dead week of the year, and since I'm awake and can't get back to sleep again I pull my raincoat on over my nightgown and climb the stairs up to the roof, look out over grey Randall Avenue, the stony grey park, here and there the dull tan of a dome, an east wind blowing over the bushy grey hedges and skylights whose panes of glass have gone black in the night and I remember drinking wine with Galbraith on another roof while the green city dropped steeply away below us and he said it looked like a green Rome, then I feel as if there's a kind of force field around my face where my tenderness for him has been waiting to feel his eyes on me. If only I could see him again and see him see me again, I'm sure it could make me feel loved enough to unlock this tenderness, first as a sort of teasing tenderness, but then if I saw it being gratefully received, as the real thing.

Only work on my novel got me through the winter's bluster and violent cold. And only work on my novel will get me through the recklessly fragrant spring, through the early summer evenings when I'm sure to be undone by some heartbroken song.

But one morning in July, I get up early and am at my desk by 6 A.M., writing about a visit with Alexander's parents at their classy hotel and their disapproval of my oversexed ruby crepe Empire dress with its sleeves pushed up into high little puffs. I write fast, try to get it all in: Alexander reaching for one of his mother's cookies and crying, "Oh,

Mama! You made *ciasteczka,* this is so fantastic," the ride up in swankness to the glassed-in brassy restaurant at the top of the hotel, its predictable splendors, the parents arguing with their son about apartheid and the war, the Cuban trio singing "Guantanamera," then doing a follow-up with a hammy version of "Stardust" in that sunny air whose dust actually did look like stardust. I also throw in a scene from another story, a story that didn't work, and after I've cobbled the disparate parts of this new story together, I decide to send it to *The New Yorker.* So that when Benno comes over late in the afternoon, I hold the story out to him. "Would you bless this?" And he passes his hand over it and says, "I bless this story and all of Thy Immortal Works."

The day after he leaves Montreal to go and look for a busboy job in Toronto, there's a party on the balcony next door to my apartment, the guest of honour a sunburned lout who has reduced his vocabulary to a single word that he repeats again and again, like a motor that can't quite get started: *cunt, cunt, cunt, cunt, cunt,* a drunken pasha in jungle camouflage gear surrounded by girls in pink shorts and white midriff tops who've been laughing at all his jokes, but now he's too far gone to make them laugh and so they begin to talk over him, around him. They don't sound like Montreal girls, they sound like Ontario girls, there's something so bored in their voices when they finally give up on him and talk only to one another, closing him out as they say to one another in their unimpressed voices, "Oh, really?"

BUT OUT OF THE BLUE a librarian who's read *The Dangerous Meadow* sends me a letter inviting me to fly east to give two readings: a reading at the public library in Fredericton, another at the public library in Saint John.

It's August when I fly east, dreaming of sand dunes and towering cliffs of sand whose plateaus of grass are bent back in the wind blowing in off the ocean, then we're landing at the tiny airport in Fredericton, the smell of grass and hay in the air. I stand reading to a small audience of polite women in the middle of the afternoon, try to respond to their questions with energy, feel unprepared, make a note to myself: never leave home without a few remarks in your pocket. Then I drive south to Saint John with Peg, the librarian, down the Saint John River Valley, its dying elms spilling yellow leaves from their crowns while in the hot car I squeeze my thighs together and with each squeeze think *Galbraith*. He's in my past now, but my car memories of him are intense and I can do this while I carry on a more or less lucid conversation with Peg as we drive past miles of scorched grass, then at last come to a great graveyard, treeless, a tawny prairie of the dead with a wide clean view of the sea, then we're here in the jumbled and mixed-up city itself, its great puffs of industrial smoke being pumped up above the churned-up commotion of its dark water, the black Reversing Falls. And black windows, still, in the old Simms Brush Factory, the city exactly itself while at the same time more jerry-built than ever with its steep seaside streets, the windblown angles of its tipped street corners. We walk to a restaurant on a forlorn street of red brick storefronts, formal in the gilded light of a lonely Sunday afternoon, then we drive past Henry and Idona's house, high up and blank-windowed on Mount Pleasant Avenue, then past my old high school, its red bricks darkened as if from depression, then on past the lighter colours of the wooden square houses with their gingerbread trim: blue houses trimmed with beige wooden lace, fog-grey houses trimmed with a dead blue, mint green with darker green, pale greys, sickly pinks.

Another reading, an evening reading, and I'm more prepared this time, I've had more time to practise being spontaneous, then it's off to the island that the people in these parts call *the Island* as if there is no other island. Red roads, ocean mist after rain—unless it's a pesticide mist after rain—and before the taxi has even reached Charlottetown, I already know it was a mistake to have come. Or it could only be the foggy bright light that's giving me a headache. In my B&B on Great George Street I swallow a 222, unpack my nightgown and toothbrush, study the collection of framed photographs of Hollywood stars from the 1930s out in the hallway, see how sleek and thrilled they are, how aware of themselves as bold and modern, the women so opaque, so creepily glamorous, their eyes saying we are here, this is now, there will never be a time more modern than now is, the men so evil and gleaming, so very stylized, non? I go down and out, walk along Euston Street, buy a map of the city, find a dive where I eat a bowl of chowder in the mild seaside light, even though Charlottetown isn't even on the sea, it's only a city looking out on rivers that feed into Northumberland Strait, if I'd wanted the real ocean I should have found myself a B&B on the east coast of the island I knew as a child, a coast as faded and decadent as a beach in Europe, magic Europe, we could have sat on the beach at Tracadie Bay and stared straight across the Atlantic at Europe if Newfoundland hadn't got in our way.

On the map I circle places whose names I like: Tea Hill (too far to go), Seaweed Road, Hurry Road, Doctors Brook, Scarlet Park, all of these places no doubt being as boring as any place could possibly be and yet I picture a flock of doctors in their white coats drinking wine on the green banks of Doctors Brook. And Scarlet Park could be turned red by trees that look like the trees in *The Flame Trees of Thika*. Or the flame trees of Anguilla. Even though it must only be called Scarlet Park because it's been named for one of the early settlers: Elijah Scarlet. Mr. Elijah Scarlet and his house of ill repute.

I wish that I'd decided to go to the other coast rather than Charlottetown because Idona used to bring Vivi and me to visit our friends the Millers in their large flat-roofed summer house on Tracadie Bay the last two weeks of every August. A grand summer place that was one spacious room after another, bamboo blinds for the wide windows looking out to sea, in the rooms at the back of the house tall yellow blinds faded to a colour like parchment in that most civilized summer house in the world, or so it seemed to me on those long summer afternoons: a seaside museum, framed maps under glass, faded Persian rugs passed down from the winter house to the summer house, the wild runs down over the dunes to the sea, then digging deep holes in the sand that we'd later race back up the beach to visit, as with barbaric cries we'd rush with our cargoes of stinging jelly fish (carried in the slings of our wet towels), captives that we dumped into the waiting holes, then we'd pelt them with handfuls of damp sand. Or we'd just stand drawing a casual foot sideways behind a hill of hot sand, then let the hot hill collapse in on them. But at last our killing sprees would tire us and we'd walk back up the dunes to spend the long dreamy afternoons sitting at the front of the house in the weak sunlight, taking turns reading aloud to one another from *Anne of Avonlea,* the first dry leaves of fall skittering across the patio stones between the veranda and the ocean.

My third morning in Charlottetown, I sit smoking on the beach and looking out over the harbour. I miss the useful solitude of being at home and writing, the solitude of travel is too aimless, it too often exposes me to the curious glances of strangers. I have a lonely supper on Euston Street, even though I quote to myself (who said this? Or wrote this?) "The cure for loneliness is solitude...." Which I know to be true or mostly true, then I go back to the B&B, spend the long sunlit evening up in my room reading Virginia Woolf (feeling in awe and inadequate) then lie back in my bath and think about the first night Galbraith came to my apartment and how I told him I used to run through Scanlon Falls on my way back from school because I couldn't wait to get home for my bath. Which is when I remember a new thing about my bath obsession: as soon as I stepped into our house, I would call up the stairs to my father and Idona, "Good afternoon, Mr. and Mrs. Haxon! I'm home from school now!" An isolated memory from childhood, still floating in the backwaters of my unconscious, it's only now that I understand why it's been filed away for all these years, it's because my parents must have been briefly sexually happy at that time in their lives, happy enough to be having sex at the end of their afternoon nap, and one of us must have blundered into their bedroom with news from school and surprised them in the act, which must have been when they told us we absolutely must call out to them to tell them we were home the very moment we stepped into the house, my hello to Mr. and Mrs. Haxon having waited all these years in the wings until it was at last ready to be understood.

I also wonder if I should squander even more money to rent a car and drive over to Tracadie Bay to see if the Miller summer house is still standing. But Dot and Abe Miller are both dead by now and I doubt that Elinor ever comes back to this sad and beautiful coast, she must have been married at least two or three times by now, must be living somewhere exotic—Rome or London or Paris or Morocco—while in a much less thrilling way (by now it's the following evening) I'm on the move too, walking in a diagonal across the city to Scarlet Park.

It's a long walk, but then the evenings are also so long down on this coast that by the time I reach the park there's still light high up in the sky. And it's just an ordinary park—green grass, no flame trees—a park reminiscent of the parks Alex and I used to take the boys to, Strathcona Park and the Rockeries, followed by drives out to Kitchisippi Beach in the late afternoons—sliding down the sandy path to the concrete wigwams where we'd change into our swimsuits, the Spanish grilles giving us a view out over the blown brightness of the river. But Tom and Benno didn't much care for swimming, they really only wanted to lie on the floor of our living room to draw their pictures of monsters and dentists, but now I have to pay attention because a pick-up truck is bumping over the green grass toward me, but no it's passing me, although a few moments later I hear it turn and follow me, there are three men in it, two of them drinking beer but the one who's drinking water or gin is the driver, three local boys who drive in a circle around me.

"Hey, baby! Go for a ride?"

"Hey, missy! Hey, Miss Toronto woman, you from Toronto?"

"Maybe she's a Frenchy."

"You a Frenchy, honey? You a Frenchy, mon amour? You Frenchy hot stuff?"

I don't look at them, I just keep walking toward the lights in the tiny houses on the outskirts of Charlottetown while the truck keeps driving around me in smaller and smaller circles. What a fool I was to come to this wide lonely park! Please let me live through this, let me live past it, the one thing I must not do is look afraid, I need to think fast before they move down the scale of endearments to shorter words—*baby, honey, mon amour, slut, cunt*—because if they drop down to shorter words there'll be no going back to civilized words again, so think of them as children, think, what do children like, what do children do, children like to give directions, more than anything in the world children like to be asked for directions and so I hold up a hand like a traffic cop, draw my map of the Island out of my bag, and the effect is miraculous because the truck also comes to a stop.

"I'm a visitor to the Island," I say, smiling a small careful smile that I hope is just friendly enough, "and I'd like to ask you guys if you could just help me out here with a few directions." Then I reach the crackling map up to the driver. "What I need to know is how do I get back to Great George Street."

They peer over one another's shoulders to frown down at the map. A little jostling here, a little male competition of important frowning and index fingers importantly pointing, and in this way I am saved.

On my last morning in Charlottetown I visit a real estate office to ask about cheap properties on the east coast of the Island and am told that there aren't any, not any more. And would I want to buy a lonely cottage down here in any case, even if I could? I don't think so. Then on my way back to the hotel, I stop off at a beauty salon to get my hair cut. I'm feeling sexually heavy, voluptuous, as I flip to a story in one of the salon's magazines about an art student in England who is approached one morning in London by a man she knows who invites her to come to his apartment close to Trafalgar Square to meet five or six friends over drinks. The art student understands, when this man tells her to wear something provocative, that she's to be paid for the evening and that the friends will be men. And so she dresses in a diaphanous black dress and pulls on a pair of unstable tall sandals that have Plexiglas heels. Like a tower of cheap stars stacked inside each spike of clear Plexiglas there's a twinkling column of rhinestones, sparkling—or so I imagine—like the stars in *Wynken, Blynken and Nod*. And after the men arrive at the Trafalgar Square apartment, they circle the black rug where she sits unzipping her filmy dress, circling and crooning lewdly adoring things to her as she moans and turns on a rug that's an oval of deep black transformed into a black oval platter, her white body the evening's sexual delicacy, a body posed in such a variety of ways that its writhing busyness must remind her of the more customary way for art students to earn extra cash: sitting naked on a kitchen chair that's been positioned on a platform for the kind of drawing classes where the model is expected to hold a pose and sit still.

The next story I flip to is about a woman pilot who crash-lands her plane on a hill north of North Bay. There's a photograph of her in her pilot's gear, a white nylon coverall with white rubber boots sewn to the legs of it. Her face looks pudgy but brave, and the story of how she walks twenty miles for help in sub-zero snow squalls makes me picture myself as the downed pilot, the rescue team tramping through the

But by the time I get back to my hotel again and am lying in my temporary bedroom in the hot June afternoon, the Trafalgar Square scenario (the invited circle of men offering nothing more scary than sexual worship, although sex too, if the art student wants it) has turned into an antidote to this story of the two terrified girls in the Illinois gravel pit surrounded by the circle of attacking boys. It's even an antidote to my having been circled by the pick-up truck last night in Scarlet Park. And even though it's hard to believe that an art student would be the owner of such tacky high heels, I can easily see myself in a pair of strappy shoes exactly like hers or even tackier than hers because when I'm feeling the way I'm feeling right now I have no standards, no fashion sense, I'm too busy being adored by the circle of men who keep prowling around me, all wanting to have sex with me in the hot sexy sunlight.

But then I grew up in a family whose religious belief was that what was homespun was holy. Flat shoes, ceramic medallions hanging from leather thongs, burlap skirts, these were the clothes meant to convey sensitivity, true emotional worth. Years ahead of her time or centuries behind it, Idona decreed that the best wardrobes (the ones with integrity, the ones with true clout) had to have something twelfth century about them, they had to look excavated.

THEN THE FLIGHT BACK, the descent into Dorval, the wheezy bus ride to downtown. At last, home: my stale apartment, its trapped sadness. I drink a glass of water, fill it with more water for the spider fern, then go back down the stairs to pick up my mail, pull out a manila envelope with my own handwriting on it. I carry it up the stairs because I don't want to meet any of the other tenants in the elevator, then let myself back into my sunlit apartment and with a gasp that's also a sigh, slit it open. The letter clipped to the story isn't from the editor who bought a story from me the one time I sold a story to

The New Yorker, it's from someone named Shirley Lederer who has written a cool two lines to me: "This is too rambling. If you can't learn to shape your stories better, and make them shorter, then perhaps you shouldn't be sending us your stories at all any more." Her words burn themselves across the wide open part of my heart where hope lives. Plot, schmot, the lack of thereof. It's like being a child again and looking out the window while behind me Idona's voice says, "Perhaps you should consider not being my child any more." A development I would never have expected five years ago, back on the day I was on my way home from work and caught sight of Benno on the other side of the screen door, waiting for me, white-faced. "What is it?" I cried, running up the steps to the house. "Are you sick? What happened?" He pulled me inside by my wrist, then took both my hands in his, speechless with news he was unable to deliver. When he could speak he said, "*The New Yorker* called, they want to buy a story from you. He's going to call you right back." Frantic, all at once unspeakably shy and afraid, I cried, "I've got to eat something! My blood sugar is much too low to talk to an editor from *The New Yorker!*" And I ran to the phone to pluck it off its hook, Benno staring at me wild-eyed. Then he fought with me, forced the phone back on the hook again. "No! He's going on vacation tonight! This will be your last chance to talk for a month!"

THE FLIMSY TUNIC Tom's girlfriend is wearing is an almost see-through grey voile, the embroidery around its neckline so eaten away by frequent washing that its stitchings might be the miniature bird-tracks of blue winter birds pecking away at a field of mist. And there seems to be nothing beneath it but her perfect brown breasts and her own perfect brown skin. "My mother is as bad as Freud," I hear Tom tell her while I'm spreading the batik cloth on the table. "All these little carpets she's dropped down over the carpet ..."

While we're having our dinner Tom and Kareen talk about Tom's job at a lab and Kareen's job at a bar and recent movies they've seen while I can hardly contain myself, I so much want to read them the *New Yorker* rejection letter, and while we're drinking our coffee I do, then get my copy of *Mystery and Manners* down from the nearest bookcase and open it to the chapter that makes fun of writing workshops, read the chapter titles to them: "The Story Formula for Writers!"and "Let's Plot!" As they laugh I notice Tom glance into my bedroom, the summer wind blowing the pale curtains in, and I wonder if they are hoping I'll go out for the evening. Tomorrow I will, tomorrow I'll offer to go out, and after dinner we sit out on the balcony in the mild twilight and talk about their professors and their friends until the talk comes back to my rejected story again (until I bring it back) and Tom says, "But you do ramble sometimes, in your stories, not in all of them, but in the ones that don't work you ramble," and I say yes, yes, I know, but I also say that I'm a believer that writing can't be taught and that I wish I could live back in the days when writers were writers and they had character, personality, harsh opinions. "But at the same time," I tell them, "the *New Yorker* letter makes me feel that I should perhaps take just one writing workshop, at Stanopolis, say. Just for one semester...."

Tom agrees. "At least if you have to go out to a class once a week, you'll meet a few people."

True, but I find it hard to believe that the kind of students I'd meet at a writing workshop would be at all thrilling to know. I picture accountants with dry moustaches, housewives in eager sweaters, cold-eyed girls in their twenties, all of them only dully wanting to know what the rules are, and once Tom and Kareen have gone off for the evening, I sit down on the sofa to read my letter again, convinced that nothing can persuade me to join the crowd, to become a student, a democrat. Above all, I don't want to become a member of a writing workshop, to choose to become competent instead of inspired. But how inspired can I argue I've been for the year and a half I've lived in this city? I'm nowhere. And what if I'm one of the ones who falls by the wayside? Falls into despair? Is silenced?

THIS MORNING the weather is foggy and cool, and after Tom and Kareen have gone out for another of their walks, I dial the department of English at Stanopolis.

"Why don't I put you through to Edison Lumley?"

"Thank you. By the way, who is he?"

The voice sounds surprised. "Our director of Creative Writing."

Edison Lumley doesn't know *The Dangerous Meadow*. "But I do know that I've heard your name mentioned when people are talking about promising fiction."

And when I tell him that I have a number of stories that have appeared in anthologies as well, he tells me to bring them along tomorrow. "Bring them along with your book, when you come to see me."

After dinner, I tell Tom and Kareen that I'm thinking of going out to a movie. "You two are welcome to come with me if you'd like to. But you're also welcome to stay here if you'd rather."

They will stay here, they would rather.

THE DIRECTOR SEEMS TOO HEALTHY and goldenly wholesome to be witty, he's too relaxed, but at the same time he's too serious a person. His eyes nostalgic or allergic, he speaks of his idyllic farm where he lives with his psychiatrist wife out in the country, not far from Saint-Pierre-de-Wakefield, then waxes lyrical about his cows and his daisies. "We have cows and daisies instead of children," he tells me, and I find it easy to picture him striding about in his fields, it's so much easier to see him in his fields than it is to picture him at the front of a classroom. To take him out of Stanopolis and place him back in the country again, I put him into a pair of breeches and tall rubber boots so he can go for a misty walk in the hills, stomping among his dogs and his cattle. But when he gets up from his chair to reach a prospectus down from a shelf, I can see that he has curiously mismatched body parts: a body that's all torso with no legs to speak of.

He asks me why I didn't go to university. "Or wasn't your family into that kind of thing?"

"They were. My brothers all went, and my sister went. But I thought I had better things to do."

"School had no appeal?"

I loved school when I was a child, loved getting away from the uproar of home but at sixteen I lost all interest in it. "My parents had a friend who owned a radio station down on the east coast and I had my own music show."

"In what city?"

"Saint John."

"And I come from St. John's. As you've probably already guessed from my accent."

"I was admiring it, actually. The lilt of it."

"So let's have a look at the anthologies. And, of course, at *The Dangerous Meadow.*"

I tumble the books down onto the table.

He picks up *The Bantam Book of Modern Canadian Stories*, then flips through the pages until he finds the story that first appeared in *The New Yorker*. "This is impressive," he tells me. "No one who's on staff here has ever been in *The New Yorker*. And you've been an editor at Basilevsky Books as well, as you say. Because of that, and also because of the various stories you've had published here and there, it occurs to me that we might just try to get you into graduate school straight away. Not bother at all with the B.A."

"I was thinking of just doing the writing workshop, actually. Just until Christmas."

"But what good will that do you? What you need to get is a degree so you can teach."

But the prospect of teaching still fills me with terror.

"Get yourself some security," he tells me. And at this he rips a sheet of paper off a memo pad, writes a name on it. "Go see Cy Stackpole," he tells me, and as I stand he gets up and comes around his desk to give me a friendly loose hug, writer to writer.

GOING DOWN INTO THE METRO is like going down into another country as in one station after another music soars up from the caverns below, angelic, primeval. As I'm sinking down into the tiled halls where the trains roar in, my heart is invariably pierced by some heartbroken song. Musicians with flutes play Bach and Villa-Lobos; a plump saxophonist in a woodsy tweed vest plays "Summertime," filling the eyes of the people who stand waiting for their trains with a stung nostalgia, then I ride up on the escalator into the clear morning, walk along de Maisonneuve to my appointment with Professor Stackpole. Who, it turns out, doesn't agree with Edison Lumley that I should go straight into graduate school. "For me to let you into graduate school with no preparation in Renaissance poetry, in myth, in the Victorian novel, would simply be irresponsible. Not that I think you should do the whole four years. I'm only suggesting a single year, a qualifying year."

The following week, the package containing the first jury's top fifty stories arrives from the Lindner Foundation. Before receiving it, I swore to myself that I would tape over the names on each story's first page, not to be influenced—one arm dramatically thrown across my eyes so that I couldn't peek at the names as I did the taping—but I now discover that my curiosity is much too extreme for me to cover the names. There are a few famous writers in the stack, it turns out, but no writer who's personally known to me until I get to the second to last writer. This writer is Professor Edison Lumley, and when I see his name I moan at the thought of having to sit in judgment on the very man who was kind enough to befriend me. On the other hand, Lumley might not even know that I'm one of the judges. But of course he will know, and must for some time have known, the judges' names were printed on the front of the competition leaflet. Then I notice something else: Lumley and the two other heads of departments of Creative Writing are the only applicants who've listed their university addresses. This ruse has apparently guaranteed all three of them a place in the top fifty. I look down at Lumley's university address in a kind of revolted wonder and resent his getting into the top fifty because he's taken a space that might have gone to a more gifted and obscure writer, a lonely and desperate writer without the protection of an impressive academic address:

Edison Lumley
Chair, Department of Creative Writing
Stanopolis University
Montreal

But I can't wait any longer, I carry his story over to the sofa and sit down to read it.

IN THE MEANTIME, Stanopolis looms: the stone lions flanking the entrance to the Arts Building, its grandly shallow flight of stone steps. On the rainy morning of the first day of classes, I walk up these shallow steps, thinking with dread of spending the next three years of my life mired in essays and assignments and know that I'll hate it here because I won't want to analyze or parse or dissect.

During the coffee break for my first class, I get into a conversation with a fair (but black-eyed) woman whose name is Brooke O'Neill and who seems to me to be perfectly named, a woman who's as bubbling and unstoppable as a sparkling brook. It turns out that she is also the mother of two sons and is a few years younger than I am. "But how come you get to do just a qualifying year? When the rest of us have to slog through the whole four years of the B.A.?"

I tell her it might be because I'm already a writer.

"Have you written a book?"

"Yes. But only one book."

"And it's been published?"

When I say yes, she tells me that she, too, has written a book "which has *also* been published. An absolutely terrific little travel book. But nobody offered a short-cut to *me*. And so just tell me this: how did you end up getting all this amazing pull, my friend?"

I tell her the story of my meeting with Edison Lumley and about the effect that my having had a story in *The New Yorker* seemed to have on him. At this, the little Brooke hisses, then bubbles up more violently than ever. "And what did you think of *him*?"

"He seemed very kind, actually."

A convoluted story then tumbles out. According to Brooke, a former lover of hers was once in partnership with Lumley back in the days when they ran a local art gallery together, "And he was such a total conniver, he was simply not to be trusted...."

I listen, trying to separate what might be true from what might only have been invented in vengeful hindsight. Lumley has been so helpful and harmless and wholesome (and handsome!) that I find Brooke's accusations hard to credit. I also don't want to hear bad things about him, I want to stay grateful. At the same time I can't stop wanting to hear the whole story. I also can't stop thinking of the story Edison entered in the Lindner competition and of his conniving way of getting the first readers to select it. But I only smile at the violently percolating Brooke. "Isn't he too bland to be dangerous?"

"Blandness is the *modus operandi* of bastards the world over. Once you've been at this joint for a week or two, you'll at least be willing to take my word for *that*."

This could very well be true, but in navigating a new world it's surely unwise to take gossip as gospel. Besides, this Brooke is so clearly a lunatic. And so I make up my mind to steer clear of her in the future.

But she is, incredibly, waiting for me after class. "Care to join me for a coffee?"

I'm about to say no, but then change my mind and say yes. Never say no: my new mantra. And so on the first day of becoming a student, I also become a teacher, since Brooke offers me a job teaching English to immigrants at a language institute near Greene Avenue. "The two classes I'm giving you each have only ten people in them. The thing is, my boyfriend is being transferred to Belgrade for a year and I want to fly over there with him, then stay with him till he gets settled."

"But I've never taught."

"I'll prepare you. I'll give you my books, everything. And the money is good."

"But won't they want to see my credentials at the school?"

"They won't give a damn. You're just a teacher I asked to cover for me while I'm away. Don't talk to anyone, just walk down the hallways looking entitled."

"When do I start?"

"Tomorrow morning at ten."

Too agitated to sleep, I get up with the sun and drink three cups of black coffee before I remember that coffee is a powerful diuretic, then sit on the sofa and make notes, eat a banana, then walk to the Language Institute, a sodden grey building on Dorchester Boulevard.

I climb the stairs to the second floor, walk past an office where I hear a man's voice say, "She's got this implacable memory," then walk down the hallway to Brooke's classroom, trying not to look as if I'm about to be arrested. So be an actor, I tell myself, act like the teachers you've seen in the movies, your students are foreigners, they won't know you don't know anything.

I introduce myself to my small audience, then turn to the blackboard to recover while I print my name on it. Then I write an assignment, click my pointer on each word as I read it aloud. To my surprise I enjoy sounding emphatic, obnoxious. I also feel so grateful to Brooke. Gossip isn't necessarily malice after all, often it's simply the longing to see justice done. As for the teaching, I can see how I might quite easily get to be good at it. Faking it. Faking it and enjoying it, even if it's still too soon to say that a star is born.

As I'm slipping out of my coat I hear Professor Flack (a small man with the luxuriant and brushed silver hair of the male academic) speak in a gleeful, piping voice as he holds forth to a group of graduate students. "Don't expect to get jobs, not if you're over twenty-six, our esteemed universities are only after young blood." It seems to have cheered him immensely to have delivered this depressing news since he's smiling as he comes walking toward me. "Oh there you are, Madame Oleski! And here am I, already making my farewells and on my way." His name makes me think of Roberta Flack singing to a lover that she only thinks of him on two occasions, night and day, then another guest comes up the steps to the porch, his army greatcoat sparkling with a haze of new snow and it's Edison Lumley, stamping his boots.

"Let me take this upstairs for you," I tell him as he hands me a snowy coat that smells of rubber boots and dogs. An even taller (and younger) man comes in behind him and also hands over his coat—I've become the coat check girl simply by standing so close to the door—but he isn't yet willing to part with his muffler. When he starts to suck the snow from its fringes and a girl in a long dress calls out to him, "That's acid snow, you cretin!" he sings to her with lazy sweetness:

Ho-ho
Acid snow
Acid rain
That's my refrain....

I come down the stairs to discover, with relief, that Brooke has arrived. I tell her that I love the jet beads and cut-glass connections of her dress as she smiles at me like a clever stepmother. "You can keep both of my jobs if you want them."

"I'd be so happy to do that. The money is amazing, I'd be lost without it, and the students are mostly really fine people too." But is this really true? By now I've been teaching long enough to know that their eyes might greet me in a hundred different ways: with reverence, with resentment, with love, with expressions of hostile boredom. "So let's get ourselves something to drink." And we go to the punch bowl where in the unreliable candlelight I talk about the Lindner Prize. The wine burning in my veins, I tell her that Lumley's story was just an essay, really— "It was all so greyly competent that it had no spark"— then after moving from one island of talk to another I don't meet up with her again until I'm ready to leave, but on my way down the icy steps I decide to go back, find her pouring herself another glass of wine out in the kitchen. I've got to get her away from here because if I leave her behind she'll confront Lumley, tell him what I said. "Let me walk you home, Brooke. Or we can get a cab."

"I just need to go and say hi and goodbye to Edison Lumley."

"Can't you do that another time?"

"There is only *this* time. And by next time, *this* time will be *that* time."

"You're drunk, Brookie, I need to take you home." And once we're down on the sidewalk I link an arm firmly through hers as I walk with her straight into the snowy breezy night. If only I knew how to hypnotize her, I could make my voice both soothing and ominous: "You will remember nothing of this evening, my little Brooke. Nothing, I tell you! Nothing." When we reach her street we could be in the Russia of the nineteenth century. Only the house she points out to me looks modern, a dark wood house that must have been designed by an architect, it looks so Japanese. When we reach its Japanese gate, she invites me in for drink. "I also need you to edit a story for me."

"I'd be happy to." And I would: this could be a perfect distraction from the Lumley revelation. I take off my coat as she runs up the stairs for her stories, then quickly comes running back down.

The first story, "The Dubliner," is about an Irish girl who comes out to Canada and ends up working as a clerk in a Calgary hotel. A serene modern fable. Who would have thought that the bubbling Brooke could have written a story as quiet as this? It needs work, though, needs to be purged of its skies like black velvet, its "wonderment," its "wondrous stars." Then I set about taking other things away: the words *stark* and *magical* whenever they turn up, cheeks that are as red as apples, violet eyes, eyes that dance, eyes looking searchingly into a mirror, merry laughter.

"I know that people think these things are clichés, but *why* are they clichés?"

"They've been overused," I tell her. "They are also a refusal to see the world freshly."

"Don't you like any of them?"

"I like her eyes looking searchingly into her own eyes in the mirror."

"Let me use it, then. People should use what they want to use."

"In theory, yes. In practice, no." In fact, I'm quite fond of "searchingly" myself. But it's been used and used. And so I can't allow her to have it. I also need to fix the syntax more or less everywhere. Where did this woman go to school? "Did you go to school here in Montreal, Brooke?"

"No. But I went to school everywhere else. I'm an army brat. But if I give you a folder of my other stories, would you edit them for me as well?"

"Yes, I would. But I'll have to charge you in that case. Ten dollars an hour."

She tells me this is acceptable and as I'm pulling on my coat she thanks me for my help with the Calgary story. "I'll also need you to write a letter to *The New Yorker* for me. To your editor there. I want you to write a letter praising my story. Once we decide which story is the best story."

On the way home I let the day drain away from me: two poems back from *Antaeus* along with a note: "We enjoyed these, but we are too well supplied with poems at the moment." Oh, how I detest that tepid word *enjoy*, it's so low bourgeois, so insulting. I would prefer to be vilified. But do I really mean this? Of course not.

AT SCHOOL I make my way through a dark forest of gossip and platitudes, with now and then the light of some tiny arrow of piercing news or theory shining through. And even though I'm as wary as ever of becoming a collaborator with whatever ideas keep puffing up from the trains of critical thought roaring through English departments all over the Western world, I'm also beginning to really like certain professors, in particular the bizarrely articulate Cy Stackpole. But also Professor Heubner, the professor I ask to recommend me for a Stanopolis Fellowship. Once she has said yes, I slip a copy of

The Dangerous Meadow into the envelope along with the application form. A week later, Heubner (so trim and adroit in her body, but her face has fallen) trips down the aisle to my desk, then breathes over me with her nicotine breath to say in a low voice, "I've been most impressed by your novel, most impressed...."

I feel too emotional to speak, I even have to try not to cry on my way home. From gratitude or shame. Or both. And am somehow not surprised when Professor Heubner asks me to stay behind after the other students have gone at the end of the next class. Perched on the corner of her desk, one leg hiked up higher than the other, a low-heeled claret leather shoe swinging, she says, "In relation to the recommendation I agreed to write for you, I'm afraid there are difficulties. The truth is, I'm completely over my head in departmental meetings and other academic duties at the moment. And so I have a proposition for you. I'm going to suggest that you write your own recommendation. Write it as if you are impersonating me. But I'll need to find you a few pages of stationery with the university letterhead on them." She lets her feet down to the floor, then neatly walks around to the other side of her desk and opens a drawer to draw several sheets of foolscap out of it, hands them to me. "You know your own work infinitely better than I do, so who better than you to write in support of it?"

"Yes," I say. "Thank you."

"I don't want you to write it by hand, obviously. I don't want you to impersonate me to quite *that* degree. Just type it up, then leave a space for my signature on it. And if I agree with it, I will sign it."

"Yes," I say. "And thanks so much again."

On my way home on the train, I remind myself that I've never had any trouble praising myself to myself within the confines of my own heart and I try to think of Heubner's gift to me as an opportunity, not a trap. But one day goes by, then another. On the night before my next class with her I ask myself: Do you want to win a fellowship or don't you? And answer myself: My life depends on it. And so I flip through *The Dangerous Meadow,* quote a few lines I admire, write of their "extraordinary intelligence and subtlety," recommend myself "very highly indeed" for a fellowship, then go to my desk to type the letter.

But when I walk into my class on Thursday afternoon all I can think is: So now here comes the hard part. After class, I wait until all the other students have gone, then pull the long white envelope out of my briefcase. "I've got the letter here," I say in a low voice, speaking as if it carries notorious evidence.

"So let's have a look at it."

Watching her draw it from its envelope, then open it to read it, I feel ill. And in fact her glance, when she looks up, is complexly academic: mocking and shrewdly admiring all at once. "Yes," she says. "Fine. I will sign this."

EXCITED SHRIEKS and cries drift down from the third floor the next time I go over to Brooke's house. Her little boy (Adam) must be entertaining a crowd of small girls. "Those shrieks are beginning to sound somewhat sexual," I say to her as I lift my feet out of my boots.

Brooke says yes, we need to go up and monitor the proceedings. And so we carry our slices of pumpkin pie and mugs of coffee upward, passing by rooms familiar to me from my last visit, and once we've reached the top floor we sit on the sofa because Adam & Company have turned all the chairs around to look out over the back garden. Brooke whispers that Adam carried all the soapstone carvings over to the table on the other side of the chairs, then placed them in a circle.

"Your son, the Druid," I whisper back as we begin to eat the pie with its heavenly silt of nutmeg and ginger, then drink from the mugs of cool bitter coffee. Between sips, I look around at Brooke's possessions: the soapstone hunters in their stone parkas, an ivory

Buddha, a landscape of winter tundra whose sandbars (or snow-bars) appear as windblown welts in the white paper—but the winter light is too bright, it fills the world with a glare, a deep but bright northern sadness, the busy voices behind the big chairs reminding me of my own children's childhood and the shrill cries of children who've discovered the most thrilling way to build or wreck something.

After we've gone over all of the stories and have chosen "The Dubliner" and I'm saying goodbye—by now the light has died and the day has gone, even the children have gone—Brooke says, "Listen, you're a sweetheart and you also seem to know what you're doing, so why don't you just take all of the stories home with you and do whatever else needs to be done to them and then mail off the story we've decided should go to New York and you can bill me for everything later."

A hot metro wind blows grit and litter up the stairs, and a wasted girl—shy, ruined, alcoholic or post-alcoholic—is standing at the bottom of the escalator in a summer dress and winter boots and singing a mournful low French version of "Waltzing Matilda," her dirge sexually forlorn.

The night is even more radiantly cold by the time I push my way out of the metro and as I turn onto Claremont, a car coming toward me dims its lights and I feel a deep tenderness for the driver, sensing behind the painfully bright barrier of the headlights the delicate flinch in one of Galbraith's thighs as he slightly brakes, then dims his lights.

A Hydro bill is lying in wait in my mailbox. Also an island on a blue sea (from William):

> Greetings from the ruins. Greece is wonderful although I've never been anywhere so trampled by tourists. I've also been thrown together with a couple from Thunder Bay, and yesterday, after hearing my presentation on choir music, they decided that I wasn't a fascist after all and invited me to spend the afternoon climbing the Acropolis.

Kind of him. Although it reminds me that my own life is so dull now. Of course there's school (a distraction) and teaching (a distraction I get paid for) but apart from my distractions, my life is lonely.

I type up "The Dubliner," then write a letter praising it, describe it as "a beautiful modern fable," then walk out to the post office with it first thing in the morning. But there are high banks of snow on both sides of the street and they seem to be calling to me as the sirens called out to Ulysses, urging me to let the story slip from a gloved hand to leave no sign of itself except for a slice in the snow like the cut of a knife. But I can't do it, all I can do is pray that *The New Yorker* will reject it. I pray the whole time I'm buying the American stamps for the return envelope. "Let them not buy it," I pray. "Please dear God, let there be justice at last."

A LONG HISS against porcelain, then the collapsed roar of the flush. But when he comes out of the washroom zipping up his fly, Galbraith doesn't look to his left as he crosses the hallway into his office and so he doesn't yet know that I'm here. But here I nevertheless am, standing in a glade, in a grove, in shade, in shadow, the room as long and brightly illuminated as ever, although my stillness makes me feel hidden, my heart a gun that keeps firing, misfiring.

I hear him say a few words, he must be on the phone. And so I should leave now, I need to get away while there's still time to run, but at this same moment, outside on the mezzanine, the elevator doors slide open and I can hear the click of high heels on polished marble, and so here comes his new woman, here she is, but to my surprise she turns out to be Magda, Magda in a raincoat, Magda apparently on her way home to Russell and her baby, and so I stand very still, trying to become part of the foliage (the foliage that doesn't actually exist) but although she glances into the long room as she passes the glass wall she appears not to have seen me for she has now hurried on by. While from the far end of the drafting room, I can hear the opening and closing of drawers, then a cough, then Galbraith comes out, turns the corner, sees me, but although he's clearly startled, he quickly recovers. "Kay," he says.

"Sorry to be an intruder like this. I actually just this minute came in. On impulse, really. I just happened to be walking by and I saw that your car was still here and all of the lights were still on."

"Well, come on down," he tells me, keeping his voice pitched too loud in a jovial way he must know I will hate. "Come on down to my office. I'm not quite ready to leave yet." And his face has become so brightly alert that he seems almost dangerous. Odd, when until now I've been thinking of myself as the dangerous one.

I walk down to his office and he ushers me in. "Come in, come in."

I hate this, I hate the way he's repeating phrases in a way meant to seem energetic and cheerful, as if I'm a woman he barely knows.

"Sit down, sit down."

"Why are you doing this?"

"Doing what?"

"Repeating yourself like this. Come in, come in, sit down, sit down. Because it's making me feel as if I'm one of your employees. Or a client."

But I can see that he's not in the mood to make light conversation, and in fact is not in the mood to listen to anything at all that I might care to say, he so clearly has things he wants to say to *me*.

"I should first of all say that I'm really glad you dropped by...."

I wait. I think I might even be praying. I am also trying not to remember that when I looked at my face in the mirror this morning it seemed marked by the tenderness of someone who's certain that another someone still secretly cares for her.

"Because as a matter of fact I have three things to tell you."

I'm quite certain by now that I do not want to hear what they are.

"And the three things," he says, sitting behind his desk and drawing the flat of his hand in a preening way down over his tie, "are as follows: I'm breaking away from this group of designers, I'm leaving the country, and I'm getting married a week from tomorrow.

In fact today is my last day here, so it's lucky that today's the day you picked to drop by...."

The news of his marriage is what wounds me the most and so I know that I must at all costs pretend to ignore it. I certainly must not speak of it if I don't want to cry. And so I ask him where he's going.

"To New York City, actually. I'll be working with a team of designers on a project in Manhattan. And the woman I'm going to marry will be working there too."

"Is she an architect as well, then?" I say this in a voice I hate because it sounds so social and unconcerned. "Is it Tess?"

"Tess?" And for a moment he can't seem to remember who Tess is. "No, no, the woman I'm going to marry is an interpreter who's just been awarded a contract to work as a simultaneous interpreter at the United Nations."

I stare at him. "She's not the woman we met when we had dinner with your cousin, is she?"

"I went to New York a few months ago, and stayed for a weekend with Monique. And Josette just happened to drop by."

"The woman you called Mademoiselle Chatterbox."

"People can change. And like so many people one knows, she's a better person once you get to know her better. As a writer, you must surely be able to accept an eventuality like that."

"I don't think you have to be a writer to accept an eventuality like that. People, once you get to know them better, are forever surprising you. For better or worse."

"If that's intended to be a rebuke to me, then I stand accused," he says, standing theatrically, then he turns to the coat rack to lift off a gunmetal raincoat that looks offensively new. "Guilty as charged." He even smiles. A sickly, ghastly smile. "When all this time I thought I was being admirably humble." But then he says in his new and terrible casual voice, "Listen can I give you a lift somewhere?"

I say no, I have a class to teach, I need to go fast on the metro.

He doesn't even ask me how I've come to have a class to teach, he only says, "I could still drive you. I have to leave here in a few minutes, I just have to make one more call, tonight there's a party called 'the burial of the young life. L'enterrement de la vie de jeunesse.'"

It's really going to happen then. I feel chastened, a frightened dignity. I tell him that I've always mixed those two words up: wedding and funeral. "Even before my own wedding."

There's a silence while we consider this. But then I stand up as well. "I have to go now." And I hold out my hand as if I plan to shake hands with him, wish him every happiness. But he doesn't shake it, he simply holds it as if he has just this moment regained consciousness and doesn't understand why he's standing in this little white room holding my hand.

But when I tell him that I really do have to go, he doesn't make any move to stop me and the rainy wind hits me as I step out onto de Maisonneuve, slips into my jacket to push at me, keeps raining down the last of the leaves as I turn the dark corner of one of the smaller streets because I can't bear the thought of his driving past me as I'm walking alone in the rain.

It's getting dark when I turn to look at a window display whose plastic men have all been cut off at their durable plastic waists. They are legs, pairs of legs simply, legs and lower bodies, sturdy male legs in grey and black trousers standing about as if engaged in polite conversation. One half man in particular, wearing black shoes and a black leather belt, is dressed in grey suit pants of the sort Galbraith used to wear, his dimensions exactly Galbraith's dimensions, and I'm gazing in at this half man, swamped by sexual desire for him. But what does it mean, I wonder, lying in bed and still stunned by the presence and force of the male legs in my dream. That Galbraith is only half mine? Or does it mean he's still half mine? Or does it mean that I only miss him sexually? This is what it has to mean most and as I shampoo my hair in the weak light I try not to be oppressed by the fascism of symbolism.

I stop off at a smoke shop on my way home, pick up the morning paper, then as I'm walking past a wall of skin magazines on my way out into the rain again I see it as a whole wall of Josettes, the younger woman's body sexily squeezed from a tube of caramel perfection.

Then home. The dim apartment gone stale and the gloomy rain saying over and over: this is life, this is life, this is life, this is life. I turn on all the lamps before I go out onto the balcony to open my umbrella, let it skitter back and forth to dry in the wind, then carry an armful of bedding down to the laundry room while I'm still in my raincoat. Forty minutes later I have to make another trip down to the steamy underworld with a new armload of shirts to be washed, pull the damp clothes out of the washing machine to throw them into a dryer, then half an hour later make another trip down to pull the first dry armful of hot clothes out and poke more damp clothes into the warm dryer again, then rise up to the top floor in the privacy of the elevator, hugging the warm towels to my face and biting them with the savage little bites a cat or a lover would take. Then I sit on my sofa and end up too lost in thought to remember to go down to fetch the final pile of laundry. I instead stare out at the mindless, enclosing rain, but when I remember it I run back down to the basement to discover that someone has already removed my clothes from the dryer and left them on top of it, not in a tumbled heap but folded into neat piles, my black lace underpants in one pile, my pale shirts and dark pants folded into second and third piles. I cringe at the sight of all this punitive order, my clothes having been handled by a stranger. This building isn't a friendly local laundry after all, it's a building where the tenants coldly nod to one another in the mornings, dislike one another on sight. I walk over to the one dryer that's ticking, hoping to open its door to see pink and white flying blots of panties, the evidence that only fussy female hands must have stroked my panties into submission in a maternal cloud of judgment, but when I open the door, then watch the damp cargo heavily flop to a stop, all I can see are black sweatshirts and giant white boxer shorts. But none of the men I know are folders of laundry. Not even Galbraith. Even the times the pile of wash was made up of only his own clothes, he'd still dump it on his bed for me to fold. A memory that ought to make me miss him less. But it doesn't.

A GREY UMBRELLA snaps open just ahead of me as I'm leaving the bank, Spanish combs pushing up the strands of white-streaked silver hair and just below the hem of the coat a long band of damp Indonesian fabric and so this has to be Giselle. We stand and talk on the street, then end up talking for an hour in her car. She was at Galbraith's wedding out in Anastasie and she tells me that Josette seemed very young the night before the wedding when she dropped by with a gift for them, that she was trying on her wedding dress, then unzipped herself from it to throw her winter coat on over her long white wedding slip so she could run out to the clothesline to peg her crucifix to it to guarantee a sunny day for the wedding. "It was a shotgun affair, I don't know if you knew that."

No, I didn't know that and didn't even imagine it, but it explains my surreal confrontation with Galbraith the last time I saw him.

"I took lots of photos of them, including one of them running down the veranda steps in a shower of snow and confetti so they could catch their plane to Costa Rica."

"So it snowed then. And so the crucifix Josette pegged to the clothesline didn't work after all."

"Everyone out there calls St. Anastasie St. Anesthésie...."

A few years ago Alex was mugged in Costa Rica. He told me the whole story when he came back to Canada. Not only the story of

213

actually being robbed but also the aftermath. The police told him that the robbers work in threes: the first robber is the one who brings the victim down by tightly looping an arm over his head (to make him faint), then once he's been placed on the ground the second robber frisks him for cash, credit cards, cameras, and the coins in his pockets while the third robber stands guard.

Not wanting to hear the windy and final crash of wedding bells or picture the bride and groom laughing as they are ducking under confetti and snow and above all not being able to bear the thought of them in each other's arms, I take Alexander's experience of being mugged in Costa Rica and transpose it to Galbraith:

IDENTITY CHORES

All he can remember is the nearly lethal hug of his breath in the few seconds before the night went dark, but nothing of what must have so quickly followed: the sprinting away of three shadows, their arms winged out, their beach bags bulging with cameras. He also remembers what he thought must be a dream when he opened his eyes to see a row of tall white towers dotted with lights and how because he so often dreams that he's looking at buildings he knew he was dreaming. But the purring of a giant cat and two giant eyes were coming towards him, but now they were the headlights of a car, although far enough off to his left to miss him, and the sound of this car was so real that he could no longer tell himself it was a dream.

He gets up, pats his pockets, but everything's gone and after he's come back into the hotel, he's borne up to the dim breezy room where a medicated heat beams at him from the sleeping Josette. He sits down on his own side of the bed to undress in the dark and is hit by a wave of heat once again: her honeymoon sunburn. And for

a long time after this he lies too wide awake in the dark, trying not
to dwell on the hallucinatory days of their rushed courtship, the
stunned days leading up to their wedding, the fact that if he hadn't
married her and come with her to Costa Rica, he wouldn't have
been robbed.

The next afternoon, after a dull morning spent trying to reclaim
his official self by doing all his little identity chores, he crosses
the patio lounge to see J's suntanned knees raised and tipped back
in laughter, a cigarette in one hand, a glass of wine in the other,
although when she catches sight of him she rocks herself forward
to set her wineglass down on the far side of her chair and must also
have dropped her cigarette into it because when she leans back in
her chair again she's no longer holding a cigarette in her hand. We
are afraid of one another, he thinks, we must be a married couple.

A sunlit world of splashes and happy cries waits for him beyond
the floral cool of the lounge, but when he steps into the late afternoon
sunshine the cries come to a stop and the other guests all turn to
watch him. He is above all being watched by the men in the pool,
the rich, hairy men who are all in love with J. Whenever he meets
them in the hallways, they stare at him with envy, with contempt.
And he mocks them too, in his heart, their grim brotherhood of
money, the hotel insignia on the pockets of their white bathrobes,
the black hotel towels flung over their shoulders.

He squats down beside J to handcuff one of her ankles. "Have
you had a good day?"

"A lovely day, mon amour. And what about you? Did you have
a good day too?"

Thinking of all the ways it was bad, he tells her it was good.
"Did you swim?"

She smiles over at the men in the pool. "I played water volleyball."

"So what would you like to do this evening?"

"Tonight's the masquerade dance and I'd like us to go as flamenco dancers."

"Sure," he says. "Sounds terrific."

In French she asks him to kiss her goodbye.

He gives her a quick peck, aware that he's being watched by the men in the pool, a Greek chorus standing waist deep in the water. "So I'll be seeing you up in the room, then." He's even sure he knows what they are thinking: The bridegroom cometh, the bridegroom cometh at last. But hey, hey, amigos, quelle surprise, the bridegroom already goeth again.

He goes up to the roof of the hotel to look out over all of San José, then does a slow turn. An architect's turn. Or a child's turn. The turn that goes with the words: I close my eyes and wherever I stop, my future will be. He cheats, decides not to close his eyes. But as he's turning west he almost cries out: a pole with a wooden skull stuck on its top stands just beyond the far side of the roof. But then he understands: it's only the top half of a dead palm tree.

Down by the lunar pool the guests are served sweet tropical drinks along with some sort of exquisite fish dish and when it's their turn to perform, J and G strictly stand, then hold up their arms flamenco-style as they stamp their way past each other's backside while looking past each other's eyes, over their shoulders. And when they walk back to their room from the party, J leans against G's shoulder and hugs him around the waist. "We danced well together, didn't we?"

"We did."

"We were the best."

He wonders if the way he smiles is sadly fatherly.

"So will you come with me to mass on Sunday morning, then?"

"I'll at least walk you as far as the front door of the cathedral."

"I think God would prefer that you come inside as well." And she pouts at him in a cool but flirty way that makes him wonder if she attributes their not being entirely in love to the fact that he's an agnostic. Or at least to his being some sort of de-mythologized Christian.

Once they are getting ready for bed he tries to make amends by telling her she looks beautiful. And it's true, she does. Or at least she looks incredibly pretty. But she always looks the same, he thinks, and already he feels bored by her. He unties his shoes, looks up at her. "I'm not all that convinced that it's such a good idea for you to smoke, though. Or drink. Not when you're pregnant."

"But I'm not harming our baby! I only take little sips, little puffs!"

"Then why did I see you hide your wineglass under your chair, then drop your cigarette into the wine as I was coming out to the pool this afternoon?"

"Because you are such a Monsieur Fusspot, mon amour."

"But what if we have a baby who's deformed or whose brain is affected?"

"My glass of wine is hardly even wine, it's mostly water."

"Jesus turned water into wine. And you're turning wine into water?"

"Yes," she says. "I am. And isn't my miracle the greater miracle?"

"To me, it is."

If it works it is.

The next night at dinner she says, "I'm being good, I hope you noticed."

"I did and I do."

She smiles a little tauntingly back at him. She's still very young after all, only twenty-two. If this were 1886 instead of 1986, he would—as her young bourgeois husband—be the one whose duty it was to give her sexual and moral instruction. It would even be his job to help her expand her mind, at least as much as was thought to be decently necessary at the time. But now she's signalling to him with her eyes: Look over there.

This is a game he dislikes, but she must want to play it because he hasn't made her happy enough. And so he looks to his left to see a fat woman whose black hair is cut in bangs. And although this woman doesn't at all resemble K, she makes him think of K because of her cigarillo and her book. He sets his knife and fork on his plate. This whole goddamn hotel depresses him, it's so sanitized by tourism. He also doesn't want to be J's accomplice in disapproval, and so he says in a voice that's even lower than hers, "Why do you want me to look at her?"

"Because she's so eccentric, her clothes, her cigar ..."

The woman looks up, apparently all too aware that she is being discussed, and it seems to G that she has a lonely face, emotional eyes.

A NEW STUDENT is sitting in the chair next to my mine. Dark eyes, tense shoulders. Lorenzo Gaddo. Whose voice, when he asks Professor Stackpole a question about one of the books on the course list, has a definite pneumatic Italian ache in it.

We talk during the coffee break, then walk through the rain to the metro after class. We talk about being the children of immigrants. I tell him how secretive this made me, how ambitious at school.

"It was the same with me and my family."

"Do they live in Montreal?"

"No, they live in Paris, Ontario."

"If you come from Paris, Ontario, what do you call yourself? Not a Parisian, I don't suppose—"

"I call myself a Parisite."

We laugh as we walk down the wet tile steps to the turnstiles and while we're waiting for our train he asks me if I know many people in the city.

"No. No one. Except for a few of the people here at school. And one of my sons. But how about you? Do you know many people here?"

"I sit all alone by my telephone."

He phones me the next night to ask me if I can lend him my copy of *The Blithedale Romance* and as we talk we quickly arrive at a state of mutual comfort that allows us to tell each other our personal histories. And more: terrible things we have thought and done.

He even comes with me to look at an apartment on Claremont Avenue. The concierge, Mohammed, is a scholarly Iranian who leads us down a terrazzo hallway linking the main building to the annex, then shows us an apartment facing a courtyard. It smells of fried onions and mould, but it has corner bookcases and shining hardwood floors. I turn from the window to ask Mohammed if there are ever any problems with mice in these apartments, and he says no, never, and while he's occupied with unlatching the doors to the balcony, I whisper to Lorenzo, "What do you think?" and he whispers back, "Take it."

The following morning, I go to Mohammed's building to meet the owner, Mr. Rastafajani, a big teddy bear of a man with a childlike smile. From the moment we shake hands I know it will be clear sailing, and so it is, even after I've told him I'm a part-time student. He seems more at home in French than in English. Or not really all that much at home in either language. "Mais prenez garde. The people who lived here avant vous was wild men. Sauvages. Very mal. I think you should perhaps to exchange your lock...."

THE WORLD TURNS green again and the next time I open the door to Lorenzo, I call him "Enzo," then worry that I've overstepped, that the name sounds too much like an experimental endearment. But he doesn't even seem to have noticed and when we sit down in the sunshine of my front room he asks me what I plan to do with my degree, once I get it. "There don't seem to be too many jobs out there for people who want to teach English lit."

"I'll be a gypsy scholar. Or a gypsy sessional lecturer."

He leans back into my sofa and sighs. "Someone pointed you out to me the first night we met. He said you were the only published writer in the class."

"When all along I've been under the impression that we became friends because you find me so intellectually and sexually alluring...."

"I *do* find you intellectually alluring," he says in a low voice. And only then does he say in an even lower voice, "And sexually alluring as well."

"Take note of the sequence."

"You remind me of an older woman I had an affair with the summer I was nineteen."

"What made it be over?"

"I made it be over."

"But what did she do to make you want it to be over?"

"She didn't do anything. Or at least she didn't do anything wrong. It was just time to move on."

"So you're blaming yourself then?"

"Because I am a gentleman." He laughs his boy's laugh. "The truth is I'm a bastard. Like all of my kind." But then he leans back and stretches. "Have you been in love very often?"

"Often enough." In fact, Galbraith has become so present to me these last few days that I often feel as if he's near. I feel it in my body, but I feel it even more in my face. These last few days are the first days since we said goodbye that my face has felt this looked at, this touched by his hand, this kissed.

Lorenzo in the meantime is confessing to me that he's having an affair with a married woman, but he's also going out with Lara, a girl from our Problems and Techniques of Fiction class. But lately she's been very moody and accusing.

"But what does she accuse you of?"

"Not loving her enough. It's what women always accuse me of, in the end. They don't put it quite like that, of course, they accuse me of narcissism instead."

I picture the bright and bitter Lara, in love with Lorenzo and enraged by her own resentful adoration. And Lorenzo being too democratic and mild to practise enough adoration to love her back. I tell him that Lara's looks fascinate me because she has two such different faces. One face—the face seen head-on—is furiously white and almost distorted from intense emotion, but her other face—her face seen in profile—is voluptuously calm and amused and seems to be borne along on a body from another era, from about 1892, say, a face that might even be patterned with little square windows of light from the chinks in the wide brim of a great straw hat heaped with roses and when she smiles in profile she smiles as if she knows that this is her best smile, her best face, a face aimed straight ahead and conveying a sensual happiness, freckled, majestic, a face bobbing along beside whoever she's walking with. "Do you think there's a chance she might suspect that you're also involved with someone else?"

"I don't think so. I think she sees my flaws as being so deep in my character that they have nothing to do with anyone else."

"And what do you think about all of this?"

"I think she's right."

"You astound me, your willingness to be hard on yourself astounds me."

"That's my trick. Anything to be liked."

"It's that deliberate?"

"Once upon a time it was, but it's second nature to me now."

I'm in no danger of falling in love with him (or so I tell myself), there's no sexual chemistry between us and he's even younger than Galbraith, but I do love to talk to him. He's a cynic. But a cynic who's willing to reveal himself. There's also a certain surprising elderliness in him, I can see it in the way he uses words like *thus* and *hence* and *therefore* and *aplenty* and other awful and fusty words in his otherwise intelligent essays. On the other hand, he has seen all, he understands all, he forgives all. Or at least he forgives all in *me* while being perfectly willing to be unforgiving of others, and it's exactly this clandestine unfairness that makes him such a fine friend.

But this is also the week my back goes into spasm, forgets how to breathe. This happened because I when I reached down to lift a pail of hot water from the bathtub, something crunched in my back, a bad twist of sound, then a snap. So that now, no matter which way I turn, I can't do one single thing to diminish that one hard and high note of pain, it's like giving birth, but higher up in my back, between my shoulder blades. I can't swim under it, crouch away from it, it's moved in to stay. And so I have to walk over to the Back Clinic.

Pinched nerve, Dr. Godbolt tells me. Flat on your back is the only thing for it.

For how long?

Six weeks.

Not possible.

"No sitting, then. Either stand up or lie down." He peers down at me: "Do you not have any friends who could help you out?"

I hear a shorter, more damning version of the question: Do you not have any friends?

"A few."

Patients line the hospital hallways, waiting to have a quick word or two with the great man.

No one sits.

No sitting! he calls out as he walks very fast past us in his flapping white coat.

Montreal has turned itself into hundreds of arrangements of hurtful light that I squint at on my way back to see Godbolt again. He tells me he'll send me to a clinic to get eight X-rays of my spine, then he gives me a prescription for ultrasound treatments at a sports clinic on Sherbrooke Street. And so every Tuesday evening I have to walk up to the clinic and wait out in the hall with all the maimed athletes. And on Thursdays I go for acupuncture treatments at the apartment of a tiny Japanese doctor who's recently shaved off his moustache in preparation for a trip to Mexico so that he'll be able to get as much sun as possible on his tiny body. On Saturdays I visit a chiropractor who tells me to give up my job at the Institute, since it involves climbing stairs. "You got a pinched nerve, you don't climb stairs."

On my way home from the chiropractor's I notice that there's a new *New Yorker* at the magazine kiosk next to Mi-hee's grocery, its cover gleaming: a pot of pink flowers in a green room. I open it to the Table of Contents and here it is: "The Dubliner" by Brooke O'Neill, page seventy-eight. But I can't look at it now, I'll have to buy it, and once I've bought it I hurry home with it, then turn to Brooke's story before I've even taken off my coat. "The Dubliner." I feel stunned by its transformation, its acquired authority. Not only by the authority of its being in this particular magazine, but also by the authority of its title. When I was doing my edit, I phoned her about the title, told her it was really much too close to the title James Joyce used for his story collection, but she refused to change it. And now I can see that perhaps the bubbling Brooke was right to stand her ground since her title no longer seems to be a copycat title, it instead bizarrely seems to have raised her story to a Joycean plane now that I'm reading it as an innocent reader might read it, pretending not to know one single thing about its contaminated history. And even though it appears not to have been altered by even one word since I mailed it off to New York.

I feel the unfairness of life, of God, of God's lousy jokes as I shower before bed, then turn the water off and hear the shower's faint echo: rain on the roof. But as I'm shaking out my damp hair I hear another noise, a noise like the echo of my own footsteps: the careful squeak of someone walking just over my head. But it can't be, it's raining up there, and dark.

I have to keep pausing in the drying of my hair in order to listen again. And each time I hear the apartment giving off its little night-time rustlings and ticks, my heart does a quick skip. I dig around in my sewing basket until I find a lone cigarette. It smells of tobacco and dry yarn as I light it. Whoever was up there must have come down by now. Either that or he's decided not to alert anyone by any more creaking. But what if he knelt next to the skylight and rubbed a port-hole in the misted glass to spy down on me as I was lathering my breasts with the shampoo-foam I pulled away from my soapy peaked hair? He could have watched me the whole time the streaming water was turning my hair into a heavy wet pelt as it sluiced down my drenched naked back. But no, he couldn't have rubbed a port-hole in the steam, the steam was on the *inside* of the window pane, not on the outside, even I, a poor student of physics when I was at school, remember this much.

I'M GOING TO HAVE to ask either Lorenzo or Benno to come over to my place and help me lift up my typewriter. Bizarre to call a typewriter heavy, but Godbolt has now forbidden me to lift anything heavier than a grapefruit until my back has recovered. I'm somehow going to have to get my typewriter up on my dresser, then type on it while I stay standing. It will be like standing and typing my essays at a lectern. But just as I'm about to dial Lorenzo's number, he calls to ask me if I want to go to a lecture on pornography at McGill, and because I never do anything social any more, I say yes.

As I'm standing at the back of the auditorium to protect my back, it seems to me that Lorenzo is looking resentfully lonely sitting all alone down in the third row. The lecturer defines pornography as a voyeuristic and sentimental reverence for physical perfection. Also as a sentimental reverence for the merely clinical. Both these statements strike me as being so right that I write them down on a slip of paper as *a voy and sentimental rev 4 fiz perf + sent rev 4 the mere clin,* although it's a code that somehow also manages to make the words look just a little obscene. I'm still standing at the back writing (my sheet of paper pressed against the auditorium's back wall) when the lecture comes to an end. Lorenzo makes his way back up the aisle to me and when I take off my glasses he says, "You look so much prettier without your glasses, you should always wear contacts." Then he invites me back to his place. "You've never even seen it."

"Am I being invited because I look so much prettier without my glasses?"

He says of course not.

I'm surprised by his place when we get to it, it's furnished with such heavy old mahogany and pine furniture, heavy armoires, carved Italian chairs. He must have driven everything here from his family's place in Paris. On the wall above a double bed that looks like a cardinal's bed, there are several framed diplomas. I peer up at them. Some of them are for academic prizes. There's also the framed diploma he got when he graduated from Western. I can hear him out in the kitchen, opening drawers, bottles. "What *is* this room, Enzo? Is this a bedroom or is it a dental office?"

He comes to the door shyly. "What's so dental about it?"

I smile up at the diplomas.

"You think I should take them down?"

"I think you should take them down."

Is he offended? I don't really think so. He likes to be teased and instructed. He comes from money, but it's new money, he wants to be taught how to be more aristocratic so he can do the right thing and when he brings the wine and crackers into the bigger room on a tray and tells me to lie down on his couch if it will help my back feel better, I feel grateful to him because he isn't miffed.

Then I stretch out, glance back at him. "Where will you be?"

"Right here."

"Are you my analyst or my father confessor?"

"I'm your analyst. Dr. Gaddo."

"You must tell me about your childhood."

"I think that that's supposed to be my line, Kay. By the way, how's the novel going?"

"I'm having trouble with my central character."

"Just don't have her living in some bourgeois dream. Not when your own life is so seedy."

"Thanks, Lorenzo. But my central character is a man."

"Don't kill him off then."

It's a mild winter night when I walk to the McGill metro, but when I come up the stairs at Vendôme, I step into wild weather. There's even the rumble of thunder and somewhere beyond the blowing snow, lightning flashes. On Claremont Avenue, I see a man sitting on the stairs next to the stairway of Rastafajani's building. When I get closer, I can see that he's Lorenzo. But how can he be? Did he take a cab to my place so that he could get here first as some kind of joke? It's unbelievable, he must be a hallucination. He smiles at me as he asks me for money and by this time I can see that he only bears an uncanny resemblance to Lorenzo. He's older, for one thing. He's drunk, for another. But acting on the belief that he must be appeased, I walk up his set of stairs to give him a handful of coins.

"Merci, chérie." And he reaches out to touch the sleeve of my coat. "Ah, c'est beau," he tells me. "Et vous êtes belle aussi, mon amour. Vous, et votre manteau, ça vous va bien."

I feel spooked, walking up the stairs to my apartment. Do we make our own fates? Once I've taken off my coat—ma belle coat—I don't want to stay in my apartment alone even though I know that the solution to this momentary fear is really only a matter of lamps and tea and reading the movie reviews and forming an opinion. And so I pick up a copy of *Le Devoir* and work my way through the movie reviews while I pretend to live somewhere more exotic and foreign. Or not even foreign. I miss St. Viateur, I miss Duluth, above all I miss Esplanade, the life I lived there. As for the poor east end of the city, the part where the elegant Sherbrooke Street is no longer elegant but lined with oil refineries for miles and miles, the area that extends out to Anjou and even farther east, that part of the city is an unknown country to me. And even though the decaying southwest is more familiar, and St. Henri is almost next door, I picture the women there as shy and at the mercy of men who are moody and often away. Away in the army or away out west. Or away in mining towns up north, towns whose names sound like the names of settlements in the interior of Africa: Abitibi, Rouyn-Noranda.

EDISON LUMLEY seems (once again) to be pretending not to see me as I'm on my way out of a class with Cy Stackpole and so I call after him, "Could I come into your office for a quick word with you?"

He ushers me in, pulls out a chair for me as I say, "As I think you might possibly already know, I was one of the judges for this year's Lindner Foundation literary prize."

He stares at me, a great clumsy browsing animal who's been startled in the underbrush. He looks as affable as ever, but I also notice—for the first time, really—that he has very shrewd eyes.

"Well," he says with an awkward little laugh after I've made the comment that his story was perfectly competent, although more of an essay, really, than a story, "that's just one person's opinion. Or, in this case, the opinion of only three people, but I'm afraid I have a few phone calls to make right now, and so I'll have to be sending you on your way...."

Walking home, I understand what a fool I was. And how enraged *he* was. His air of calm was too calm, a calm biding its time, an academic calm, the most vengeful calm of all. It must seem to him that I broke our unspoken agreement by not rewarding him for his earlier kindness to me. I also listened to Brooke's gossip ("all art is gossip") and without even being aware I was doing it I must have given him puzzled looks. Or worse: darkly puzzled looks. My money situation is by now also very bad. So bad that I decide to try to get Idona to pay back the money she asked me to give her the summer of the year I got married—three thousand dollars from my education fund—because she needed money for renovations for an old house she bought for five thousand dollars.

"Dear Idona," I write, but the words don't sound effusive enough. "Dearest Idona," I write, but this seems too dishonest. And "My darling Idona" is out of the question. I go back to Dear Idona, followed by a description of the calamity that has befallen me and as I seal the envelope I can almost hear a foghorn doing its melancholy oompah out over the harbour in Saint John, the visibility nil or almost nil on one of those mean east coast snowy mornings, the postman coming up the steps of the yellow house on Mount Pleasant Avenue with his damp sack of letters, Idona watching the letter slot being forced open by the morning's cascade of postcards and letters. A faithful correspondent, she writes to friends in Rome, Athens, Stockholm, Madrid, and after the postie has gone back down the steps to the street, I see her scoop all the postal loot up in her arms and carry it to the den. After she's read my letter she'll hand it across to Henry. "My firstborn daughter," she will tell him, "is a specialist in the past." And after he's also read it she'll say, "She could have been a cabaret singer. She could be living a glamorous, unbitter life, but she chose not to, she chose to be a writer."

When I get a letter back from Saint John, I stand down in the lobby reading it:

Our dearest little Kay, We have no problem at all in empathizing with your financial plight....

But then it goes on to say,

We've been there! And we are on our way there once again! The house Henry and I bought for the two of us to live in after our wedding has become a bottomless pit. (It needs a new roof, it also needs extensive work on the plumbing.) All this extra expense and turmoil has left us cash-poor, and so we are so very very sorry not to be able to be of help.

> Much, much love, etc.,
> Idona

I write to Freddie, ask him to intervene on my behalf. "My situation is a little bit desperate, although I'm hoping only temporarily so."

A letter from Freddie then brings the news that Idona has agreed to pay back the money. "But only in instalments so at this rate it'll take you almost three years to get your three thousand." Ten days later Idona's first cheque arrives, for one hundred dollars. In its bottom lefthand corner she's written "Bursary." It's clipped to a note bearing the news that some money has "fortuitously been freed up," now making it possible for her to pay off the debt. "These transactions are so important in families," she writes. "We must all do our best to be decent and loyal, to treat each other with honour, decency, love, and respect."

I write to Alex, but he doesn't write back and so I make another trip to the welfare office. It's a dismal cool morning and my back has gone into spasm again. I feel stiff, ancient, wait in line until I'm ushered into a cubicle to see a Mademoiselle Breau who tells me that a Monsieur Muldoon will call on me Monday at two.

Toast smell, fried sizzle. The excavated aroma of strong coffee. Followed by a rushed morning of scouring and mopping and forcing piles of papers and bills and magazines into cupboards and drawers. The deceit of good housekeeping. Or the deceit of bad housekeeping. But at last the place is as superb as I can make it: low black coffee table with its bowl of lemons, cushions lined up on the red sofa, the bright little rug. All in all, I feel pleased and exhausted, as if I've escaped something. And yet what I've accomplished is madness, I should have been trying to preserve the chaos, I should have been trying to look poor.

When I open the door to Monsieur Muldoon, he gazes past me to give my apartment a professionally assessing look. "Beautiful place you got here."

I'm a fool then, this man's admiration for my beautiful place proves it.

"And so many books!"

"I'm working on a second novel."

"Any idea when you'll be getting some kind of monetary return on it?"

"I don't know. I haven't finished writing it yet."

"How much rent you pay here?"

"Three hundred and fifty a month."

"I believe we might be able to cover that for you."

"I'd be incredibly grateful."

"But only as a loan and only for one month."

Delicately, I ask him how soon I can have it.

"Come to the welfare office on Monday morning."

On Monday morning, even though I can spare only half of the cheque for Mr. Rastafajani, he insists that I come in for a cup of tea. I stay standing while I drink it, but he can't bear it. "You must sit, my friend." And so I do, then turn the pages of an album of photographs he opens for me. There's a story for every face, but finally I have to stand and fake an extreme interest in his azalea plant to give myself the right to keep standing after I've gone over to inspect it.

The physiotherapist I go to see after lunch catches my neck in a carefully calibrated headlock. She has a deep tan and she's wearing fringed white moccasins even though it's snowing outside the clinic's tall windows. When she tells me that she has just come back from a holiday in Venezuela, I imagine that I can smell bright Venezuelan sunlight in the short sleeves of her white cotton shirt. But now she's asking me to roll my eyes to the right while she exerts an exquisitely subtle counter-pressure on my neck. Next she tells me to raise my hips while she slips a pad of wet cotton beneath them. When she clicks on the machine the wet pad is hooked up to, my lower back is bombarded by a rain of miniature and painlessly tap-dancing needles: an effervescence, the tingle of ginger ale in the small of my back.

She also gives me a dozen red moon stickers to put up in my apartment, little red moons to warn me to be careful when I'm bending down to lift a bowl of adzuki beans out of the fridge, a sticker for beside the bathroom mirror to remind me to not lean too far forward when I'm doing my eyes.

But it isn't a red moon that Lorenzo speaks of when he phones me this evening, it's a blue moon. "Last night there was a blue moon, did you see it?"

"Can a person actually see such a thing? I thought it was just an emotional state for singers to sing about—"

"No, no, it's an actual celestial phenomenon. Two moons in the same month. The second one is the blue moon. They only come once every two years or so. That's where the expression comes from, 'once in a blue moon.'" And he laughs a happy panting laugh. A dog's laugh, a boy's laugh. "And once in a blue moon I go to bed with a man—"

"Who?"

"Denny Koepp ..."

The student who sucked the snow from his scarf fringes. "How did that happen?" But then I don't like the jealous force of my question and so I say in a more rational voice, "I mean, were you expecting it to?"

"I knew he had a thing for me. And then last night we had dinner together out at his place in Anjou, and afterwards he asked me. And I couldn't really think of a good reason to say no. I mean it seemed sort of unkind not to just let it happen."

Is he going to say more? But he doesn't say more and so I tell him that the summer I was fourteen a woman fell in love with me. "Or at least I think she did, she just made me feel so looked at. She never touched me, but I had the feeling that she walked around thinking about me all the time. I loved her too, I think. She was just so manly and decent. I kept wishing that I knew a man who was as manly as she was. But that summer I didn't. Except for my father."

"What did your parents think of all this?"

"I don't think they noticed. She was a weaver who'd come out to their workshop with her lover, a woman photographer, and they'd pitched a tent down by the river. But when people of the same sex were involved with each other I don't think my mother thought that actual sex was involved. I think she thought they just liked to give each other hugs. Or else they sometimes had little tiffs."

Lorenzo laughs.

"So how was it? With Denny?"

"We were both pretty nervous," he says.

ALEXANDER (back from Poland at last) called me last week and when he heard the story of my back pain told me he'd be willing to help me. But even his help might not be enough for me since my boss at the Institute, a man who wears elderly cardigans and the kind of black patent leather shoes a jazz musician might wear, the kind that look like svelte slippers, is beginning to give all the new work to the younger teachers.

But this afternoon when Alexander's cheque for two thousand dollars arrives, along with a letter begging me to get my life (and above all my finances) in some kind of sensible order, my eyes burn. How I wish I could write to him: "At the time of our divorce I asked you for nothing. Nothing! And now I'm even being given a lecture." I cry from pure shame and pure gratitude.

A LOUD KNOCK on my door, then Rastafajani's voice: "Good evening, my friend! Forgive me for disturbing you!"

I nudge my notes under the sofa, with my foot. "Coming!" I call in the melodious soprano of a hostess. I turn out the lamp to make the room flutter in nothing but candlelight, scoop up a handful of orange peels and drop them into one of my pockets, then snap out the kitchen light on my way to the door.

The candle flames go wild in the draft as Rastafajani enters. He says in his tenderly mournful voice, "Ah, my dear friend, I do hope I am not disturbing you—"

"Not at all. It's just that things are a little bit untidy in here."

"I just have to take a look at your bathroom, there's something leaking down below."

I slither past him to turn on the light in the hall, feel his elbow's startled contact with a breast.

A few moments after he leaves, the phone rings. Feeling blurred, I go to it quickly. But it's no one, a wrong number. I go into my bedroom to change into tights and a sweater. The phone rings again while I'm at the bathroom sink, splashing my face with warm water. Distrustfully, I go to it.

"Hel*lo,*" says a male voice, deep and coy with the offensive intimacy of the wrong kind of stranger.

"Who is this?"

When he doesn't answer, I take the phone off the hook, then go out to the kitchen to start supper. But the call has made me feel spied on, shivery. I yank the curtain across the rod so that it covers the glass door to the fire escape, and wait till I've had my soup before I set the phone back in its cradle again.

Toward midnight I go to my bedroom window to look down at the narrow street behind the back wing, at the slow progress of a line of cars capped with snow. But the phone rings as I'm getting ready for bed. I should have left it off the hook, but now that it's ringing I can't not answer it. It could be one of the boys. Or it could be Lorenzo.

"Kay ..."

"Lorenzo!" But at once Lorenzo begins, inexplicably, to sob. "Lorenzo, what is it?" But the sobs only go on, wrenching, horrible, my ear is stormed by them. And then I understand: it isn't Lorenzo and it isn't sobbing, it's a stranger who somehow knows my first name, it's the orgasmic sobbing of telephone lust. I unplug the phone, then stay primed for the tiniest creak for nearly an hour. At last I get up again, go to check the door to the balcony. Also the front door. There's also the glass door that leads to the fire escape. I hurry down through the dark kitchen and pull back the zebra curtain—the red between its black stripes by now bleached to a wrinkled pink by the city's night sky—then open the inside window to check on the lock on its outer frame, and as I do, the cold snow blows up my wrists.

MOHAMMED HAS NEWS for me when we meet on the stairs. "Mr. Rastafajani is going to arrange for an exterminator to go up to your apartment. The tenants who lived up there before you saw a mouse."

"Oh no...."

Before I go to bed, I set a white paper napkin on top of the stove between the four elements, then place four green peas in a square in the middle of it. If there's a mouse in this apartment, it will surely eat these peas during the night. On the other hand, I could wake up to find the four peas sitting on their white napkin in untouched formation. I bow to the stove. "Please be here, peas! I beg of you, please. Please please me, peas."

I read for ten minutes, then pad out to the kitchen, snap on the light. The white napkin is still on the top of the stove, but the four peas are gone. I run back to my bedroom, close the door fast, pray that I'm closing the mouse out of my room, not trapping him inside it with me for the night. But after I turn out my light, I remember how night after night the summer I was nine my toes would brush a ball of fluff at the end of my bed, then retract as the fluff—with a quick touch of bad magic—turned into a mouse, and I'd call out to my father in a frail voice, "Daddy, come quick! There's a mouse in my bed!" And he'd come up the stairs and pull the bed apart to show me there wasn't any mouse hiding anywhere in my bed or the bedding.

In the morning I open the door to a tall man in a navy coat who ducks in, peers all around, then squats beside the tall bookcase to shine his flashlight behind it, a doctor shining a light down a long dusty throat. "It's a mystery to me, how mice are getting into this apartment. I have not been able to find one single hole."

If I don't see it or hear it, I might be able to bear it. But I also seem to be eternally braced against seeing or hearing it and sometimes when I come into the apartment at night, after walking home in a fresh night wind or rain, there's the mousy smell of fur and fear, tiny terrors.

But now that I've begun teaching again, I've also noticed that Stefan, a Polish geophysicist, seems to have turned against me, and one spring morning I see him exchange a look with a sleek young woman named Simone. When they come back from the break they're both seriously listening to a woman named May who has a sulky mouth and is wearing a quilted jacket with silver buttercups stencilled on it, and I get so distracted that I can't pay proper attention to anyone else all through the second half of the morning.

After I've dismissed the class, my three spies stay down at the back of the sunny cold room, in deep consultation. Even Stefan, who once smiled at me with such easy affection, now glances up to watch me shrewdly over the words of the two women as if he has just made the decision never to smile at me again. But Constanza has also stayed behind and now comes up to my desk to ask me to explain, please, the difference between a pullover and a pushover. Ordinarily this would be an entertaining and useful question, but this morning I don't feel equal to it. Still, I must try to be. And so I explain the difference between push and pull by hand gestures, then sit down at my desk—*No sitting!*—and make a quick sketch of a sweater. "Pullover," I tell her. But how to explain pushover? I stand again, lift her right hand in mine, plant the flat of it on my own shoulder, then instruct her, "Push at me." She doesn't wish to (what an idea!) but with one eye on my enemies I tell her she must. And so when she halfheartedly pushes at me I stagger feebly backwards, then plunk down in my chair, noticing as I so forcefully sit that I have streaks of chalk on my black skirt, clouds of chalk dust on the sleeves of my black sweater. The three gossips down at the back of the room are now gazing at me, dumbstruck. If only Costanza would get into the spirit of it all a bit more so that my spies would understand that I'm only doing a bit of innovative teaching! But when I try to explain myself to them as they are on their way out, they only smile at me with a frighteningly glassy approximation of harmlessness that must mean that they've written me off and so they don't want to hear.

MY WORLD RE-ORDERS ITSELF. What's heavy is bad, what's light is good. When I hand out work to my students, I make the assignments short and to the point. "Write a six-line poem," I write on the blackboard, then I collect fifteen lightweight pages of jingles that I take home on the train with me. The poem by Miroslav, my exuberant Russian, even makes me smile so much that I decide to give him an A on it:

> *We luff*
> *with the seasons*
> *and hate all the time*
> *the Goodness of God*
> *how I wish it was Mein*

Hıgh above the trees at the back of the park, fast-moving summery clouds here and there reveal winter's piercing stars, and as I hurry to Stanopolis the first school night after the holidays, I compare Montreals: the Montreal of a childhood visit, a city that was grand and summery and dappled and monumental and static. The city of my early marriage, a city where a calypso band seemed to be playing "Yellow Bird" in every bistro and the cold slush kept freezing my feet in my low boots. The city the city became when it turned into a city of bombs exploding in mailboxes on peaceful and snowy winter nights.

Lorenzo is already sitting at the seminar table, all brushed and shining in a new sweater the texture of porridge but with a thread of red knitted into its collar. "Let's split the cost of the books. That way we should each save fifty bucks."

Professor Hamilton Swanson—in a peacock-blue pullover, tall, medieval, dark, amused—stands at the far end of the room eating an apple. Between bites, he tells the class that he's brought two stacks of books along with him to give away to two lucky winners. As it happens, I'm feeling very lucky already, having received news in this morning's mail that I've been awarded a Stanopolis Fellowship. "Everyone guess two numbers between one and twenty-five,"

Professor Swanson tells us, indicating with his half-eaten apple the two stacks of books, "and whoever comes closest to the number I have in my head for *this* stack will become this stack's owner. And the same goes for *this* stack."

A tall woman in a black turtleneck, a long-necked Alice in our postmodern wonderland, calls out, "Six and thirteen!"

Next comes a young woman who speaks in a soft but distrustful voice: "Thirteen and fourteen."

Then it's Lorenzo's turn. "Five and nineteen."

I decide to call out the first two numbers that pop into my head, but then wonder how Swanson will pick a winner if the number he has in mind is four, say, and someone chooses three but someone else chooses five. In order not to have a dispute, he'll have to choose one and twenty-five, or so I decide, and so I call out "One and twenty-five," and Swanson chalks my name and the numbers 1 and 25 in the column next to Lorenzo's numbers.

When he has printed everyone's name and guesses up on the blackboard, Swanson turns to face the class. He tosses his chalk up into the air and the whole class watches him catch it. He takes a festive bite from his apple. Does he enjoy having a roomful of people watch him chew? He appears to. He says, "So many names, so many numbers," and we laugh.

"Makes a person feel quite ontologically giddy."

A voice calls out flirtatiously, "Are you going to keep us in suspense forever then?"

"Indeed not," says Swanson. And he tosses his apple core into the wastebasket and returns to the table. How handsome he is, in his tall and grim way! He stacks one pile of books on top of the other pile and walks down the length of the seminar room with them. He sets the stack down between Lorenzo and me. But of course. Lady Luck has always loved Lorenzo.

"Winner take all," says Swanson, but he isn't speaking to Lorenzo, he's speaking to me.

"Are you clairvoyant?" is the question everyone keeps asking me during the coffee break.

"I just thought he might have a system."

"Really quite awesome, the way you guessed both the numbers," says a tall fair-haired young man with a prominent bony nose. He has a sunburned British look, like an advertisement for something nautical. But he says he's a Greek. "From Griss," he tells me, with a lofty smile.

I find him appealing and wonder how old he might be. "You look and sound British. And how can you be a Greek and have a name like Charles?"

"I don't know how I did it, but I did it. My name is Charles and I am a Grik."

HURRYING ALONG Sherbrooke in a snow squall, I bump into the bear hug of an unexpected embrace and look up to see William Lindstrom.

"Hey, Kay! Are you living in this part of the city now?"

We hustle down to Encore Une Fois, come into it to see that there's no one in the place but the owner. As we're pulling off our coats, I say in a low voice to William, "Look at what he's reading."

William glances over at him. It's *Daniel Deronda*. "Montreal," he says. "The literate city. Except that it's not, since everyone does nothing but speak Franglais here." But the owner is already on his way over to take our order, and while we're ordering the pumpkin soup, I can feel William study me with his sad blue eyes. Something lost about them, some old desperation.

Because I'm afraid that my sweater might be grubby, I stroke my silk scarf outward so that it nearly covers the front of it while I tell him what it's like, being a schoolgirl again.

"I wrote to you a few times, but the letters came back."

"The last time I moved, I didn't fill out the postal form with my new address on it."

He stretches and sighs. "The really weird thing about my running into you like this is that I was recently in a position to do you a favour. You remember my friend Lew Quick?"

"I met him once. But this was years ago."

"He's editing a series of short novels for Macmillan and when I suggested you he said yes, I definitely want her in my series. The problem was, no one knew where to find you."

"I'm even working on a novel that I soon hope to finish."

"What's it called?"

"Mr. Taciturn."

"So what's it about?"

"It's about life's pettiness and cruelty. There's also a lot of sex in it." His smile is uneasy.

"At first I wanted it to be about a writer. And about the second chance the writer gives to life itself, plundering it in the name of art. But now it's about an architect who is unjustly accused of something. I might have a beautiful building he designs collapse because of a terrible mistake one of his contractors makes. The contractor he calls Mr. Taciturn. Who gives him bad advice and who is, essentially, a fool."

"Am I in it by any chance?"

"Why? Would you want to be?"

"I wouldn't mind."

"Okay then, you are."

"I thought so."

But while we're drinking our coffee he asks me if I do much revising.

"Thirteen ways of looking at a blackbird. Fifty ways to leave your lover ..."

Later in the evening, smoke blows into my bedroom from the direction of the hospital smokestacks at the Queen E, and when I go over to my window to pull down the sash I can see that it's snowing again. I want to use William in the novel, want to use the afternoon with him in the Lord Elgin Hotel. I could make him small, French, pale, black, Indonesian, American. But then he will no longer be the same person. I want to use Professor Heubner too, the way she lunges toward the blackboard to draw excited diagrams with her chalk while she wildly calls back to the class over a shoulder, "Primary mimesis! Secondary mimesis!" Also want to catch her eccentricities, making it clear that I understand why eccentrics are surprised that anyone else should find them eccentric. They are deeply practical people, but they have too much imagination to be practical in any sort of ordinary way. Their practicalities are bizarre. But not to them.

I DECIDE TO KILL two birds with one stone and use some of the material from my Modern American Lit class for my first paper for Hamilton Swanson. I could call it "Good Writing, Bad Writing, Old Writing, New Writing: An Examination of Minimalism Using *King Lear* as Paradigm." But when Lorenzo calls me on Thursday night and I tell him my title, he laughs. "I don't know if Ham will go for it though...."

I say no, no, listen, he might, and I read him a few lines from the part of my paper that deals with *King Lear*: "At times the writing descends to the simple diction of a first-grade primer with its 'Help, help, O, help!' and its 'Run, run, O, run,'" then I tell him that I'd love to use him as a model for a character in my novel. "Because I need yet another shrewd handsome man."

"Use me, baby."

After we've said goodbye, I pull on a sweater, then sit at my dining-room table to write: "In reviewing or analyzing a work of fiction, how much does lifting lines out of context violate the bond of trust between writer & reader? And if the lines—"

But now the phone is ringing again, it's Lorenzo again, and so this time I carry it into my bedroom, then lie stretched across my bed with it placed on my belly. After we've talked for nearly three hours and seem to be on the point of saying goodbye he tells me that he's been feeling that our relationship is ready to move onto a new plane, that we're very close now, true, but that our relationship now needs to move into an even more intense closeness. By this time my right ear and my right wrist are aching. I move the phone to my left ear, loop its cord around my most achy wrist.

"Something is missing right now," he tells me.

I ask in a small voice, "What's missing?"

"You're my best friend," he tells me sternly. "And since you *are* my best friend, I don't see why all my needs can't be met."

It's the most unromantic sexual invitation that I have ever received, there's nothing about his being attracted to me, nothing about desire. I know all about his deficiencies as a lover too, from the terrible things the young women have accused him of. And then he has also, just as often, accused himself. It's one of his great charms as a friend, the fact that he never makes self-righteous pronouncements. I suppose what I want, really, is to keep him as my best friend forever. I also can't help paraphrasing, but only to myself, those eternally useful lines from Marvell ("The phone's a fine and private place, but none I think do there embrace …") and so I only say, "You must know how much I value you as a friend."

"How much?"

I'm uneasily flattered to hear how raw with hope his voice sounds. And after warning myself not to say "with all my heart," I finally give in and say it.

"Oh, *that*." His voice so flat with disappointment that we both have to shakily laugh. And into the half ease of that laughter, I quickly say, "It would be insane for us to go to bed together, we both know that."

"We don't know that."

I admire him for saying this, even if he doesn't really mean it. But toward morning I dream that he comes to my door with snow in his hair and he's carrying his distrustful boy's look high up in his eyes. He follows close behind me as I walk down the hall to my room, then makes tenderly violent love to me on the top of my bedspread. During part of the dream he's Galbraith. Then he's himself again and making some joke about the bedspread being plowed. I wake up with a nearly unbearable ache in my back.

After breakfast I remember that I've promised to critique his novel (he's calling it "Sophia") and I pull it out of its envelope. "Possibly needs another title," I write. "Something more pictorial, something with more of a narrative in it." But as I begin to read it I'm back in the Italy of 1938, the sun hot on the streets of Florence. A young doctor is cycling past the Duomo on his way to his hospital for the evening shift. When he gets up to his ward the nursing sister leads him to the bed of a new patient, a beautiful young widow who's been admitted with weight loss and fever. "What virtues does this woman possess," I write in the margin, "besides being beautiful?" The best scene is set on a cold grey winter day on the Ponte Vecchio. The doctor and the widow are choosing a ring for her at one of the tourist jewellery shops, a yellow stone shop that's less tacky in January than in summer. "This is wonderful," I write. But by this time I've skipped ahead, then gone back to the middle again, and so I know that Sophia (who's not so young, really, she's actually twelve years older than the doctor) has been diagnosed with tuberculosis and that at the beginning of the second week of World War II—by now it's October in Tuscany—she will die. The novel's final scene is of the doctor walking with her two little boys on Via Guelfa, taking them out for ice cream cones the day after her funeral. I praise it, but about several of the other scenes I write "Possibly omit" or "Too stodgy" or "This whole section could go."

On Thursday afternoon I give my seminar on *The Late Bourgeois World* and on our way out of class Lorenzo tells me it was good. But you kept saying 'vunnerable' instead of 'vulnerable.'"

"Oh damn, I always do that. But I only used it once, didn't I?"

"Actually, you used it twice."

Which is when it occurs to me that now would be as good a time as any to give his novel back to him and so I pull it out of my briefcase.

He smiles his irresistible smile. "Were you kind to me?"

"Off and on. But why does every male writer have to kill a woman in his first novel? You sit in your little garrets all over the world and you all get struck by the same brilliant idea: kill a woman."

"I promise to kill a man in my next novel."

ANOTHER SNOWY AFTERNOON and no letters, a dull fact that makes me feel tired of everything. But when I let myself into my apartment I see that I was wrong, there's a letter after all, someone has slid an envelope under my door, square and white in the afternoon gloom, and it's as if I exist once again. I even feel lighthearted as I turn on the lamps and go into my kitchen to run water into a saucepan for soup. Then I go back to the door to pick up my envelope. It doesn't have anything written on it, and so (mystified) I pick up my butter knife to slice it open, then unfold it to read:

Dear Kay,

If we are to remain friends, then perhaps it will be best if you don't read (or at least don't comment on) any more of my work.

Lorenzo

How direct this is, how much more direct than I could ever be. It makes me realize that I should have said more kind things, I should have commented on his eloquence, his fine gift for pacing. But how sensitive men are. So deeply tactful, so easily hurt. At least the best of them are. I'll just finish my soup, then I'll call him.

But he isn't at home. And so I begin to work on my poem. If it's good enough I'll send it off to a contest I saw announced on a flyer I picked up at school last week. One of the jurors is Georgia Switzer. I consider possible titles: Letter to a Younger Man in Another Country, She Bends to Praise Him, I Think of You All the Time. But Georgia will never choose my poem, to her I'll always be the girl she didn't choose to be Joan of Arc. But then I look down at the contest rules to see that the contestants will be identified only by numbers. I could cry with gratitude, and even though I know I should be working on my novel, I want even more to work on my poem, I want the woman in the poem to discover that there's only one letter waiting for her at the post office, a letter she feels a flash of hatred for because it comes from the wrong country. By bedtime I've finished the third draft. I feel so grateful to Galbraith. I feel joy, gratitude, tenderness, heartlessness. With the magic wand of two hundred words and more emotion than I've ever used in writing about him—writing to him—I've turned him into material.

Aɴᴏᴛʜᴇʀ ɢʀᴇʏ ᴅᴀʏ, greyly snowing, grey snow falling beyond the tall windows of the correct narrow room as I study my classmates. So many snowed-in, tired faces. Even the plaid skirts and Icelandic sweaters are all grey and white and the parkas are either gunmetal grey or the kind of dull police blue that might just as well be grey, to go with the winterized grey raincoats. Only two spots of colour, both at the far end of the room: Hamilton Swanson, today in an apple-green sweater and, to his right, his apple-green apple.

I glance over at Lorenzo to see that he's staring with severe fatigue down at his notes, then open my notebook to a clean page to write: "What is a Canadian? Someone who smiles too much, above all someone who smiles too much in the winter. Smiles in pain against the unbearable cold," then I write: "Hey diddle diddy, I'm ontologically giddy," and I do a little sketch of a roast pig on a platter, its mouth propped open with a perfect polished apple. Underneath it, I print ʜᴀᴍ ᴀɴᴅ ʜɪs ᴀᴘᴘʟᴇ. Not that there's anything particularly pig-like about Ham, he's too noble and handsome (in his own sour way), a sour, displaced monarch who makes me wonder what colours a king would wear if he inherited a whole kingdom of sweaters. Ruby would be one, but if Swanson owns a ruby pullover he hasn't modelled it for us yet. And sapphire: I seem to remember the night he wore a sweater that could be called that. I draw whiskers all around the word *ruby* and am drawing a plump little blue bird in a scratchy blue nest in the word's whiskers when I change my mind and decide to do a quick sketch of the tense little person Lorenzo has secretly nicknamed Sparkle Plenty because she wears so many diamonds: diamond studs in her ears, a diamond bracelet, tiny diamond-embedded silver lobster claws attaching her watch face to its diamond watch-band, a woman drained and tanned and bleached and hardened and frightened by money, a woman who lives at the top of the mountain and yet says unbelievable things like "I'm a single mum with three kids, I've paid my dues." But then I change my mind and instead decide to draw Shannon, a woman who sits across from me and who often makes me laugh. I draw her Bo-peepish face and her short curly grey hair and her curly darker grey cardigan whose curls are so tiny and tight they almost look pubic. Since she looks so much like a sheep (but a ravishing sheep) I picture her singing with a musical group called SHANNON AND THE SHEEPETTES. I've just printed SHEEPETTES under the sketch when I hear Swanson's voice say "Kay? You've been taking a good many notes, I see, and so perhaps you'd like to give us your thoughts on this point."

I close my notebook and look up. At Swanson first, then at Lorenzo.

Lorenzo pretends to scratch at his head and tips back in his chair to tilt up his book so that I can see its title: *The Taming of the Shrew*.

Thank you, my friend.

I'm still at a loss though. "I'm sure this will seem to be awfully remote from the discussion at hand," I say, "but it's something I've been planning to bring up for quite some time … it really isn't at all academic though, but it still might be a point worth raising—"

My classmates are watching me with a glazed communal expression of exhaustion and boredom, and here I am, stalling, then hopping from foot to foot. "…But in a book I've been reading recently, a sort of compendium of sex questionnaires, one of the women being inter-viewed talked about how she wasn't able to have orgasms with her lover...."

The other students seem to rouse themselves out of their long winter nap at this point and turn to me with one face, one heart. And it's an amazed and tender face, it's a grateful and tender heart. Even Swanson—or perhaps Swanson most of all?—is gazing at me with a shaken look of real affection, as if his whole life he's been waiting for someone to say exactly this. Only Lorenzo's expression conveys alarm for me, the startled concern of a friend for a friend.

"—and her lover wanted to help her—" People are now nearly smiling, but at the same time they seem to be feeling too sexually serious to smile. "... and so he said it made him feel very very sad that they couldn't have orgasms together, that he so much wished there was something he could do for her, and it was at this point that she decided to tell him that she'd always had fantasies of being spanked. And so, although he had never done that kind of thing to anyone before ..." I pause, not for effect, but out of the breathless fear that I just can't go on. "But I have to warn you that this is not at all academic...."

"On the contrary," says Swanson. Then he tells me that it's very *much* to the point of the discussion we've just been having. "Please," he says, looking ill with the desire to have me continue, "carry on."

Beyond the classroom's closed door, I can hear someone call out to someone. "So then he did," I say. "Spank her. And it really worked. After a while she even discovered that she didn't need him to do it any more. Because by then it was clear that she could have orgasms without—" I stop. I really can't go on any longer, I'm too afraid I might laugh. Laugh or cry.

"Without the spanking?" Swanson tenderly asks me.

I tell him yes and when the class is at last over, Lorenzo formally stands. He looks like a man on the point of asking a woman to dance.

I gather up my books to go to him, but Charles is all at once at my elbow, but keeping his voice low. "Say, Kay, listen, if you ever need any help with research for an essay or anything, just give me a call, okay?" And he prints his phone number for me on the top page of my notes.

On the way out of the class, the other students smile at me with amused affection. Only Lorenzo and Shannon are not sending entertained little glances my way. They don't even seem to want to discuss what happened in class as we're walking across the campus in the misty snowy night. Shannon instead talks about being the theatre seamstress for a local production of *As You Like It,* and when I ask her if this means she has to sew all the costumes herself she says, "Mostly I glue things."

As we're walking down the steps to the quad, Lorenzo glances over at her. "Glue things?"

The library building is already looming to our left. "Glass gumdrops on velvet!" she calls over a shoulder as she's turning onto its path with her armload of books.

But as Lorenzo and I are walking on through the foggy falling snow to the metro, he's smiling into the air just above my hair. "So how old would you say Charles *is,* anyway? Nineteen? Twenty?"

"I don't know. Maybe twenty. And I'm really, really hoping he won't call me."

"He won't, he'll be too shy to. He's just hoping that you will call *him.*"

"But the story I told in class was an endearing story, I thought."

"Uh-huh."

"Very human."

"Very. But doesn't the potential for violence bother you? Or do you see it as a playful enacting of the violence that men have been subjecting women to, over the centuries? Or forever, basically."

I tell him that I'm afraid of any kind of violence but that anything that turns it into something playful interests me. "And spanking and hitting are so totally different. As different as sky-diving and porridge."

"So which is the sky-diving and which is the porridge?"

But as we step into our train, I only smile.

He smiles too. "And who's to say it wouldn't have led to wife-beating in the end? Something like that, how can you tell what way it'll go? It's like playing around with the occult."

I glance down at the book on his knees, Foucault's *Discipline and Punish*, a book I haven't even begun to read yet, even though I'm supposed to have finished it by now. "Possibly women letting men do this to them gives men a false sense of power, now that the days of their real power are gone. And as you say, it can also just be playful and innocent. Look at little boys playing war games. They aren't going to grow up to join the army just because they've played at being soldiers."

"You don't know that."

"But I do. And so do you."

"No, I don't."

"Little boys have played war games since time immemorial."

"We've also had wars since time immemorial."

I picture Tom and Benno as children, firing at one another with their fake silver pistols, then ducking and running while trailing joyful long hissing noises. They were the tanks and planes, but they were also the wounded, falling to the ground within a breath of each other's faces.

"So," says Lorenzo, getting to the heart of the matter. "Did you ever have it done to you?"

"A few times. It was with someone I loved, but I don't see him any more."

"Where is he now?"

"He's married to a woman who works as a simultaneous interpreter in New York City...."

"So tell me what it was like."

I look out the window and see our reflections as the black brick walls of the tunnel go flying by. "It felt just wrong enough to be fun. As if we were children again and pulling off clothes and rolling around on the grass. Spank, spank. Bad, bad."

"But what about this whole questionnaire business?"

"The questionnaire as confessional. The reader as priest."

But we're already roaring into Lionel Groulx and I need to change trains.

Alone on the platform I feel regret. Fond as I am of Lorenzo, I regret talking to him about Galbraith. I feel like a milkmaid who has spoken a forbidden word, done a forbidden thing. Now I will never see my darling prince again.

Wᴴᴱɴ ɪ ᴛʜɪɴᴋ of the differences between being friends with a man and in love with a man—not that I consider myself any kind of expert on men as either friends or lovers—it seems to me that the conversations with the man who's the friend are more thoughtful, but with the man who's the lover it's all improvisation, it's all repartee. But it's repartee with an agenda—"I'm going to charm you into giving me everything I need and you will give it gladly...." Or so I decide, turning my head on my pillow to look up at a row of pigeons posed with such heroic rectitude that they must be pretending to be falcons or Mexican stone birds as they guard the roof opposite my open window against the dawn's early light. But at this same moment the phone shrieks, scattering them into a flurry of more ordinary birds (pigeons, for example) and I glance down at my watch to see that it's much later than dawn, it's nearly ten, and the woman at the other end of the line is telling me she's the secretary for the League of Poets and the reason she's calling is to let me know that my poem about the younger lover is the winner of this year's L'Heureux-Chandler Prize. "It won the first prize, actually, the catch being that the two other winners are first-prize winners as well. Our usual practice is to award a first prize of a thousand dollars, a second prize of seven hundred dollars and a third prize of five hundred dollars, but this year the jurors just couldn't decide between the three of you, you are all just too too wonderful, and so we're spreading the joy, so to speak."

I should spend the rest of the day on school work, but the news of the prize has had such a corrupting effect on me that I spend it walking along Sherbrooke Street, daydreaming and visiting dress boutiques where the dresses hang in recessed archways, hit by spot-lights, and every time I walk down the steps into a boutique it's like visiting a museum exhibition on the history of the dress, then on my way back home (minus a new dress) I go down more stone steps to a basement gallery to visit a neo-minimalist exhibition of the work of a group of South American painters, purely for the reason that it's just been in New York and so there's a chance that Galbraith might have seen it. The predominant colours are blurred reds, strong blues, fog greys, faces outlined in thick black—Rouault comes to Guatemala—along with one large mural that looks as if the painter dipped a giant brush into a pail of urine mixed with gold paint, then drew the brush in a bubbled trajectory across the huge canvas. And it could be anything—a comet, a field of wild grasses and buttercups—but when I stand reading the list of terrible ingre-dients printed in a box of text I see that the paint was made from human cadaver grease, rendered from body parts after autopsies, that it's a mural painted in a context in which premature dying and murder have become everyday phenomena. This news, along with the squeamish sensation I've been feeling ever since walking down the steps to the gallery and the smell of at least forty years of paint and dust, makes me hurry up to the street again to breathe the somewhat less contaminated air, and after dinner I make use of the gallery material for my novel, picture G as he visits galleries and museums until his eyes feel like "museum eyes," they keep burning because he keeps forgetting to blink.

MUSEUM EYES

He goes to the Whitney and the Frick and the Met, he walks the
upward spiral of the Guggenheim—the museum he once told K is
the world's most revered parking garage—and on the way down he
stops to look at paintings saturated with colour—reds, browns, bold
bars of black—and next to them the inevitable painters' manifestos.
Then he visits two or three galleries in Brooklyn and when he comes
out of the final gallery he goes into a nearby hotel for dinner, the
voices of a group of male singers singing "How deep is your love ..."
over the sound system as he walks back into the lobby after eating a
bowl of soup and a sad salad in the dining room. The voices of the
singers sound supremely self-satisfied, like a barbershop quartet, but
there's something soothing about the musical arrangement too, an
undersea heartbeat, a sub-aquatic boom-boom that lulls him as he's
crossing the lounge but just as he's about to push his way out to the
street he's thunderstruck to see K waiting for the elevator, her by
now darker hair brushing her shoulders, the laddered grey strap of
her Guatemalan shoulder bag completely familiar to him as she's
standing talking to a tall man who looks Swedish or German, and
he sprints to the elevator, reaches it just in time to squeeze into it as
the doors are closing, but the woman, seen from the front, is of
course not at all like K. He nevertheless follows her and her friend
when they get out on the seventh floor, then walks behind the
woman because she has turned into K once again, but after he has
followed them for ten paces or so, she glances back at him, suspicious,
and so he turns a corner, walks along another hallway and ends up
looking down through a window at a view of a red clay Brooklyn
tennis court with green nets, walled at its far end by the blank wall
of a tenement that's painted a utilitarian warehouse grey.

Two WOMEN POETS are spastically dancing together in a spoof of a jitterbug and we (an audience of poets) are all watching them, the male poets in their leather jackets, the women poets in their snazzy dresses. One of the dancing women looks hyperthyroid, but she has expressive eyes and she's wearing her hazy brown hair brushed high into an upsweep, its platter of frizz tipped forward like the tilt of a hat and her long debutante gloves (black gloves, not white) go with her 1940s dress of black and white silky stripes slashed on the diagonal. She makes me feel that I ought to have bought myself a smashing dress too, but what I really ought to have done was buy myself a pair of high-heeled black shoes so that I could elegantly cross this shining floor to claim my money and read my poem. Now I'll have to schlep up to the microphone in my heavy monk's sandals, then stand reading my poem while looking sternly artistic and drab and I'm also feeling too swimmy in my head, as if I might faint, and now the music and dancing have come to a stop, the dancers are already on their way back to their chairs and there's the clear ping of a spoon being struck against a wineglass at the head table as a portly poet in a tuxedo comes to the microphone and raises it to the proper height to make a little speech about the pleasure of having so many wonderful poets in attendance, "along with the whole crowd of poets who are sharing the first prize"—this gets scattered laughter—"and we are also delighted to also see so many enthusiastic supporters from the great city of Montreal, in fact we've had a remarkable response from both town and gown. But now, dear friends, without more ado, I would like to introduce the first of our three winners. Ladies and gentlemen, please honour Katarina Oleski ..." and he looks out over the crowd for me, but I'm already hurrying behind the outer tables by this time, then approaching him from behind his right elbow.

"Ah," he says. "Katarina. Here you are ..." And he lowers the microphone for me.

I read my poem, not knowing if everyone can hear me, not knowing what sort of reception it's getting since I'm too shaky to look up, I'm only convinced that I'm reading it in a voice pitched too high into an unnatural, pigeon-toed voice that everyone must be hearing as the voice of a woman who has never been loved, a woman who has never loved. On my way back to my table, a male hand even shoots out, pulls me to sit down on the empty chair next to him. "So you wrote a love poem. But haven't love poems gone the way of the dodo?"

"Shhhh!" hisses a woman on the other side of the table. "The next reader is reading...."

The next reader—it's the woman with the long black debutante gloves—reads a poem that is short and sunny. But the third poem feels too forced and baroque.

After dinner, when coffee is being served by a flotilla of students, the lanky poet sidles up to me once again, asks me the dodo question once again.

"It's true," says a woman in a lace dress who's standing next to me. "Love is no longer a proper subject for poetry. Not in the twentieth century. Now that we live in the age of irony, in the age of the mundane, in the age of despair."

"In the age of remorse," says one of the men from our table.

"In the age of *Schadenfreude*," says a clever man whose entertained eyes gleam at me.

"In the age of all that jazz," says a boy dressed all in black.

As soon as I decently can, I go off to find a washroom and on my way pass a crowd of poets whose eyes are medieval as they watch me walk by. I feel certain that they must have just been saying harsh things about me or my poem, and once I'm in the washroom combing my hair, a younger woman comes in and begins to do her eyes, and I get the impression that she's mainly doing them so she can watch me in the mirror.

"Your poem was great, by the way," she tells me, surprising me. "I loved it. The way you were reading it, it sounded as if you just sat down and wrote it in five minutes, it was that inspired."

Grateful to her, I turn to tell her that I actually worked on it night and day.

"That's good to know."

Then I study her in the mirror too, this mischievous, generous poet in the red Spanish dress with a diagonal flounce and the pattern of big white camellias on it, the matching white flower in her hair, her dancer's slim torso suggesting the red stem of a flower, now she's washing her hands, then flapping them to dry in the air, then she's poking around for something in her tiny beaded white evening bag. Her lipstick. When she uncaps it, it's as red as her dress, and after she has applied it, she turns to glance back at me. "Your poem was the real winner, as a matter of fact. It was the real and literal winner of the first prize, but then the jury decided to take the prize away from you and split it with the second and third prize winners, thereby also depriving you of a thousand dollars."

I stare at her in the mirror, then turn to stare at her actual self.

"Giving you, however, a consolation prize of seven hundred bucks."

"But why ever would they do a thing like that?"

"Because once they'd turned the winning numbers over to the League, and the League matched the winning numbers with the names, it was discovered that you were that most unholy of unholies, a fiction writer. You'd also never had even one poem published in a magazine, you hadn't written a single poetry book, you were not a member of the League, you hadn't paid your dues, baby...."

"My mother knew Georgia Switzer years ago," I tell her, hugging myself darkly. "They were part of the same crowd, and when I was ready to send off my poem, I worried that Georgia would never vote for it, that to her I would always be a child, but then I remembered that my name wouldn't appear anywhere on the poem and so I felt safe."

"After all, the whole point of a blind competition is to prevent exactly the kind of thing the jury was doing—"

"Yes," I say. Yes, yes, *yes*. "And how could Georgia justify such a thing to her*self?*"

"She belongs to the school that believes jurors should first of all look after their own."

"And so are the other winners her friends?"

"They are. But then again the poetry community is so very tiny in this country, everyone knows everyone." She snaps her little purse shut and gazes into my eyes. A deep look that's somehow both distrustful and tender. "So you knew the Switzer family well, then?"

"I didn't know Georgia well, but I did know her younger brother well because he came to stay with my family the summer their mother died. And Georgia was also my teacher for one year in high school...."

The door is pushed open, a plump woman peers in at us, then comes trotting in, her tiny steps unsteady, her bracelets drunkenly tinkling and jingling.

My informant and I exchange a glance in the mirror. No more talking. But in spite of resenting what was done to me by Georgia and her jury, I also find myself feeling excited: when all I was expecting was a dull evening of speeches and the agony of reading my poem to a company of strangers, I've become a party to the conspiracy of being human.

"Listen," I say, "I want to really thank you for telling me this."

"Tales from the League," she says in a low voice and she signals with her eyes toward the cubicle where the jingling woman is peeing. "Listen, I've got to go."

As I'm on my way out of the main hall an hour later, the awards ceremony over at last, a stocky man in a tan coat who's with a tall woman in green comes walking toward me as if for some time he's been planning to speak to me. "Kay!" he calls as he's on his way over to me. "We really enjoyed your poem!" When he reaches me, he warmly takes both of my hands in his and talks on for a bit: tremendous poem and a great little crowd too, town and gown, etc. "It's thanks to Georgia, really, that we're here," he tells me. "Mimi and I are living out in Pointe Claire, and Georgia invited us to come along for the dinner. She was on the jury that picked your poem, as you probably already know."

So this is Derek, then. A short handsome man who is the prototype for the small army of men I've fallen for, over the years.

"But is Georgia here tonight?"

"She's living in San Diego these days, but she must be here somewhere, because we have her coat…." And I begin to be afraid that I'll have to talk to her and I all at once want to get away before she comes, I'm also afraid that he'll suggest that we all get together for an evening of biscuits and sherry, I'm already trying to think of reasons why I won't be able to go, and yet it isn't that I hold our sexual encounter against him, our single ten minutes of love in the afternoon, it's simply that I don't want to return to the past. "But you're a writer," I can hear a voice cry. "The past is the writer's stock in trade! The past is the writer's *life*." Yes and no. Or yes: my own private past is my stock in trade, but I don't want to go back there to see what happened to the people I used to know back then. Not even the people I especially liked. I especially don't want to meet the people I especially liked! But he doesn't suggest we meet again, he doesn't have the chance to. "Oh, here she is," he says and we all turn to await the arrival of Georgia, walking toward us with her brilliant gaze—walking toward us like a prophet out of the Bible, the woman who cast a vote (or a stone) against me—she's in a long white caftan with a grilled gold bib inset at her throat, her pinned-up fair hair going white at the temples. She clasps both of my hands in hers as she says in her deep sexy voice, "So this is Kay," a voice I now tell myself I ought to assess for deceit. "And I must tell you, Kay, that when I first read your poem I simply fell on it with a cry of joy, it was so much more emotional than the other poems …" and I forgive her for everything. On my way down the stone steps into the cool spring evening, I even ask myself: Who knows how these decisions are made? Georgia might not even have had all that much to do with it, but on the way home on the bus I remember that even when she was a young woman she had the gaze of a very old and powerful man, someone military, she had such penetrating eyes, eyes that said, "Whatever you know or think you know, forget that you know it."

Waiting in line for the mirrors and trying not to listen to the trickles that are followed by pushed crashes of water, the short pink doors that snap in and out, each woman waits as if she's holding her breath while thinking sad thoughts. Even the younger women seem sad, although less so, as they study their faces in the mirror with a workmanlike calm that suggests they aren't yet ready to believe that the future will ever happen to them.

When I come back into the lobby, Lorenzo is talking to Lara, who has come on her own to see *Amadeus*. We talk for a few minutes, then Lorenzo looks at his watch and says that he has to get home and finish his essay on *Discipline and Punish*.

"When I came out into the lobby," I tell him as we're walking along Sherbrooke Street, "from the way you and Lara were talking, you looked like lovers."

"We might have looked that way, but that's not what we are."

And so I can't ask him anything more, it would be prying. But when I get home, out of loneliness I look for Galbraith in the new phone book and find a listing for an M. Galbraith in Dollard-des-Ormeaux. I get out my street map. But Dollard-des-Ormeaux is a patch of barely inhabited green, a green country of golf courses and miles of green land waiting for the armies of developers, not Galbraith's sort of place at all, and so I doubt it can be him. Even so, when I sit down to write about him, I write about him as if he also saw a movie tonight in the cinema complex where Lorenzo and I saw *Blue Velvet:*

CRIMES OF THE HEART

What they have in common is their baby boy, when he comes home from work at night they sit on the sofa and worship their small son together. He's their church, he's their new religion. But he's also a religion they need to get away from in the evenings, and on the nights that he doesn't have meetings they go out. To the movies, to bars, looping down from the mountain and into this theatrical city whose topography has become almost as exciting as the skyline of New York. In the lobby of the movie complex, G lights a tense cigarette, then as he tilts his head back to exhale he looks up to the upper level to see K riding down on the escalator. Here she is, sinking past him, her eyes looking straight ahead. She's wearing a man's white shirt tucked into one of her narrow black skirts, and on this rainy but cold spring night she's also wearing her winter boots. She's also looking fatter around the waist and her expression of dreamy but dignified myopia makes him realize that she's not wearing her contacts. She also appears to be alone.

But he's wrong about this, as the escalator slides its bottom steps into the floor, the dark young man who's been standing two steps below her (the man whose back she bumps into at the bottom) turns to say something to her, and when he does she shoves back the cuff of one of his jacket sleeves so she can check the time by his watch. Over his other arm he's carrying a raincoat that must be hers because what she does next is dip her hand into one of its pockets and fish out her glasses. He wonders if this guy is Italian. He must be. Spanish or Italian. He has a riverboat gambler's moustache that gives his good looks a dangerously Sicilian touch. But by now fifteen or twenty people are drifting over to stand in line for *Blue Velvet*—K and her friend among them—and the usher is already unhooking the red velvet rope so that the line-up can move forward.

G detours close to her on his way to buy more popcorn but she doesn't see him and so she doesn't know the hold she still has over him: her nearsighted but serene charisma, her hips in the well-fitting black skirt. As for the Italian, when the usher unhooks the red velvet rope, he walks behind her with his arms hanging down. Like an ape, thinks G, like a rubber-kneed boy or a baboon whose arms are hanging so low that his knuckles nearly graze the carpet, he doesn't even rest his right hand on her lower back as he steers her into the dark cave leading to their movie.

But now G has to go with J into the other theatre, the one that's showing *Crimes of the Heart*, the magnified American voices speaking in their echoey accents from the Deep South making him feel apprehensive as they walk down the aisle to find themselves seats, he's going to be trapped with these loudspeaker voices inside a hollow tin drum and won't be released until the movie is over. After half an hour has passed, he whispers to J, "Need a smoke and a piss," then he's on his way up the dark aisle, overjoyed to be making even this small escape from the magnified twang as he follows the sign to Toilettes, then comes back out again to stand in the lobby, smoking and hoping that K will come out because she, too, will need to find a washroom. She has to come, every goddamn movie he ever saw with her had to be interrupted by her excusing her way past at least three pairs of knees, but she doesn't come, no one comes, and so he walks from poster to poster, rehearsing a look of surprise and reading the movie times for *Blue Velvet* to discover that it doesn't get out until twenty minutes after *Crimes of the Heart,* although even that will still be a whole hour from now, and a mad thought occurs to him: he could go into the wrong theatre by mistake, look for the gleam of a white shirt in the darkness, sit somewhere near it or behind it, bump into her on their way out, but how could he ever explain his long absence to J? The whole scheme is deranged. But on his way back to see what's left of *Crimes of the Heart,* he changes direction and he goes into the theatre for *Blue Velvet.* He slips into the darkness, then goes down to the front, finds himself a seat in the empty front row, gets trapped down here in the depths, assaulted by new giant faces and new magnified voices for three or four minutes, then he gets up and slowly walks up the aisle, looking to both right and left. And easily spots K and the Italian sitting about ten rows back, their eyes aimed in solemn unison at the screen. He bends to tie a shoe, and when he stands straight again he fakes a coughing fit. But no one looks over at him—no one!—and so he has no choice but to keep walking up the aisle and return to *Crimes of the Heart.*

"I saw a cockroach two days ago," I tell Benno in a low voice, as if I'm afraid Mohammed and his wife (Kelly) might overhear.

"So? Everyone's got them."

"And so I went out and bought a Roach Motel. And then almost right away a cockroach walked into it." I go out to the kitchen, then come back to the front room with the little brown box. "But look—"

He peers inside it. "What's all that stuff around it? Like soot—"

"Babies!"

"You're in luck then, you've annihilated a dynasty."

But the poor little cockroach, caught when she was pregnant. And the babies too, coming out into a world that's a glassy pavement of glue, but I know better than to say so, Benno will only accuse me of crying crocodile tears. "So they must be all over the building then.

Which means that any day now Mohammed will knock on my door and tell me that he's been given orders to spray."

"You can refuse, can't you?"

"But then they'll make a mass exodus from all the other apartments and come up to live at my place."

The next night as I'm working on an essay for my Woolf class, there's a knock on my door.

I open it, trying not to look guilty.

Mohammed, spiffily dressed, is gazing too deeply into my eyes. "Seen any roaches?"

"Only one," I tell him.

"There is never only just one cockroach," says Mohammed.

"I hope you aren't going to spray, I really can't stand the fumes." A reek I remember all too well from my Randall Avenue days: the lethal blend of pesticide spray and floor wax.

"It's a powder this time, perfectly safe, we're doing both sections of the building, we do it at least twice a year, no complaints. Just make sure there are no pets in here. And no children. And put away all your food. And your dishes."

Then how safe can it be? But I have no choice, I do as I'm told.

WHEN I GET BACK home at six, cockroaches are crawling out of the woodwork. They wobble and fall and pitifully struggle up to try to walk once again. They are as dusted with the poisonous white powder as miniature workmen—tiny men in dust-whitened overalls who have to work up in the high scaffolding of a heartless high tower.

I wake up in the morning to feel a fly close to my throat. But it isn't a fly, it's a dead cockroach, lying like a reproach on its back, where it has now slipped down close to the décolletage of my nightgown. I carry it out to the kitchen, drop it into the garbage pail, then pull off my nightgown and drop it to the floor. My throat is dry and I begin to worry that the cockroach walked over my mouth with its tiny poison-dusted feet while I was sleeping. In the kitchen I wash my hands and then lean down and cup both my hands to wash out my mouth with tiny pools of stale-tasting tap water. I'm on my way to the bathroom for my shower when I remember that I'm naked. I pull a dishtowel off the towel rack and hold it in front of my breasts as I go to yank the curtain closed—another thing to remember, I must throw this possibly poison-dusted towel and my contaminated nightgown into the wash when I'm on my way to the shower—which is when I see a flash of white shirt moving away from a window in one of the apartments on the other side of the courtyard. *Damn,* why didn't I think of pulling on my kimono? But I know why: I didn't want to contaminate it with the poison dust. Still, the choreography that led up to this particular series of star-crossed events makes me feel a bond with the dead cockroach, makes me see him as a doomed pawn in the great (and also doomed) toxic pond of the world.

At bedtime I go down the hall to the kitchen to check the fire-escape door. I picture a face at one of the courtyard's dark windows, watching me. And it's a job that even an amateur could do, breaking in.

In bed I lean on an elbow and read from a book of haiku:

> *O, don't mistreat*
> *the fly! He wrings his hands!*
> *He wrings his feet!*

And at some point during the night I sit up, my heart wild with the imperative to listen. Then I get out of bed and walk down the hall to the kitchen, try the lock on the fire-escape door once again. But it's intact. I peer up at the sky above the courtyard. There's no moon, only the grey sky of four o'clock on a city morning.

In the evening I phone Lorenzo and we talk about Foucault and depression and whether Lorenzo (in an essay, footnoting a book by Lentricchia) was or was not flirting with Cy Stackpole the time he spelled Lentricchia's name Lentriccccchia. We also talk about his women, his problems with women, his fantasies about suicide, his father—"Although I've given up on God and my father, Freud is my father now"—then just before we say goodnight, I tell him about the dead cockroach.

"Christ," he says. But he laughs. "On your *breast?* What a story."

"You find it entertaining?"

"God, yes."

"Don't tell anyone!"

"My lips are sealed—"

"It always makes me so nervous when you say that...."

But in spite of having sworn him to secrecy, I end up telling Shannon about the cockroach when she calls me about an assignment after my next class with her.

"I'd break my lease, I wouldn't stay there a single night longer, there's no way I'd live in an apartment with cockroaches."

"What about mice?"

"Mice are darling, mice are mammals, I had a pet mouse when I was a wee girl."

Y ESTERDAY MORNING it was sunny and all at once spring again, so that in the late afternoon when I was walking out of one of the ground floor elevators at Stanopolis reading "The High Brutality of Good Intentions," I was shocked to look up and see through the dark institutional glass that another crazy snowstorm had blown up. I wasn't even wearing my winter boots, but I had no choice, I had to venture (or slither) forth. On the ride home on the train the other passengers looked saturated with damp, alone, deeply depressed. I got off at Vendôme, then walked down the slippy street in what had become a snowfall turning into rain.

But this morning the rain is blowing like smoke as it sweeps across the needled lake on the flat roof of the building next door, giving me a thrill as I look out at it. Then another thrill, but a bad one: on my way back to the sofa, I catch sight of a blur of movement on the little red rug. A grey mouse is making a beeline for my bedroom. I jump up, do a frantic sideways skip to head it off before it reaches the open door. I'll never sleep again, not if it ends up hiding anywhere in my bedroom! But the long bookcase offers it an escape route and after it has dashed behind it, I pull the shade off a lamp and click the lightbulb on, then shine its light down a narrow tunnel of darkness. Nothing down there but old fluff. But then I can see that one of the balls of fluff has eyes, glassy as boot buttons, and I crouch, a wad of paper towel in one hand, wait for it to make its dash for freedom. When it at last races out, I sideways-skip along beside it again, then pluck it up with a section of the towel. My hand feels crazed holding it, and in an attempt to calm myself I make a small joke: If Mohammed won't come to the mouse, then the mouse must come to Mohammed.

But walking down the stairs to his apartment, I'm trembling at holding something so small and alive in my hand. I'm also praying that Mohammed will be the one to come to the door, not Kelly, I don't want to have to deal with Kelly's prim nurse act. Mohammed is kinder, an Iranian dreamer. But I can't believe that I am actually doing this, holding this mouse that for months has been a rumour, then a swift blur, then an actual mouse that's making me feel a zinged electric pulse in my wrist, in the cup of my hand. As I'm on my way down the final stairway, a curious thing even happens: although I continue to be afraid of it, I also find myself falling a little in love with it. Peering out of its hood of paper towel it's looking so trustingly bright-eyed and adorable, it isn't all terrified heartbeat the way a baby bird would be.

Mohammed, holding his little son in his arms, answers the door, then does a double-take when he sees the mouse. But Anooshiravan, who's dressed in a yellow dress that makes him look like a fat little girl, seems much more pleased than shocked: first to see me, then to see the mouse, peeking so anthropomorphically out of its hood of paper towel. He whimpers and squirms, bleats to be let down. "No, you don't," says Mohammed. "You're not going anywhere."

Anoo throws himself violently back and forth in his father's arms, then sets up such an irritating cawing that Mohammed lets him slide to the floor. But Anoo, instead of reaching up to touch the mouse, laughingly takes off in a run on his hands and knees down the hallway, leading Mohammed to lunge after him, then swoop him up. Then they are back in the doorway again, father and son, staring at the little mouse, exactly as before. "What are we going to do with him," says Mohammed. "What." He stares at the little mouse, then makes a pronouncement. "Flush it down the toilet."

"Oh," I say. "But do you think that would be wise? Wouldn't it ... clog up the plumbing?"

"Not at all," says Mohammed, in his rather firm British English. "Not the least bit."

I try to hand the mouse to Mohammed, but Mohammed only holds fast to Anoo. "I'll press the flush. And you will drop it in."

Feeling doomed, I follow him into his dim apartment. The bathroom, fragrantly muggy with the smell of nylon stockings drying out, is fitted with a child-sized toilet. A mauve nylon blouse of Kelly's is presiding over the scene with its tall row of pearl buttons.

"Ready?"

As ready as I'll ever be. But as the little mouse goes flying down to its death in the whirling water and I'm both touched and horrified by Anooshiravan's shriek of joy, I understand that it's only a baby, and after the harsh gasp has sucked it away, I can hardly bear to look at Mohammed. He seems ashamed too as he kisses Anooshiravan's neck, then plays some guttural and nuzzling game with him.

THE WHINE OF A VACUUM cleaner up on the third floor spirals down the stairs, and on the way up, I catch sight of Kelly yanking it across the floor of one of the empty apartments. She glances back at me over a shoulder, then pulls the plug out of the wall to yell over its dying moan, "Mohammed says you threw a mouse down the toilet!" She turns to face me as she makes an ugly, prissy sound, disgusted.

I want to tattle on Mohammed, want to say, "Well, sweetheart, it was your *husband's* idea," but instead I try to sound merely curious: "Have you and Mohammed had any difficulties with mice yourselves?"

"Oh, sure, we get them every year, this morning I found two babies in a canister of flour."

"What did you do with them?"

"I threw them out the window?"

Some people have no guilt, I tell myself, going up the stairs to my apartment. Some people feel free.

I'm deep in my essay for Swanson when there's a knock on my door. I don't even know what time it is. Close to supper, still raining, getting dark. When I open it, Mohammed is standing out in the dark hallway. He smells of a racy male cologne and is dressed in a white shirt, undone at the throat. Anxiously on his way out somewhere. Unless it's the anxiety of dealing with more mice. "I'll have to come into your apartment, try to deal with the mouse situation."

"The exterminator was here just before New Year's and he couldn't find any holes, even."

"Perhaps I will be the one to find them."

"Now that I've caught one, possibly that's all there will be."

"There is never just *one* mouse," says Mohammed. But he can't find any holes either, and as he's leaving he tells me he'll ask Mr. Rastafajani to call the exterminator first thing in the morning.

Two hours later, I go down to the kitchen. I rub two chicken drumsticks with oil and basil, shove the Pyrex dish into the oven, strike a match for the gas. But at the pop of the flame's rippling blue ring, a small black projectile comes leaping toward me above the loop of blue fire, then lands on the floor to the left of my left little toe.

I run down the stairs to Kelly and Mohammed's apartment, knock hard on the door. But there's nobody home.

And when I get back to my own place I carry my supper into my bedroom, then call Lorenzo.

"A circus mouse," he says, laughing.

And it's true. With an inventiveness that's almost comic—although nothing is comic to a phobic—the little mice have jumped through hoops for me. He tells me to go out and buy myself a trap. But I'd never be able to bear taking a mouse out of a trap. "Besides, once I've caught one, there will be others. Replacements. Exterminators keep coming, but no one has been able to find even one point of entry."

I'm beginning to feel sorry for the little mice too, much as I dread them, they are so hunted down, so beleaguered. If only I didn't fear them so, if only I could see them as unpredictable pets, entertainers: but a phobia is a condition that never lets up, it's just always there in the wings, waiting. As long as I'm phobic I'll be condemned to remember. If I could afford it, I would go to a hypnotist and have the hypnotist take me back to what happened the night I was nine and was being wakened in reluctant stages by an enormous purring while something slumped and silken and heavy was being dragged back and forth across my mouth as I was fighting to stay asleep, my rocking back and forth fighting with the back and forth of the heavy weight being dragged across my nose, across my eyes, up into my hair, then back down to my mouth again, rhythmically, a monotonous and insistent figure eight, dragged back and forth, and then something else too, a dragged tickle, a cold shoelace or tail, until I was at last awake enough to shove my cat off my mattress, to hear the thump below the bed as he made his leap free of it. If only I could have gone back to sleep at that moment, instead of deciding that I had to see for myself, instead of staggering up to reach for the string hanging down from the lightbulb, the small click of illumination showing me what I hadn't yet dared to imagine: my cat sitting down on the green linoleum floor with the big grey mouse that he'd brought as a gift for me, my shriek so extreme that my father, pulled out of his own sleep, came running to my rescue, my cat not understanding why I couldn't see what an honour it was that he, my darling

Poppins, was so proud when he caught his first mouse that he'd brought it straight to me, the little girl he loved so much that he must have decided that I too was a cat, this was why he'd dragged the mouse back and forth across my sleeping mouth in the first place, he'd meant for me to eat it, this was how much he loved me.

Deep in revisionland, I write about G flying east with no thought of K:

UP IN THE AIR

G is back in Canada again, flying back to Montreal from a visit to a site out on the west coast, now and then looking up from the papers he's reading to gaze out at air so clear he can see all the way down to the snow-dusted prairies east of Saskatoon, the fields as ugly as streaked floor tiles: dun fields, pale orange fields, striated slate fields with here and there a black chip in them (a lake) and here and there a black lizard (a much longer lake) and black rims around so many of the other lakes (like licorice, or like the mad-eyed rims on certain African fabric designs), not knowing that J is waiting for him in the airport in a puffy parka or that she has a sore throat and their baby is cranky, but all too soon the plane comes down in the sunny cold of a bright Montreal early spring afternoon and he disembarks to walk into the airport at Dorval whose air, for some reason, is contaminated by a toxic caramel smell.

But when I go down to the kitchen to get a glass of beer, I cry out when I feel the fur swoop of a tiny belly and panicked claws racing across my

276

bare feet, my heart all at once beating everywhere, a deranged drumbeat making the walls of my apartment breathe in, breathe out, as I run through the throbbing dim rooms turning on lights—lights, lights, radio, radio—because if I can't quickly calm myself down with bright lights and loud music I know that I'll die of a heart seizure.

And so another exterminator arrives. More peering and squatting. "You need a glue-trap."

But there has to be a limit to how much cruelty I'll support to stave off my own terror. And besides, the thought of finding a little mouse with its stem-like little legs fixed in the pale honey of the glue is just too terrible to bear.

The voice is professionally soothing. "They're very effective."

"Thanks. But no."

He's older, more exhausted than the other exterminators. He places foil plates heaped with pink poison behind the stove and inside the bottom cupboards, and once he has gone I gather my papers together and leave for Stanopolis.

Swanson hands back my paper on Foucault's *The History of Sexuality*, a book I enjoyed although I waited so long to write my paper that I had to wing my way through it. I'm surprised to see that he's given me an A plus on it, and wonder if this magic mark has anything to do with my comment that this "isn't a young man's book, but for those of us who consider ourselves to be battered survivors of the sexual wars or even over the hill, sexually speaking, it could act as an agent of consolation."

After class, when I ask Swanson if he would consider giving me an extension for my final essay he hesitates, and so (hoping to charm him) I tell him that sometimes my students say entertaining things to me and that one of them recently asked me, "Mees? Could you tell me please the difference between a pullover and a pushover?"

He gazes at me, his eyes dark with distrust. "You see me as a pushover?"

"Oh, *no*," I say, speaking with unhappy force. "I wasn't thinking of that part of it at *all*. I was only thinking of your pullover."

He glances down at it—tonight's model is a lemon cashmere—to say that he's rather fond of this particular one himself, then he surprises me by granting the extension. "But I must warn you that I will be expecting something unusually good in that case."

When I step out of the bath at bedtime, I realize that I forgot to bring my flip-flops into the bathroom and so I arrange a towel in a U on the floor, then shimmy my way across the tiles, my feet on the arms of the U and shuffling on them as if they are snowshoes, I'm that afraid of getting the mouse poison on my bare feet. During the night there's such a ferocious scrabbling inside the walls just behind the stove that I barely sleep. Awake, I dream of moving to another apartment, another life.

I BEGIN WRITING letters of application for teaching jobs in Ontario, even consider moving back to Ottawa again—ersatz, water-sparkling, Never-Never-Land Ottawa with all its admirals and initials and acronyms and flowers and all its cars darting in their surreal way in and out among trees and across lawns (although really only appearing to) if you look across to the university as you walk down the town side of the Canal.

While I'm waiting to hear back, I visit an art supply store and buy a sheet of blue Bristol board and a tin of play dough, then make a Dutch door for my bedroom by pressing long strips of the play dough up and down the door frame to hold the Bristol board upright. No little mouse will be able to climb up this slippery wall, I tell myself, and it's the best bedtime story until I realize that a mouse could easily make its way up the sides of my Dutch door where I've pressed the play dough, like pie dough, into the door frame. And when it does occur to me, I pray that the mouse isn't a clever mouse.

But as I'm wrapping myself in a towel after I've stepped out of the tub, I feel I'm being watched. I stay very still, peering out into the dim hallway at the tall bookcase with its rows of gleaming books, at the braided blue-and-grey rug on the hardwood floor. The apartment is more orderly than usual and this makes it seem somewhat sinister. But there's no one until I glance to my left to see a small mouse sitting up on his hind legs and watching me. I gasp, then make a guttural sound that ends in a pinched whimper. But a few hours later I feel that I could almost have loved this little mouse too, I can even picture him buckled into a pair of pink overalls like a mouse in a storybook.

After my class with Cy Stackpole I stop off at the graduate studies office to leave my novel with Merrilee. "Do you know who my thesis readers will be?"

"Edison Lumley is the only one I know so far…." And in a hushed voice she tells me that Professor Lumley has made a special request for it.

"He's my enemy, Merrilee."

And as if to prove to myself that my own words are true, I twist my ankle as I miss the bottom step of the stairs on the way down.

I'M RESTING my sprained ankle on a chair when Edison Lumley calls to ask me if I can be a replacement for a poet who's unable to give a reading at LaLa Barn Bar. I'd have to be there by eight and I'll be paid forty dollars and so I say yes, then I jack open the ironing board to press my grey silk shirt, whimper as I lunge from room to room collecting my scattered poems, call a cab, limp down to the street to wait for it in the November night, not daring to go back upstairs to phone again for fear I'll miss my ride. By this time I hate every cab sweeping past that isn't for me and when my cab does slowly approach me and my cabbie leans over to open the door for me as if we have all the time in the world, I tell him I have to make a speech because a speech sounds more adult ("I'm already twenty damn minutes late for it") and so we flee across the dark city while I keep trying to get my poems in order and in a way it feels like flying since I'm also seeing myself as someone who's come from nowhere to here, to this dramatic moment in this dark fleeing car, someone who's being borne across a great city at high speed to read her poems to strangers, to a future in which people wait for my arrival, but at the same time the realist in me pictures an opposite scene: coldly amused patrons smoking in near darkness and making unimpressed remarks about the entertainment. It's like a blind date, really, with a whole crowd of strangers—they didn't choose me, I didn't choose them—and it's real life when I get here, real life with an aura of purgatory about it, it's a music barn with acres and acres of people drinking and shouting while Edison, majestic and superbly calm, comes sweeping toward me. "We were afraid we had lost you!" Behind him comes a boy with pre-Raphaelite hair who leads me to a washroom mirror among a labyrinth of black partitions and smeary red lights, then squires me back through utter blackness to the main barn again where the second reader has just been called up to read first: a big man who mounts the stage to face the crowd with a scowl, then begins to alternately roar and whisper, dropping his voice so low that it becomes fraught, then letting it rise to feebly bleat out *"Ezekiel!"* then letting it drop low once again. He knows all about drama, all about timing, he'll be a hard act to follow. And then the student MC (Jean-Luc) who's sexily pudgy and dressed all in black jumps up on the stage to announce the next reader.

Up on the platform, I can get the attention of only half of the audience, loud talkers down at the back still need to be harshly shushed, and I read badly too, wanting only to get it over with. When I do, I'm helped down the steps by Jean-Luc, then limp back to the table where Edison and the pre-Raphaelite are sitting, squeezing behind chairs to here and there pass by a kind face turned up to thank me. Between sets, Edison talks about inviting American poets to come up to Canada. But they want such very high fees. To my "How high?" all he will say is "You really don't want to know." At some later point, emphasizing something or other, I place a hand on his thigh, then forget to remove it again. And so how long does my hand rest there? To paraphrase Edison, I really don't want to know.

LORENZO DROPS BY this evening after dinner. "So this is it, the infamous mouse-wall...." He squats to inspect it, amused by it. "Is Rastafajani going to get another exterminator?"

"He said he would. And he's been good about that always. It's just that the exterminators have never been able to discover how the mice are getting in."

"They need to fumigate down in the basement and garbage room. That's where the real problem is."

"But the other tenants who've had them have managed to get rid of them and so I decided it must be because I was too casual a housekeeper."

"Hell, no. The problem is down in the basement."

"Here's something I've been meaning to tell you, Enzo. Edison Lumley has made a special request to read my thesis and this is making me feel very afraid. But when he asked me to read a few poems at a bar two nights ago he was surprisingly friendly...."

"This means nothing. The man is a great actor."

"You think he would actually stay bitter for so long?"

"You hurt his vanity, Kay."

"You always hear that Newfoundlanders are so terrific. But Edison Lumley is from St. John's and he is utterly devious. So isn't it amazing? The gift he has for looking so harmless?"

He smiles a smile that seems to say: This guy is banal, but he is evil.

Later in the evening Benno comes over to use my typewriter for typing up an essay for his art history class. Then he too makes the tour, squats with the flashlight to look for holes behind chests of drawers, then agrees with Lorenzo: I need to set traps. "I'd come over and empty them for you."

But I can't bear having traps in my apartment. "At least not yet."

We sit in the front room and talk about movies. "Go see *Stranger Than Paradise.* Or *El Norte.* No, don't go to *El Norte,* there's a scene in it with hundreds of rats running down an underground tunnel."

"I could always cover my eyes. But Lorenzo says that Rastafajani should get the fumigators in."

"But by now they're living in the walls and there must be a hole in here *some*where."

"I don't know what to do, I keep changing my mind—"

"I recently read somewhere that doubt, too, is a dogma."

A GREEN CAR FLASHES past me in the rain, then backs up to park just ahead of the bus shelter where I've been waiting to catch a bus going west, then the driver (whose head appears to be the head of a nodding enlarged insect) leans over to open the front door for me. When I run through the rain, then duck down to the window to see who it is, I see Professor Heubner peering out at me from within a sectioned clear plastic rain bonnet. Her car radio is still on as I slide in beside her, solemn voices are singing the praises of someone who has died, one of her pointed claret leather shoes resting lightly first on the brake, then on the gas pedal as each solemn voice says something kind: he was always so thoughtful and helpful to others, no one ever had a bad word to say about him, he had no enemies, he will be deeply missed.

If a hearse could be a voice, this is the voice in which a hearse would speak. But Professor Heubner reaches over to snap the voice off. "What a terrible thing to say of a man who's no longer able to defend himself: He had no enemies. Would *you* like that, Kay? After you're dead? To know that people are saying only fatuous and kind things about you?"

"I wouldn't mind. I think I might love it, actually."

"But why would you love it?"

"I'm not sure it would be so strange to want that."

"Not so strange, no, but depressingly predictable. And do they really mean it? I doubt it. At least if you had a few enemies, you'd know that you'd stood for something."

Is this a reference to my having agreed to write my own recommendation letter? But she only says, "Look, where can I drop you off?"

"Right here would be perfect. I can get the metro from here."

"By the way, did you ever get the fellowship you asked me to recommend you for?"

"Yes, I did," I tell her, leaning in to talk to her through the open window. "And I was so grateful to you, thanks again."

"Well, that's excellent news." Her smile enigmatic, academic.

And the windshield wipers thrash like mad wings as she, the angel of charity, the professor-grasshopper, speeds away in the rain.

ONE SUNNY AFTERNOON last week, a man who had such a stitched freckled look that he made me think of an octogenarian thug was crossing Sherbrooke toward me. And when I saw his glance take me in, then heard his dry "Bonjour, ma belle. Bonjour, bébé," I was so grateful to him that I wanted to drop to my knees and kiss his puffy freckled feet. He even made me feel so happy that I went into the deli to buy a bag of croissants, then stopped to give money to the aristo-cratic tall man with the silky orange beard who has recently set up camp in the alley that leads to Bulmer Street, a man whose eyes are intellectually unforgiving, the eyes of an academic who's been kicked out of some institution or other for being totally impossible. But when I tried to hand him a five-dollar bill, he turned on me as if I'd dared to disagree with him in a classroom discussion on critical theory, then snatched it out of my hand to toss into the litter that had sifted in among the roots of the wine-red bushes behind the deli. And he yelled at me too, a professor's accusatory "Bah!"

A week later, when I was walking out to Sherbrooke via the alley-way with my novel (or a version of it) to be mailed to Lew Quick, I could see that Professor Bah was asleep, his head supported by the black plastic garbage bag filled with his belongings. I glanced over at the hedge and spotted a flake of blue caught among the layered faded pink and grey leaves. Pretty blue Canadian money. If it's not wanted, I thought, why don't I just retrieve it? God knows I need it. And I went over to the hedge and curtsied to it as I delicately detached the blue paper from the leaves and litter, then glanced back at Herr Bah (he was still asleep) before I hurried home with it shoved into a pocket. Because even though he was offended by being offered it, I still felt like a thief.

In need of an encounter that was morally ambiguous, I worked this episode into the story I wrote for Cy Stackpole's workshop, and tonight is the night we'll be discussing it. There's such an air of polite butchery in this workshop, it's so opposite to the workshop I once imagined, there are no accountants or housewives in it, the students are all planning to be novelists or poets and they crouch darkly at the seminar table, little animals guarding their stories as if they believe them to be dying fires. So here we all are then, sitting in silence until Cy Stackpole comes in, a lanky male flower in his aqua shirt as we all turn to him. Or we are the flowers and he is the sun. Lara arrives last, white-faced as she sweeps into the workshop at five minutes past eight, her hazy brown hair hidden inside the raised hood of her rain cape. Fierceness and an apology for being late light up her already incendiary eyes. She is frightening—to me, at least—her critiques are marked by such a principled savagery. But are her opinions to be trusted? Sometimes she admires work that seems so affected and hokey, although often she's right to condemn what she so harshly condemns. But she sees narcissism everywhere. On the other hand what she loves she loves with her whole heart.

Cy casts his long glance down the table and when he gets to Lara, her voice is hoarse as she stiffly says, "First of all, to begin on a positive note, this could be a really great story if the central character could be made less obnoxious and insane. When she steals money from the homeless man, for instance, I couldn't believe it, she's stealing from a homeless person, she's really despicable."

I turn to her. "But he didn't even want the money! So how could what I did be called stealing?"

There's laughter at my having revealed the true pronoun, then a student at the far end of the table says he would have liked to see all the characters brought together at the end of the story.

"The real problem," says Lara, "is that the central character doesn't change or grow."

Lorenzo smiles coolly at her from above his crossed arms. "Grown-ups don't change or grow," he tells her.

When Lara hands my story back to me I see that she has written "I love this" next to one section and "Wow" next to another. I smile over at her to say, "I forgive you for everything." And on the way to the metro, I talk to Lorenzo about her. "It's so clear that she's still in love with you, Enzo."

"She just wants to fight with me."

"That could be love."

"Then I'm too tired for love."

I can understand this, I've so often felt this, but I doubt I would say it. I would be too proud to say it. But my admiration for him is great because he's been willing to say it.

I'VE RECENTLY THROWN A SWIMMER into the mix, a swimmer who travels to races in distant pools, distant cities, she could be the one the architect falls for. He builds towers that rise into the air, she plunges deep into inverted towers of water. Being a swimmer could also be a metaphor for being a writer: the obsession, the plunge into the subconscious, the euphoria, the dive, the long hours of moving through layers of memories and cold, the integrated wave-wash, the deep but also somehow comic personal revelations. Or do I flatter writers too much? When I write, I feel like God or a gossip. Unless it's not going well. But when I meet with Cy Stackpole in his office in the

English tower, he urges me to cut the overgrowth. It's like working with a gifted surgeon, but because he's a fan of sentences that are short and unadorned, I can't stop missing my own way to write: the tangents, the second thoughts, the sideways shuffle, secretly I vow to protect all of it from him as I nod and agree with him, feeling duplicitous, devious. But once I'm down on the quad and walking toward the lights and traffic of the great world of the city, it's what I imagine it would be like to come out into the world after working under brilliant lights to save a life—the world was here all the time, but we forgot it, we were working in such fierce concentration up there, to save the word, to save the body—and now I've come down among the infidels from that devoutly fussy and hermetic place.

I GO FROM one carousel of bright books to another, lift down book after book to read the opening page before moving on to find the writers who've saved my life simply by writing about their resentment or their shame or their fury or even what they love. I stand reading them long enough to make sure they can still shine with the goodness of their invigorating rage or their self-castigating sorrow before I move on to the books of writers I have at least now and then loved, although when I look at the books of writers whose work is not alluring, at least not to me, I begin to feel like a child who's spent the long afternoon of her childhood in a window seat reading—*Heidi, A Tale of Two Cities*—while her younger brothers and sisters were growing up all around her, growing up and fulfilling her secret ambition to be a writer, for here they all are, all off and running, hundreds of thousands of them all running as fast as they can while fanning out toward a horizon of readers. While I've been spending years testing the water with a single hesitant toe and my one slim novel and my tiny output of stories, they have been finding themselves confidence, publishers, brilliant haircuts. And when I turn away from their books to move back to the more

alphabetically obscure part of the store where the O's are I discover that
The Dangerous Meadow is not on the shelf where it should be—where
is it? My child! It should be here!—and it's at this moment that I seem
to become defiled. Defiled as a reader by being turned into a writer and,
what's worse, the wrong kind of writer. A writer whose relationship to
her work is custodial and public, not exhilarated and private. Even
walking into a bookstore and seeing *The Dangerous Meadow* with my
name on it used to make me scurry out of the store so I could breathe
again. But now all the worlds have changed, the so-called real world
and the literary world, and I want my book to be here and am enraged
that it isn't. Even though it's not how many lovers or how many readers
that counts, it's which reader, which lover, which is when I see that
Della Kuhnert's new novel is out and so I pick it up, read the ecstatic
review quotes on the back cover, open it to read its first page. And am
unable to decide if it's fake or actually brilliant in an arch way, or simply
stylish but banal, another bloodless coup that emotionally lets her
readers down once again, which doesn't mean I won't want to read it.
But even greater than my longing to read it is my longing to get away
from it (the dark force of its entitled brightness) and so I move from
one shelf to another shelf, reading opening pages and longing for
another writer to talk to, and on a hunt for such a writer I begin to look
at the photographs on the insides of the book jackets. Above all to
look at the photographs of the women writers. And so see that most of
them could have been anything, anything other than writers: aerobics
instructors, real estate agents, athletes, interior decorators. Their dark
lipstick shines and their dark eyes shine, and so does the sleekness of the
shine of their hair. Some of them are even tilting their heads so far to
one side that a single earring hangs down in front of the dark cave made
by an elegant wing of dark or fair hair. These single earrings, like a
single chain of glitter, make me think of a chain on an old-fashioned
toilet tank, and every time I see a face that's tipped into such a coy tilt

that its ear drips an earring in front of its fall of gleaming hair, I long to give it a hard pull and hear the crash of a flush. It's a wish that makes me feel I've got to get out of this place, but first I have to take another quick peek at the Kuhnert novel, I flip through the pages until I'm stopped by a dramatization of the afternoon Della and I had coffee in the Ottawa deli next door to Stationery House—how long ago was this?—for here I am, disguised as a woman named Rae Padolski who "talks ad nauseam about her inability to get a decent night's sleep or finish her novel (apparently it's a good deal longer than her slim first book—something fields? *Dark Fields? The Dangerous Dark?*—and although I try mightily to be kind, it's hard to see her as anything but a sly dirty blonde who by a curious fluke once managed to sell a story to *Esquire,* her secretive smile suggesting that *she,* Rae Padolski, is the better writer...." By now my heart has gone into free fall and my back feels chilled and afraid. That I should have happened to read this when I have no one. Two pages later, the Della character is saying about Rae/Kay to a friend, "Wasn't there some talk, years ago, of her having been a singer? But talk must have been all it ever was, since no one has ever heard her sing. And she apparently hasn't had a lover since the day her fantastic husband walked out. But as I'm pondering the ramifications of Rae's celibate life, she rudely blows smoke in my face, in the process releasing an odour of cheap perfume from the sleeve of her boxy blue Oriental jacket...."

I feel the full force of Della's orderly fury. It's the best writing she's ever done, and to think that *I* (Kay/Rae!) was her muse. I turn back a page to read about Rae once again, then remember the afternoon Della came up to my place for tea and how I praised a few images in her latest book but then was unwise enough to say what I said to her and even though I have to admit that it was, in its way, a blow, it was also the truth. "Anything in particular that you're looking for?" I hear a man's voice call out to me, and I mumble no, sorry, then I hurry out

Happiness is the engine that drives you to even greater happiness and what happens tonight proves it when I get a call from a Professor Calhoun offering me a job as a sessional lecturer at York. I sit down after his call, rest my head sideways on my hugged knees while I cry for two or three minutes from gratitude and surprise. Now at last I'll get away from this haunted city, I'll have a second chance, I can begin again. But at the same time I fear the irony of a comeuppance. Irony as instruction. Irony as the black engine roaring out of a dark fate. When I think of the past I think of humiliation. When I think of the future I think of triumph. When I think of happiness I think of when it will be taken away from me.

And when I get up from the sofa to go into my bedroom for a sweater, one of my feet gets trapped in a loop of the phone cord and I pitch forward, my fall broken by the mouse wall. Herr Maus Wahl, my hero. But in spite of the fact that it has protected me from breaking my arms and smashing my face, I decide that it's time to dismantle it.

There's been a carnival air in the city these hot early days of spring, women walking coatless, men walking with their suit jackets unbuttoned, but my apartment was so cool when I was leaving it that

I pulled on my coat and now I can't be bothered to go back up to the top floor to put on a jacket instead.

I stop to look at the pails of red tulips outside Mi-hee's store, the way they cup light, then look up to see what can't be possible: Galbraith standing in the shade in front of Terre Etoile.

I need to escape. I need to escape into Mi-hee's to peel off my ugly coat, then duck behind the counter with it, fold it over two crates of oranges while Mi-hee is busy at the back of the store. Then I peer out at him through the dirty window to see if he looks happy, but it seems to me that he's looking severe.

"I'm leaving my coat with you, Mi-hee! But I'll be back for it in five minutes!"

Mi-hee is angry. "Why you do that for?"

But I'm already on my way back out into the sunlight.

He walks out to the street to meet me and I warn myself not to be affected as I bump against him when we hug. But we only end up holding hands. "You're wearing the necklace I gave you."

I reach up my free hand to feel the hexagonal beads. "I do wear it now and then."

He smiles as he tells me that he's a father now, he has a baby boy. And when I say that this must make him really happy he says yes. But his yes doesn't sound like the whole story and to relieve the awkward silence that follows it, I tell him about being a student at Stanopolis.

"How have you been finding it?"

"Demeaning in some ways, boring in some ways, although in a few other ways it's been weirdly thrilling."

"So things are mostly good for you, then?"

"Most of the time. And how about you?"

"Ups and downs, but more or less fine."

And when he asks me if I'll be staying on in Montreal after I finish school I tell him no. "I'm going to be teaching at a university in Toronto in the fall."

"So you too have been seduced by Toronto."

It's just that there aren't enough cities in this part of the country. Not real cities. "I mean," I say in my *Blue Angel* accent, "vhot's a girl to do, if she's only got two? But I hate leaving *here*," I tell him, putting so much emphasis on the "here" that I think he might hear it as *you*.

"How soon is this going to happen?"

"Five weeks from tomorrow."

Too long a silence makes me feel the need to say more. "And so once again I'll be moving on. Shedding skins, lives, acquaintances, beliefs, opinions …"

"And shedding me?"

"I hope so."

When he smiles, I draw an arc on the sidewalk with the toe of one of my shoes. "And don't you hope so too?"

"I'm not sure."

Then he tells me that he looked me up in the phone book one night. "After I moved back here from New York."

"When was this?'

"Just one night when I was thinking of you."

"But you never called."

"I actually did call you one night, but I only let the phone ring once because I realized that you might not even want to talk to me. After all I'd put you through...."

Something about this, or the way he says this, makes me so unhappy that I feel the need to say, "But why am I the only one this is supposed to have been an ordeal for?"

"You're right. I'm sorry I put it that way."

But now a man's voice is calling out of a slowly passing car, "Hey,

Galbraith! Hey, man! I'll be seeing you down at Encore Une Fois some fois or other!"

We look up at him, disoriented. But then Galbraith holds up a hand with his five fingers splayed, and after his friend has driven off, he says, "That was Gus, the friend I'm supposed to be meeting for lunch. But I've just had a brilliant idea. I can go down to Encore Une Fois and tell him I'll meet him tomorrow instead. And he'll be sure to understand. This is Montreal, after all."

"And then what?"

"Then we could buy a bottle of wine and go back to your place." He smiles at me, one of his old cocky smiles. "Or maybe not. So just walk with me down to the restaurant then."

And so we walk down the street to Encore Une Fois and when we get there he tells me that he'll just go in to get Gus to order for him. "Then I'll walk you over to your place."

Gus (a bald, benign man) peeks out the window at me, then turns to say something to Galbraith while out on Sherbrooke Street the siren of an ambulance is being raced across the early afternoon. Then Galbraith comes back out into the day again looking careful and alert and as he walks me home he keeps up a stream of talk, his voice so jaunty that when we get to my street I'm not surprised when he says, "So. Can I come up? Just to see your apartment?"

We don't talk as the elevator rises and after I've unlocked my door he follows me in, looks all around. "Hey, this is great. You've got so much more space to work with here. Great space and great light."

And I'm grateful that my place is so filled with sunlight and smells so mopped and so fresh as he opens the door to the balcony and steps out into the sunshine and the bright noontime air, then I tag along behind him as he walks from room to room, wanting to hear him talk in the waylaying voice that's holding off the moment that he'll have to go, a voice that's as filled with dreamy invention and evasion as the voices of Tom and Benno used to be when they hoped they could stave off forever the moment of being sent up to bed.

But he seems to be barely looking. "So what other amazing things have you accomplished, during the time you were free of me?"

"I wrote a poem that won a prize. And a novel. Just a short one. But probably no one will bother to read it."

He sits on the edge of the window seat. "If you'd like, I could start a rumour that you plagiarized it from an impoverished Third World woman writer who has mysteriously gone missing, I bet that would make your sales skyrocket."

"It would."

"But I understand what you're saying and I hope it can be otherwise."

I feel close to tears from his kind jokes and sympathy.

"So what's it about?"

"It's about your life as I imagined it, while you were away from me."

He looks startled, humble, yearning, and wary all at once. "Really?"

"Really. It's about an education of the heart. And other body parts."

"The education of the other body parts sounds intriguing." But then he quickly adds, "And so does an education of the heart. Or is it," he says, smiling, "an education of the pancreas?"

"To put it another way, it's about someone I used to love once."

"Someone who has been relegated to the past tense, I see."

"Isn't that the best place for you to be? All things considered?"

"All things considered, I've always been a really big believer in the present tense. And you know what? I think we should talk. I keep feeling we haven't talked."

"What about Gus? Isn't he expecting you to come back and eat the food that he ordered for you?"

"Not especially. In fact he was all in favour of my preferring you over him."

He walks down the hall to the doorway of my bedroom and when he asks me if it's okay if he goes in, all I can think is how lucky it is that I decided to dismantle the mouse wall. Because the mouse saga is just not a saga I can bear for him to hear. "It's a bit of a mess," I say, coming over to stand next to him so that I can gauge the possibilities for embarrassment in the flowered underpants and scatter of sandals and papers on the floor next to my bed.

But he doesn't seem to either notice or care, he just sits down on my bed while I stay standing in the doorway, buoyant but uneasy, there's something I need to remember. But it could only be the dark days when I was so lost from the loss of him, the whole front of my body defined by a tingling hollowness too painful to bear. I should look at my watch but I must have left it on the counter in the kitchen, next to the sink. "What day is this?"

"What?"

"What day is this?"

"It's Thursday...."

"And what *time* is it?"

He looks down at his own watch. "It's twelve-thirty."

"Oh no! I have a class to teach, I have to be there at one o'clock!"

He stands, he looks shaken. "I'll drive you there. But first you'll have to tell me where it is."

"On Dorchester, close to Greene."

"What do you still need to do?"

"Pee and eat."

"Pee, then. And I'll go get you an apple."

As I'm splashing my eyes with cold water, I hear him go down to the kitchen and am relieved that I don't have to see his look of horror when he gets his first view of the jungle inside my refrigerator, the dim bulb shining down on a forest of carrot tops and green fronds.

"Here are just a few of the delicacies I found in your fridge," he tells me as he comes back into the front room, and he holds out an orange that looks as hard as a bullet, then brings out the hand he's been holding behind his back to show me an atrophied apple, all the while smiling a flirty little smile—mocking, affectionate—but when he goes back to the kitchen to get me a peach I find myself thinking *no* without even knowing why. It seems to be no, I don't need to be smiled at. At least not like that and not any more. Even if at the same time I don't at all mind being teased and even love the way he seems to be amused by himself for still being at least a little bit under my spell.

On our way to the Institute, though, there's a melody I can't get out of my head, a low warning howl about some woman's poor heart being on the mend and some man deciding he might just pass her way again. But I forgive Galbraith as I'm getting out of his car because the long look he gives me is so much better than the wrong kind of kiss.

Lorenzo calls, wanting to tell me that his relationships with the two women he's currently involved with have reached a new level of maturity. "I spent Tuesday night with Lara and Wednesday night with Patty, and I didn't have sex with either one of them."

"Oh Lorenzo, you two-timer you."

He laughs, he's so obliging. "But I really called to tell you that I picked up my essay from Swanson's mailbox this afternoon, and when I saw that your essay was there too I picked it up as well. I figured I could drop it off to you tomorrow night on my way to Lara's place."

"Could you just open it now though? Tell me what mark I got?"

I can hear the envelope being ripped open. "There's a letter in here."

"Is it long? Could you read it?"

Lorenzo, hamming it up, clears his throat, then with the overprecise lilt of someone mimicking someone—but the someone he's mimicking isn't quite Swanson—he reads, "Dear Kay, This is an intelligent, lively essay, written with your usual lucidity and strength...."

"So," I say, smiling. "The man liked it ..." But he doesn't go on, and so I say, "Lorenzo! Please! Don't just read it to yourself!"

"Hold everything," he says. Then there's another long pause. "This is really bad news—"

"How do you mean?"

"He says he's going to fail you."

"I don't believe this. Read the rest. Please."

"Okay, but brace yourself." And he reads:

But I don't see how I can pass you for the course. First of all, and least important, the paper is three weeks or so late—that is, you had three weeks extra to do something unusually good. Second of all, the essay really isn't unusually good. It's good, maybe even very good, but that's all. Third, and most important, the essay has nothing to do with the course. Apart from "bad writing in *King Lear*," which is just a hook on which to hang the essay, any connection either with the material of the course, or with the critical methodology of the course, is purely coincidental.

I'm not happy with the prospect of not passing you for the course. You're brighter and more interesting than other students whom I have passed. All this doesn't mean I'm changing my mind: I have to play within the rules of my own game, even as I recognize that they are different from the game you are playing. What I am saying, however, is that I would be willing to cooperate with any attempt to transfer the evaluation procedure to a version of your game, or a similar one. In specific terms, what you might want to do is apply for a reread by people of your choice. Maybe there are other things you could do as well to get us both off the hook. But for the time being, I am reporting your grade for the course as unsatisfactory, though indicating to the graduate Program Director that he might want to sit on the grade for a bit, in the expectation that he will probably hear from you.

I'm sorry. I really enjoyed meeting you and talking to you as well as reading the papers you submitted to me during the course of the semester.

Hamilton Swanson

"Do you think I should ask for a reread?"

"They're a club, they stick together. Just remember: they have to say good morning to each other for the next twenty years. And you're just passing through." When he was an undergraduate he requested a reread, he tells me, but his mark wasn't altered. "It would be better to write a new paper."

As I think of the hours and hours of aching hand, aching eyes, my voice gets untethered. "I'm just so tired. And why does he begin the letter with all that misleading praise? It seems so sadistic."

"He wants you to think he's a nice guy, but at the same time he wants to fail you."

The following evening when I call Swanson he tells me I was trying to kill two birds with one stone in that essay. "Not that it didn't have some original ideas in it."

But when I tell him that I want to write a new paper he sounds surprised, then speaks of the various directions my essay might go in. Then he stops, says he would like to organize his suggestions and send them to me by mail. He'll try to get them off to me before he leaves for Stratford to see *The Taming of the Shrew*. "I'll never forget the afternoon in class when you brought up that story about the woman who had fantasies of being spanked by her lover...."

I experience a gone sensation in my belly, press the flat of my free hand into a thigh. I could be seventeen again. This is what terror does to you, it makes you young.

He seems to be at a loss for words as well. "Well," he says at last. And then after another difficult silence he tells me that he'll be able to give me till the end of July to do a new paper, but that I should feel free to contact him if I have any questions. "Call me, if there is anything at all you feel the need to discuss."

A long, careful document arrives two days later. He has included one of his own papers on new historicism. "Optional reading," he has written across the top of the first page. But his letter ends with a warning: "These are only suggestions. Deviate from them as you wish, but also at your own risk."

I make notes for my paper over the next three days, but it isn't until Friday night when the sun is trying to burn its way through a polluted sunset that I lift my typewriter onto the dining room table and (the door to the balcony open) begin to type:

But is this bad? For a critic to be lively? When Norris, toward
the end of his essay, places Dr. Johnson near the beginning, and
F. R. Leavis toward the end of a certain dominant cultural formation
in the history of Shakespeare studies by saying "It is an effort of
ideological containment to attempt to harness the unruly energies
of the text to a stable order of significance," he makes it clear (with
his harness and stable) that *he* hasn't driven out metaphor with a
pitchfork—

The phone rings. I pick it up, then carry it, still ringing, out to the big room to set it down on the coffee table, pick up the receiver on the twelfth ring to hear the eternally familiar voice say, "Hello, Kay." I take it off the hook, go back to work, but the insinuating tone of the caller's voice keeps me looking too often toward the balcony, the dark night. I also keep checking over my shoulder to make sure there's no one standing behind me, then I turn on all the lights and make a tour of the apartment, close and lock all the windows, take my flashlight with me to beam it down at the phantom ankles of long skirts, long pale cotton pants, then type until the sky lightens. At sunrise, I lock the door to the balcony so that only the sapphire plastic blades of the electric fan stir the stale hot air, then fall asleep in the dim bedroom.

It's a hot Saturday afternoon when I get up, my sheets damp from my shallow and uneasy sleep. I tell myself that I'm far from being the only woman in this (or any) city who gets anonymous phone calls, but all I can think of is how much I envy the thousands upon thousands of women who were allowed to sleep through the night in breezy peace, their balcony doors and windows flung open. The rest of the dull afternoon passes slowly by my windows and by suppertime I've come up with a title: "Despair and the Critic." A useful title, because it can cover both kinds of despair: bad despair, good despair. The bad despair I qualify as "Postmodernist's Complaint," the complaint being that most postmodern criticism is, as one of the critics I've had to study so presciently puts it, "doomed to be forever unreadable and unread." To support my analysis of why this is so, I only need to quote part of a sentence I plan to call a monstrous syntactical horror: "The most severe problematic of proto-professional ideological production denied autonomous political weight in a society struggling to preserve the hegemony of an aristocratic class-ideology is here displayed to illustrate for the reader the dichotomy between—" And the good despair will be the despair that accompanies change and the resistance to change. By this time I have my comments on good despair and they have such an elegiac, summing-up ring that I decide to work them into the essay's ending.

A BUDDHA CAT, its gaze serene, its front paws tucked beneath it, is lying on a green lawn in front of a house on de Maisonneuve, then a few minutes later on another lawn I see another cat, a cat with a white diamond on its throat. As I'm passing it, it bounds to a nearby tree, then begins to claw in a showy way at the trunk. "Hello, pretty kitty!" I call to it, and it seems to me that it's smiling as I hurry on by. The other cat was a charmer too, they were both such cool little cats.

As I cross Mountain Street, a church bell tolls the hour. But how *can* it be? I look at my watch and see that it has stopped. It must already be ten then, but the traffic is too heavy for me to dart across Sherbrooke. On this morning of all mornings. But while I'm waiting for the light to change I hear a meowing behind me and by this time I'm certain that the two cats were the same cat and that this little cat has followed me across this vast distance, its cries sounding like "Miaow, mama, miaow mama!" I pick it up, then stand for a moment trying to decide what to do with it, I shouldn't have smiled at it, now it thinks I'm its mother, and in desperation I push through the revolving doors of Holt Renfrew and set it down on the polished marble floor, feel its rigid resistance to being abandoned while at the same time I'm telling myself it's the only way, now the clerks will gather around it and a rich customer will take it home and feed it saucers of cream, and when it turns its head away from me for an instant, I push out into the morning and it's such an awful feeling, as if I've abandoned one of my own babies, but I have to run to Stanopolis, and when I get to the top floor, I can see a small crowd gathered at the door to the seminar room for my thesis defence. Cy is there too, and when I get closer to him, I can see how distraught he is, how wildly pale. "Why didn't you tell me you'd sold your novel to Macmillan? Because what's happening here is so bad for you."

"What's happening?"

"What's happening is that Edison has given everyone A's. Except for you. He gave you all B's." But at this point he has to stop since we've all become aware of a grand ripple in the morning as Edison, mammoth and golden (although also short-legged), arrives.

Edison: "Good morning, all."

All: "Good morning, Edison."

In the seminar room, Cy looks apprehensive, as if he's afraid I'm going to say something much too convoluted that will come out of left field, something too crazily engineered to be misunderstood. Edison in the meantime has begun to raise several objections to the sections of my novel that he's highlighted with a yellow marker. But I have an ally in Marvin Glisper, my other reader. And in Cy.

At long last it's over, but did it go well? In a roomful of dissemblers, it's impossible to tell. I also can't bring myself to take my second essay to Stanopolis, I'm too overwhelmed by second thoughts. The inspired ideas I had at the beginning are starting to fall apart, disassemble. And so I phone Lorenzo. "Can a person use the terms postmodern, post-structuralist, deconstructionist and new historicist more or less interchangeably?"

Lorenzo's voice has a fatherly smile in it. "More or less interchangeably?"

"Yes. More or less."

As Lorenzo explains the differences between them, I try to listen, but it's like having a mechanic tell me what's wrong with a car, I can never keep definitions in my head for more than a minute before they vaporize, they bore me so.

Day of the deadline comes (last day of July) and I take the metro to Stanopolis, then walk through the hollow hallways, poke my essay in Swanson's mailbox, walk across the campus to the Peel metro. I so hate the thought of moving, beginning somewhere new. Coming up into the sunlight at Vendôme I even love Montreal, love it more than I've ever loved any city, I can't bear the thought of leaving it, the city where Galbraith is, even if he has disappeared from my life once again, and on my way up the stairs of my building, I meet Mr. Rastafajani on his way down. In his shaggy brown sweater, he more than ever resembles a big friendly brown bear. "I hear from Kelly and Mohammed that you are going. And I tell them: No! I no want my dear friend to go!"

"Yes, to Toronto," I tell him. "Although I have loved living here."

But when I let myself into my apartment, I see Montreal as a city of mice and high-up hidden gardens. City of Galbraith. I picture him feeding his baby son apricot purée. He doesn't talk to his little son as he holds him on his lap and spoons the awful baby food into his eager mouth, he instead gives him the best gift he knows how to give him: perfect silence while he blows on his hair and bounces him on his jiggling knees until his baby begins to discover his voice and make little shy sounds, then tries to capture his father's shirt cuff as it starts to rain. A dense August rain begins to fall, a night rain that I wish would make him wonder what I am doing at this minute or even wonder if I ever remember the nights we would stay in on rainy evenings, the deep stillness in the big front room of his old place on Esplanade, the way we sometimes wouldn't speak for hours, the way if I got up to get a glass of water or pee and passed by him he'd grab my hand and kiss it, or I would lean over and kiss his forehead, three little bumps of kisses, then we'd go back to our own worlds again so that for a long time there would be silence except for the flick of a page being turned.

A scatter of pebbles thrown against the window could startle him as he carries his glass out to the kitchen, then he could realize that it's only the rain. Or he could look out through a window to see that the night is wild, a night from a life in which he wouldn't have been able to imagine himself ending up in Dollard-des-Ormeaux. He could dream of moving back downtown, to a top-floor flat at the end of Jeanne-Mance, close to the park with its great ancient trees. Or he could come back to the den to see that the movie has already started. A woman could be pulling a sheer black stocking up a raised leg in such a wittily fondling way that she would make him want sex. But he could also want more than sex, he could want what men have always wanted from women: consolation, conversation, to be truly seen by the other person.

IT's EARLY AUGUST by this time, and when I open the door to Lorenzo, he's standing at least six paces back from the door, the manila envelope held up like a STOP sign. "All I can say is: don't shoot the messenger."

Lorenzo the Magnificent Realist. But I'm also reminding myself of all the times I came to Swanson's class ten minutes late, all the times my mind wandered. I even went so far as to write him a little note to let him know that work pressures had prevented me from having the free time to read his paper. Why had I found it necessary to do such an ungracious thing? There is really no hope for me. I slit open the envelope, draw out both essay and letter, then clear my throat to read the letter aloud to Lorenzo:

Another good paper (in fact a very good one: nice light touch and a graceful choreography of important ideas), once again not particularly on topic. Closer, though. Wittgenstein et al. need only to be tipped slightly in one direction (no doubt leftwards!) to get to the argument that would have brought you more centrally into new historicist claims: namely, that "good writing" is just another ideological construct. For the record, I will defend to the death (well, at least to the point of minor physical anguish) your right to claim that good writing, whatever it is, should be hung on to—we should grapple it to our souls with hoops of steel, etc. Not because of any particular commitment to free speech, that sort of thing, but because I agree with you. I'm just an old-fashioned liberal humanist type myself. The thing is, though, that the kinds of liberal humanist arguments you make, while I might agree with you, do nothing for you against the new historicists. Either you've got to refute them on their own grounds (i.e., show how writing well doesn't make you a fascist bad guy), or show why their premises are wrong, or not the best place on which to construct an argument (e.g., show how their kind of criticism doesn't make the world safe for the good guys any more than does the criticism of some of the supposed bad guys).

You don't do that, so I'm left with some of the same complaints I had the first time round. But enough is enough. You've certainly made the effort necessary to get credit for the course. I'm submitting a grade of C+ for you. It's a stupid grade for all the reasons I suggested earlier, since it derives from some wholly conventional considerations—like whether you did work that was specifically relevant to the demands of the course, whether you were able to do it on time—rather than from my beliefs about your intelligence and your ability to write well in some more general and freer context. But then grades themselves are pretty largely conventional things, and I take some comfort from the fact that you just want to get the credits under your belt. And best wishes for the summer—what's left of it (whatever happened to the summer, anyway?). I wasn't sure whether I was supposed to return either the latest paper or the earlier one, but here they are.

Kind regards,
Hamilton Swanson

I feel curiously flattered, even though the grade is really terrible news. "Do you think Swanson is intelligent?"

"Why do you ask? Do you want him to be?"

"Yes. Because he thinks I am."

"But there's something missing in Swanson...."

"A soul, perhaps?"

"He's an academic. We have to make certain allowances. I'm sure that to Swanson the soul is a truly amusing concept...."

"A relic. A sentimental and repellent artifact. I even gave him a good evaluation on the teacher-evaluation sheet—"

"And now you regret it—"

"I regret it."

When the phone rings he picks it up because he's the one who's closest to it. "Just hang on a minute, she's right here...." And he hands me the receiver, then goes into the back room for a smoke.

I go to sit in the window seat. "Hello?"

"You have visitors, then."

"Just one."

"Just one. And why should I find just one visitor reassuring?"

I can't help smiling when I say, "Just a friend."

"So could I come over then? Once you're alone again."

"That would be good. Come after nine." And then I tell him about my thesis defence, I even tell him about the mouse running over my bare foot. And the upsetting calls from the spooky caller.

"I'll buy you an answering machine then, I'll buy it on my way over to your place tonight."

After he's heard me put down the phone, Lorenzo comes looking for me. "I have to go, I couldn't stay all that long in the first place."

We hug goodbye at my front door and at the top of the stairway he turns to look back at me. "I've never told you this before, but back in the days when I was feeling so depressed, I would have killed myself if it hadn't been for you. All those hours we spent, talking on the phone. Looking back on it all now, I know that you saved my life."

I stand listening to his footsteps go down one set of stairs, down the next, then can hear a noisy crowd of people come in through the back entrance four stories below, which is when I'm struck by my own lack of gratitude, and so I run over to the banister to call down into the stairwell, "Lorenzo!"

From far below me, he stops to look up, then his face is briefly hidden by the people coming up to the next level. Once I can see him again, I want to call down to him, "You saved my life too!" But this will embarrass him and so instead I call down, "It was the same for me!"

The drunken others, by now having reached the top floor, are letting themselves into the apartment across from mine when one of the men glances back at me, his sidelong smile entertained. "Ah, bon. And so eet was good for you too?" And once the door is closed behind them, I can hear their voices on the other side of it extending the joke: "Did la terre move pour toi, mon amour? Did la terre move for you *too*?"

It's raining by the time Galbraith arrives with the answering machine at twenty past nine.

He kneels on the floor to speak into the tiny microphone: "We can't come to the phone right now. Leave us a message." He presses and clicks a button on the machine. "Here's another thing I neglected to mention: the added benefit of having me speak on the tape is that whenever you get lonely for the sound of my voice, all you'll have to do is dial your own number."

"Then I'm sure to call myself every day." And then after a few minutes I also tell him that the poem that won the prize was written to him.

"Why didn't you tell me this before?"

"Because I was afraid you'd want to read it."

"And so I do."

Although I wonder if he doesn't also feel a fear of it too. Of not liking it, and my getting upset. Or just a fear of not feeling anything at all about it.

"So get it for me, Kay."

"I just don't want you to feel obliged to say kind things about it."

"If I don't like it I've already made up my mind that I'll lie to you about it. I'll lie to you with a clear conscience. A clear Catholic conscience. And I swear to you there's no clearer conscience than that."

I go into my bedroom to find it, bring it back into the front room to hand it to him. Then I make my escape to the kitchen. But once I get out there I find myself on a cliff, the high cliff of being judged, found wanting, and when I open the fridge I feel its cold air come down on my arms. I pull out a cucumber, slice the rye bread, lift out the heavy cloved ham and slice it. But it's already been too quiet out there for too long. He must be trying to think of something to say about it. Something polite. Polite and quelling.

He doesn't glance up when I set the ham on rye in front of him, he's looking down at the poem.

I go back to the kitchen, drink a glass of water, and when I come back to the front room again I'm in agony as I sit down beside him and listen to him chew. The fact that he has just read my poem makes him seem like more of a stranger. "I like it because it's more angry than sappy," he tells me. "And I also don't think it's only because I'm the person that this poem is written to that it's had such a big effect on me ..." and I look down at it to see that he's underlined the lines he likes best, two of the four lines also being the lines I like best. This makes me feel too emotional to say anything to him. But then he doesn't speak to me about my poem after all, he instead talks about two buildings his firm is building overseas, one in Munich, the other in Tel Aviv, then tells me that every Montreal architectural firm needs to be made up of a prescribed trio: a partner who's a Jew, a partner who's French, a partner who's Anglo.

"And so did you send your Jewish architect to Tel Aviv?"

"I'm the one who got sent to Tel Aviv. Our Jewish architect we sent to Germany."

When I smile he says, "But it's true. There's all that deep guilt in Germany, and who better than a Jew to go over there and exploit it?"

I tell him about finding Della Kuhnert's portrait of me in her latest book. "And it just so happens that I know why this writer wanted to pay me back. It's because three or four years ago I couldn't resist telling her that, overall, one of her books suffered from an unbearable lightness of being."

He stretches out his legs and yawns a little. But he knows how to make a yawn look like an affectionate act. How does he do that? It's the way his eyes smile. "That's pretty all-inclusive...."

"I would never have got over it either, if another writer had dared to say such a thing to me. And yet writers say things like that to each other all the time. And besides, I felt she deserved it."

"A man would just laugh at another man who said that to him, or try to beat the bastard at squash."

"But women never forgive. Who said that? Virginia Woolf, I think, in *To the Lighthouse*. No, she didn't say that, she said children never forgive. But she didn't say that either: she said children never forget."

But Galbraith wants to talk about Josette. "The thing is, she means well. And then I also have to travel a lot. Which is a great relief really, because when I'm home it's like living inside a cage filled with birds. Before our baby was born, she used to have to go out to work every day, but now she's at home except for the days she's offered contract work. And so it's hours and hours of chirping. To me, to the baby, to her sisters, to my sisters, to her thousands of women friends...."

What about sex, does she chirp during sex? But this is a question that can never be asked.

"And because at work she has to repeat the words of other people so constantly, she wants to use her own words when she gets home, she just can't stop the flow."

I listen strategically, like a therapist. I listen like a woman who doesn't chirp.

"When we first started going out together, we ate out at a different ethnic restaurant every goddamn night. When we ate at Russian restaurants she'd talk to the waiters in Russian and they would fall in love with her. Same story with the German and Italian and Spanish waiters. And the more I could see other men falling in love with her, the more desirable I found her. Eventually, though, I woke up to the fact that we had no relationship to speak of...." He stops abruptly. "You don't find this boring, do you?"

"Not at all. Please go on."

"So one night when we were eating at a German restaurant, I suggested that although we'd had a good time together, from now on it would probably be best if we could both start to see other people, and that's when she told me she was pregnant. And so by the time we'd both had three more glasses of wine I'd convinced myself that I'd always been too demanding with women and here was this beautiful multilingual woman who would give birth to beautiful multilingual babies and so I asked her to marry me. And by the next afternoon already, all of her sisters and all of my sisters were in on the act and my life had turned into a maelstrom. Shrieks, consultations with florists, tickets to Costa Rica ..."

"And so how is it now?"

"It's fine, really. Because when all's said and done, we get along fine."

Fine, then. But it doesn't sound fine.

"We never fight, what's there to fight about, she just chirps and I listen."

I picture Josette's animation as a flash fire roaring across their marriage, leaving behind it a black field where nothing can grow.

"Or I don't listen. As the case may be." He turns to me. "So tell me how you are, then."

Without warning my eyes fill. But it would kill me to be his wife, it would kill me to be the one who has to wonder where he is and what time he'll be home. Or to go out to parties with him and have to pretend not to notice the way he's pretending not to look at other women. "I suppose it's a dangerous plateau to have reached, the plateau where writing has become the life, and so-called real life is an intrusion...."

He looks over at me, then looks quickly away, seems to call himself to attention, leans forward to rest his arms on his knees. "You mentioned a mouse running over your foot. Have you seen any others?"

"There have been. There have actually been whole armies of them." And I tell him about my phobia and how it began with the gift my cat brought me in the middle of the night.

"Did I ever tell you about the time I opened a kitchen cupboard and there was a mouse sitting on the floor beside a bag of potatoes? Just a little thing, I picked it up in my hands."

"Did you take it outside and set it free?"

"I gave it to my cat."

When I stare at him, he says, "I look at it this way, your cat gave a gift to you, but I gave a gift to my cat."

We both have to laugh at that. "One afternoon a few months ago, one of the senior architects in this new firm I'm with cried out for help and we all rushed into his office, afraid he was having a heart attack. But when we got in there he was standing on top of his desk, terrified because he'd seen a mouse run across the room. And he's a huge guy, he was a football star back in his university days."

A story I'm grateful for. But now he too must make the flashlight tour, his tour like the tours of all the exterminators, he even follows the same exterminator itinerary. "Sorry," he says at the end of it, handing the flashlight back to me. "But what a mystery."

Just before he leaves, he decides to take one last look, and I follow him out to the kitchen again, watch him lower himself flat on the floor next to the cabinet that's under the sink. He looks like a man about to do push-ups, but then he collapses and lies completely flat, slides a hand under the door. "The door doesn't fit flush with the door frame down here and so I've found it. A good-sized gap."

"This is so brilliant of you. Because everyone else has also always looked down there."

"You have to actually lie down beside it to find the lopsided error in the carpentry that's been allowing all these armies and plagues of mice to run in and out."

How incredible that this tiny entrance into my life has been found so late in the day. When he stands up, I hug him. "Irony of ironies. I could have stayed here."

"If only I'd called you sooner and you'd told me your mouse story sooner you might have stayed here forever."

"It's true, I would have."

It could even have been the perfect arrangement. Just enough anticipation, just enough solitude. But it's not going to be. On the way to the door we are even a little formal with one another, we even step back from one another a little as we say goodbye.

I STAND IN MY DOORWAY to listen for the sound of footsteps coming up. But there aren't any footsteps coming up, instead it's the elevator that's hitching and rising. And when the doors slide open, my visitor is Humpty Dumpty. Or at least this particular pair of spindly legs in striped tights (horizontal bands of red, bands of white) seems to be connected to a body that's a giant egg of flowers sheathed in squeaky clear plastic. And no human head in evidence until a delivery boy's face peers around the great floral egg. "Madame Oleski?"

When I say *oui,* he places the flowers, like a giant floral baby, in my arms, and after he's gone, I cut the sweetly funereal forest out of its oxygen tent and extract a small card:

For K,
I'll call you, G

I sit down beside them to breathe them in and it's like sitting down next to a tall leafy man. But they also make me uneasy, because they seem to mean goodbye, and after I've climbed into bed—it's raining tonight, a light summer rain—I feel tearful as I open my jar of night cream and make a face called "the Lion" that involves sucking in my cheeks and raising my eyebrows in an unimpressed way, then forcing my tongue out of the contracted "o" of my mouth. I so dread getting old, dread the prospect of having people speak to me as if I'm a not very bright toddler. I dread people's smiles, even. Dread seeing men walk toward me on the street and not pay any attention at all to me, not see me, even, dread the terrible future days when I'll be of no more interest in the landscape than a park bench or a pebble.

But I have to get up again to brush my teeth and on my way back to bed turn the corner to meet my flowers. I drop an aspirin into the water before I turn out the lights, inhale the damp leafy fragrance with its scent of decay. In two weeks I'll have to go to Toronto to look for an apartment, with great good luck I might even find one that's close to the lake. I try to see the city as thrilling beneath the façade of its staid reputation, see boardwalks running next to the lake's glitter, the long slope of green parks in the shady green afternoons.

More and more students come up the stairs to my floor as the summer moves toward September. They stand shyly in each of my doorways as if an invisible rope is holding them back from going near the bed on display, near the table that's on display with its African batik. This is what it must be like to be dead. When I'm dead I'll look down (or up) from wherever I am in the afterlife and see those who are still among the living as they draw back the curtains and let the morning sunlight in. But after a time no more visitors come, the apartment must have been taken. And Galbraith doesn't call. So the flowers really did mean goodbye then, I at least know enough about the world to know this much.

So I'm going, I'll be gone, and so I phone Tom.

"But you'll never be able to afford it here, it's out of sight. So why don't you just take a room here and keep your apartment in Montreal? You can commute back and forth, get the best of both worlds."

"The only problem is that my apartment here already seems to have been rented out to someone else. At least it must have been, no one has come up to look at it lately."

"But Ma, that's a tragedy, that's a terrific little apartment, you've got to start doing what you're always telling Benno and me to do: you've got to think ahead."

When I go downstairs to knock on Kelly and Mohammed's door, Mohammed opens it.

"I've been wondering if my apartment has been rented out yet."

"The last people who saw it were going to take it but they never came back to sign the lease."

"So it's still free, then?"

"It's free."

MY FLOWERS HAVE has by now dried down to withered licks of pink and purple, their green leaves gone tan, tan papery leaves ending in slimy grey and tan stems, done for. On my way down to the basement with them, I hear my bell ring. Is it him? It has to be him and I don't even know what I look like, but I uneasily keep on going down until I get an almost aerial view of a tiny man and woman in pale raincoats on the far side of the heavy glass in the lower door, waiting.

Idona and Henry, how can this be?

But here they are, I let them in.

"Hello, little Kay," says Idona. "We're in Montreal for the day and so we thought we'd drop by."

Henry smiles one of his ancient smiles, looking more like a turtle than ever. A virile turtle, but a turtle nevertheless.

Idona doesn't ask about the flowers, oddly enough, and once we're up in my apartment, I poke them into a garbage bag, then pour out three glasses of apple juice and carry them into the front room on a red tin tray.

"It seems that it's been quite some time since we've been in touch, sweetie...."

"I've been meaning to write you. To tell you I'll be moving to Toronto. To teach ..."

"And are you excited by that?"

"I have mixed feelings about it, actually."

"Who were the flowers from, darling?"

"From someone I love."

"Oh, do tell. Do tell us more. How did you meet him, for instance?"

"Through Alexander. Crazily enough."

"Alexander introduced you to him?"

"Not directly. But it's still because of Alexander that I met him. I got a job with a cousin of Alexander's just after I moved to Montreal and the office where this man was working was down on the mezzanine level and so eventually we met."

"Was he that lovely young man you were with the night you came to have dessert with us at the Ritz-Carlton?"

"Yes," I say. "As a matter of fact he was."

"But what happened?"

"His work took him to another country." And I escape out to the kitchen to put on the kettle for tea. Out in that breezy privacy, I run a blast of cold water into the kettle, then rip open a packet of oat cakes. But I can tell you this much, I say to Idona, to myself: I still get flowers sent to me even if the one who loves me doesn't even know he loves me.

BENNO COMES OVER for dinner two nights before he's to fly west to study marine biology at UVic, and while we're drying the dishes I remember that Victoria is allegedly druggier than druggy Montreal. "Bennie, you won't take drugs, will you?"

"I'm an alkie, remember?"

"Yes, but do you do drugs at all any more?"

"Hardly ever."

How often is hardly ever? But I don't dare ask. "Just one thing: you wouldn't ever take acid?"

"Mum, *no*. I told you, years ago. I'm finished with acid." And he does an imitation of the drug dealers on St. Denis adding and dropping *h*'s as they go: "'Ash, hacide, mescalanh, coke ...'"

I walk with him down to the street. Down by the back entrance, we embrace shyly. God be with you, my son. But I can't say it, he would hate it. I stand watching him walk away. In his long coat he carries himself very straight, his shoulders tall. I watch him turn right onto de Maisonneuve. He does not look back.

A SLIP OF PAPER that has a telephone message from Professor Calhoun written on it has been left on my bed by my new landlord, Señor Mendoza, the night I arrive in Toronto:

> I'm afraid that we have a bit of an academic emergency here. Please call me immediately upon arrival, no matter how late your train gets in.

I sink down on the bed in the unfamiliar room. My dark academic history has been discovered, then. Which must mean that York insisted on seeing my transcripts and therefore my adventure in the wide world is already over. But Professor Calhoun, when I reach him, sounds amazingly grateful to hear from me: "Would you be willing to take on another workshop? One of our instructors has intractable back pain and will be dropping one of his workshops. This way we can pay you sixteen thousand for eight months instead of a mere eight." And after giving me this astounding news he even thanks me for saving his life.

Two mornings later, I teach my first class. It's not in a classroom, it's in a seminar room, my students are seated on both sides of the long table and are looking relaxed in a way that suggests they all know one another from other classes. I stiffly stand at the teacher end, dressed in a slim skirt and a strictly tailored red linen jacket that's equipped with the monster shoulder pads that are all the rage this year, and I read from the notes I've written (a mix of theories and quotes and ideas about fiction) while they gaze at me as if they think I must be a novice, someone they'll have to help along with advice, the facts of life, the facts of fiction. Later I learn that I should have done what all of the other instructors do, I should have lolled in a chair at my own end of the table and asked people to introduce themselves, tell the class why they want to be writers.

The following week I wear a black silk shirt with shoulder pads, the red jacket with its monster shoulder pads again, then top my outfit off with a raincoat that has significant shoulder pads. I think I must look as ludicrously padded as a football player as I cross the field to the tower I teach in—give me a tap, I'll topple over—and on my way to a staff meeting after class I wonder if it's the authority in so many pairs of shoulder pads that has made my workshop go better.

"Just remember this," one of the poets on staff tells me (he's sitting next to the poet bpNichol, the instructor whose back pain is so severe that it's given me the gift of the second workshop). "If you can flirt with your students, you can teach them. Teaching is all about flirting."

This is advice that helps me when I'm marking their work on the train to Montreal and can't think of a single word to say about it. It helps me write to a young man who has floppy hair and sad clever eyes: "What can I do for you, apart from trying to rein in your runaway syntax?"

I HEAR A MALE VOICE call out to a student who's taking a drink from the water fountain in the main hallway of my tower, "Beepee died, man!" And I suppose that this Beepee must be a student, some lonely and unlucky East Indian student who has died of a drug overdose.

It's only as I'm on my way to my office that it occurs to me that Beepee is bpNichol, my benefactor poet. I run up to the second floor to talk to the secretary for the division of Humanities. "Did bpNichol die? I thought he just had back pain."

"They discovered too late that his back pain was a tumour on the spine. But it wasn't the tumour that killed him, it was the operation to remove it. It lasted over thirteen hours and he died on the operating table. His students are in shock."

I hurry across the campus to the bookstore to buy a book of bpNichol's poetry because I'll have to tell my students that he has died and it will be so much better if I can make the announcement a tribute to him. I also can't stop thinking of how much my life was changed, not by his death but by the pain that led to his death, as in life's endless shuffle, life's perpetual longing for transformation, someone's bad luck was converted into someone's good luck. But to be the beneficiary of such spectacular sorrow is humbling, almost scary, and so to cheer myself I buy a book of poems about Kafka called *K. in Love* that I'll give to Galbraith if I ever see him again, and once I've got back to my classroom and my students are already filing in, claiming their usual spots on both sides of the table, I bring *The Martyrology* to the front of the class with me, then print from it on the blackboard in large letters:

A
LAKE
A
LANE
A
LINE
A
LONE

They'll love this list, they'll love the fact that it's vertical, musical, and once everyone is settled, I tap the blackboard with a pointer, speak each set of words aloud, find them pleasing to intone, even if I'm also afraid the formal solemnity of my voice will make me express my discomfort by laughing. "Do any of you recognize these particular words?"

No, they don't.

Already regretting my innovative way of announcing such terrible news, I tell them: "They were written by one of the poets on staff here."

A tentative arm goes up, the arm of a nervously pale girl at the far end of the table. "I think they might have been written by bpNichol."

"Excellent," I say. But how can I follow my "excellent" with today's shocking news? My announcement will seem too much like the punch line to a sadistic joke.

"Think of these lines as a sort of epitaph," I say and I begin to feel shaky, as if I might not laugh, but cry. "Containing words that will live on, after the poet. Words that convey, in this distilled manner, not only his method but also his gift for evoking, in words that are almost a code—and a code that's a terrifically rhythmic code—this city with its great lake and its lanes, as well as the news that we are born alone and we die alone ..." But now I can see that I've lost them, that they hear this kind of talk as professor talk. Or as parent talk, the talk of a parent who fears dying, growing old.

Another hand goes up, the hand of a male student with combed-back yellow hair and ambitious eyes who's sitting two students down from me. "Professor Oleski?"

I respond with what I hope is an alert but dignified "Yes?"

"We've got a whole load of work to get through today, so maybe we should consider getting this show on the road?"

"Fair enough," I say, startled. "But I first of all want to reassure everyone in this class that my remarks were not idle chatter, they were in fact the introduction to very sad news. The poet who wrote these stunning words, bpNichol, died yesterday."

There's a shocked silence, then a girl in pink overalls moans *"No"* as she gathers up her books and hurries out of the room.

ALL THE WINDY DAYS of the damp fall, I keep two gooseneck lamps aimed at my bed, two bright pools of light in the hideous polyester hideout of my tiny apartment, on the bedside table a stack of books, a bowl of apples.

On the first Tuesday in November when I walk with my landlord out to Bloor Street in the dry frosty air, he tells me about how he came to meet his wife, a few years after the end of the Second World War. "It was at almost the exact mid-point of the twentieth century, it was in June, 1950. I was conscripted into Generalissimo Franco's army, there was no way to escape it. I was posted to Barcelona, but while I was on vacation visiting my family on the Costa Brava, in a town where I have many cousins, one of my cousins asked me if I would do his patrol for him for two hours. He was in the Civil Guard and his patrol was the beach. He loaned me his uniform and his rifle and so I went down to the Mediterranean to impersonate him to the waves, to the seabirds. I was expecting a pleasant but dull afternoon since there were so seldom any visitors to that part of the coast. Instead I was surprised to see a girl sunbathing all alone. She was fair, like you. I thought she was Danish. Danish or American."

"Which did you want her to be most?"

"Danish, because Danish girls were supposed to be—" But words fail him and so he only smiles.

"Quite wild?"

"That's what people said. And so I paraded up and down that same stretch of beach until she called out to me, 'Señor! Por favor!' She had a cigarette in one hand and was digging a hole in the sand with the other, but as I got closer to her, I could see her drop her cigarette into the hole, then smooth the sand over it, and I wondered if she was afraid I would shoot her for smoking."

"Could she speak any Spanish?"

"A few words. Hasta la vista. Vaya con dios. I laid my gun on the sand and she handed me a bottle of suntan oil. But the only English words I knew were the words 'Well, hell, buddy, that's real swell.'"

"Words you got from the movies?"

"Yes, exactly. From American movies during the war. Then she scratched her name and the name of her hotel in the sand with a stick. She had the same initials I do. Joyce Miller, Juan Mendoza. And that seemed to me to be a very good sign. I picked her up at her hotel when my shift was over and we went out for a drink. I'd changed into a white shirt and slacks by this time and I was sitting on the patio of our local bodega with my arm around her when a member of the Civil Guard came over to us. And what he said will give you some small indication of how repressed Spain was at that time. How devout. Because what he said to me was, 'Sir! In *my* country, that is *not* done.' I responded, 'Well, hell, buddy, that's real swell.' He was scandalized, but what could he do? He couldn't very well apprehend a man he took to be an American tourist."

And the town, he told me, was Palamos, a town I incredibly once lived in for three weeks. "With my husband the first year we were married. We drove out to the beach every morning on our motorcycle, we had the place all to ourselves. We must have been lying on the same beach where you met your wife."

He's older than I am and so he doesn't find this nearly as amazing as I do. Or so I conclude when I get back to my room and record our conversation, feeling like a perpetual magpie as I write in my notebook: "He loaned me his uniform and his rifle, and I went down to the sea to impersonate him to the waves, to the seabirds."

COMING BACK to Montreal on a Wednesday is like coming back to it on a Sunday afternoon at the end of summer, it's so deserted and sunny. Like London on a Sunday afternoon after World War II. It even makes me doubt the wisdom of keeping my apartment here because of what use is it, really? I never see Galbraith.

But then on Saturday I do see him. I walk over to Westmount Park, pass through the muggy Victorian greenhouse that's attached to the library, then walk down the library steps and out onto the sunlit grass to see two men in the middle distance throwing a Frisbee to three children. One of the men is Galbraith and the other is Felix. Now and then they aim the spinning white saucer down low for the children to catch, but most of the time it flies from one brother to the other, a white moon sailing high and wide in the sunlit sky. I walk part of the way toward them, then lean against a tree as Felix whirls and throws the Frisbee, then I watch Galbraith come racing toward it, the sun in his eyes, but he's still able to manage (with a sideways leap) to intercept it. I feel camouflaged, hidden within the dappled shelter of the leaves and while I'm leaning back against my hands, braced against the tree trunk, I make a bargain with myself: if he glances in my direction within the next fifteen minutes, I'll walk out into the sunlight to meet him. But if he doesn't, I'll go home, I'll give him up forever. I look at my watch, look out at him, look at my watch again. Eventually the fifteen minutes go by. And so I let another ten minutes pass, then another ten until at last the shadows lengthen across the green grass and the two brothers call to the children and they all walk away up the brick road to the far side of the park.

Wʜᴇɴ ᴄᴏʟᴅ ᴡɪɴᴅs ʙʟᴏᴡ up the canyons of Toronto this morning I pull leg-warmers on over my tights, blurred brown birds and stars knitted into the tubes of coarsely swollen grey wool. I've decided to stay here this week, holed up in my green cave to work on two poems to send to Clifton Field, a York poet who's just published a fine first collection of poems that I recently bought at Book City. After my Monday class, a student we have in common is the emissary who takes him my poems along with a fan's notes on his work. I also send him my long poem about a baby deer my father found in the woods and then brought back home for us to raise until the day it was shot by an idiot hunter from the city.

The following Wednesday the emissary brings a note back from Professor Field: "Could we do coffee next Monday at four? At the faculty club? Being a sleuth of sorts, I've already ascertained that your last class gets out at four. Your poems interest me a great deal, by the way."

On Monday afternoon, as I'm crossing the campus with two of my women students, we all turn to glance at a giant of a man who's wearing his raincoat collar turned up as he's talking to a tiny girl just beyond the entrance to Vanier College. A courtly hawk in the freezing rain, he's the sort of man a woman might be willing to throw herself over a cliff for. "Who is that?"

My students smile at me, their eyes teasingly shine, the more mischievous one even watches my eyes as she says, "That's Professor Field, isn't he adorable?"

At five past four I find Clifton Field sitting at one of the tables next to the windows of the faculty club, making notes on a stack of papers. Up close, his hair is in three colours: tufts of white, strands of grey, claws of black, the claws branching out from his head like hacked-off slices of crow wings. When he glances up and sees me, he gets to his feet to shake my hand, and once we've sat down he immediately begins to butcher each of my poems for the greater good of the poem, although he seems to be quite fond of what he calls, with a sideways smile, "the Bambi poem," and particularly seems to admire "that pious shark of a Chrysler" (the idiot hunter's car), and the fawn's spots fading to a "muddied snow in his coat of adulthood."

"So you're the nymph complaining of the death of your fawn," he says, then tells me that "The Nymph Complaining for the Death of Her Fawn" is the title of a passionate poem of loss written by Andrew Marvell. And he quotes two lines from it for me:

> But all its chief delight was still
> On roses thus itself to fill

"Eight beats per line, and therefore it has a much more formal rhythm than yours. And of course it's either confined or liberated by having its end words forced into rhymes, depending on your point of view. Whereas your lines, which also refer to a fawn eating flowers in a garden—four hundred years pass and fawns are still addicted to flowers—are more casual. And the beats are more uneven, nine in the first two lines, ten in the third, eleven in the fourth, eleven in the fifth...."

When I say that I never count beats, he tells me that the odd thing about going with form, with limitations, is that one is forced to be resourceful. He points to a weak section of my poem and asks me to read it aloud, but slowly. And so I awkwardly clear my throat to read:

> *he stayed with you all of that summer,*
> *chomping the tops off all the blossoms*
> *in the back garden, everyone's darling,*
> *so spotted and shy above the backed-up stilts*
> *of his legs. All of July and August you*
> *had to know where he was every minute,*
> *you could not bear to go to bed in the evenings*
> *while he was still allowed to be up with the grown-ups*

"It's a bit prosy, don't you think? And even though there's more orig-inality in your poem than there is in Marvell's poem—your use of a verb like 'chomping,' for instance, which in Marvell's defence might not even have existed back in his day, and 'the backed-up stilts of his legs' which catches the fawn's skittishness so very well—I'd have to say that Marvell's poem is more luscious than yours, the roses are more dewy, its confinements force it to transmogrify into a truly gorgeous mouthful of blossoms. Or a mouthful of petals. Come to think of it, it's actually somewhat vulvular although it's the sibilance of the sounds—'chief, itself, still, fill, roses, thus'—that gives it such a heady impression of sweetness and moisture."

Outside the tall windows snow has erratically begun to fall and inside the faculty club people are rising and yawning, then pulling on their coats. After another fifteen minutes or so, Cliff and I also stand to pull on our coats and as we're walking across the campus together I tell him that all the pets we had in my family came to bad ends. "Not just the pet deer who got shot by a hunter on the first day of hunting season, but also a pet crow who flew at our windmill in the middle of a storm and was decapitated. And my sister and I had two turtles,

Victoria and Albert, who died from a massive overdose of turtle food. We were the ones who killed them." We killed them, not knowing we were killing them. Every night we fought over whose turn it was to feed them because we so loved to watch the turtle powder sinking down into the aquarium's lamplit water like golden snow.

A WIND-SANITIZED MORNING blows across the city after the first crowds of leaves have been driven from Montreal's trees, but now dark rain clouds are moving in, pushed by a warm wind, almost a summer wind in November. I want to go out for a walk in it, but just as I'm about to leave, the doorbell rings. I go out into the hall to see the shiny yellow hard hat of a construction worker coming up, but as the owner of the hat turns onto the final stairway, I see that the not truly unexpected has happened: he's been transformed into Galbraith.

"I've just been inspecting a site near here with the fire chief," he calls up to me. "And so I thought I'd drop by to see if your name was still listed in the lobby directory."

The wind beyond my balcony is shaking the leafy crowns of the trees as he comes in, then there's a wild attack of rain, we can hear it hitting the skylight over the bathtub like hail.

He takes off the yellow construction hat as I pull off my raincoat and dump it over the back of a chair. "So you're still living here then."

"Off and on. I was sure that my apartment was taken, but then it turned out that it wasn't. And so I took that as a sign that I shouldn't let it go. And then the first night I arrived in Toronto I was offered another workshop at York which means that I can keep the apartment here and a room in Toronto and still have enough money left over to travel back and forth. But would you like a drink? Although I only have tonic water."

He seems preoccupied and I'm not even sure that he's quite taken in what I've just said. But then he says, "Water, tonic water, anything, anything at all would be fine."

I go out to the kitchen to get us glasses of tonic water and on my way back to him, when I detour into the bathroom to spray cologne onto my wrists, I can hear that the rain on the skylight has subsided.

"How amazing," I say when I go back to him and hand him his drink, "that the rain, just like that, has already stopped," but then I worry that he'll be able to smell that I've put perfume on. "So let's go for a walk to the park."

"But do you really want to? It's going to be so damn wet out."

"I have books that I need to take back to the library. And this could be the last warm day till next summer."

"True."

As we go down into the damp day he talks about his year in New York. Then I describe the wicker armchair painted a hideous dark green that's in my room in Toronto and the green wallpaper with pink rosebuds on it and the Spanish shutters painted a darker green and a cushion stitched to look like a puffy beige heart. "Along with thousands of knick-knacks and what-nots...."

"It sounds pretty horrible."

"It's very horrible."

We leave my pile of books on the library desk, then go down the steps into the green world of the park to find it a little unfriendly after the rain. The leaves drip heavy drops of water on the great lawns, the wet grass drags a tickle across my bare feet in my sandals. But what I feel most of all is too heavy in my hips, over-sexed from the sex we didn't even have.

"One Sunday afternoon when I was still in New York I bought your book."

I thank him. "But did you have a chance to read any of it yet?"

"I did. But because I know you so well, I'd start thinking of you, thoughts of you kept on keeping me from reading your book. I also really wanted you to only be intimate with me, I didn't want you to be intimate with thousands of strangers." But then he looks at his watch. "Listen, I have to nip over to Verdun, to rue de Sébastopol, to look at an old warehouse so I can come up with a plan to convert it into studios for painters and sculptors, a project financed by a local tycoon. Want to come with me?"

And so we drive over there, walk into a dim utilitarian tower, a wainscotting of chicken wire protecting the glass of the lower windows although the higher windows have a clean view of grey sky. Feathers drift into the corners like eiderdown as we try not to breathe in the mould and old urine smells, while it's also hard not to find the soaring height of the walls oppressive, hard not to see Galbraith, pacing back and forth, as a prisoner pacing the circumference of a contaminated well.

But when we get back to Claremont we sit slumped in his car. Exhausted by the rain, by the day. I lean my head back on the seat and turn to look at him. "I kept your flowers alive for a such a long time…."

"How did you do that?"

"I dropped an aspirin into the water every night before I went to bed."

"How did you know that would work?"

"I read it somewhere. In a magazine, probably. But I never thanked you for them…."

"So why didn't you call me, then?"

I tuck a leg beneath me and shake my head.

"So on a whim I innocently send you a bouquet of flowers, but then it turns out that it's not a bouquet of flowers after all, it's a faux pas, maybe even a criminal act."

"They weren't a bouquet, they were a whole garden. I also didn't know what they meant."

"They didn't mean anything, they were flowers."

"So did they mean hello or did they mean goodbye?"

"They sure as hell didn't mean goodbye."

"Your note also said you would call and then you didn't call."

"It's true that when I didn't hear from you, I decided not to call."

"I didn't even know where to reach you."

"I'm in the phone book."

"Please don't play games with me. I don't even know what this new firm you're with is called. And I knew I couldn't call you at home."

"Speaking of calls, I have a few people I should be calling right now and if it's all right with you I'd like to call them from your place."

Up in my bedroom he holds the phone swinging between his knees while he talks and I lie on the bed behind him and rest the palm of a hand on his lower back, sending warmth into it since it so often causes him pain, then close my eyes, hear him end his call with a "salut," feel him lie down beside me.

"You've bought yourself a new mattress, I'm happy to see. This one feels so much firmer."

"I had to get a new one because the old one was so shot."

"Thanks to us, I hope."

"Thanks to us, thanks to you. Thanks even to me, all by myself alone …"

He bites the fat part of one of my fingers. Bites it with one of the holding bites of a cat. A bite that doesn't hurt, but a bite that won't let my finger go either. But then he does let go of it to say, "To go back to the mattress again. Have there been others?"

"Other mattresses?"

"Other lovers."

"I got to be very close to a guy I met at Stanopolis."

"Did you become lovers?"

"He wanted us to be."

"How do you know that?" His voice skeptical. A husband's voice, skeptical but threatened.

"Because he asked me, Galbraith."

"What did he say?"

I don't want to tell him that Lorenzo propositioned me on the phone and so I only say, "I think it would be really disloyal of me to tell you that."

"And so I suppose he's a reedy and pale little guy? A bit wispy? An academic type?"

"Not really. And not reedy either. And not pale and not little. But possibly just a wee bit academic. Although most certainly not wispy. In other words not at all as you apparently imagine him to be. In fact he's an Italian. An Italian who, as a matter of fact, happens to be magnificently handsome."

"Is he gay?"

"No."

"Is he more handsome than I am?"

"Yes."

He strokes back my hair, rhythmically, almost feverishly. "Is he taller?"

"Much."

"And so do you love him too?"

"I've already told you."

"What did you tell me? Tell me again. I forget."

"That we got very close."

He pulls me on top of him, then shoves two pillows under his head so he can raise his head high enough to give my nipples the same tiny pulling bites he gave to my finger, tiny bites that make me remember so many of the ways I've felt in bed—like a storm, like a baby, like a pony, like a man, like a rider—I even love the fact that we're keeping our clothes on, at least for the moment, it's like being back at the beginning of sex all over again.

But after he leaves me, I can't settle down. And for hours, for all night and all the next day, the skin of my inner arm (my right arm) carries the memory of standing with him down on the sidewalk in the lonely early evening, and the way my arm around his waist kept feeling the breathing warmth of his skin through the drier warmth of his cotton shirt.

November rain beads on the windshield and so it must blur us to anyone who might come walking by, although in a reversal of the usual state of things (since Toronto is the more tropical city) it's snowing all along Lake Ontario by the time my train comes into Union Station.

It's still snowing on Monday evening when I run into Señor Mendoza on his way out as I'm on my way in. He lifts his fedora. "I was hoping to encounter you, Kay. I would like to invite you to dinner at my restaurant on Sunday night. The Manoir Mendoza, on Yonge Street. My son will be there also, and perhaps also my daughter."

I feel the old terror of having my time frittered away by social occasions. "That's really so kind of you, but I'm actually in Montreal on Sunday nights. I take the train in the early evening and I don't actually reach Toronto until close to midnight...."

Actually.

"But Tuesday night is perhaps free?"

How can I convey my gratitude while at the same time turning him down so I can keep the evening free to work at my work? I feel a kind of hysteria from the thought of the squandered hours. After all, what is free time for, except to write? Write and make love? But Señor Mendoza believes me to be a teacher. He is also my landlord and has been remarkably kind to me, and so I say yes.

And the dinner is fine. Mendoza and his son eat with me and just as we are finishing our paella and some kind of fish in an oily orange sauce, the daughter comes in, a gold silk scarf puffed out at her perfumed throat. Polite questions, polite answers, an exchange of cigarettes and cigarillos (we all smoke, although we are all trying to stop). "But even if the whole world stops smoking, smoking will make a comeback," says Mendoza, "Because everything does. Someone will think of a way to make smoking healthy. Cigarettes made of oxygen. Oxygen and fire. The perfect combination!"

"Smoking kills smokers," says Mendoza's son. "But why wait years to die? Be efficient! The new improved oxygen cigarette will make you die on the spot!"

We all laugh, the way people laugh when they joke about death, and then Mendoza and I, walking home to Borden Street, also talk about death, the death of Mendoza's wife in a hospital in a town not far from Mexico City. From a water-borne illness. "We were drinking bottled water, but she must have forgotten the danger momentarily and taken a few sips of the local water."

"Was it cholera?"

"No, it was an illness that affected her kidneys."

I listen to the loneliness in Mendoza's voice. I fear loneliness, too, in every way it can be feared, but I fear the loneliness of others too, especially if it's a loneliness that interferes with the solitude that I require to write about, among other things, loneliness. But if I were writing a certain kind of novel, I think, letting myself into my bedroom above Mendoza's bedroom, if I were writing the kind of novel that ends with all the characters rounded up like cattle for the epiphany, the character based on me would be paired up with Juan Mendoza, a widower after all, and a kind and thoughtful man who is older than I am and who even happens to be taller. But I hope never to write this kind of novel,

it's so much my fate to continue to be the lover of the more inappropriate man. Which makes me wonder, as I've wondered all evening, if
he has called me, but there's no red light flashing on my answering
machine. I sit down on my bed, overcome by sadness and even fear
because he hasn't called, a sadness that's emerging from a more general-
ized sensation of loss, the squandered hours in which I didn't write.

It continues to snow while I'm brushing my hair. I watch it fall
beyond the window with its interior green shutters pinned back
against the pattern of roses on the wall. Galbraith was supposed to
arrive in Montreal at eight tonight after a day of meetings in
Edmonton and it's now nearly eleven. How would I ever even know if
anything bad happened to him? Who would tell me? I feel afraid in
the way I felt afraid when my children were small and one of them was
fifteen minutes late coming home from school. The questions I asked
myself are even the same questions. How can I live? How can I live in
this world without this person I so love?

I carry the phone into the bathroom with me so that if it rings while
I'm taking my shower I'll be able to hear it, and discover something I
forgot I knew, that the water from the shower rings like a phone ringing,
it rings and rings, and (as always) each time I turn it off, the ringing stops.

It's just after midnight when I turn out my light. I don't close the
shutters, instead I lie in the dark watching the illuminated snow
falling in front of the pink brick wall of the house next door to the
Mendoza house and my aloneness is as alive as an animal, as alive as
my own heart.

I'VE BEEN INVITED to go to lunch with Mira Brukova a week from Tuesday. "She's a legendary Czech poet who lives out in the country near Kleinburg," Cliff tells me as we're walking across the campus on Monday night. "And I'll need to pick you up on Tuesday morning no later than eleven." After we've said goodbye, I walk to the division of Humanities to check my mailbox and find an envelope returning all of the poems I recently sent out to a local poetry magazine. They've come back too fast, were perhaps not even glanced at. On the train south, they lie in my lap, white pages turned into white petals with my life written on them, their quick return a sadness like no other. I decide not to tell Cliff about getting them back and when he comes to pick me up for our visit to Kleinburg, bounding up the stairs to my rumpled room pumped up with vodka or vitamins or whatever damn thing he eats for breakfast, he's looking like a huge happy hybrid, some kind of puppyhawk, the black leather tongue with his car keys clipped to it hanging from the grip of his bared teeth as he pulls off his gloves.

When he helps me into my new coat—a long tan coat that I bought last week because its feathery black collar blooms up close to my face—he gives me a startled look, as if up till now he's always thought of me as a nondescript woman, even plain, but fur near my face must do something alluring for me, then we clump down into the mild morning to find Mendoza scraping the snow off the front steps with his shovel. But he takes off his fedora and bows to me as I come down the porch steps. "Buenos dias, Kay."

"Buenos dias, Señor Mendoza."

Cliff has already swept past him. "So here we are, then!" he calls back to me. "Here's my pious shark of a Chrysler!"

Once we're on our way, I glance back over my shoulder. "I really ought to have introduced you to Señor Mendoza."

"The debonair guy in the fedora who was bowing and scraping?"

I try to think of a way of defending Mendoza without seeming to be sanctimonious about it, but Cliff is already singing "Spanish Eyes," then he glances over at me to say, "The señora has very wistful eyes this morning. Why so wistful, Señora?"

"It's nothing, really."

"So it's nothing, really. That sounds fairly serious."

And so I tell him.

"What did you send them?"

"All of the poems you and I worked on together."

"Then I'm offended as well."

This makes us laugh. So how much better it is to have confessed. To have confessed and to smile in the company of another writer. Not to be swamped by a lonely and cranky melancholy. Now he's even telling me school secrets to cheer me up, departmental gossip. "Alas, poor York ... I knew it, Katarina...." And it *is* crazily soothing, as gossip so often is, it even makes me feel happy and philosophical about life as we drive through the bleached industrial landscape that lies on both sides of Keele, past factories and faded industrial billboards and smokestacks puffing out big white puffs of poisonous smoke, then on past the dull grey dormitory skyscrapers of Student City, the fields of dead grass under grey winter skies.

"So how's the teaching going? Mostly going well?"

"Mostly." But then I say, "Oh God, I don't know. I think they think I'm insane, actually...."

"So let's see how we can orchestrate this into an advantage for you."

"You think we can?"

"Why not? Here's my own annual insane thing to do: every year on the first day of class I swing into the classroom, then stagger backwards until I feel my back hit the blackboard, then I let loose a great anguished howl: 'Who *are* all these people? Arrest them!' And once I've got them to laugh, I scowl at them, then tell them they should think of me as 'Da enemy, man, they should think of me as da *foe*.' And I swear to God they walk out of that class so confused that they are actually in love with me. Not that I'd recommend this kind of behaviour to a woman instructor."

I smile in uneasy agreement. I can sometimes make my students laugh, true, but (it must also be confessed) not always intentionally.

"And when the day comes for the dreaded teacher-evaluation forms to be handed out, I sashay into class looking intimidating but humble, noble but humble, confident but humble. Humble, humble, humble, humble. But also gimlet-eyed. And I'm here to tell you they get the message."

"I've been doing it all wrong, I can see. I've only mastered the humble part."

"You're right, that *is* wrong. You will suffer deeply for this."

But his methods, although fascinating to me, make me feel apprehensive. "So what's Mira Brukova's poetry like?"

"Heroic. Stalingrad and hunger. And more melodramatic than mellow. Not that one would want one's work to be either. She's a big fan of Akhmatova. Not that that's bad, but in her case it's not good."

"So why is she so legendary, then?"

"Because the trick she performs is called Living Too Long. By now her critics have all done her the favour of dying. Which in the case of some critics is the only favour they ever do any writer...."

We laugh again, lulled by all the talk of flirtation and death, lulled by the monotony of the landscape as we keep driving north. But at some point Cliff whistles, then turns off the narrow paved highway into a gravel pit where he does a relaxed stretch, turns off the ignition, then does another stretch that's like a morning stretch, a stretch that's the body's idea of a smile. "Looks like we're lost. I should try to see if I can unearth a map somewhere in this chaos."

But how sinister a gravel pit is, in its own utilitarian way. The country we've been driving through also adds an eerie cast to the early afternoon, it's so uninhabited, so desolate as the pale grasses move slightly in the wind and now and then a lonesome car glints darkly by on the oddly distant small highway.

It's AFTER ONE by the time we reach Mira Brukova's little white summer house, set far back on a parched lawn that's walled in by chewed-looking hedges, and Mira comes to the door in a shiny black dress with a mandarin collar, small and stooped from osteoporosis, her eyes brightly blue with what looks like a bitter nostalgia.

When we apologize to her for being so late, she says in a deep musical voice, "I did wonder," then leads us down a short flight of steps into the back of her house. The brunch, set out on a long table in the chilled sunroom, at first looks terrific but it turns out to have the dying taste of food that's been sitting out on plates for too many hours, the anointed taste of a meal that's been painfully concocted with an eye more to colour than what will taste good with what: a wilting salad of escarole and spinach leaves whose main seasoning seems to be black pepper, and just beneath the shelter of a bouquet of shedding tea roses, a platter of assorted sweaty red slices of salami. Chinese porcelain bowls heaped with glistening black caviar have also been set out on a black tray painted with the same species of roses that are the centrepiece for the table, and next to the painted tray there's a blue plate of cookies along with a platter of devilled eggs snowed red by paprika, and a giant glass jug of pink lemonade, the main course being a lukewarm asparagus soup that tastes unpleasantly of tin. So much of tin, in fact, that I make the excuse that I need to get a drink of water, then go out to the kitchen to dump it into the sink.

After lunch, we go up into the kitchen where Mira serves us a fragrant Chinese tea in delicate maroon china teacups that feel greasy and unwashed. I breathe in the sweetened steam and pray not to live to be as old as Mira, then go over to the screen door to see that it's snowing. I hear Cliff come up behind me, feel him clamp my shoulders with his immense hands in a way that feels so husbandly that a sexual shiver gives me the chills. I hope it doesn't mean that I'm attracted to him. In the mists of pre-history, I suppose I would have wanted to be part of his herd of women. A man who could protect me, a man with giant hands, giant feet. But now he's only quoting the final two verses of my November poem for Mira:

by noon
what's delirious
forced into storage

while bats of snow
blown to the windowscreen
peer blindly in

I should help Mira sit down before she says something terrible. But at the end of Cliff's recitation, she seems to have already forgotten the poem or was perhaps all along thinking of something else. Her childhood, perhaps. Or her need for a nap. And so there is silence in the winterized kitchen, the silence of snow falling on a dry lawn in deep country.

She could also be wishing that Cliff would just leave. Or she could be meditating on the fact that when he was reciting these few little verses by his new inamorata, she kept forgetting to listen. To her they might have sounded like nothing at all, as she would long ago have concluded that all poetry does in these dull modern times. She might instead be thinking of her own poems, so political, so glorious, so much more modern and dramatic than anything being written in this ironic but essentially shallow decade. Glory must be what she's wanting, glory and words that are violent, her thoughts so confused by old age or too many glasses of toxic lemonade that she's in the Russia of Akhmatova in one thought and in Kleinburg in the next thought: in a time of war and famine, women standing barefoot in the snow outside Russian prisons, flowers that bleed. But at least they seemed to enjoy the food.

As we're driving against the blowing squalls of snow on the way south, Cliff talks about one of his sons again (an elaboration on his revelations about this boy when we sat and talked for almost an hour in the gravel pit), then we're back to talking about "all this critical theory voodoo" again and when the conversation gets around to the pink lemonade, I tell him that at the turn of the century cooks turned lemonade pink by dropping a red necktie into it, leaving it there for ten minutes or so, then lifting it out while wringing the final squeezed drops of red dye into the drink.

"Jesus, Kay, why didn't you warn me? That lemonade tasted vile. Mira used to have lovers and some of these lovers must have had neckties and some of these ties would have had to be red. And so I suggest that we find ourselves a bistro where we can begin the disinfection process. Vodka first, then a bottle of wine along with something fantastic and foreign to eat. In fact, there's a good little place I know on Harbord Street where they serve lamb cooked with almonds and apricots." Which is how we end up drinking a lot of vodka and wine, then eating pouchy warm apricots along with a great deal of spiced lamb followed by tiny cups of coffee so strong it tastes as if it's been dug out of the darkest earth, then simmered all day on the back of the stove in Mira Brukova's kitchen.

In Montreal the snow must also be falling as Galbraith tries my number one last time before he goes home for the night. I picture him having to listen to his own voice on my answering machine, it must be like living inside some dark story of deceit. I see him stand at his desk in his coat and try my number one final time and when I get back to Borden Street and run up the stairs to my room, I go to the phone before I even take off my coat. Three calls from him and two clicks. I dial his number at work, but there's no answer. I eat an apple, then pick up the proofs of my novel, but I can't concentrate and so I finally give in and call the number in Dollard-des-Ormeaux, my heart doing a hop and skip of fear. If Josette answers, I must be quick to hang up. But Galbraith is the one who says, "Allô?"

"Are you alone?"

"No."

"But could I just tell you a few things that might be important?"

He hesitates, then says, "That should be possible."

"I know that you called me several times and I'm so sorry that I wasn't here."

There's a long silence before he finally says, "That was my response to the situation as well."

"I had to go out to the country to have lunch with Mira Brukova, a Czech poet who's so old she's a legend. And on the way back to Toronto we had to drive through a blizzard and when we got downtown some of us went out for dinner because we knew we'd be too tired to cook by the time we got home."

Some of us, some of us, some of us, and when he has nothing to say to some of us, I picture Josette sitting on the big bed beside him, painting her toenails. "Just one more thing," I say.

He says in a cool voice, "Which is?"

"Will you still be able to meet my train tomorrow night?"

There's another long pause until he says that he's expecting that meeting to go ahead as scheduled.

"Good night, then...." Although after a tiny silence I do dare to say in a low voice, "my darling."

"Right you are then, we can tie up all these loose ends at tomorrow's meeting." Then he quickly hangs up before (as he would see it) I can tell him any more lies.

I lie awake trying to picture what he does next, see him hand the phone over to Josette so she can call one of her sisters, see him shove his feet into his slippers and shuffle down the hall to the bathroom to lean his arms against the wall next to the shower. He could feel nauseated from the toxic odour of the nail polish, he could think "I can't breathe the air of my own house" as he listens to Josette's laughing voice cry into the phone, *"Mais non!"* and *"Tellement bon!"* But as I roll over, I catch sight of a white envelope illuminated by the band of light under my door. I get out of bed and go to it quickly, then open it to see that it's from Mendoza, I must have walked over it without seeing it when I came back from Kleinburg.

It is now close to 8 P.M. and this is just a brief note to say that your friend in Montreal called me almost an hour ago because he had been trying to reach you all day and was concerned about you. I told him that I saw you leave just before lunch and he asked me if you were alone when you left. I was not quite certain how to proceed in responding to such a question (not knowing the nature of your relationship with the other gentleman) but I must confess that I did tell him that you went off with a gentleman in his car. I must also confess that I now begin to worry if I did the right thing and can only say that I hope so.

If only I could have seen this note before I called Galbraith, because now there's nothing to do but lie awake the rest of the night thinking of how much he must be hating me now.

CLACKING ACROSS WINTER FIELDS, the train flies past hedges and the backs of towns while all my hopes and thoughts are only on Montreal—*get me there, get me there*—but in the meantime I have the student work to distract me. It's either very good or very bad and after I've read a sentence that makes me feel as if I can't bear to go on ("She was supposed to be dead by already as per her physician's prognosis …") I move on to livelier work, then after an hour or so lean back, looking with half-closed eyes at the rising pale rounds of my knees in my black pantyhose, then secretly study the woman sitting across from me who's smoking and looking out the window. Combed-back black hair, plum eye-shadow, plush lipstick, a heavy young woman whose hips are huge enough to look upholstered when she gets up to walk to the back of the train. I look out at the flash of a town, the random lights that signal more darkness, more stars shining down on more fields of snow, then fall asleep an hour before the train comes into Montreal to wake up thinking of Galbraith and what would this city (or this life) mean to me if he isn't here? But as I walk out of the station I can see his car is waiting for me, one of three cars waiting with their headlights on in the clear night.

I slide in beside him, lean over to kiss him. But he keeps his mouth stiffly turned away from me.

"What is it?"

"When you called me last night you were so clearly lying to me."

"Yes, I was. At least partly."

"You admit it then, that's at least a start."

"I did it for your sake. So you could get some sleep. You sounded so tired that I decided to tell you what would console you the most."

"This is beginning to sound incredibly disrespectful toward me, Kay."

"But you haven't even let me begin to explain...."

He stares distrustfully at me and I wonder if my coat, the most sexy coat I've ever owned, makes me look slutty and deceitful, its feathery collar is so frou-frou and flirty.

"I don't want you to explain, I want to ask you questions. And I want you to swear that you'll tell me the truth."

"Fine," I tell him.

"Do you swear?"

"Yes, of course."

"Did you spend the day and evening yesterday with just one person?"

"Partly."

"Did you have sex with him?"

"No."

"Are you in love with him?"

"No. He's just a professor who's helped me a lot with my work. And if it was a flirtation at all, it was only a methodical flirtation...."

It's clear that even in his present state he doesn't consider a methodical flirtation exactly flirty.

"I got so worried about you that I actually called Mendoza."

"I know. He slipped a note under my door."

"I don't believe this. He wrote you a note about it?"

"Just to be polite, just to let me know that you'd called."

"Unless he was writing to warn you to dovetail your story to his story ..."

"I'm sure he wrote to me for that reason too, but he barely knows me. And so how could he know that you're the one who means everything to me?"

He turns on the ignition and in silence we drive to Claremont Avenue, then up in my cold kitchen he uncorks a bottle of wine while he's still in his coat and I take out the treats that he bought for us, their crisp foreign fragrance stapled away inside the warm paper bags, then raise my hands to the feathery collar of my own coat, feel the tickle of its feathers brush my fingers. "Do you like my new coat?"

"Yeah, I do." He studies it briefly, his eyes unyielding. "It's sexy." But his voice is sad. Still, he must be deciding that he doesn't sound convincing enough and so he says, "Sexy and funky."

But when we begin to eat we go back to being silent again. And once we've had our coffee, I go into my bedroom and lie down on my bed, then call to him to come in and be with me. But there's only silence in the next room and gradually this silence undoes me and I can feel my eyes fill. As if this is a signal he's been waiting for he sighs, then comes into the darkness to lie down beside me and we rock back and forth, biting and crying, his warm body and his hot face pressed against me.

SPRING HAS COME sporadically early this year: cold one day, balmy the next, and tonight, my last night in Toronto, a weirdly mild wind blows in off the lake. We walk east in it, looking for a restaurant where Galbraith can stand up at the bar and eat. Because of his back pain it's best for him not to sit. Unless it's the flu. His face felt too warm when I kissed him hello. Once we've found a dark and noisy anonymous place where we can stand at a bar and have lobster salads with our beer, we talk about our future. "I think I could like it very well," I tell him. "Coming back here again. The solitude. Broken now and then by the pleasure of your arrival."

He takes a sip from his glass of beer, but it's clear that it hurts him to swallow.

I also liked being elegantly trapped on the train and marking student work while racing across the landscape to meet him. Canada: the country of the long commute. "I loved coming to see you on the train too, I loved getting closer to you with every mile."

"But you hate and fear teaching."

"Sometimes I do. But on good days it's like being in love, there's nothing like it. I might even come back here to teach again in the fall."

"If we can afford it," he says, like a husband. "You might also consider applying for a job in Montreal." And when the dessert turns out to be such a slippery junket that it must be coolly sliding down his painful throat, he talks about how forgiving the French view of life is. "To know all is to understand all. Just another cool little maxim from Maximland. Or it's to understand all is to forgive all. Or it's both. That's why the French have so many affairs. We're forever understanding all, forgiving all."

After we've moved to the big wall of tinted glass we stand looking out over the dark lake and I tell him that sometimes my students used to write me little notes. "One of them always used to begin his notes to me with the words 'Esteemed Oracle.'"

"I wish someone would call *me* Esteemed Oracle. All I seem to get these days is Silly Dadda."

"But I was under the impression that this student was mocking me."

"Mocking is flirting." But then he sneezes. "Kay, I'm going to have to get some sleep, I'm getting delirious," and as we're walking toward the coat rack, I can feel his hand guiding me slightly, then he lifts out my coat, holds it open for me.

"Señor Galbraith! Come sta, mein Herr? Und guten Abend...."

We move quickly away from one another as we turn back to see someone Galbraith apparently already knows and then I see this man (Leon) glance down at my left hand as it pokes its way out of my coat sleeve. There's even a ring for him to look at since I'm still wearing the Mexican silver ring Galbraith bought for me from a street vendor so long ago.

"Prosit," says Leon, raising his glass because, like everyone these days, he has a mongrel vocabulary of international words at the ready: *adios, prosit, arrivederci, hasta la vista, salut, ciao,* it's the nature of modern life. Even in Canada.

On our way back to the car when we pass a photographer's window, I stop to study a photo of a bride and groom who've clearly been ordered by the photographer to kiss. But they are looking backwards from the camera to lean into the privacy of it, the bride's body (in an unadorned long white dress) facing the camera while her white swan's neck is turned back and away from it, her hands tightly holding her bouquet while the groom is also tipping back toward the kiss, his arm (the one arm I can see) hanging down with a shy formality at his side.

Galbraith comes back to join me, jingling his keys in a pocket.

"What I like about this photograph is the way they're turning their faces to look behind them, into the kiss, you can't even tell what their faces look like, they're keeping the kiss so much to themselves...."

"Sounds like us. And therefore incredibly touching. Now can we go?"

When we get back to Borden Street, he sits slumped on the side of my bed while I'm in my tiny kitchen, brewing him a mug of tea with brandy and honey in it, the brandy courtesy of Señor Mendoza. When I sit down on the bed next to him, tipping it slightly, he opens his eyes against the glare of the light. "These two aspirins will be safe, since I'm only giving you a wee bit of the brandy...."

He lifts them up from my palm, then his eyes wince against the flash of light as I snap the tall lamp on, then off, and the smaller lights scatter. "I can drive us back tomorrow. I learned to drive when I was fifteen, and I'm incredibly fast."

"Fast," he says in a dubious voice as I brush my hair, then I click the room into darkness and slide into bed behind him in my slip, my toothpasty breath cool on the back of his neck, or so I imagine as I whisper that I've been driving for years and have never had an accident.

"I feel so lousy I almost feel good," he whispers back, then his breathing becomes so adenoidal that he must be asleep.

I lie in the dark and think back to the night he mimicked himself sitting hunched up at his desk the year he was in grade two, then showed me the way he'd speechlessly nodded when his adored teacher had come down the aisle and put a hand on his shoulder to tell him she was skipping him ahead to grade three. Years before

that, when I was the same age he was back then, Idona had a necklace
that I called her ruby necklace even though its stones were too
murky to be rubies and one night when she was having a party I got
so excited that I pawed through her bead box until I disentangled it,
then fastened it on and ran back downstairs again, wearing nothing
but the necklace and my tiny pink bathing suit. The laughter of the
grown-ups shocked me as I dropped on one knee to beg Idona to
give me the necklace, but she only regally tapped me on the head
and said no, I won't give it to you to keep, but I will let you borrow
it. And so I ran up to my room in a fury because I was too young to
consider a concept like the pathos of ownership. And because I knew
that if I could only borrow it, my whole life would be nothing to
me because I would die. But if I could get to keep it forever, I would
live forever. As for Galbraith, a future life with Galbraith, couldn't
this happen? Even when we are very old, or at least when I am very
old, we could keep on with our arrangement. Or it could be this
way: his marriage will break up ten years from now, he'll leave his
house to his wife, he'll find another house for us and I'll live with
him in it and we'll be a couple of sorts, dressed in the gypsy style of
the artistic old, a style distinguished by an offbeat (if decrepit)
glamour, Galbraith wearing an awkwardly striped bright serape
pulled down over his steel-grey hair, and me, either addled and fat
or ravaged and frail, dressed in a long red skirt, my embroidered
shirt dragged down by the weight of a brooch as oval as an engraved
silver clam shell. A time when I'll be for him what I want him to be
for me: a refuge, not a habit.

But no, it can't last. Nature is harsh. Nature is obsessed, as nature
has always been obsessed, with usefulness. What I've been forgetting
all along is that Galbraith will be more and more drawn into his
other life. He will have more children, will get a dog, will get cats,
will build a summer place, will travel to more and more countries,

will have less and less time for me, even if I stay lucid enough to remain his confidante, his best friend. But I can't bear the thought of not staying close to him, our good years together could just be beginning. Could be, but won't be, because as I'm drifting off to sleep another voice makes its own dark pronouncement: These are the last days of your happiness.

The cool breeze blowing in through the window makes me shiver and wake up, then I roll over to see that Galbraith is waking up too. "Did you sleep well?"

"You kept pulling the blankets off me, Kay." His voice still sounds sick, it still has such a deep croak of reproach in it. "And so if we ever do end up living together we might need to get separate beds."

"We might even need to get separate bedrooms, separate houses."

"At least I hope we'll be able to live on the same street."

We eat bacon and fried bananas in the stale kitchen, not talking, passing sections of the morning paper back and forth. And then as I'm rinsing the dishes he calls to me from the bedroom, "All set?"

I pull *Love in the Time of Cholera* out of my knapsack. "I just have to sponge out the fridge and wrap up this book for Mendoza, then bring it down to him...."

"Kay, no, you'll just get into one of your endless conversations." He comes out to the kitchen, pulls me into a hug. "Do this for me, sweetheart. My meeting's at three, and I really do have to get there on time. I'll sponge out the fridge, you wrap up his gift and write him a note."

I hate not going downstairs to say goodbye to Mendoza, but he's right, we would talk, be polite, it would take at least ten extra minutes. But then I look over at him. "The title of this book has the word 'cholera' in it, and Mendoza's wife died of a water-borne disease."

"But was the disease cholera?"

"No, it was some other disease."

"I wouldn't worry then, people who've suffered a loss are accustomed to pain. And so they are far beyond getting offended if someone happens to make a mistake and allude to the pain...."

"That's very profound, really."

"Well, you know me. I'm a pretty profound sort of guy." Then we're running down into the foggy wind and I can't help but picture Mendoza waiting for us to come up to say goodbye, then when he doesn't hear footsteps he'll go to his window. And when he looks down on the street he won't understand how I could allow my lover to just drive away.

Because he won't know that I'm the one who drove away, he will have been away from the window. Or so I hope, seeing the spatter of rain in the mist as I turn onto the ramp to the 401, then we're joining the racing stream of cars and it's like joining a relay race for the damned, the traffic is moving at such a great clip that it makes me horribly regret my boast that I'm a good driver, because now I'm afraid, the cars fleeing out of the city on both sides of me keep dancing and bouncing in the rain, in every car the serious profile of a face that knows where it's going, so many thousands of racing faces and cars terrify me, but when Galbraith calls out from the back, "Flash your right signal, then cut over to the next lane on your right!" I do as he tells me, and soon, almost soon, we're leaving Toronto and its endless satellite towns and cities behind and as sails of water fly up in the rainy morning, I become seduced by the highway and drive faster and faster, now and then glancing into the rearview mirror to check on Galbraith. Wrapped in the duvet and deeply asleep, he makes me think of my children the times they used to fall asleep on the back seat, he even makes me think of my cat Poppins on the day he died, how he looked laid out in his cardboard coffin—imperious, elderly, human, Oriental—but this spooks me and so I decide not to edge past the towering transport truck I'm already driving too close to, I instead sink back, let other cars pass me.

Mendoza could have forgiven me by this time, but not my country. In Toronto the rain could even be blowing into snow by now, snow squalls were predicted, a spring squall that will obscure the new green on the trees. Sometimes he must hate this cold continent, sometimes he must believe he's the only Spaniard living in exile this far north, the only Spaniard in Toronto. After all, what Spaniard would ever feel a need to leave Spain? Except for love? And yet if Joyce had been a Spanish girl, he would have had nothing more than a boring exchange of words with her, would have asked her, in Spanish, "Do you come to this beach often?" It was because his hands made an acquaintance with the Canadian girl's body before she scratched her name in the sand that they fell in love.

I see him open his gift and hope he'll decide I'm a decent person after all, see him as a character in a story I might write, wonder if he already knew he'd end up with the Canadian girl when they invented the game of getting to know one another without resorting to language, the way children do, see him kneel on the sand to smooth suntan oil on her back, see the way she has to walk on her knees in a half circle to face him as she flicks the wheel on his lighter, inventing fire (at least for him) with the quick hello of its flame, think of other trips in the rain, but now the rain is changing to snow, ten minutes before Lake of Two Mountains, a snowstorm of white sand blows against the green leaves, then a cold sun comes out to illuminate the damp afternoon as I turn off the highway to park at a lodge on the Montreal side of the lake.

Walking past the big windows I see two women sitting across from one another in the new sun, the elbows of the one on the left propped up on their tiny table so she can hold her hands straight out to roll her glass of beer back and forth between her two palms in such a sadly thoughtful way that they can only be talking about the thrill of dealing with some complicated man and I know that I'd rather be her, that I'd rather be bemused and analytical and afraid, than be what I most fear becoming: the sort of woman who laughs and says in a brash voice, "All my relationships with men are platonic and this is a relief, not a tragedy." I go into a washroom that's panelled in pale wood and spruced up with an egg of blue soap and the smell of pine deodorant, its single pane of glass looking out over the lake and I feel hopeful as I splash my eyes with cold water—driving has done this for me, safely getting us this far—but when I look out over the water all I can think of is what a failure I've made of my life. I did everything wrong, I did everything too late.

Once I'm out in the dining area again, paying for the coffee, I look out through the wide windows to see that Galbraith is out of the car and leaning back against it as he tries to wake himself up in the sun. No, we will never live together, I know this as I walk down the steps with the white cup in one hand, the steam blowing up in the breeze as I make my way back to him in the cold sunlight.

A HIGH SCHOOL BOY who has skipped his last class of the day is at this same moment driving home from school in his father's Jeep, hurtling toward the bridge over Lake of Two Mountains. Halfway across it he sees a woman who's holding a white cup in one hand as she walks across a green lawn toward a man who's leaning against a car, watching her. He sees the woman give this man the cup, sees the way the man sets it on the hood of the car, sees him hug the woman with his free arm, then smooth a hand back over her hair the way a father would do to a little girl who's fallen and hurt herself, but slower than that. So they must be lovers then. They must be old, though, at least over thirty, maybe even as old as his parents, but what the hell, let them be happy, let them be happy at least for a time, and he salutes them with the careening whine of his horn as he goes racing past them, sending them news of his mocking approval.

Acknowledgments

I am very grateful for the financial support given to *All Times Have Been Modern* at various stages over the last twelve years by the Canada Council, the Ontario Arts Council, and the Toronto Arts Council. Parts of this novel have also appeared, often in quite different form, in *PRISM international*, *Event*, *Quarry*, *77: Best Canadian Stories*, *The Malahat Review*, and in *Turn of the Story: Canadian Short Fiction on the Eve of the Millennium*. The chapter in which Kay Oleski meets William Lindstrom at an Ottawa restaurant appeared in *Turn of the Story* under the title "Down with Heartbreak." Part of the novel's first chapter was originally published in quite different form as "One Whole Hour (And Even More) With Proust and Novocaine" when it appeared in *Event*. It was subsequently chosen for *03: Best Canadian Stories*.

The book Michael Galbraith is reading from on page 168 is *Soft City*, by Jonathan Raban.

The story of how pink lemonade was made at the beginning of the twentieth century on page 345 comes from a revelation Jane Jacobs made when she was being interviewed by Eleanor Wachtel on CBC Radio's *Writers & Company*.

The two lines from a song that are quoted on page 297 are paraphrased from Gordon Lightfoot's "That's What You Get for Loving Me."

The lines quoted on page 322 are from *The Martyrology*, by bpNichol.